THE STORY OF THREE SAD WOMEN

Dropseed

NETTIE MARIE MAGNAN

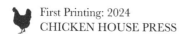 First Printing: 2024
CHICKEN HOUSE PRESS

Library and Archives Canada Cataloguing in Publication
CIP data on file with the National Library and Archives

ISBN trade paperback edition: 978-1-990336-74-4

The King James Bible, public domain

Cover art by Nettie Marie Magnan; cover design by Alanna Rusnak

Chicken House Press
282906 Normanby/Bentinck Townline
Durham, Ontario, Canada, N0G 1R0
www.chickenhousepress.ca

To my Mother

Table of Contents

Dropseed: The Story of Three Sad Women

Nettie Marie Magnan

CHICKEN HOUSE PRESS

Sally

The note is in the middle of the dining room table. When her husband reads it, he'll believe she's with her mother, a little more than a mile away. Her mother still lives in the old white farmhouse, two storeys, the kind still scattered across the prairie, tired and weather-worn, but dignified because they've outlasted the rest. Right about now, the mid-afternoon sun will be lighting the yard in yellow tones, the grass and gravel still shimmering and wet from the overnight rain.

The city, Sally thinks absently, always has the feeling of another realm. The sky seems less noticeable here, the eye is kept too busy with other things. It's been several months since she ventured into the city, and the difference between this view and the view from her own kitchen window is jarring, almost shocking. She watches the men and women below, miniature-looking from this height, passing between the tall buildings. She envies them, if for no reason other than their freedom to go about their afternoon, unconscious of the cold white walls in a clinic high above them. They're concerned with ordinary things, ordinary errands. Elm trees punctuate the sidewalk, their leaves littered along the wide pavement in shades of orange, yellow, and green.

About an hour ago, after crossing a sprawling white foyer, she was shown into this room. She was asked to remove her clothes and to dress in what they referred to as a gown, which is really more of a smock with side-snap buttons attached to tattered blue fabric. A young nurse was there, performing a series of transactions; her blood pressure reading was taken, questions about her medical history were asked and answered, an intravenous line was inserted on the inside of her wrist.

Left to wait, she has absorbed herself in the city scene below, particularly in the archaic beauty of an old Catholic church, with its grey stone walls and curved cobblestone pathway leading to arched wooden doors. Tall bursts of bright green grass poke through some of the rounded stones, a thing that strikes her as hopeful, for whomever laid the pathway left the grass beneath it to die under the weight and lack of light, yet here are the stubborn green blades, giving life another try.

The sight reminds her of the cobbled lanes in Europe, a place she's never been, but in her mind, the European continent and a picturesque cobbled lane seem perfectly synonymous somehow, like an early autumn evening and the full red shimmer of a harvest moon, or an old wooden rocking chair and a screened porch. She muses over the word cobble, the meaning of which is to produce or put something together quickly or roughly. Yet that's precisely what makes them special, why they're the subject of so many photographs, and why they're so often revered and painted and written about. They're usually made from limestone or some other natural stone, but she can't tell what this accompanying church is made from, this antiquated structure rising high and separate from the straight lines of the downtown surrounding it, unaware of its own elegance. But it doesn't matter that she can't differentiate one type of stone from another. Stones, cobbled and lime, rounded or squared, are merely something to keep her mind away from the whiteness and sterility of this room. Stones, right now, are a beautiful, exquisite distraction.

It's not too late, a voice tells her. You can have this thing pulled from your wrist, put your clothes back on, forget this clandestine trip to a whitewashed clinic in the sky. She watches meditatively as the slow drip of fluid descends through the long thin tube, and her breath catches in her chest as she's afflicted once again by the enormity of her decision. There's something cruel about this, something sinful. She thinks of her husband, of their house, the clean, quiet rooms. She sees in her mind the succulent plants on the ledge of the kitchen window, the ivory curtains she soaked in the sink then hung on the line to dry. She recalls the black-capped chickadee perched on the branch of a poplar while she finished her coffee, the wooden wind chime outside the dining-room window, making hollow sounds, and the apprehensive kiss placed on her cheek when her husband left for work. Because she loves him, it's better to leave him in the dark. Her secretiveness is an act of kindness, the best way to protect his heart, which would probably be pulled to pieces if he knew. He would insist on being here to support her, or worse, and more likely, pleading with her to change her mind. He would have weakened her resolve, and she probably would have submitted.

An urge to submit, then, rises inside of her suddenly, and she feels consoled by the thought of returning home to the ivory curtains, the wooden wind chime, the waiting note. Yet just as suddenly, the feeling abates, and when the young nurse comes to lead her down the hall, Sally says nothing to stop her. The intravenous line attached to the wheeled metal pole makes her nervous, so she walks stiff and upright along the tiles as if balancing a wickerwork basket on her head.

When they arrive at a larger room, Sally is guided inside. Despite being brightly lit, the room is depressing, with a procedure table covered in a thin white sheet. There is a knowing silence, deceptively calm, with an air of people who know something immense is about to happen, at least for the patient; something beyond words, something ineffable, even if commonplace for the others. There's a sterile, chemical sort of smell, a doctor with his back turned, and a stout, elderly-looking nurse writing in a chart. When the door closes, the doctor turns in his stool and asks Sally, rather unemotionally, if she has any questions. She notes his large pale hands and thick white hair.

"I'd rather not be given a sedative, and was told I could refuse it, if I wanted to," Sally says. "Is that still an option?"

"Yes, some women prefer to go without the sedative," the doctor responds impersonally, then eases his expression into something more reassuring. "Let us know if at any point you need me to stop, or if you want something more for the pain. We'll have it ready, just in case."

Sally nods. The doctor turns around again in his wheeled stool. He writes something in a chart, closes it, places it on the counter. The younger nurse assists her onto the sheeted procedure table and in a quick, habitual way, helps to lift Sally's legs into the stirrups. They've performed these tasks many times before, Sally gathers; all these easy, inured movements to show that this day isn't any different from the day that came before or the day that will follow. The sordidness is forgettable, and the lady sinner in stirrups is just one of many on the list.

Sally lies quietly, listening to the wind and the clanging of instruments as they are set down on a metal tray. The white-haired doctor wheels himself in front of her and says, "Just another moment and we'll begin."

Sally's eyes shift to the narrow window, the only one in the room. It's splattered with dry raindrops, which blend elegantly together in a way that reminds her of an expressionist landscape, the genre of paintings once described by her professor as being metaphoric in emotion. Any emotional response brought about by the image, he said, is more indicative of the observer than of the artist. The image can then be thought of as a kind of mirror, and in this moment, this ash-toned, expressionistic raindrop arrangement on a windowpane elicits from her a mix of grief, fear, claustrophobia, and loss. And so, she pictures in her mind that pretty pathway of cobblestones, smooth and multi-shaped, with the occasional burst of determined green grasses, pushing their way through.

The young nurse extends her hand, offering it to hold, but Sally ignores the gesture and turns away. The muscles tense all over her body and she has to consciously keep from wrenching herself out of the stirrups. She feels with all her heart, to the core of her being, this thing happening, the innocent speck of life about to be taken. She is immediately, immensely ashamed, and humiliated. She feels something cold and closes her eyes.

The boughs of grown poplars and poplar saplings line the south end of their four acres, shadowing the ground but letting through enough dappled sunlight during the day to nourish a small bush of raspberries. Behind the poplars, the earth dips naturally into a shallow ravine. The small stretch of ground between the poplars and ravine, only a few feet wide, is lush with couch grass and dotted with yellow lady's slippers, a thing Sally is always tempted to pick but never does. A lover of flowers shouldn't pluck away the only wildflower. She's plucked other things though, usually the prairie dropseed that she likes to put in a vase once or twice a year, or a few of the little water-polished stones for her flowerbed. She goes there to be alone sometimes, to sit under the canopy of leaves and listen to nothing in particular, just to enjoy the quietness and tranquility of a place where, beyond the ravine, there is nothing to see but the immenseness and splendour of the neighbour's golden hayfield. Once the bales are carried away there will be nothing in the way of the flatness, no tree lines or hedges or bungalow houses, just the undisturbed vastness of the prairie stretching out ahead. Sally sat under the poplars for over an hour last night, avoiding her husband and reflecting on the day ahead, on the afternoon appointment at the clinic that would change her life. The experience would change only her inward life; outwardly nothing would be different.

Sally lies quietly in her bed, her mind still lingering somewhere on the edge of a deepened sleep. The fitful yellow light pouring in through the curtains is what woke her a few minutes ago, brushing her eyes gently, but insistently. It fills the room now and emblazons the yellow wallpaper. She raises her head slightly from the pillow, glances at the clock on the nightstand. It's twenty minutes past seven. From the kitchen she hears the underlying sounds of an ordinary morning, the crackling voices of AM radio, the wind chime, doors of the cupboard opening and closing. Her husband often wakes before her.

She looks sleepily at the yellow wallpaper, listening to Jaime move around the kitchen and a faint chorus of crickets outside the bedroom window. They're searching for warmth, probably, and most years when the air starts to cool, she finds at least one or two sneaking in by the entrance. Some days the unrelenting trills and chirps are maddening, yet this morning the sound gives her a surprising sense of quiet and relief. Their strange cheeping melody, her husband's movements in another room, the thick bedcover, and the illuminated yellow wallpaper all seem to draw themselves into something perfectly consoling and familiar, for she has awoken this way thousands of times.

Sally moves the covers away and rises from the bed. She steps toward the full-length mirror that hangs on the back of the bedroom door, turns to her side, strokes her belly softly. She tugs at the nightgown from behind to assess any change in size, but of course she can't; it's too small, nothing is visible yet. The appointment was finalized two weeks ago, and up until last night, this procedure had seemed like an abstract thing. However, last night under the poplars, and right now, stroking her belly, it became something more perceptible, more tangible, as if it were now a tactile thing, begging but paining her to feel. It was the distant echo of something, narrowed into clarity. She considers how much physical pain might be involved, and what might happen to her conscience once she's gone through with it. It's one thing to be confident in its rightness beforehand, another to be confident in its rightness afterward. Yet this isn't the sort of thing one can feel right about, or confident about, at least not fully. It wavers, and perhaps when she gets there she will be wavering still.

She shivers, wraps herself in her pale purple dressing gown, then slowly makes her way down the dusky hall. It's late September and crisp autumn air encroaches its way through the house every morning, cooling the floors. She pauses for a moment before entering the kitchen, gathering her thoughts, readying her expression. She's been mindful lately not to make any unconscious show of emotion. Better to be reserved; better to have a morning of acting stiff than to falter and give anything away. She hears a clatter of dishes in the sink, the sound of running water. From outside comes the song of a bird, a loud, inelegant descant overriding the dull tones of the wind chime. A kind of swallow, Sally imagines, or a sparrow, but she doesn't know birds very well.

She steps into the kitchen feeling disjointed, slightly

unmoored, then catches the sheer, leaf-patterned curtains in the corner of her eye, billowing gently across an opened window. She must have forgotten to close it last night.

Jaime, sitting by the back door and readying his new pair of work boots, runs his fingers through blonde hair and glances up at her with the weary brown eyes that often hint at sleeplessness. It's a strained expression at first, one he wears when his thoughts are on work or something acutely worrying, but his expression relaxes when he sees her standing in the doorframe. This expression is softer, more emblematic of the gentle, equably stoic man she has been tied to romantically since the age of 17, a man who seemed to view the birth of a son less than a year out of high school as a grand adventure rather than an obstacle. Looking back, Jesse's unexpected entrance into their lives managed to be both. The little boy offered her bliss and amusement one day, struggle and true inconvenience in the next.

"Good morning," Jaime says. "I hope I wasn't making too much noise."

"Not at all."

"There's coffee."

"How was your sleep?" she asks, shivering again as she steps across the cool linoleum toward the wafting curtains.

"Full of noisy crickets, but fine."

Sally closes the window, fills a cup with coffee, stirs in a small amount of milk. He must have noticed her long avoidance yesterday, she suspects, for something about the low tone of his voice brings into the room a kind of dank sensation, one more or less akin to the feel of an elephant lingering in a room. She warms her hands against the side of the cup, scolds herself for not waiting until he left for work to leave the bedroom. Again she hears the bird's melody, a quick song sounding both fierce and careless, as if the bird were prompted into a spurt of sound only to hear itself, or to break the quiet. She half-smiles at the thought of this bird, admiring the illusory look of it, bright-feathered perhaps, competent and confident, with nothing to do but sing.

"What is that?" she asks.

"What?"

"That bird."

"I didn't hear it," he says distractedly, for his efforts are concentrated now on weaving a new pair of laces through the boots, and again his expression is one that seems full of grievances. Still, this is an ordinary morning for her husband, one that is utterly forgettable, and in all probability believes that his sense of ordinariness is the same for her. She sips her coffee.

"You have that worried look on your face again," Sally remarks.

"What worried look?"

"The one you wear when you're worried," she says wryly.

"We've been having some trouble with one of the repairs. It's nothing I'm too worried about though. It'll work out."

"Yes, it usually does," she says, then sighs desolately at the thought of her own mounting paperwork at their auto-shop; normally, two to three days a week she makes her way to the shop's office to manage invoices, outstanding payments, the bi-weekly payroll, though lately she's fallen behind on the tasks. It's too repetitive, too sedentary, too subversive to more peaceable things like having a quiet morning to oneself while coffee brews and a bright-feathered bird sings merrily from a branch.

"What are your plans today?" Jaime inquires. "Are you going to your mother's?"

"In the afternoon," Sally says, not quite meeting his eyes. She sets her cup down somewhat unsteadily and wipes the counter with a damp cloth, calms the taciturn thoughts somewhat, subdues her own pulsating sense of wrongdoing.

"What time will you be home? Jesse mentioned that he and Valerie might be stopping by."

Sally sets the cloth down. "For dinner?"

"I don't think so. They just want to discuss a few more details about the engagement party, something to that effect."

"Alright," she says, after a pause. "I don't think I'll be any later than five."

"Good. And it will probably rain again today. They mentioned it on the radio."

"Well, maybe we need it after the dry summer," Sally says, quietly wrapping her mind around the considerable strength it will take to endure a gathering, even a short one. She had been hoping to come home tonight only to quietness, a long rest, to go to bed early and be listless.

Sally reclaims her cup of coffee from the counter, raises a hand to her hair. "Jaime, he's too young to be engaged."

Jaime releases the laces and lowers his head in a way that professes, to her, his profound discouragement. She immediately regrets the impulse to speak, for there's no sense in mentioning the engagement. They've been over this before.

"Yes, I know you think so," he sighs at length. "But they've been together for a few years now, and they're happy. There's not much we can say at this point."

"No, I suppose there isn't," she says despondently, watching her husband as he finalizes the tie of laces on his boots, carefully through one hole, then another. She sips her coffee and glances out the window, past the filmy curtains, recalling the night her son announced his engagement. He was short of breath, as if he'd rushed to their house immediately after the moment to gather their blessing. She could see that he was overjoyed. She could see that he wanted her to be happy. She could see that an endearing element of his personality had not changed since that afternoon when, as an 8-year-old, he arrived from school with a wooden wind chime, the one that still hangs outside the kitchen window. He had run into the house without removing his shoes, and handed it to her. The white oak chimes fell roundly from the hanger, each with a copper weight bound by threads of dark leather. He had watched carefully for her reaction. The chime was beautiful, she had to admit, this decorative ornament he managed to put together himself, and privately she doubted that the other boys his age could produce one as attractive or expertly made. Her little craftsman, she had called him, playfully messing his hair. He had smiled shyly, knowing he'd done well and that he'd pleased her. He has always been that way; eager for approval, and somewhat fragile, his confidence swayed too easily one way or another by what others did or didn't say.

Jaime clears his throat. "How's your mother been this week? You haven't said much about her lately."

"Oh, I'll have to speak with her doctor again about her breathing," Sally replies. "She's short of breath so often. I think the staff are starting to have a hard time with her, trying to convince her to walk a little every day. It's especially hard getting her to eat. She argues with them."

"That does not surprise me one bit," Jaime says flatly. "The arguing, I mean. I wish she'd let us take her to a care home."

"Yes, but the nurse is handling her medication at home now," Sally says, while pulling a frozen container of vegetable soup from the freezer and placing it in the fridge to thaw. She will take it to her mother's tomorrow. She adds, "Between the nurses and the other caregivers, she probably gets more one-on-one time than she would in a home."

"But you say they're having a hard time."

"Not the nurses, my mom wouldn't refuse her pills, but the other caregivers are, yes. They'd have a hard time at a care home too, though," she says definitively, feeling again the encroaching wintriness in the air, and warming her hand against the side of the cup. When a crackling voice on the radio confirms what Jamie has already told her about more rain to come, Sally considers her mother and how the higher levels of humidity have aggravated her arthritic hips and hands, though with the steady spread of cancer it's difficult to say these days whether the symptoms are rheumatoid or tumorous. She moves her body less and less, the ailments consigning her to a life of sitting still and ruminating quietly, for she dislikes the radio and television. Most days, Sally finds her mother facing the bow window in her armchair, staring indolently ahead, listening to the wind and birds, maybe, or thinking deeply about something or other before tipping her head to the side and nodding off again.

"Day by day, I suppose," Jaime says, rising from the stool and putting on his coat.

"Exactly. Day by day." Sally brings her cup to her lips. "She would never agree to a nursing home, anyway. You know her."

"Yes, I do," he smiles airily. He will not confront her in any way this morning for her recent avoidance of him, she concedes, rather, he will be Jaime; lenient, undemanding, sweet-tempered.

Sally sets her cup on the counter and goes to him, inhales the smoky scent of his shirt. Already, he must have had one of his cigarettes. He smiles down at her, dimly, almost bashfully. He is transparent in his love for this moment, for she is rarely awake to see him off.

"This was nice," he softly tells her. "Seeing you before I leave."

"I know, I've been sleeping in too often."

"No, don't worry about that. It was just nice to see you before work. That's all I meant."

"Yes, it's nice," she repeats.

Then there are the awkward yet tender parting movements of a loving but detached husband and wife. He says I love you; she says I love you too. He draws her closer. He hesitates, then kisses her cheek.

"Have a good day," she tells him.

"I hope things go well with your mom," he replies as he steps out the screen door, and for nearly a full minute Sally stands perfectly still, sunken by his final words, so offhanded and well-meaning, then listens until his truck reaches the road. She allows a few tears to fall, then turns to the window. The sky is slightly leaden toward the west, and she recalls the warning for more rain. She realizes, suddenly, watching the leaden sky, that she is not likely to be home by five, that she may not, in fact, arrive before six. She will leave a note, she decides, on the dining room table. She will tell him that the care agency isn't able to send anyone before six, and she wants to stay with her mother until then. No one will question it.

Sally switches off the radio, preferring quietness in the morning, then steps absently with her coffee across the hall into the small, cluttered corner room bearing her easel and canvas. These days it's a room less fit for artistry than it is a repository of things; books, papers, and old tubes of watercolour lie in crooked mounds on the bookshelf and chair. Still on the canvas from several months earlier is the straight line of garnet-coloured paint, meant to be a horizon, the lower edge of it dripping like red rain into the ground until it gathered and dried in blotches at the bottom of the canvas.

It's on quiet mornings such as these that she tends to wander into this corner room, a room considered to be hers, only hers, to sit in front of the easel, or, these days, merely to stare at it. It used to excite her, being in this well-lit, south facing room, but sitting in front of a canvas now fills her with uncertainty. Too often, she's been disappointed by the outcome of her paintings. They fall short of her vision, and finally, convinced of her own inaptitude, she sets the brush down and leaves the room to busy herself with something else. Her ability to enter the spirit of it, as she calls it, that glittering, indiscernible feeling, the inexplicable dilation of the soul, comes and goes, rises and falls in unpredictable waves. These waves come to her naturally, but can never be called upon.

Staring at the garnet horizon, she reminisces the time in her life, years ago, when the crest of one of these waves was at its highest. She would rise early in the morning, a muted morning such as this, kiss her husband goodbye, and with the baby washed and changed and napping, she would sit, thrilled, fresh and hopeful, in front of the canvas. Only when the house was quiet of other footsteps did she feel secure enough to emancipate herself into that parallel world—the place of unusually florid visions, as if she were stepping over the threshold into a brilliantly lit landscape not entirely unlike this one, but more amplified, more embellished, where sheets of watercolour further unveil themselves as big sunny rooms with clay vases and strands of ivy wavering in a window. There is the stir of life all around; there are long gardens of brash bluebells that carry their scent for miles; there are sculptures of angels with seeing eyes. Whenever she could pick up a paintbrush and get herself over that threshold, her mind angled itself in a way that felt more organic than it did at any other time. She might have called it a trance, a kind of fleeting departure. She was sitting in a quaint countryside bungalow while a baby slept and a refrigerator hummed, but in her mind, she was there, the light of her soul swaying feather-like among the brash bluebells and wavering strands of ivy.

Sally taps her fingers against the side of her cup, thinking reverently of the ivy strands and bluebells, then mournfully at the thought of all the galleries and exhibits of her past, which now seem frivolous. Usually, the scent of her morning brew is soothing, but today it only aggravates the murky, ever-increasing sense of queasiness and unease. That she can't assuage herself temporarily with a coffee or a paintbrush and canvas is disappointing, unsettling, and distinctly tragic, for these were once the dependable manifestations of comfort.

She turns to the little wire-rimmed clock that hangs on the wall opposite the bookshelf. It's a few minutes before eight. She still has time. She washes her cup, returns it to the cupboard, retrieves the broom and mop from the hall closet. Movement helps the queasiness more than rest, and she finds a certain consolation in cleanliness, a restored sense of balance, a sense of rightness. And so, for the next hour or so, she finds herself in a combative mood, cleaning furiously, sweeping then mopping the floors in the dining room, hallway, and kitchen. She unhooks the ivory curtains from the steel rods in the bedroom, soaks them in warm water, steps outside the patio doors and hangs them on the line to dry. By the look of the clouds, there is still some distance between the start of rain and the fluttering, pale-ivory fabric. Such a pretty pattern, Sally thinks as she watches the high fluttering curtains, embroidered so delicately with swirls of leaves and flower petals. She crosses her arms and roams slowly around the yard for a while with the strange, mindless hope that she'll hear that bird again, and soon she does, its distinctive melody seeming more cheerful this time, more optimistic. She sees the bird, too, a blackbird of some kind, not as brightly feathered as she had thought, or hoped, but larger, with a spot of red on its wing that reminds her, somewhat, of the garnet-coloured line of paint.

Sally returns to the clothesline, strokes the material, unclips the curtains. Their sheerness means they usually dry quickly in the breeze, and besides, the rain has started; a thin, mournful drizzle. She returns the curtains to their rod in the bedroom, and as the clouds darken, switches on a lamp in the dining room. The sky rumbles ominously and the wind starts to pick up along the sides of the house, a long whistling at first then a grim, deep howling.

Sally showers and dresses, then under the light of the lamp, writes the note.

A sense of relief crept quietly through her body toward the end, little by little, and overall the pain was less than she expected. But as she redressed, the relief became too muddied in shame to let her indulge in it for too long. Relief seemed an unwarranted emotion, as if relief were not a feeling but a kindly offering, reserved only for those who deserve it—the destitute, the unjustly persecuted—and really, nothing inside of her felt gratified. She wondered, as she started the car, whether an emotion like relief could ever be felt in a pure way. Relief never rises to fruition on its own. It's always knotted with something else; some hardship must come before. She told herself the best way to get through the rest of the day would be to pretend that this was merely an errand, one both benign and entirely expected, like stepping out for groceries, during which one typically feels nothing.

Now at home, she has bypassed the house and gone to her leaf-canopied area by the ravine. They might have heard her pull into the yard, they may be waiting, wondering, for Jesse's car is in the driveway and it is already past six. Yet she needed another moment to herself, here in the twitch grass, to wrap her mind around this new suffering, to hear the strange yet soothing euphony of crickets, bellowing furiously over nothing, and to gaze out at the browns and yellows of the hay field where the bales have yet to be carried away. Above the field, the sun continues its slow descent, sending long threads of pink and orange light outward across the horizon. The threads taper off slowly into a vapourish blue, but at the brightest points of light, the sky seems almost a glittering red, ruby-coloured, the burning waves of cloud stretching long but harboured in place by the golden sun. When she would paint her prairie landscapes, such a magnificent sky would allow for a kind of recklessness, for such a free-wheeling use of brush strokes that even the unexpected errors seem full of meaning.

She looks at the grass, at the coppery-toned leaves that have fallen there. There is no sign tonight of the singing blackbird. A single tear slides down her cheek and she wipes it away. She is physically sore, regretting the deed and not regretting it at the same time. She recalls, solemnly, the white walls, the clanging sounds, the greyish splattering of raindrops on the glass. She had weaved afterward through the unconcerned crowd as a mere reticence of a woman, drifting ghostlike an inch or two above the wet pavement, like the detached head of a lily floating nimbly in a bowl of water, unbodied and separate. The sensation of detachment, of non-presence, clings similarly to her here, upon this dampish stretch of grass, a miasma-like woman set adrift, yet anchored in place.

A few drops of rain fall against her skin, then subside. She wipes away another tear. If they hadn't heard her car in the driveway, they might phone her mother's house soon, looking for her. She breathes a sigh of thankfulness for this moment of tranquility under the sunset and turns unhurriedly toward the house, toward the dim, motion-censored light beside the porch which was already set off when she crossed. She could be satisfied as one of those threads of light in the sky, a ruby-coloured tendril that inspires onlookers for a while, then dissipates; no one misses it, no one wonders where. The ruby tendril weaves through her mind now, a whimsical image, soft yet playful, so removed from these worn wooden steps with shallow puddles at their centre, so wonderfully traitorous to a warm walled room where people mingle and pour drinks, where certain expectations are held.

Sally enters through the back door, opening and closing it as discreetly as she can, though she knows they're fully expecting her. The soft, cheerful voices of her son and his fiancée are already wafting toward her from the living room and suddenly, strangely, with the familiarity of their voices and then a moment later by her husband's laugh, quick and full of his usual mirth, the permanence of the loss becomes clearer. The results of today's procedure are adamant and final. This morning she carried a life; now that life is gone. It's inextricable. She wants nothing more than to bypass all of this without a word, and lie down.

"There's more than enough room for guests in the yard," she hears her husband say with an enthusiasm that surprises her, yet it shouldn't, for he has long been in favour of the engagement. "The evenings are getting cool, but we'll have a fire."

"I'll help you split some wood over the weekend," Jesse offers.

"My mom and I are taking care of the dinner," Valerie adds effusively. "I might ask Sally if she can handle the cake."

Sally steps forward slowly and carefully, scarcely lifting her feet. She stops anxiously when the sounds of their voices stop, measures her ability to endure their glances and well-meaning company should she enter the room, and wishing to conjure up some thought or image that will quiet her nerves, pictures herself aside the ravine, among the tall grass blades that swayed so peacefully this way and that, shadowed in some spots while illuminated in others by the remnants of sun.

"She hasn't been eating well, or very much," she hears Jaime say, and she carefully steps forward again.

"Maybe she's coming down with something," Valerie suggests. "It's that time of the year, flus are going around."

"It may have something to do her mother," Jaime continues. "She's, well, it may not be too long now."

Jesse says, after a moment of quiet, "I can't imagine not having my grandmother at the wedding."

Sally reaches the edge of the foyer, hearing their words but perceiving them as when one sees something from far away, muddled, half-lit, unable to identify with certainty or follow with reason. She spots the peperomia plant, just visible now on the dining room table, its green tips curling meekly and dryly inward for lack of water. The sight of it on the table depresses her, for she had written the note there, and its wilted shape further enmeshes her mind in the details of her wrongdoing, of her willingness to lay still upon a sheeted procedure table and allow the awful withdrawing sounds to continue. Memories are tied to inanimate things, after all, whether good, bad, or middling. She had a similar thought this morning when setting the wind-dried ivory curtains onto the rod, that she may never again feel their softness, or run her fingers along the rougher feel of their seams, without feeling sad in some way. And so the more noticeable things of the day; the wind chime, the blackbird, the ivory curtains, thinned by years of sun, and even the sight of dried raindrops on a window, might always be reminiscent of this immoral act, of the stealth plotting that led to it. For all those things already seem to intimate in her mind a kind of mournful tenderness.

She hears her son add, "All I can hope for, I guess, is that she isn't in pain, because I know she's been in pain."

"The pain is better handled now, from what I understand," Jaime confirms.

Sally envisions her son, a tall, keen-eyed blond, the kind other men might describe as capable, yet overly soft, and Sally's mind wanders to all the sentimental souls in the world, to those easily broken or easily moved by others, by the inevitable ups and downs, by the lilting prose of life itself.

Sally knows intuitively that she will not join them. She will continue ever so quietly down the hall, for she can do so without being visible to them. They will gather before long that she is home and has sidestepped them intentionally and gone into the bedroom. In this moment, she won't allow herself to care. The floor creaks.

"Mom?" Jesse calls.

Sally stiffens. A wave of both love and fear runs swiftly through her at the sound of his voice, a cadence that pulls her by sudden gravity to the trueness of her being. Compared to the tragedy of the afternoon, everything had seemed small, featureless, obscure, whereas now, she must admit, she is here, in the thick of tangible things, bounded once again by dimly lit rooms where clocks tick and floors creak, where a son calls out for his mother. There's no avoiding them now. Sally leaves the hall and crosses the dining room, willfully yet somewhat sorely, as if yielding to a finer power, an amateur delinquent caught in a poorly planned escape. For fear of rattling the hangers, she hadn't removed her raincoat, and in taking a single step into the living room, is aware of her disjointed appearance, her damp, dishevelled hair, her heavy eyes. She straightens her shoulders.

"Are you alright?" Jaime asks. He leans forward in his seat, ready to stand.

"I'm fine, I'm just not feeling well," Sally says, motioning gently with her hand for him to stay seated. She hears the eloquent stirs of the wind chime. "I'm sorry, but I think it's better if I go lie down."

Sally avoids her husband's eyes, lest she begin to weep or shatter like a shivery fretwork of glass on the floor with the three of them watching. For in each of those shattered glass parts they would see her for what she was—an inefficient wife and mother they didn't know quite as well as they thought. They would be shocked by the glass piece that revealed an initial wave of relief after what happened today.

Jaime asks, "Did you eat?"

"Yes, I had something."

"At your mother's?"

"Yes."

"How is she?" Jesse inquires, and though she avoids his glance, she can see that Valerie is rubbing his shoulder, soothingly. She's a gentle type, Sally concedes, bohemian-like in appearance, and Sally has come to understand what her son finds appealing about her; in her presence everything seems smooth and light, all ruffles levelled-out and properly tended to. Sally resolves to do what Valerie hasn't yet had a chance to ask of her; she, Sally, will take care of the cake.

"She's okay, no change," Sally proclaims, with surprising ease, and in speaking about her mother, feels herself longing for the following morning when she will be with her. She will rise early, perhaps, before the sadness begins to claw at her too thoroughly, then head to her childhood home, where the outstretched willow shades the yard as it always has, where framed photographs sit all in a row. She will rest for a while on the old chesterfield and listen amiably to the low terseness of her mother's voice, regardless of their disputes which, though frequent, tend to dissolve rather quickly into something peaceful, like jagged scraps of ice set into warm water. "I know you had planned on discussing the party, but maybe the three of you can take care of that, just for tonight."

"Sally," Valerie begins hesitantly. "One thing, quickly, before you go lie down. My mom and I were hoping to stop by one day, before the party. I know it might seem unnecessary, but she wants to know what she can help with."

"Yes, that's fine," Sally assents, trying not to sound too impatient, only she feels as though she may faint if she stands for too long. She wishes for them to carry on with their discussions, to forget her presence as anyone would one of those ruby-coloured wisp in the sky, here one minute then gone the next, to let it go wherever it wants to go, and to be unceremonious about it.

Valerie smiles. "Great."

"Well then, I'll go rest," Sally says, turning to leave the room.

"Good night, mom," Jesse says in a quiet way that seems to show his concern, and Sally can't help but turn to him. His face is sweet, pensive, beautiful. She could never admit that she finds him beautiful, a man wouldn't want to be described in such a way. Now that he's grown, she is, at times, astonished by him, for there he is, looking at her in such a complete way, a perfect soul borne then moulded by her. Despite the years of worrying, despite the struggle to act in consonance with the sort of mother he deserves —firm and confident, effortless and affectionate—there he is, despite her, entirely happy.

"Good night," she says, smiling wistfully, and he returns his attention to the others.

Sally steps soundlessly down the hall, and as she draws farther from the light of the living room and closer to the unlit bedroom, she feels herself overcome by mournful, disordered thoughts, and she envisions a flurry of things: her mother's arthritic hands, the brilliant strands of ruby-coloured sunlight in the sky, the varied shapes of cobblestones, and the ridiculous attachment earlier to the blackbird's song that seemed so unreasonably reassuring. She thinks of what they may be whispering about her in the other room, if anything. They'll think of her tonight as rude, perhaps, an odd neurasthenic who shouldn't be bothered, a troubled woman in need of a rest cure. And so she may be.

She laments the neglected canvas and tubes of paint in the corner room, for the simple yet exceptional act of raising brush to canvas was once the go-to cure for all that ails, the most useful distraction, her true bedrock, her centrepiece, the thing she has been most caring and protective of. Yet a person shouldn't need distractions if they're living in a good way, she concludes suddenly, and this conclusion pulls her into a deeper despair. It seems impossible after a day like this to ever again refer to hers as a good, pure life. The opportunity to live decently was there, within her, but was shrugged off, banished, tossed aside, and the gallant strand that tied her to anything innocent has been severed.

She feels, deep within her skin and bones, blemished in an unalterable way. From here on, it's her own ugly secret, her own private, distinct cause of loneliness. It's a forever type of memory, she knows, the kind that will continue to web itself in her mind, unvanquished, coiling around her insides in a way that won't let her heal, but won't allow her to be killed by it altogether. She'll have to fight off this shame over and over as if it were a living organism.

Finally in her bedroom, she closes the curtains. She decides that these elegant ivory curtains and the splattered raindrops on the windowpane, even the peperomia plant, will not explicitly remind her of this day, for somehow the memory is already etched into everything; the purple dressing gown hanging from a nail behind the bedroom door, the sight of bread in a basket, wet, coppery-toned leaves, the chirps of crickets. Sally goes to the ensuite to clean herself and deal with the blood, which is less than she thought. She changes into her nightgown, places her clothes in the laundry basket, and feeling a sudden disgust with herself, avoids the mirror completely. She switches off the ensuite light and cautiously lies down on the bed, for there is still a twinge of pain. After covering herself in the heavy quilt, she stares for a few minutes at the yellow wallpaper, lost in wonder at the loss of life, at the surprising amount of fear she felt on the procedure table when it started, the metal instruments, the doctor's white hair and unemotional voice, her failure to say anything to stop it.

"Are you alright?" the nurse had asked somewhere near the beginning. She didn't answer, because she didn't know.

Sally lies on her side, very still, listening to the chastened sounds of voices, crickets, and wind. The moment she closes her eyes she is asleep.

Her mother still lives in the family home where Sally and her brothers were raised. They've always called it a farmhouse, even though the adjacent field was sold off a long time ago by her father, before her parents were married. Although raised by a farmer, her father had no ambition to become one himself, and her mother, perhaps, had no interest in being a farmer's wife. Sally and her brothers slept on the second floor in small, claustrophobic bedrooms, and for as long as she can remember, the house's wood siding and trims have been marred by severely splintered white paint.

Lately, the splintered paint conjures up inside of her a peculiar sense of peacefulness and abandon. There's a certain morbid charm to it, like a prickly weed that produces at its tip a broad-leaved purple flower, or a pretty wrought iron gate with rusted hinges that creak and whine. Like the splintered paint, there's a morbid charm to a lot of things that remind her of her childhood—the red-brick fireplace in the living room stained black on the inner borders from soot, a million poplar leaves trembling, the wildness of the prairie wind that littered their yard with torn branches, and once, the intricately woven nest of a robin. It was her father who identified it as a robin's nest when she found it in the grass, and when she cried over the vulnerable little eggs, he lifted her above his shoulders so she could replace it in the trees. She recalls her father, a rather reserved man, and the way his eyes would rest contemplatively on things—those trembling poplar leaves, his row of evergreens that he grew from seed, the weeds that poked stubbornly through the gravel in the driveway, but most especially the flickering in the fireplace on colder evenings. A man must love a fire to stare at its wavering flames, nearly motionless, for hours.

All of these things she daydreams about as she drives to her mother's house on the other side of town, over the bridge that covers the narrow Sylvia River on its way to the immense Sylvia Lake. Beside her on the seat is the thawed container of soup from the fridge.

She turns onto Main Street, passes the manicured hyacinths along the soft-cornered brick walls of the Eleanor Hicks Presbyterian Church, and decides to make a stop at the florist on the nearby Weiser Crescent. This already has the feel of a difficult day, the memory of the one before still too raw, too unsettled, and flowers are, in a way, medicinal to melancholy. Also, if her mother is upset with her for not visiting yesterday, for normally she stops by every day, then she might be sated by a bouquet of roses. Indeed, both Sally and her mother adore flowers beyond what might be considered average. Flowers have the kind of beauty no room or yard is complete without, her mother often said, and if you can learn to properly care for flowers, you can learn to properly care for anything.

When Sally arrives at the florist, she parks the car, and steps onto the curb. The town's quiet streets seem quieter than usual, grim and overcast, unable to rid themselves of the nocturnal quality that settled here a week or so ago with all the heavy rain. Sally pushes open the door and is immediately, wonderfully enveloped by the scents of irises and orchids, hydrangeas and lilies, carnations and roses. The air is cool yet humid, the wide room dimly lit. The walls are a dark oak panelling, and birds of paradise vertically decorate a column near the centre. She meanders for a few minutes before finding the perfect bouquet of long-stemmed roses, cream coloured, their petals not yet opened in full. She thinks, rather mindlessly, that yet another reason to fall in love with flowers is that they know nothing of what she did the day before. They are just the soft, bright, indifferent blooms of a plant, concerned only with themselves. They mean only to stay alive long enough to brighten a room, and whose room they brighten is of no consequence; they brighten the cell of an inmate as proudly as they would the sanctum of a priest. She feels oddly, stupidly in love with all the inanimate things that could never judge her—the angled shelf that holds the greeting cards, the stacks of filmy wrapping paper, the single violet in a small ceramic cup by the window, almost starting to wilt. It would be easy to lose herself here for a while, for today this place seems to carry the feeling of a different realm, but her mother is waiting, and the female employee is looking at her strangely from above her frames. Sally heads to the counter. She nods when the woman asks if she would like to include some baby's breath. Both are then wrapped together in thin, filmy green-and-white-patterned sheets, and Sally carries the bundle, dripping, back to the car.

She pulls back onto Main Street, passes the lumber yard, crosses the train tracks, and continues north on Elnor Road, slowing slightly as the blacktop gives way to lose gravel. Soon the farmhouse emerges through the trees, its walls of splintered paint surrounded by the wrap-around porch that leans slightly to the west. Sally pulls the car up to the end of the driveway and steps out, carrying the container of soup in one hand and freshly wrapped flowers in the other. The yard remains in a frozen scene of disuse; the swing set is weather-grazed and orange with rust, weeds and thistles peek out from the dilapidated garden trough, while under the shadow of the old willow are the calmest memories of childhood, a cozy and wispy little sanctuary. A place to read or paint, a place to wonder, a place to hide.

Sally was—it was never made secret—an accident, the unplanned child of her mother's middle age. Her brothers, twins with fourteen years between her and them, fled to the west coast while she was still quite young. They are the dark-haired men who resemble their father, who send Christmas cards, who phone now and then to ask about their mother's health. She's not an only child, but a drum in the vein of an only child, and so the appointments, the decisions, the managing of finances—she handled all of it, ordered her life around whatever needed to be done. She did have a knack, her father would say, for keeping things shapely and under control, and her parents—and her brothers—certainly leaned on that quality. Yet once a family member takes on that role of caregiver, it's either very difficult or impossible to get out of. Still, that was the father she loved, this is the mother she has, and these are the things that daughters are expected to do.

Sally steps past the old flowerpot that sits on the porch, the decorative one that never held flowers; instead it had always been the keeping place for garden shears and muddied garden gloves. She opens the door and enters the house, immediately taking in the familiar smells of humid wood and the creaks and bends of the old floorboards. As she places the container of soup on the table and enters the dining room, she catches the other smell that lives here. It's a rank, unwavering odour, faint yet distinct, the smell of illness. She notices it some days more than others.

Sally sets the wrapped roses on the table and crosses the linoleum, which opens broadly into the darkened living room, for the curved bow window is draped with curtains heavy enough to shut out most of the daylight, but there is still enough light coming through the willow branches outside to form a delicate, lattice-like shadow pattern along the more sunlit areas of the curtains. The pattern reminds her of the white forests that grow out of the frost crystals on a poorly insulated window in the dead of winter. One of the thinner willow branches has grown long enough to reach the house, and it taps gently against the windowpane. In the armchair facing the window is her mother, just beginning to wake, a pretty moss-green afghan splayed across her lap. Sleepily, Mary turns her head toward Sally.

"Hi, Mom," Sally says quietly.

Mary gazes at her for a moment, seemingly bewildered by the presence of another person in the room, then slowly turns back to the window. "Are the tapping sounds of a branch against the glass as depressing to you as it is to me?"

Sally descends the single step into the room and kneels beside the armchair. "I'm sorry I didn't come yesterday, Mom."

"It's alright. I wasn't sure whether you had," Mary says. She closes her eyes, opens them again, rather languidly, still trying to pull herself from sleep. "I was dreaming about sunsets."

"Sunsets?"

"Last night's sunset was beautiful. There hasn't been enough of those lately. They've been dull, most of them. Not enough colour."

"Well, it's been cloudy."

"I love watching the sunsets through the trees. The colourful ones. With orange and crimson."

"Yes, those are nice."

"Bright crimson sunsets," Mary says absently.

"I brought you some soup."

"I'm not hungry."

"You don't have to eat any right now. It's still early," Sally says, feeling more conscious now of how warm the room is. The house is overheated as always, at her mother's insistence, for she seems to feel the cold more and more. "We'll have the soup at lunch."

"What I would rather have right now is one of my pills."

"Mom, not yet," Sally sighs. "The nurse comes at eight to help with your pills, so it's too early for another one. It's only nine thirty. I'll give you one when we have lunch."

"For heaven's sake, I wish you'd let me manage it," Mary says irritably. "They're my pills, aren't they?"

Sally looks at her mother and sees an expression that somehow seems as tender as it does malicious. But Sally knows better than anyone that her mother, beneath the thick outer shell, is entirely lacking in malice. She's full of contrition and spite, but never cruel.

"I'm not denying you the pills," Sally says wanly, loathe to engage in the same argument she often has with her mother. "You were taking too many on your own."

"Better than being in pain."

"I'll give you one when we have our lunch, like I said."

"Two."

"Fine, two," Sally relents. "But two is the most you can have at one time. And I'll leave a note for the staff so they know you've had it."

Sally walks toward the long curtains and pushes them open impatiently. "It's always too dark in here. No wonder you lose track of what time it is. It's these horrible curtains that make it feel so depressing in this room. Much more so than that tree branch."

The sky and yard are bathed in a dull steel-toned light, yet Mary raises an arm to shade her eyes. Standing directly in front of the window, Sally sees, to the east, a pale blue clearing on the horizon.

"It's not very cheerful out there today, is it?" Mary quips.

"Well, it's better than keeping the curtains closed all the time," Sally says decisively. "I'll talk to the doctor again about your pain management, if you feel it's not enough. Alright?"

"That doctor is useless."

"No, he's not. I don't know why you always want to blame him for everything."

"He left me in pain for months because he thought I'd be turned into an addict. Imagine! A woman my age who will probably be brown bread in a matter of weeks." Mary pauses for a moment, regains her breath, then continues. "If I'm to die as an addict, but without pain, then so be it. It should be my choice."

"Mom, please don't get upset. I don't want you getting short of breath. And like I said, I am not trying to deny you any medication, but there is such a thing as taking too much of it. I don't want to worry about you overdosing yourself."

Mary lowers her arm and rests her head against the back of the armchair. "You do what you think is best. I'm not in my own hands any longer, it seems."

Sally kneels again beside her mother, takes her cold hand and warms it inside her own. She runs her fingers along the raised bones and soft veins, looks up at the hollowness of her mother's changing face, the still thick mass of grey-white hair loosely pinned back. When she kneels this close, Sally can smell the familiar scent of her mother, behind the scent of illness, a consoling quality she could never quite put her finger on. It's the smell of something powdery and fresh. Her mother must have allowed the staff to help her with a shower this morning.

"I'll talk to the doctor tomorrow," Sally reassures her, still stroking her hand. "I'll see what he says. Maybe there's something else we can try. But today I want you to promise me that you will eat a little bit. If you don't eat, you'll get weak. In fact, you're already weak. And you told me you don't want to go back to the hospital. You told me you wanted to stay in this house for as long as you can. So, you have to eat."

Mary lifts her other hand and rests it, very gently, over Sally's. "Alright. I will eat."

Her mother's softer side is starting to warm through, and Sally knows the day will be easier from here on. Wistfully, wearily, they smile at one another.

"I brought you some flowers."

"Did you?" Mary says, lightly clapping her hand against Sally's. "Bring them in the room. Let's put them beside me, here on the table."

"Alright. I'll get them."

Sally goes to the kitchen, takes the container of soup from the table and places it in the fridge. There is a thin layer of dust on the countertops and stove, so she takes a moment to wipe them. As she's wiping around the sink, she sees a note, addressed to her, sticking out from the locked cupboard that holds her mother's medications. She quickly recognizes the distinct cursive handwriting that details the small events of her mother's morning; the shower, the shortness of breath, the refusal of food, the pain rated at a six out of ten. The nurse arrived to administer the medication around nine thirty. Beth, one of her mother's caregivers, often left behind these helpful little notes.

Something about the singular scrawl reminds her of a woman she passed on the sidewalk after leaving the clinic, when she had been a mere reticence of a woman hovering along the sidewalk, weaving through the unconcerned crowd. She sees them all in her mind—the modish men and women in handsome and tailored suits, some with their hair left shaggy, some a little more coiffed, their shoes and briefcases matching or not. Distinguished from all the harried movement was a young woman with a short poem or verse tattooed on the side of her leg, who accidentally hitched the scalloped edge of her sea-green dress on a metal rail, unhitched it, leaving it to once again drift and billow in the breeze in a way that reminded her of seaweed dancing side to side near the shallow end of a lake. Sally had caught only a few words of the verse, something about a deep breath, something about a braggart heart, something that distracted her and gave her a vague sense of renascence.

In the kitchen pantry, Sally finds a glass vase. She fills it with water then unwraps the roses from their sheets, trims the thorny stems, and carefully arranges them before returning to the living room.

"I see Beth was here this morning," Sally remarks on her way in. "She left me a note."

"Yes," Mary says. "I'd forgotten her name."

"I'm glad you let her help with a shower."

"Only because she's good about it. Some of the girls are in such a rush, turning and flipping me like a piece of meat on a grill."

"I can't imagine any of the staff doing that."

"Well, imagine it or don't imagine it," Mary snaps, then turns to the window.

Sally places the vase on the small round table that sits between the armchair and floral sofa, thinking the new cream-coloured roses seem fitting on a table in a room with a bow window and a hopeful stretch of blue on the horizon. Her mother often remarks that flowers complete a room, and they do. This room in particular is ingrained as the most familiar in Sally's life, for this room, where the family spent most of their time, has inhabited her since childhood, far longer than the rooms of her married home. The room exists in a world of its own, apart from all others, where everything speaks directly to her own history, a history that solidifies itself into objects so completely that even the metal fire pick leaning on the soot-stained brick implies a lengthy story of some kind. Her childhood wasn't perfect, but it was good, and this is still the place where life relaxes its grasp a bit, and where time feels slightly less defined.

"Cream-coloured roses," Mary says, leaning into them. "Lovely. Of course, I would have preferred lilacs."

"That surprises me. Since when do you prefer lilac over roses?"

"Lilac was my mother's flower. I suppose it would just be nice for a change, to smell them again. The kitchen especially would be doused in the scent of lilac when they were in season."

"I think I remember you mentioning that, once or twice," Sally says reminiscently. "But September is almost over, so lilac season is long gone, unfortunately."

"So, it is," Mary laments, rather more to herself than to Sally.

"Those roses remind me of something a florist told me a long time ago. She said that all roses have a certain meaning, depending on their colour. Yellow roses represent joy and friendship, lavender roses symbolize enchantment. The cream-coloured ones are supposed to convey charm, and something else. I think it was thoughtfulness. Anyway, that's what she said."

"Sounds like hogwash."

"Well, maybe so."

Mary adjusts the vase slightly, leans into them a bit closer. "You were friends with her, were you not?"

"The florist?"

"No. That girl. Beth."

"Oh, yes, we were friends. A long time ago."

"I remember you used to go to the river," Mary remarks redolently. "You and your friends, always running away. You kids would be gone for hours."

"I haven't thought about that in years," Sally responds dismissively. Indeed, it has been a long time since Sally even considered Beth, the quiet, magnanimous friend of her past, outside the present context of being a caregiver to her mother. They drifted apart naturally, yet Sally has held on to a vague, distrait affection for her, the endless sort of affection one often has for anyone tied to their youth. Beth remains unmarried and childless, unbound by anything or anyone in town aside from her own mother, whom, to the best of Sally's knowledge, lives in the nursing home. Sally envies Beth, suddenly, unaccountably, almost to the point of resentment, for still having any number of paths open to her, for being as free as a bird now as she was when they were teenagers. Hasn't she noticed that there is nothing tying her down? Why does she not simply take off?

"You aren't friends with her any longer? With that girl?"

"No, not really."

"Why is that?"

"I suppose there is no reason," Sally says, after considering the question for a few moments. She goes to the small radio that sits on a shelf above the television. She switches it on and adjusts the dial until she tunes clearly into what sounds like old folk music. She leaves it there; the room is otherwise too quiet, too vulnerable to unwanted questions. As she turns toward the sofa, she is taken by a sudden jolt of pain across her abdomen. A cruel reminding, for she had a few isolated minutes of forgetting all about it. She takes a deep breath and experiences an unexpected, fragmentary vision of the child's face, heavenly and ashen, completely beautiful and innocent, a face she's never seen, but will see every day.

She places a hand over her stomach as she lies down on the flower-patterned sofa, her knees bent, feeling the tips of its rusted inner springs beneath the thin upholstery poking into the small of her back. She can't stretch out on the sofa completely; the end is covered in books and papers and miscellaneous junk. She will have to tackle that small mess, sooner or later. It's unlike her to ignore any kind of untidiness, but that seems a more hopeless kind, for in addition to books and papers are old letters, photo albums, and other keepsakes. Her mother understandably wants to hold on to them, and Sally finds the thought of shuffling through them daunting, too bleak, almost funereal. For in examining them, she will have to decide in her mind what should be kept, what can live on, and what will eventually be left to moulder somewhere in the filth of a depot or landfill. Grainy black and white photos of her unsmiling ancestors rotting alongside a single-use food container; it's the most disheartening thing she can imagine.

"Are you having a nap?" Mary asks.

"No. Just resting."

"Well, rest then. You look exhausted, quite frankly. Your age is catching up with you, finally. Your face is starting to look as though someone let a layer of air out of the tire."

"You're on form today," Sally says plaintively.

"Oh, come on now. You're very nearly as beautiful as you ever were. Older, yes, which no one can help. I only meant to say that you look tired. Go ahead and rest. Myself, I won't nap. I feel all I've done for two days is nap. As a matter of fact, I feel quite awake."

"Good. Are you hungry yet?"

"No," Mary rebuffs. "But I would like a pill."

"Mom, please." The pain in her abdomen has passed, but she leaves her hand resting over her stomach. She was expecting more pain in the days that followed, but thus far the discomfort has been very little.

"Yes, I know," Mary says in equal measure of glumness and defiance, snapping Sally out of her reverie. "I'm sorry. I'll behave. I will wait for my pills until lunch. I will eat my lunch. Maybe even a glass of wine to wash it down."

"Very funny. How about some water. Or juice."

"What kind of juice?"

"I don't know. I don't remember what you have in the fridge."

"Your father always had orange juice."

"Yes, I remember that."

"He would be upset with me for making a joke about wine. Guilt me over it, in his own quiet way. Your father smoked in this house for all the years I knew him, and I never once made him feel awful about that. It was his house, but now it's my house." Mary pauses for a moment, regains her breath, then continues. "I avoided that wretched habit all my life and here I am. I'm the one with lung cancer, left to rot, while your father was blessed with a quick and peaceful death in his own bed after an ordinary day, asleep like a baby."

"It wasn't quite that way. Dad was sick for a long time after his heart attack. Remember? He was so weak on some days, he could barely get anything done."

"Even so. Never more than a day in the hospital. He died easy, your father, if you ask me."

Sally doesn't respond, and after a minute the two of them settle into a comfortable silence.

From when Sally was very young, the arguments that ensued between her mother and brothers were often followed by her father's pleas for them to calm down. She would lie on her bed, her little hands hollowed over her ears, waiting for the bad sounds to stop. People bear witness to a myriad of wounding things in life, then over time let the resulting emotions settle, like ashes coming to rest after a fire that destroyed something precious. Sally envisages herself as a little girl, rising to her bedroom window on tiptoes to watch her brothers get into the car, knowing, by a kind of disenchanted, childlike clarity, that they wouldn't come back. It's the first feeling of profound sadness she can remember.

Her mother never disclosed the details of those years, what Sally has come to call her drinking years, so Sally is left to assume that she drank for her own private reasons, whether it was to muffle an obscure feeling of misery or to repress a well-known demon. Sally couldn't appreciate the depths of her mother's unhappiness, yet it's also true that she hasn't fully explored the present depths of her own, nor found a cause, that is, if a singular cause is needed. Often one's sadness is vague and can't be isolated to any one thing. It can be caused, it seems, by nothing at all. And so, Sally muses, perhaps their unhappiness is merely a continuance of the endless, ancient stories of sadness, the same kind that has preyed upon centuries of minds—lost fortunes, failures, unrequited love, disconnection, undeserved illness, or nameless pain of any kind. There is nothing new about wanting to hang a veil between sadness and sober conscience. If her mother's chosen veil was alcohol, then hers must be art.

"Tell me," Mary begins. "If you haven't fallen asleep. How is Jesse? Has the party already happened?"

"No, it's on Saturday," Sally replies, her eyes settling casually on the brick fireplace and leaning fire pick. It was largely her father who brought in the firewood and tended to the fires. After he died, no one bothered, and the fire pick probably hasn't moved since he last set it down. Now the furnace huffs and clicks from October to May.

"I think it's silly to rent a hall for that sort of thing," Mary remarks.

"It was supposed to be at the hall, but now it's all changed," Sally says. "We're hosting it in our yard."

"In your yard?"

"Yes, so hopefully the weather cooperates. It's supposed to. We'll have food, drinks, a fire, tables and chairs, maybe some music."

"Well, cheaper I suppose than renting a hall, but it still seems to me like a lot of fuss for an engagement party," Mary announces.

"Yes. I have to agree with you on that."

"But he's doing alright, is he?"

"Yes."

"And how are things between you and Jaime?"

Sally raises her head and looks at Mary, who is leaning into the flowers and stroking one of the petals. "Why do you ask?"

"No reason in particular, only you never say very much about how things are."

"You never ask," Sally remarks.

Mary lets go of the rose petal and fixes on Sally.

"Well, today I am asking," she says shrilly. "I sit here all day and all night, by myself, thinking of you. I think of my children. I think about your father. I am dying all day in this house and thinking about all of you."

"You're right, I'm sorry," Sally acquiesces.

"Go on then. Tell me. Tell me about your life. Tell me if you've been happy."

"If I've been happy." Sally repeats the words to herself.

"Yes. That's what I asked."

"No, I haven't been very happy," Sally says after a pause. "But I have no right to say it."

"Nonsense. You've every right, if it's true. But you were happy at one point, I remember. When Jesse was young, and you took that silly college course."

"Art history."

"Whatever it was," Mary says, with a wave of her hand. "Tell me. Does Jaime know you're unhappy?"

"No, I don't think so, and anyway it's not his fault. He's a good man, you know that. He's been good to me, and good to Jesse. I imagine he thinks I've been just fine. Which I've often been, I suppose."

Mary leans her head, wearily, against the back of the chair. Then she half-sings, unhurriedly, in a falsetto voice, "It is always the men who believe everything to be fine."

"Maybe so," Sally acknowledges rather distractedly, facing the bow window, where a little robin hops unconcernedly along the windowsill. At least, she thinks it's a robin. It looks pretty, like a piece of moving art, a perfectly sculpted mass of feathers. It twins its head awkwardly to the side and takes off from the porch rail, circles in the air, then rises and swoops out of sight beyond the stand of poplars. Sally watches after it with envy, then feels herself mentally dragged back to the time, years ago, when it became obvious that she would have to stop going to classes. There was Jesse to worry about, but really, it was about the money. She recalls replacing the phone on the receiver after informing the school of her decision and, standing in the silent dining room with a few tears welling in her eyes, had thought to herself very sullenly that the world of art, whatever that may be, does not exist for her, the ordinary housewife in an ordinary housecoat. It exists only for the supremely talented, the lucky few, the elite. Just as there are ancient stories of sadness, so there are ancient stories of artists doomed to live their lives in comfortable homes, caring for husbands, caring for children, their physical needs met, their days uneventful, tortured and taunted by an indifferent world. She would be outwardly indistinguishable from everyone else, and inside, an embittered remnant of something that might have been great; the presentiment of something that should have been, but never was.

And so, she imagines herself now as she imagines the other obscure artists of the world, like a multitude of shells at the bottom of a lake, beautiful in their varied colours, but unknown, thickly covered by layers of earth, never to be seen.

"Art history," Mary says thoughtfully, interrupting the silence. "I suppose that makes sense."

She pauses, then adds wistfully, "My beautiful artistic daughter."

"Your once artistic daughter."

"You don't paint often, do you?"

"No."

"You used to put on shows, whatever they're called, in the city."

"They were exhibits. I put on a lot of exhibits, a long time ago."

"That's right, and there was one at the gallery here in town. I remember. I was there, at the little gallery."

"It was just a small exhibit at the library, but yes."

"And you never graduated from the university."

"No, we couldn't afford me going back and forth to the city. And Jesse was so young then, just a baby," Sally says, feeling a sudden mental fatigue. She wishes she could sit quietly for the rest of the morning, without being impelled to discuss anything at all, especially the matter of her happiness, or lack thereof. Yet she hasn't been altogether unhappy. The day-to-day process of living seems neither melancholic nor enthusiastic, for those emotions are simply too large to pass through a membrane that has grown perpetually complacent and numb. It's a thick, stubborn layer, unwilling to break, but she can still feel a flicker of enthusiasm burning somewhere beneath that sleepy membrane. It's far away, but it's there, glimmering, wanting to get out, eager for a chance to pass through and bring itself to light.

"Is that when the unhappiness set in?" Mary inquires.

"Mom, I don't know," Sally says, a bit too impatiently, rubbing her forehead without realizing. "And I haven't been unhappy, necessarily. I just remember that when I was in school, it seemed as though I was at the beginning of something. And I was hoping for ... well, I don't know what I was hoping for."

"Something else?"

"Yes. Something else."

Mary pauses for a moment. "I see."

Outside the wind picks up and the thin willow branch resumes its soft tapping against the glass. Mary can hear the tapping, but can't see the branch; the bulk of the tree is hidden behind the wall and the corner of the window still shadowed by the curtain's edge.

"You'll have to be very careful with those thoughts," Mary cautions. "You're right when you say you have a good husband. As daft as men can be sometimes, he is still a good man. And you have your son. He doesn't come around to visit me anymore, but he seems as good as his father. You should not—"

"I know Mom," Sally interrupts. "I understand what you're saying. I have a lot to be grateful for."

"Wait!" Mary says abruptly. "I'm never allowed to say

anything. All those girls come to wash me and throw me in and out of bed, then scamper out the door so quickly I can't get a word in. And your father is gone. He's gone, but at least he listened. Your brothers don't call because I said so many things wrong."

"Please, don't get upset," Sally pleads tiredly. "You made some mistakes, everyone does. But you're not a fool."

"Well listen to you, being so kind. You were always that way, so perfect and well-mannered and kind, the apple of your father's eye." Mary's voice carries a hint of irony. "But I was indeed a fool. Foolishness defeated me many years ago. It did me in. I drank and drank and then I drank some more, ran my mouth and off they went. And now I sit alone in this damn chair, and that old branch keeps hitting the window. It's enough to drive anyone crazy."

"Mom, I really don't want to get into anything right now."

"I suppose I shouldn't be surprised that you'd have a problem. The kindly daughter, the artist, the oh-so-sensitive soul. I must coat my words in sugar for you."

"That isn't what I meant," Sally says despondently. "I just don't want you getting short of breath. You don't have the oxygen tank yet and it scares me when you get so out of breath."

"Oxygen tank?"

"Yes, they're delivering a portable oxygen tank for you. We've discussed this. You don't have to use it all the time, but at least it will be here if you need it."

"I won't need it."

"Yes, you will."

"I'm only short of breath when I'm upset."

"That's not true."

"You just don't want to listen!" Mary scowls. "I'll never be comfortable living in this house without your father. He was a good listener."

Sally sighs exhaustively and sits up on the sofa. She needs to forget about herself for a moment and listen. These are the sort of ministrations a daughter must perform, unselfishly, for a dying mother. A decent daughter, a decent person, would be only too glad to do so.

"Alright, Mom," she says, meeting her eyes. "You're right. I'm listening."

Mary raises a long, arthritic forefinger and points it at Sally as though she caught her in a lie. "You forget that I was once young, and like you I never appreciated it, not properly. I can see your unhappiness. You're my daughter, after all. I can see it in your eyes. I can see your boredom."

Mary lowers her finger, sinks back into the chair, and draws a deep, moist-sounding breath. "Maybe you're disappointed because you made certain agreements with yourself, that you would never settle for one thing or another, that if you wait and hope hard enough and long enough your life will someday turn out this way or that. It is a stupid mistake to believe that your life is supposed to be any certain way, because let me tell you, it isn't. There's a lot of unhappy women in the world, and I'm ashamed if you're one of them. It's a tired, ugly thing."

Mary stops for a few moments to regain her breath and continues, looking at Sally with a motherly guile. "I don't think you're quite old enough to understand what it means to waste time. I had the perfect man, and he gave me good children. But I tossed my time with them aside. Don't be that way. Don't let your pain be your own fault. The time I lost haunts me like a phantom now that I'm alone in this house, now that they've gone. Your husband, your son. That is your history. It's what you have built, you can't take it back now. That is your life. And it is a good life. Happiness, much like your unhappiness, is just a way of thinking, a frame of mind, and looking at things the wrong way can soak up a lot of your time. Take a silly course here and there if it pleases you, paint again if you wish. But do not be a woman who waits for more. You will wait, and you will wait, and you will wait."

At first Sally can only look furtively at her mother, the exceedingly gaunt, indelible woman she adores yet has always felt suffocated by in equal measure; the woman who so rarely shows her vulnerability. Her mother is watching her curiously, as if some sort of grand proclamation is now due, in turn, from her. Sally has scant idea of how to respond, yet quietly resolves to give more attention to her mother from this moment until she passes.

"Mom, I—"

"I'm not finished," Mary interrupts again, and her expression shifts from aggravation to concern. "I want to tell you not to let your marriage become one where the only words you bother to speak are the ones he wants to hear. If you're unhappy, I'm sure he knows it. So, let him listen to you, and make sure you listen to him too."

"Okay," Sally says, nodding.

"I listened to your father, but not as well as I could have." Mary's tone is distant. "I should have died before him."

"Okay, Mom, I understand," Sally says, slowly and somewhat absently. The air around them feels changed from the usual, letting an unfamiliar calmness into the room, as if her mother's words are peeling away a layer of dissonance that has always hung between them.

"Good. I'm glad you do." Mary peers once again into the roses. "But now I'm tired, and the ache in my back is worse. I want one of my pills."

"It's still too early," Sally reminds her.

"No, it's not," Mary responds derisively. "Give me one. We agreed that I would have two pills at lunch, so I'll take one now, and I'll put off the other until lunch."

"Fine," Sally relents. "One pill. I won't argue."

"Thank heaven for that," Mary says, wincing.

"Are you alright?"

"No." Mary pushes the green afghan off her lap. "I have to go lie down. I don't know what's made me so tired all of a sudden, but I need to lie down for a while."

"Okay, I'll help you up," Sally says, rising from the sofa. "I'll get your pill before we go to the bedroom."

"No. Help me to the bedroom first."

"Alright. Do you need the washroom?"

"No."

Sally wraps her arm around her mother's waist to help her stand. "Maybe you'll feel up to going outside after lunch. We can sit on the back porch together, on those old wicker chairs. We haven't done that for a while."

"Yes, maybe so. But let me lie down first, for heaven's sake."

They step away from the chair, and for a few minutes are absorbed in the task of moving up the single stair from the living room, through the dining room, then down the hall. At one point, they stop and stand still for a minute while Mary catches her breath. Sally gently runs her hand up and down her back, as a mother would affectionately to a daughter, in a propriety sort of way, full of maternal reassurance and warmth.

"I'm sorry," Mary says when they reach the bedroom. "I've been hard on you. You're a good daughter and I'm nothing more than a burden."

"Don't worry," Sally says calmly, almost in a whisper. "Sit

down and I'll go get your pill."

She goes into the kitchen, opens the locked cupboard, and removes the white cap from the tall orange bottle. She hears her mother trying to cough. It's a pained sound, weak and wet. Sally fills a cup with water, returns the medication to the cupboard, locks it, then goes to her mother. The bedroom, like the other rooms, is overheated, damp smelling, and darkened by curtains. A lit lamp on the nightstand emanates a dim, muted light beneath a green shade. Mary sits at the side of the bed as a child would in waiting for a parent, eyes half closed, hands at her side, waiting to be tucked in.

"Here, Mom, take your pill," Sally bids tranquilly.

Mary takes the little green pill and places it on her tongue, relieved. She sips from the cup of water, some of which dribbles down her chin, then hands the cup back to Sally.

"Can you lift your legs onto the bed?" Sally asks.

"I think so."

Mary lifts her legs slowly onto the bed, inwardly grateful for her daughter's help. Sally runs her fingers once along her mother's hair, kisses her forehead. Again, she inhales the familiar scent of her mother, powdery and fresh.

"Have a good rest," she whispers.

Already her mother's eyes are closed and Sally hears the thin rattle of her breathing, slow and shallow at first, then laboured. Her breathing is strange sometimes, as if her lungs could vanquish her at any moment. Sally folds her arms and watches her calmly. Her mother appears even more fragile when she's asleep, frighteningly vulnerable, almost insufficient, and self-effacing in a way, as though the hugeness of her personality should imply an equally great size. Yet here she is in her bed, surprisingly small.

The edge of her nightgown is bunched above her knees, leaving her swollen calves in plain sight. If only she wouldn't refuse the compression garments; if only she didn't always have to be so defiant. Sally lifts the comforter from the foot of the bed, covers her mother's withering body, and tucks it gently around her shoulders. Quietly, she switches off the lamp and backs out of the room.

Without pausing, Sally heads straight out the back door, onto the porch, and takes the garden shears from the flowerpot. She descends the steps, goes around to the front yard, and begins trimming any willow branch within a foot of the windowpane. As it falls, one of the thinner branches carries a ladybug down onto the overgrown grass. Sally crouches to watch the displaced creature, its six little black legs scrambling to pull itself upright. It depresses her unexpectedly, the desperation of this little bug, knowing she's to blame for its fear when it went from crawling innocently along a branch to being cast adrift when that branch was sheared loose. With one of the fallen twigs, she helps it over, then watches as it struggles to make its way up a blade of grass. Sally is relieved when after a moment, the ladybug takes flight, and she watches it weave and crisscross through the air in a frantic yet delicate way, redeemed, presumably, but still fearful.

When the path of the winged bug crosses the horizon, Sally realizes there's been a change in the weather. Instead of the distant blue line on the horizon that was visible when she arrived, now the blue is stretched out above the house, and the clearing allows the sun to brighten the yard and fields in a way it hasn't for days. The breeze is still cool, but it may not be too late in the year for an outdoor engagement party after all.

She walks around to the shady side of the house and dwells, wearily, on the wind-bitten paint and sun-blistered curtains that she can see hanging inside some of the windows, their bluish floral pattern falling in soft, tarnished pleats. Weeds are growing tall around the porch, reaching halfway up the side and through the wooden boards. The house and yard will need plenty of work before its resale, but decides it's too soon and too depressing to worry about those things. She squints up at the second-storey window of what was once her bedroom, then looks directly up to the sky, which seems amplified, like an exaggerated version of itself. It's blue and bright with pillowy, slow-moving clouds that remind her of the paintings Jesse used to bring home from school, the vivid, cartoon-like skies children tend to make before embracing some degree of realism. And in her observation, Sally recollects it was precisely that—realism—which became her first true love in art. To capture on a canvas the beauty of an ordinary moment—a farmer standing in a purple field of ready flax, a couple sweeping leaves from a porch onto wet grass, a woman standing with garden trimmers in the broad shadow of a threadbare farmhouse—then to slant her mind perfectly, like an ornate kettle tipped forward just so, and let that captured image spill out of her mind and onto the canvas. There was, and is, no better feeling.

If only she hadn't given up her ambitions so easily. If only she hadn't lost the glimmering, consuming part of herself that made her want to paint all the time, that mysterious flicker of light that made her an artist. If only she could once again find pleasure in her life, as her mother says, just as it is. She feels a sudden divisiveness between the woman she was prior to stepping foot in that clinic, a sad woman full of flaws, but still clean in a way that the woman she is today, standing here on the grass, who had her womb scraped empty at that clinic, can never be again. She knew she would feel guilty, but she didn't know she would start to feel dirty. She misses the clean, innocently flawed version of herself, a woman who once found a great inner peace through her art, who never would have had the thought she had yesterday before going to bed, that there is something wrong with having distractions. For to concentrate on the finer features of life—the cobbled stones along a pathway, the streams of sunlight falling waywardly along a kitchen table, a singing blackbird, and the exquisite act of painting—is to touch with one's spirit the prose and poetry of life itself. Sally feels a sudden conviction with these thoughts, that the intricacies of life, the threads of its tapestry, are the essence of life, and thus, of art.

Sally climbs the porch steps and returns the garden shears to the flowerpot, envisions in her mind the way things used to appear in this yard, her mother in a rimmed sunhat bent over the garden, tending to rows of carrots and beans, then in the kitchen, shelling peas and canning tomatoes.

Her death is very near, Sally knows and thinks of this often, yet it's difficult to imagine this house being absent of her, death itself being such a difficult concept to imagine. Death is the inevitable ending for everyone, but it's a distant, abstract event, an event too foreign from the daily experience to grasp in its entirety until the moment it arrives. And even then, it's impossible to say whether the dying can claim a better understanding of death than those who stand in the room around them, watching. It's also difficult to say if it's preferable for death to reach out in a quick and unexpected way, rather than to watch it seep into someone slowly. The slowness feels like a punishment, as though one is made to view the ticking of a clock while strapped to a chair in front of it, waiting for the invisible. Yet as Sally looks out at the garden troughs, which remain picturesque despite their neglect, she feels herself passing into a more peaceful realm of thought; maybe after such a prolonged period of pain, dying is not such a dark thing. It's not something vertiginous or cruel, but something calm. Her mother will simply fall asleep late one night, or earlier in the day, and once her eyes close there will be a very gentle drawing away, followed by a slight pull into whatever happens next, if anything. It would be the sense of something faint yet distinct passing by, one as natural and as peaceful as the blue clearing that drifted, with slow-moving clouds, across the horizon. It could feel that passive, it could be that serene.

Sally goes back inside the house and into the dining room. She opens the window slightly to let in the fresh air, then looking around the room, decides the best way to pass the time before lunch is to clean. She's the only one who does, and she's been neglectful. She starts by dusting the living room, then empties and wipes the shelves of the fridge, and scrubs down every surface in the washroom. She takes the unwashed pile of sheets and stuffs them into the washing machine, and as she steps into the hallway, considers her earlier thought of death, and the speck of life no longer inside of her. The life that somehow feels both given away freely by her, yet unjustly taken by another. It could have happened in a similar way, she wonders, she hopes, not as something awful, but as something passive and soft, a blue clearing in the sky that opened, then was reached, and through there, only calm, only light.

Sally glances at the clock. Over an hour has passed since her mother fell asleep. She goes to the kitchen, takes the soup from the fridge. She fills a pot with the soup and sets it on the stove to heat. From the cupboard she takes two bowls, then from the drawer she takes two spoons, lying them across from one another on the dining room table. She places a napkin on each of the placemats. She feels a twinge of excitement about sitting down for a bowl of homemade soup with her mother. Rather, she feels suddenly wrapped up in the nostalgia of these creaking floorboards, these blue earthenware bowls, this set of cutlery, as if she's caught herself in one of those rare moments where one recognizes the preciousness and frailty of life, the fleeting nature of it, of simple things, like the powdery scent of her mother and the prettiness of a set dining room table, which is only missing one thing. She goes to the living room, takes the vase of roses from beside the armchair and places it at the centre of the table. Yes, Sally observes, they really do complete a room. She plays again for a moment with the arrangement, stroking the soft petals, breathing in their perfume.

It is time to wake her mother. It is time for lunch.

A small framed print of her favourite painting hangs on the wall next to the window, behind the easel, in the corner room ineffably cluttered with art history books, stacks of paper, and half-painted canvases. Early this morning, after Jaime left for work and the dishes were washed and put away, Sally went to the art store in town for supplies and, impulsively, to the florist for fresh flowers. It's the sort of bouquet she prefers, not of one particular kind of flower, but a colourful, varied mix. She inherited this love of flowers from her mother, but rather than creamy roses or white orchids, Sally prefers the brighter, more cheerful qualities of tulips and carnations and gerbera daisies. When she got home, she trimmed their stems, placed them in a vase, then set them down next to the window in the cluttered room.

It's been one of those rare and singular mornings where she felt very awake and eager to begin the day; the sort of eagerness rendered only by thoughts of painting. The thoughts came to her during the night as a vague inner pulling, a faint, shimmering feeling, and so in pursuance of that feeling, she started the day with the hope that she might be able to set the guilt aside, if only for a short while, and paint. It was a silent crossroad reached unexpectedly in the early hours, and it seemed suddenly that she had no choice but to either try to paint away the shame, somehow, or drown.

But she isn't prepared to let the cold water take her, doesn't want to lose the good part of herself, has no wish to sink into the shores of that dreadful world where so many humans live; that forlorn recess of the mind where the most powerful depressions thrive, where black shadow ribbons cling like seaweed around the ankles of the saddest beings, until they finally pull them under. She had visions of that terrible shore, last night, half-asleep in the dark, but the part of her that loves life rejected it, and she opened her eyes. This is the time to swim, to push forward, to heal, to set a course for self-reparation the same way an addict readies themselves for the first step in a recovery program; they simply open the door and step inside, knowing that the first step is the hardest and most necessary. It seems suddenly clear to Sally that she can survive, even thrive, if she can paint again, if she can step through the gate and enter that portal. After all, peace has come into her life by placing brush to canvas more than by anything else, and so maybe if she forces the first painting, more will freely follow.

She has the house to herself, and fresh supplies. The last half of the morning has been spent transforming the cluttered area into a more workable space, and now with the vase of colourful flowers by the window, the room already feels airier and less gloomy. She sorted through everything, arranging old books, tossing away tubes of dried paint. The environment in which one works is important, she muses, and believes an improvement of this room might release a newness of inspiration. That's the hope, at least.

Now, with all that done, it is shortly before one o'clock. Sally is sitting straight and upright on the stool in front of a freshly unwrapped canvas that rests on the easel. The paintbrushes are propped inside a cup of warm water, and a row of watercolours wait at her side. She wonders, for a few minutes, what to paint.

She turns instinctively to the print of her favourite painting, the one that depicts a young woman paralyzed as a child by polio. She's wearing a yellow dress and crawling across a grassy field toward her father's farmhouse. Sally recalls her first view of it, the painting called *Cristina's World*, lit across a projection slide during one of many prodigious lectures at the college of art. The professor was an older, genteel man, yet when it came to bandying the relevance of certain paintings or art forms during their time of production, he spoke very animatedly.

"Look at the colours," he said, pacing back and forth beneath the projection light. "They're too dark, far too dark. The image appears barren and muted. Many describe it as dull. The discussion had shifted in its favour over time, but I tend to agree with the original, lukewarm reception of it."

"Why was it criticized?" one student asked.

"I wouldn't say criticized, necessarily," the professor replied. "More largely ignored when it was first shown. You see, *Cristina's World* is merely the result of a painter looking out his window one day and seeing his neighbour's disabled daughter crawling through the grass. What's important to remember is that these were the years following the War, and some felt that a disabled girl in a field was too dull and depressing during an already depressing time. Following the war, there was a developing need for positive energy. For colour. For excitement. For art that was joyous and fresh and new. And that's precisely why abstract expressionism started to grow in popularity. This coincided with a resurgence of the old thought that to be an artist is to be part mad. It was felt that in order to paint with the kind of messiness associated with abstract expressionism, one would have to be unbalanced, or deranged in some way. Yet artists were believed to be rapt with fascinating visions, visions that offered the kind of escapism that was so craved at the time. It became less popular, then, to simply paint whatever was in front of you, in this case a young woman with polio in a field. Especially with such a dull colour pallet."

"How can a painting be criticized for its colour, when those colours might match exactly what the artist saw when he looked out the window?" another student asked. "Isn't that what realism is supposed to do?"

"Again, that this painting followed the War played a role in how it was received," the professor explained. "But there is also such a thing as language of colour. Realism calls for colour and shading according to subject matter. We'll go further into colour usage in a few weeks, but it involves knowing when to go from light to dark, and from dark to light. Shadows, for example, should be painted as though there is a light source coming from behind the painter, and so should take on a deeper tone of the local colour. *Cristina's World* doesn't abide by those rules, which is why they say it has an off use of colour … which we'll talk about more when we delve into colour use later. Here's another slide.

It's a Barnett Newman, expressionism at its best. Here the painter connects with the hidden emotion within the subject, meaning the inner world is shown without a dependence on the outer. It's a show of inner feeling, all that is felt within a moment. It ignores the reality of the external and finds the spirit, the truth, the madness ..."

Sally loves art in all forms, yet never had the desire nor the ability to undertake an abstract or expressionistic painting herself. The images in her mind's eye simply haven't poured out of her in that way. And she believes that when one sits down to paint, that which pours out of a person should come organically, through your soul to your hand, or not at all. Sally's forte has been in capturing the prairie landscape—the mercurial gold and yellows of the fields, the prairie grass gathered around the post of a barbed fence, the grain elevator standing high along the side of the tracks. It mattered to her that these scenes were captured in careful detail. She believes, still, that nothing in art or life could possibly be more beautiful than these things. She also believes, like the painter of *Cristina's World*, that inspiration can be found simply by looking out of one's window, for those are the images that cultivate a kind of storied expression of everyday life. And Sally envisages her paintings in that same way—an illumination of the ordinary things around her.

Gently, she runs her fingers along the row of paints meditatively, picks up a tube of burnt sienna, absently sets it down again.

It's a show of inner feeling, all that is felt within a moment. It ignores the reality and finds the spirit, the truth, the madness.

She looks at the canvas, the rectangle of white space where she is free to do anything. She tries to recapture the vague, shimmering feeling that she had earlier in the morning, the anticipatory feeling that comes with new supplies and a house to herself. She picks up the paintbrush and glances at the flowers, at their cheerful mix of pinks and reds and yellows atop stems of green. A flush of excitement passes through her, faint but distinct, enough to feel confident about unearthing some worthwhile part of her talent, of having a chance to step away from these shadows and move, as in the professor's words, from dark to light.

She will start simply, with a familiar subject, the lovely still-life image sitting right next to her; the vase of fresh flowers. She pours a small amount of Payne's grey onto the pallet, then imbues the tip of her paintbrush in the watercolour. She starts with the contour of the vase, a thin, curved line. Next, she paints the bottom half of the stems, the part immersed in water. For the stems above water, she'll have to dilute the paint a little less to darken their colour. She'll save the petals for last.

A sound drifts in. Someone is tapping at the back door, and Sally is wrenched out of her blissful trance, as when someone rips open the blinds unexpectedly in a pleasantly dim room and lets in a harsh burst of light. She's quickly irritated by the interruption. For the first time in a long time she's painting in a pure, faithful way, having finally entered the spirit of it. She knows that this is the sort of feeling that may not survive a distraction. She can already feel it drifting down to the depths from which it inexplicably rose, back into incoherence. The visitor taps at the door again, louder and more insistently. Wanting nothing more than an afternoon of solitude, she briefly considers ignoring them. Instead she sighs and places the paintbrush in its cup and the colour dilutes from the bristles and fades into the warm water. She rises from the stool. As she reaches the foyer, she hears Valerie's voice, then another voice, this one unfamiliar. Suddenly, Sally remembers that she'd arranged for Valerie and her mother to come for coffee this afternoon to discuss the engagement party, and the wedding. The fresh, damp canvas, the feelings of faith and replenishment, the row of watercolour; all of it would have to wait.

Cold coffee from the morning sits in the pot, she has no snacks to offer, and some papers and miscellaneous things cover the dining room table. But she can't leave them waiting on the porch any longer. She straightens her hair and blouse, looks longingly over her shoulder at her canvas and the grey outline of a vase, then opens the door. Standing on the porch is Valerie's mother, a robust woman several years older than Sally, whose name she can't remember. She seems meticulously put together, though, with a beige dress coat and short, coppery-blonde hair. Valerie, who with her long hair and willowy stature is very unlike her mother in appearance, holds a plate of muffins.

"Hi, Sally," Valerie's mother says. "We were just about to give up!"

"Hello," Sally says, "I must have lost track of time. Come in."

"Are you sure we're not interrupting anything?" Valerie asks.

"Not at all. Hang your coats and I'll get the coffee started."

Sally goes to the kitchen and dumps the coffee from the pot. She scoops fresh coffee into the machine, pours water into the reservoir, switches it on. Quickly, she goes to the dining room and moves the mess of papers and miscellaneous things into the top drawer of the sideboard.

"Come, have a seat at the table," Sally calls to them, laying a few napkins onto the table. She muses sullenly that such day-to-day obligations are damaging to the creative soul. There are too many persistent little demands. Life is a tiring string of distractions; a steady and injurious wear and tear that goes on and on. Which would all be more tolerable, much more tolerable, if it didn't leave her with such a dank feeling of self-suppression. The suppression is not optional, but mandated, if she is to perform these tasks efficiently; the setting down of napkins, the tidying of tables, the planning of parties.

Yet this censuring of life's little demands is always quickly followed by a sense of guilt, for who would not want and love these things; the setting down of napkins for guests, the tidying of tables around which to gather and drink fresh coffee, the planning of parties.

Her guests hang their coats and make their way inside the house. Sally absently straightens her blouse again, deciding that life is somehow both too short and too long, too empty yet too densely packed.

"You're working on a painting!" Valerie exclaims. "It looks nice so far. Are these flower stems?"

"Yes," Sally replies, coming around the corner. "I only just started it. There's not much to it yet. Can I take those muffins?"

Valerie nods and hands over the platter, her eyes roaming from the canvas, to the fresh flowers, to the meticulously arranged row of fresh paints.

Valerie's mother seems more focused on the damp outline of the vase. "It's beautiful already."

Sally turns to the table with the plate of muffins and hears her say, "It must be wonderful to have such talent. Valerie, wouldn't it be wonderful? What a gift. I could never draw worth anything."

"Me either. Just doodles and stick men." Valerie says jokingly.

Sally waits equivocally in the dining room as the two women, who have stepped uninvited into her corner room, examine the paint on the canvas. She should have draped the canvas before answering the door, or set it down on the floor behind the easel, facing the wall. It bothers her when anyone sees an unfinished project, keenly aware that an incomplete painting can look like a clumsy, amateurish placement of lines or colour, resembling very little. At least, that's how she imagines her unfinished paintings might appear to others who have no foresight into what they will be.

"Come have a seat in the dining room," Sally urges them. She returns to the kitchen to retrieve three cups and three teaspoons, and pours a small amount of milk from the carton into a white creamer. The blue glazed sugar bowl is already on the table. As the women take their seats, Sally sees that the little peperomia plant on the table, the gift from Valerie, still needs watering. The fringes of the top leaves appear tawny and gloomy and half-curled into themselves. She feels the familiar wave of uncertainty that comes over her in these moments. This is her own dining room, her own cups and teaspoons, yet the wave causes her to feel unusually detached and unsuited, as though she were the unwanted visitor, or a lost intruder, an inadequately rehearsed understudy who wandered onto the stage at an inappropriate time. She chastises herself for falling into these ridiculous moods whenever she is made to host, or socialize. Suddenly, she remembers the woman's name.

"Linda, how are you? I haven't seen you since—"

"Last fall, I believe it was," Linda interposes. "A dinner at the community hall."

"That's right, a fundraiser for the school. I suppose it's been nearly a year already."

"Time goes quickly," Linda remarks. "Honestly, I don't remember what they needed the funds for."

"It was for supplies, I think." Sally knows, but doesn't want to appear self-serving. "To replace some things in the music room, maybe for some new books or instruments."

She recalls the fundraiser, sitting next to Jaime at one of the rows of long white-clothed tables in the auditorium and feeling quite disinterested. She was once a student at that school, where gold star stickers were pasted to her art projects, and where she would sometimes disappear into the small room near the auditorium if the world felt thin and she wanted to be alone. It was more of a large closet than a room, where the theatre props and costumes were stored. She would hide there, running her fingers along vintage hand-held mirrors and the beads of silk gowns, and slip away into an intense state of daydreaming, her mind drifting to the mystical faraway places to which it seems only a child's mind can drift. In the back of the closet was a wooden armoire, and at the bottom was a drawer of hair clips and prop jewellery. She once draped herself in a green velvet cloak smelling of moth balls, donned the elaborate bracelets and pearls after the run of a play had come to a close, and twirled in front of an oval mirror. She was someone else, somewhere else. In the middle of that fundraiser, where the world again seemed thin and the air too close, she longed to do just that—walk without a word past the crowd as she had as a child to hide in the closet with the beads of a baroque silk gown, daydreaming about a whimsical faraway place.

Valerie unwraps the plate of muffins. "They're homemade. We baked them this morning."

"They're blueberry," Linda adds.

"Thank you," Sally says, and in looking at them, is reminded of the little raspberry bush by the ravine. She laments this summer as the first of many where she hadn't bothered to make jam out of the raspberries. Usually she gathers enough for three or four jars—one or two for herself, one or two for her mother.

She adds, "I wouldn't have had much to offer in the way of snacks, I'm sorry to say."

"It's nothing at all," Linda says cordially. She takes a muffin and gingerly starts to peel away the paper. "Well, then. About the party. Please, tell me what I can do."

"There isn't a lot more that needs to be done," Sally says. "Jaime and I will get the yard ready, and Jesse has already put some firewood together. We'll have a bonfire when it gets dark, which Valerie probably already told you. Only I haven't decided what kind of snacks to serve. Some bowls of chips and a few other things, I suppose. Oh, and a cake. I will make a cake." Sally suddenly recalls her earlier commitment to do so.

"No, you're doing too much," Linda decrees resolutely. "Having to host is enough trouble. I can make a cake. No, two cakes. Fifty people calls for a lot of cake!"

"You don't have to do that," Sally says.

"But I'd like to. It will make me feel useful."

"Well, alright, but we can split the cost of baking supplies."

"No, no, no, certainly we don't have to. I enjoy baking, as you can see." Linda gestures toward the plate of muffins. "Like I said, hosting is already a strain on you and your husband. I would have been happy to host, but we don't have nearly the amount of yard space you do."

"Alright, Linda," Sally says, somewhat relieved. "If you insist, I'll leave the cake, or cakes, to you."

"I insist." Instead of biting into her muffin, Linda has broken it into small pieces with her fingers. After the first bite, she dabs her mouth with the napkin.

Though they live in the same town, outwardly living similar lives, it somehow feels as if they, Linda and Sally, are somewhat subversive to the other's world. Linda is crisp, composed, the sort of woman who carries an air of domesticity into every room, quietly convincing everyone of her competence. Sally envisages the look of Linda's house, furnished in a minimalist way, full of clean lines, like the glossy image of a home-design magazine that dictates to readers what they should desire for their homes, and making them feel behind the times if they don't. Sally wonders if Linda senses the difference between them as well.

"In fact, I would also like to take care of the other snacks," Linda continues. "You're already having to spend time preparing your yard, so please. Let me take care of the food side of things."

"I think that's too much, Linda."

"Sally, my mom lives for this sort of thing," Valerie remarks, a bit ironically.

"She's right," Linda nods. "I'll take care of the food. If you want to split the cost for the snacks, I'm fine with that. Just some trays of vegetables and crackers and cheese, that's what I had in mind. I'll bring drinks too. I'm not sure what I'll bring, but people aren't too fussy. Then all you'll have to do is get the yard ready and decorate."

"Decorate?" Sally says, bemused, thinking again that too much fuss is being made over this party. Fuss, however, seems too light of a word. She is utterly overwhelmed.

"I'd assumed there would be decorations, but don't trouble yourself too much about it," Linda says warmly, "I would be happy to help in that end as well."

"Right," Sally says, vacantly. It's not a hat she wears comfortably, that of an amiable hostess. One or two guests for coffee is enough to unsettle her. Maybe her worries have been unreasonable, however, as this should be considered, more or less, a casual outdoor gathering. And she will have help in making sure things run smoothly. Jaime will be here, and Linda, it seems, will be happy to keep things organized. Yet despite the presence of a husband at gatherings, the overall duty to host in a gracious and structured way always seems to fall on the wife. If a party is disagreeable or disorganized, it's the wife who is commented upon, not the husband. Women, not typically men, take turns entertaining; it's what's expected. Women are still governed, Sally muses, in so many ways by traditions handed down. And how many women are there who continue to host gatherings not purely out of love of family and tradition, of cakes and decorating, but out of obligation and avoidance of shame?

Valerie turns to her mother. "What sort of cake will you make?"

"Vanilla with a strawberry topping, I think, and chocolate for the other cake. That can be topped with strawberries too. Or maybe a fudge topping."

"We can go to the store today," Valerie suggests. "The grocer on Richland Road has a bigger selection for baking supplies."

"Yes, alright, we can do some shopping this afternoon."

"We should buy pink and yellow icing!"

"Now that's a nice idea," Linda says enthusiastically. "Your colours."

"Colours?" Sally asks.

"Yes," Valerie says. "I've chosen pink and yellow for the wedding colours."

"Oh, I see. Pink and yellow. That will be nice." Sally says airily, yet dolefully, then wonders whether Jesse is aware of this colour scheme. Likely not, for men are often on the sidelines for these decisions, acting as well-dressed bystanders at their own decorated head table, overlooking the sort of details women agonize over. Some women. "Excuse me for a minute, the coffee should be ready by now."

She leaves Linda and Valerie at the table. She goes to the kitchen, envisages a room of round tables clothed in pink and yellow table runners, vases of pink and yellow flowers throughout, even Valerie in a pink-hued dress, cupcake shaped. As Sally removes the pot from the element, she realizes that she'd counted on Jesse changing his mind about the engagement, perhaps more than she realized. Yet Jesse seems more certain than ever and the wedding arrangements continue to move forward uninterrupted. Her earlier hopes for her son, then, have been dashed; she imagined he could go the places she hadn't gone, accomplish the things she hadn't accomplished, as though by marrying Valerie he was denying his own mother some vicarious satisfaction. If her life is squandered and dull, fine, but her child should rise above her to succeed at something. Anything. When he was a little boy, running through the grass in the yard while she affectionately watched, she envisioned such grand things for his life. Perhaps that's the most dangerous delusion a mother can have, that her child is meant to do great things, whatever great might mean, when it's such a subjective thing. For subjectively, in her bias, Jesse is doing great things already. Indeed, she thinks so highly of him that she can't help but see everything he does with an attitude of adoration. That white oak wind chime, bound to copper weights by threads of dark leather; he made it himself as a boy, and so isn't it the most wonderful wind chime of all wind chimes? Isn't her son the most handsome and compassionate young man of all the young men? Yet if she pauses to look at things objectively, her son, though nearly perfect in her biased eyes, is not in any way rare, separate or above the rest, and really, neither is she. They are ordinary people leading ordinary lives in an ordinary place. That's just the way it is, for most of us. Destiny reveals unsurprising lives more often than it reveals the shine of golden gems.

Sally starts back into the dining room, but stops for a moment, listening to her future daughter-in-law and her fervent mother discussing potential catering companies for hire. She feels a sudden stab of anger toward Valerie. Tears start to well up as a riot of overwhelming thoughts press upon her like hot waves— her infant son in the grass, the unfinished painting in the next room, pink table runners, the strange, unexpected loneliness of being a mother, the disappointing, wandering irrationality of life. She clings tightly to the handle of the coffee pot. She shouldn't lose herself like this with guests in the next room. She inhales deeply, three times until she calms herself, then steps into the dining room.

With the particulars of the engagement party resolved, the conversation has shifted to the wedding. Valerie is complaining about the difficulties in finding a suitable dress.

"Lace is too old fashioned," she complains. "It will look like an old woman's dress."

Sally notices, as she approaches the table, that Valerie seems to be eyeing her strangely.

"Nonsense," Linda tersely replies. "Lace is popular these days. I've seen a lot of girls with lace on their wedding dress."

"Coffee?" Sally extends the pot forward, ready to pour.

"Please," Linda smiles.

"Valerie?"

"No, thank you. Sally, Mom thinks I should choose another kind of flower for the bouquets, but I really want calla lilies. What do you think?"

Before Sally can respond, Linda says, "Valerie, calla lilies are fine as a centrepiece, but there should be something different for the bouquets."

"But I like calla lilies," Valerie says quietly, furrowing her brow with the obvious sadness of a young child who doesn't understand why she can't simply have it her way. "And they represent purity and faithfulness. I love the idea of holding flowers with a meaning like that on my wedding day."

Ostensibly unmoved, Linda pours milk into her coffee, stirs, then continues to assert her point. "If you and your bridesmaids are holding the same kind of flowers that are on every table centrepiece, it will be too much of the same. You need some variety."

Valerie's expression becomes one of weariness, as though on the receiving end of a long, gruelling cross-examination. It's possible that a young woman, even one as girlish and excitable and as deeply in love as Valerie, is vulnerable to the repetitive discussions over the details of a wedding. Regardless, Sally is annoyed that Linda would be so critical; a woman has a right to choose whatever flowers she pleases. Sally feels, on this matter, a sudden flicker of kinship with Valerie, as though they are joined imperceptibly by an awareness of what flowers can mean, each singularly tuned into the ways in which a bouquet of flowers can brighten a room and heighten a mood. On the other chair is Linda, a woman seemingly unable to tune into the general theme of what Valerie and Sally are tuned into, which is that the selection of flowers is so invaluable, and so completely personal, that the assessments of others are immaterial.

"If you want calla lilies for the bouquets," Sally says sympathetically, "then have calla lilies. Have buckets upon buckets of calla lilies at the reception if you want. It's your wedding after all."

Valerie's expression brightens, as if finally having found an ally in a battle she's grown accustomed to fighting alone, and Sally feels ever so slightly less cynical; a gentle and motherly beacon of encouragement rather than the moody, dark-eyed villain of their engagement. Linda, meanwhile, intent on her coffee a moment ago, now looks disapprovingly at Sally. For the first time since she arrived with her daughter, she appears slightly uncomposed.

"Of course, you may find that you don't have enough of a variety," Sally amends, with a consolatory nod in Linda's direction. "But if you think you've already given it enough thought, and you still want the place swimming with calla lilies, then do whatever you want."

"Thank you, and yes, I have thought a lot about it," Valerie affirms.

Sally once again detects Valerie looking at her strangely, almost concernedly, as though she might somehow be able to see directly through her pensive, introspective mood, which she had thought she had concealed carefully.

"Just know that some things look better in our minds than when it's finally put on display," Linda says matter-of-factly, then adds, "You still have a year to think about it."

"Yes, I do," Valerie says placatingly.

For the next half hour, the conversation centres around what the three have seen at other weddings—flowers and decorations, dresses and music, dinners and desserts. Sally makes another trip to the kitchen to refresh the coffee for her and Linda. They speak briefly about the recent changes in the area, most notably the new development expanding on the north side of town. Linda and Sally agree that the newer homes are built too closely together, and can't imagine how anyone would tolerate neighbours so near on either side.

"You can't swing a cat between those houses, is how my mom likes to put it," Sally says. "She has her own way of describing things, I guess you could say."

"Will your mother be joining us on Saturday?" Linda inquires. "I know she hasn't been well."

"No, she's not well. But I'll bring her for a while. She won't be able to stay long; she tires easily."

"I've only met her once or twice, but even so, it will be nice to see her again," Linda says.

"I have to warn you though, she might not remember you."

"That's alright," Linda says empathetically.

Valerie examines her nails, an impeccably shellacked mauve, then runs her fingers through her hair. "Jesse will be happy to have her here. He thinks about her a lot, I know, even if he doesn't say."

"Well, Valerie," Linda says, setting down her cup and glancing at her watch. "Shall we do some shopping before it gets too late?"

"Sure," Valerie says, then looks at Sally. "Thank you for having us."

"You're welcome." Sally rises from the table, grateful that their conversation has come to an end. The long exchange of lighthearted words seemed to make more weighted and more painful the awareness of an abandoned canvas in the next room. This room is dull with small talk, crumpled napkins, and lukewarm coffee, while across the hall there awaits a parallel world, where strands of ivy wisp across a landscape of seeing sculptures and sentient water lilies. One cannot properly live in this world when there is such an easy access to the next. She thinks distractedly again about all the women who seem to love and feel gratitude for these things; the napkins, the coffee, the tidied table, the chatter.

Linda, seemingly intent on at least one act of servility, carries the cups and spoons into the kitchen. Valerie and Sally listen as Linda places the dishes in the sink and runs water over them.

"You seem kind of sad lately," Valerie says quietly. "It's none of my business, but I only wanted to say that I hope you're alright."

Linda steps back into the dining room before Sally can respond.

"Thank you for the coffee, Sally. Ready to go, Valerie?"

"Yes," Valerie says, then smiles in a surprisingly tender way at Sally, and for the first time, Sally saw her future daughter-in-law not only in a kindred sort of way, but as a sensitive young woman, a kind, attentive, compassionate soul. A woman caring enough to have noticed and then attempted to peek beneath her thin veil of melancholy. Sally takes a moment to absorb her son's fiancée from this new point of view, this altered shade of light, a light that only seems altered because, perhaps, Sally judged Valerie unfairly in the beginning.

"I'm glad all the arrangements for the party are settled," Linda says as she slips on her boots, then bends down to tie them. They were the sort of boots Sally expected a scrupulous, reliable woman like Linda would wear; a soft, beige-coloured suede, clean, and rising just above the ankle. And with a practical half-inch heel. Linda, surely, is not a woman whose soul is easily overwhelmed with life's persistent string of demands. Rather, she thrives on them.

"Me too," Sally says, opening the door and holding it for them.

"See you on Saturday," Valerie says with another tender half-smile.

"See you Saturday," Sally replies.

"Bye," Linda says.

"Bye," Sally says, then finally closes the door.

She listens as their footsteps cross the porch and the car engine starts before she returns to the dining room. She folds her arms and stands quietly, her eyes fixed on the dehydrated peperomia plant. She feels, above all else, depleted, as if this minor social gathering had exhausted her only energy reserve. The depletion is not only mental and emotional; a physical effect has come over her, one leaving her eyes sore and heavy, her legs weak. She thinks worriedly of her upcoming hosting duties, of Valerie and her kindness, her tender smile, then gathers into herself, drawing her arms tightly around her waist. She feels entirely removed from the earlier half of the day, where she felt more animated, rejuvenated, as if some long-dormant fragment of her soul had been set alight, when she bought a bouquet of flowers and came home with fresh supplies. She knew, somehow by the sight of the petals and the feel of a new brush, that she would be able to paint. Yet the presence of other people has a way of pulling her out of the spirit of creativity—that mystical feeling expanding in the mind, or heart, or wherever the potent, mighty urge to splash colours on a canvas comes from. She wants desperately to return to her canvas and moves tentatively in that direction, then stops, feeling the mood has already been spoiled, and feeling her mind pulled once again toward her husband, her deception, and the growing apprehension that he knows something is wrong.

"People hide. Hide, hide, hide, and all to gain a thing that doesn't matter more than what was lost in the hiding. They hide, but their eyes give them away," her mother had recently told her, resolutely, and in a way that showed she was in a sombre mood. Her mother is a vanishing woman, full of generalized musings these days, oracle-like, and sometimes, with her white hair, silk dressing gown, and crochet afghan in the sunlight, a whole catalogue of old-world feminine beauty. "It is sometimes better," she said, "to read eyes than hear words."

"Maybe people see what they want to see," Sally countered. "It could be subjective. Maybe I'll look in someone's eyes and see dread, while another sees anger."

"In your eyes it is only possible to see a curmudgeon who always argues," Mary said, by way of small revenge, yet somewhere within their expressions, a great affection was insinuated from one to the other.

Sally hasn't phoned the doctor yet to discuss pain management, as promised. She checks the time. Already it is nearly three o'clock; her husband will be home in another hour or so, and the doctor's office will close an hour later. She decides definitively to abandon her painting for the day and start supper. She goes to the freezer and takes out a bag of green and yellow beans leftover from the garden, and a small roast. She switches on the oven, takes a few red potatoes from the pantry, pulls out the cutting board. Later on, she'll bring a plate over to her mother, and stay until the evening caregiver arrives.

She knows her mother's current living situation can't continue this way for much longer. Four months ago, she was still moving around the house on her own, but in the last two months the illness has tightened its hold around her body and kept her in the front room of the house, an illness with invisible chains, grim restraints that her mother seems less and less willing to fight against. Yes, something has crossed over in that house. The atmosphere has changed, become more solemn, the air itself implying that her mother is through with the miseries that accompany a hopeless battle and the ongoing strains of sleepless nights. Yet when the time comes to leave the house, her mother still might kick and scream and rail against it. It's an agonizing image, but not all problems have attractive solutions.

Tomorrow afternoon, she will go shopping for the necessary party supplies. She will buy napkins, plates, cutlery, and, reluctantly, a few decorations. Everything in yellow and pink. If there is time after that she'll go to the shop office to complete the payroll, which should only take an hour or two. Following that, she'll return once again to her mother's side. Tomorrow morning though, she is free. Tomorrow morning, she will paint, and let nothing interrupt her. Sally uses the knife to glide the sliced potatoes from the cutting board onto the roast, then places it in the oven. She'll add the beans later. As she steps out of the kitchen, she can't help but smile outwardly to herself, for she can feel a profound, glistening anticipation for the following morning. She'll wake early to complete the first painting, and maybe there will be enough time to start another. Flittering around in her mind, as she searches for the number to the doctor's office, is this renewed love of painting, the wonderfully romantic process of setting a brush to canvas and giving birth to something new, and the curious ways in which the painting itself communicates to the painter, by slow and varying degrees, what it ultimately wants to be.

With a restored sense of clarity, Sally sits on an armchair in the living room, picks up the phone, and dials the doctor's number.

For the second time in a week, Sally has gone into the city without anyone knowing. Of course, it would not have mattered to anyone that she chose to shop in the city rather than in town, but it was not until she got into her car and pulled out of the driveway that she suddenly decided, definitively, to escape. It could be consoling, even recuperative, to take leave of the quietness and lose herself for the afternoon in a bustling, faceless downtown. It also seemed that the experience of walking would be more satisfying if she could do so clandestinely. She used to know the area well, the web of streets called the Warehouse District. The little gallery where she once held many exhibits is on a narrow stretch called Ripon Way, and if she can remember her way, she'll stop at that gallery to see their current exhibit, whatever it may be.

She had spent the entire morning lost in the parallel world, the world from which the result is her most expressive and inspired work, a world where numinous things like polished cobblestone lanes and white butterflies exploding into the air from the shallower roots of oak trees, their wings shaped more like feathers, must exist. And somewhere off that cobbled lane, sipping wine and in a cozy café, is an alliance of artists similar to herself, but there are also musicians, poets, historians. She, Sally, would be nearby, in a wide studio room of her own, with high red-brick walls and a glittering skyline. There she lives an interesting life, a woman who never found herself pregnant or in love, because she is a woman in love only with her paints and her canvas and that brazen shimmering world.

Within four hours, she had two canvases covered, and was unwrapping and starting on a third. She set the brush down precisely at noon, confident that the third canvas will be something bright, brighter than anything she's made, livelier and more energetic than the others.

It's a peculiar thing, Sally reflects as she parks the car and pays the meter, that the true origin of one's desire to create, the initial kindling of inspiration, that first generative seed, is always more or less unknown. The source of one's creativity seems to evade a clear-cut understanding. No clear analysis can be made. It's too subjective, too multifaceted. An artist can recount their reasons for what might have given them the idea to paint, sing, or write about this thing or that, but it remains a mystery how one person can experience the strange, inexplicable wave that leads to an idea, and then is pushed further by an impulse to pick up a tool and give birth to that idea, while another person, simply, cannot. Sally likes to muse on this sometimes—why does the world shape itself differently for some, and why don't we all move through life using the same set of eyes—but it's impossible to know the reasons why. They are as random and unforeseen as the fluke windfalls that shudder past her house, rattling the walls and sending the wind chime into a fit.

Sally steps onto Notre Dame Avenue and wonders, as she disappears into a subdued afternoon crowd, whether this renewed desire to paint after so many years of creative drought stems from the feelings that come with renouncing her unborn child. Well, of course it does, she decides quickly, shaking her head. It's purely escapist; creativity, at least for her, always starts with pain. The emotions that invaded her heart following the procedure, and the isolation of being the only one who knows that it happened, was the wave that grabbed her. That was the doleful shift in the wind, quite possibly the worst moment of her life. And now, following her along the pavement, is a melancholy sentiment, that because she went through with it, she is somehow less human, or at the very least, less of a woman. Mostly because of the act itself, but partly because she successfully hid so much of it; the queasiness in her stomach, her expressions when the nausea was at its worst, her phone calls and whereabouts. And then she had repressed the feeling that her husband, even at this late stage, would have loved a second child. She shakes her head again at the foolishness of her early hope, that once it was over, she could forget about it completely. It's true what they say, then; denial is a frighteningly powerful thing, a thing so dangerous that it wreaks a quiet havoc on all kinds of aspects in one's life—relationships, self-perception, self-respect, the pathological or non-pathological ability to lie to someone's face, once, maybe, or a hundred little times.

Sally turns onto McGill, a winding street with high elms that arch over the sidewalks. The pavement is littered gorgeously with autumn leaves. There are brick and mortar shops, restaurants, a used clothing store called Revivals where vintage-style dresses are displayed prominently in the window. A young, dilettante-looking woman steps out of the store. She glances at Sally dismissively, then continues past the patrons of a sidewalk café with her shopping bag in hand. Her thin floral scarf trails behind, drifting blandly side to side in the breeze. There's a beatnik kind of look to her outfit, a deliberate poverty, as though she chose her clothes —torn pale jeans, tweed coat, a felt hat—specifically to match the current notion of nonconformity. Sally smiles to herself, half-pitying the girl for being so careful about fashion. Yet the other part of Sally feels envious. She would like to be that young woman, or some version of her, a free spirit, a flower child, probably spending her days doing some rousing and creative things, with the future still open to her.

She, Sally, was once a version of that girl, if less caring about fashion. Twenty years ago, on these same shaded city streets, it was Sally, an unfettered woman with an open future, an art book or canvas under her arm, on her way from an art class or a show at a gallery. The years are so easy to waste, Sally laments as she turns off McGill Street and onto the leafy quietness of Ripon Way. She stands still for a moment in a fit of nostalgia to admire the quaintness of the street corner, for the little café still has its mismatched iron chairs and tables along the sidewalk, and the high mural of a woman with blue feathers for hair still reigns over the treetops. Sally smiles to herself, then walks on.

The Ochre Gallery, where she held most of her exhibits, is only slightly changed. The colour of the lettering outside has gone from red to black, and through the large white-trimmed windows she can see they have added rows of modern track lighting on the high ceiling. She pushes the door open. The wide white-lit room is perfectly clean, exquisitely quiet, and Sally steps onto the polished hardwood as a congregant steps onto the polished floor of a temple, full of esteem and reverence.

A cordial-looking woman in a navy dress appears from the back room of the gallery.

"Welcome to The Ochre Gallery," she says affably. "Is there something I can help you with, or are you here to look at the exhibit?"

"Only to see the exhibit," Sally replies.

"We're featuring an exhibit by Mikael Cahill, a popular local artist. We try to feature local artists here, as you might know. He's used charcoal drawings to depict a sequential story, if you'll start over here with this first drawing, of a British woman immigrating to Canada after the second world war. Actually, this exhibit was inspired by the artist's grandmother."

"That sounds interesting," Sally remarks, peering around at the white walls punctuated by stunningly detailed, yet dark, shadowy sketches.

"Enjoy the exhibit," the woman, whose name tag reads Luanne, says cordially before adding, "I'll just be in the back. Let me know if you have any questions."

"Thank you."

Luanne disappears behind the back wall, and Sally moves slowly toward the first sketch. It depicts a rather lithe, yet dignified woman from behind, dressed heavily in early twentieth century clothing, standing on a wooden dock, holding the hand of a young boy. Their joined hands give rise to reflections of her own son, once a young boy, holding her hand in a similarly comfortable way. It's one of the softer aspects of motherhood, the simple hand holding, until one day he doesn't require it anymore, and probably a mother never remembers the last time she held her son's hand to guide him safely out of a room or across the street. Sally sighs mournfully, thinking of Jesse's once little-boy hands.

In the next sketch a large passenger ship has pulled in, while crowds of men and women wait with grave expressions. There is a wicket gate in the far right of the drawing, and a man stands behind it, looking on. It would have taken a considerable amount of time to complete all these, to draw out each detail so vividly, to consider each line and knot in the wood of the dock, everything carefully shaded, each of the passenger's expressions mediated until they are fully brought to life.

Sally crosses the wide room to see the rest of the sketches, her boots echoing hollowly against the hardwood. She stops in front of a view of a dining room on the ship, then moves to two men smoking while playing cards as children play on the decks with a string and spinning top. The dignified woman is either in the background or the forefront of drawings, her essence one of mixed fatigue and stateliness, a weather-beaten goddess growing weary from her battles yet refusing to appear as anything less than poised.

The entire exhibit has the feeling of an ancient folk-tale—someone hapless or deeply unhappy pushing out of their conditions, conquering the odds, conquering an ocean, attaining something valuable they didn't have on the first page. The type of tale that leaves you with a certain faith. Sally slips into a whimsical vision of the woman, industrious in her former land, doing needlework perhaps, weaving a lively pattern on a mat and dreaming of the grand ocean, its unfathomable depths, its mysterious caches and treasures, and seeing it as a great laid-out carpet of limpid blue, summoning her to a fantastic place.

In the final drawing, the woman is again standing against the rails of the ship with her son. Through the fog, she sees what she's attained, has finally caught sight of the incredible thing she didn't have at the start—a faint, vaporous stretch of novel land where hope resides and anything can happen.

Sally envisages this artist, the man named Mikael Cahill, hunched over a drafting board with his row of pencils, rapt in the intricate, graphite images, sketches full of people and things as tangible in his mind as the pencil in his hand. This illusory image of him in her mind, hunched over sketches, resonates with some profound part of her spirit, a bright, idealistic, essential aspect of her being. He has a simple notion, an idea, an errant brainwave with no known origin, and so he picks up his chosen tool with nothing more on his mind than to turn this new idea into something. He hopes, maybe, that it will become something great, something others will not only stop to see, but be moved by, captivated by, lingering with them long after they leave the gallery.

There are many people out there who see themselves as artists, she reflects, whether it manifests by way of painting, sketching, musicianship, or writing, who possess the kind of gifts others commonly regard as brilliant and powerful, even mystical.

Artists tend to feed off that regard, some more than others. She
did too, to some degree, when she was young, naïve, and maybe a
little odious, especially following a successful exhibit. She had, in
those days, an explicit faith in her ability to put brush to canvas
and convey exactly what she wanted, and with a certainty that
yes, this is right, it matters, and it is powerful. She felt herself
marked in some unearthly way, touched by that brand of
mysticism, singled out from the rest, called to create things. She
envisioned it almost like fairy dust falling on her head from an
opening or tear in the lining of the sky. But maybe there is no
such thing as being marked. To think so is suddenly consoling to
her, and freeing in a way, even if makes everything seem suddenly
more secular and mundane. Her little corner room at home, for
instance, a place of great creativity this morning, where a varied
mix of flowers bloom upward from a vase and canvases are set
against the wall to dry, is really an unremarkable room,
commonplace, just a room with things in it, no energy to it at all.
Indeed, it's mostly full of ordinary things—a thin layer of dust
atop the easel lamp, an old wooden stool, a clock radio, a line of
paperbacks with white crackled lines of use along the spines.

It is difficult for herself, and presumably other artists, to have
faith that their art is both important and precious, whether or not
it is recognized or renowned. These days, the criterion by which
an artist is judged is too harsh. It's too much about money and
notoriety, and it seems that an artist who manages to attain some
degree of money or notoriety is the only one encouraged to
continue. Like the falling tree in a forest, art that is not widely
known or heard fails to make a sound, and even if art manages a
sound but is not widely heard, it ceases to be of any relevance.
Art is considered nothing if there is no echo to follow that initial
playing of the note. History is full of artists who die in obscurity,

without accolades, their work discarded like scraps of paper in the wind.

Sally mind drifts again to thoughts of the parallel world, of that amplified, embellished place, and of herself, painting in a great red-brick studio with high windows, where outside there are things like broad pink lilies that never wilt and spirited lovers lying in the twittering grass of a shadowy park. She imagines all sorts of animated things about this parallel world, which is what makes it so exciting—it can go anywhere, it can be anything. And the particulars of that world have never been tied to money or power or sovereignty; it isn't interested in those things at all. It was about the act of painting itself, the moment something is conceived in the mind, then planted, watered, and grown. For the most interesting visions that an artist can have are hidden not within their celebrity, but within the brush strokes they leave upon a canvas. The work matters enough on its own, and should be regarded by the artist as magnificent, with or without another voice to proclaim it so. It is, at least, a more optimistic way of looking at things.

Sally gazes fixedly at the final sketch, at the curved graphite lines and shadowing depicting the novel stretch of land where the woman will set foot. This exhibit, draped prettily along the walls of The Ochre Gallery on this cloudy, final day in September, is spectacular, just as it is. From the tip of her eye, Luanne emerges from the back room. She asks Sally if she enjoyed the exhibit.

"Are any of these for sale?" Sally inquires.

"Absolutely," Luanne replies energetically. "Is there one in particular you're interested in?"

"This one." Sally points to the final drawing of the woman and the foggy stretch of land. In her mind she has already picked a place to hang it in her corner room.

"Great. I'll mark it down as sold. You can pick it up once the exhibit has finished, in another four days, but we would need you to make the payment today."

"That's fine," Sally nods.

Luanne asks Sally to follow her to the back room of the gallery, and as they walk across the hardwood, past the charcoal drawings that punctuate the high white walls, Sally is struck with an idea. It pierces the air suddenly, as though some great pendulum swung past her in a wave that forced her mind in another direction. She will hold an exhibit at The Ochre Gallery. The thought of her paintings being hung in this wonderfully hushed, immaculate room is somehow as dazzling and remote as it is perfectly familiar, and so clear and obvious a thing to do that she questions why it hadn't occurred to her until now.

"Do you have an application process?" Sally asks eagerly when they reach the office.

Luanne, who has just opened the top drawer of a file cabinet, turns to her with a surprised expression.

"I used to exhibit my paintings here," Sally explains. "But as I said, that was years ago. I'm sure the process has changed."

Luanne smiles warmly, unlocks the top drawer of the filing cabinet, removes a sheet of paper, closes the drawer, and then opens the next one down. "I've been working here for about ten years. I don't think you'll find the process has changed very much. You'll have to bring a few sample pieces, and even if you've had an exhibit here before, the manager might want to have you in for an interview."

She hands Sally an application form and another form listing the rules and requirements for holding an exhibit. Sally pays for the drawing of the woman on the ship, then furls the sheets of paper together and holds them up to her chest protectively; the dry feel of them in her hands assures her that there was a sly, mystic providence in being drawn to the city this afternoon. They also carry a feeling of something lost being reimbursed.

Luanne closes the drawer to the filing cabinet and locks it with a key.

"Thank you for your help today," Sally says, with contained excitement.

"You're welcome," Luanne replies, then adds heartily, "I look forward to seeing your work."

Sally crosses the high white room. She feels, as she opens the door and steps off the paved stoop of the gallery, that she has slipped into a modified version of herself. Or more precisely, that a pre-existing part of herself has superseded another, switched places, the woeful, distracted woman of years past now submitting to the richer, unfeigned version of herself. She is a semi-unravelled, semi-mended woman walking along a sidewalk littered with yellow and copper-toned leaves outside an art gallery, outlining the look of her next exhibit. Her mind stirs.

She turns off Ripon Way and meanders down McGill Street with a kind of lightness, glancing into the window of an outlet shop, then an antique jewelry store where emerald-green earrings and gold brooches line the display. The bakery next door shows raisin bread and glazed rolls arranged in fresh, orderly rows. The party supply store is only two or three blocks ahead, if she remembers correctly, but as she walks she's easily averted by the busy sights—the festooned mannequin outside a shop door, the soda advertisement streamed along the side of a passing bus, the grave expression of a lone busker strumming a ukulele for change. Across the street a shabbily dressed man nods off on a wooden bench, and the round coloured lights of a one-room theatre reflect and spread outward from edge to edge on the puddle in front of her like a butterfly's wing. She smiles involuntarily; everything about this area excites her. Its facets merge in a way that exude a fascinating mix of modern and old, an area that is both shoddy and illustrious, with elements that contrast in unexpected yet seemingly expected ways—a manicured courtyard that is home to the homeless, an upscale restaurant adjacent to a derelict pawn shop, a raggedy-looking car leaving the underground parkade of the regally gothic Minster Hotel.

Waiting to cross King Street, Sally shudders against the wind, which is cool, but not uncomfortable. Still, she is glad to have worn her heavier fall coat. There is a fruit and vegetable market between herself and the red swinging sign of the party supply store, but the mere sight of that sign, with its oval shape and dull rust-colour swinging languidly in the breeze, suddenly dulls her mood, slants her spirit toward the lesser version of itself, the woeful self who must run a simple yet meretricious errand. The purer version of herself, the one who accepted the gallery's application form and then peered acquiescently into the display windows of jewellers and bakers, wouldn't be made to shop for an engagement party she has no wish to host.

The light changes and Sally steps off the curb and weaves through the busy market, where a restless child cries loudly in their mother's arms, where a man in a Panama hat lifts a pear, tests its ripeness, sets it down again, negotiates the price.

As she passes a table with little baskets filled with chokecherries and saskatoons, Sally mourns that purer version of herself, of her spirit, the same spirit that seems continually denied the air it needs to flower properly. She's tired of mourning it, tired of the self-pity, but while she tries to ignore it, she nevertheless feels it coming—the sadness, the self-reproach, the fatalistic mood that interrupts the prosperous part of her soul, as a prickly weed disrupts the flourishing of perennials, undaunted by the silver sheers that attempt to slice it away. No amount of slicing, no amount of willing or unwilling will remove the old, rancid feelings of disappointment, and to make matters more difficult, now she cannot even claim to be good. She scorns herself for the lightness and contentment she felt only a few minutes ago on the other side of King Street. It was undeserved; she is impure, unclean, a weak, tainted woman who lies to her husband, who ran away on a cloudy afternoon to expel then abandon her responsibilities in the small sterile room of a clinic.

"It's over," the young nurse said. "Let me help you down."

As Sally was helped off the sheeted table, she felt the first rush of blood leaving her, and lightheaded to the point that, this time, she accepted the nurse's hand to hold. Yet her kindness only exacerbated the shame. If the nurse had retrieved a leather whip from a drawer and proceeded to lash her across the back, it would have seemed more suited to the moment somehow, a better match for how she felt about herself than a warm hand to steady her.

"She's going to be a princess," the young nurse said to another nurse once they reached the recovery room. They were discussing their children's Hallowe'en costumes. That the nurses would discuss such a triviality in front of her in such a moment, about children no less, may have lowered her opinion of them if she felt in any way a right to heighten herself above anyone. For those nurses it was, she reminded herself, an ordinary day.

"My boys both want to be vampires."

"Do they want to match?" the young nurse asked, still clasping Sally's hand as they made their way slowly to an empty recovery chair.

"They don't want to match. One Dracula, one Orlok."

"Orlok?"

"He was a vampire in an old silent film."

"Never heard of him," the young nurse said, assisting Sally into the chair before finally speaking to her directly. "Everything went well, as the doctor said. Can you lift your arm for me? We need to take your blood pressure again."

As the cuff tightened around her arm, she stared numbly straight ahead at the wall, more specifically at a flake of chipped sky-blue paint an inch or so above the door light switch. Then she caught a quick glimpse of another lost woman being led into the adjacent room for her turn, and Sally had thought, what is this feeling of emptiness compared to whatever happiness might have been if she had let him, or her, grow? What is this new freedom in comparison with the loss she endures for her freedom? That little speck of life bearing her own blood wanted only to be born, then loved.

Keeping all this to herself, she ruminates, has started to feel much like an infection, as though in that clinic room she rid herself of one living thing but inadvertently picked up another nefarious thing that now slithers inside of her. It seems apt to describe the guilt as an infection, for it's an invisible thing that hurts only herself. That is the organism she will need to fight off, or live with, one she will attempt to lessen or purge from her body over time by painting, by spending as much time as possible in the light and colour of the parallel world.

It will be a varied and ongoing battle, with some moments more or less successful than others. For this morning, when she finally set the brush down into the cup of warm water and watched the brightness of the paint fade and dilute into something bland and lifeless in the water, something inside of her did the same thing. The longer the paint diluted in water, the more she felt herself reminded of everything else. She had started to move around the house, cleaning a few things that really didn't need to be cleaned before getting ready to leave, because an encroaching sense that she might be unworthy of the joy and enlivenment that comes through painting made her physically uncomfortable.

She begins to suspect, as she makes her way along the pavement, kicking a few leaves aside, that a true healing may only be possible through a mix of painting and of something else—a renewed sense of rightness in her core, a sense of integrity and kind-heartedness. Yet the notion of trying to be a good person, while still being dishonest to her husband, seems too contrasting when set against one another.

And so, what had initially been the right thing to do— keeping the pregnancy and procedure a secret—flipped over suddenly in her mind to be the wrong thing after all. As a cleansing act, she could tell Jaime what he has had a right to know all along—that as much as she loves their child, she doesn't have the strength or interest in another. If secrecy is the poison, then a confession should be the poison's cure, a way to kill the slithering thing. For the concealment of the deed has perhaps caused her more misery than the deed itself. This idea of confessing, she muses, seems almost biblical in its simplicity and meaning. She'll confess to her husband like a worshipper to a priest, and be at his mercy, come what may. A few sentences, a few sober facts, some gentle variation of, 'I was pregnant, and now I'm not. It wasn't an accident; it was my decision. It's done, and cannot be undone. And now we must move on.' Then she'll accept her penance, do whatever she needs to do to be absolved. Maybe Jaime's face, when she says the words, will contort into varying expressions of anger, or resentment, or bewilderment, or all three, or none of the above. Maybe his face will melt into something loving or sympathetic. And as she visualizes her husband's ever-shy smile, Sally smiles to herself, and there in the middle of McGill Street, the whole plot to keep this secret from her husband fell in on itself. In the middle of this bustling market covered in pretty autumn-toned leaves, the resonance of it dies.

Sally stops on the pavement, glances up at the unattractive oval sign that creaks and seems ill fitted to the brightly coloured things in the adjacent window. She carefully folds the sheets of paper from the gallery into her purse and pulls out her list of commissions, which is mercifully short,

The store is surprisingly crowded, so she takes a basket and decides to shop quickly. Most of what she needs is found in the second aisle, where angled shelves bear plates and napkins seemingly in every shade imaginable. Valerie, she reluctantly concludes, is not so myopic after all; indeed, she has shown herself to be kinder and more layered than Sally first gave her credit for, and so she disregards the cheaper white plates and places a stack of the bright yellow ones in her basket. She chooses a lively shade of pink napkins, yellow table covers, and streamers and balloons in variations of both colours.

Then, at the continued sight of these pristinely stacked cloths and varicoloured plastic cups, her thoughts of confessing flip back suddenly the other way. Confessing seems rather like a cruel thing to do, an act more malevolent than benevolent. She will hurt him too much in doing so, and she'll be no better off. It's not up to him to save her or offer deliverance. She will not bring him into her battered little world, with her covert trips to the city, her momentous blackbird melody, her secrecy. She made her choice, it's her long and lonely burden, her cross to bear. She will move forward; she will take life day by day. She will focus her mind above all else on her painting, and get all she can out of that. It is, at least, pacifying, and momentarily curative.

Sally lifts a small ivory candle from the shelf, twirls it between her fingers, sets it back down because of the cost. It carries a faint scent of vanilla. It could be for a wedding, this candle, though she knows it's contrary to Valerie's tastes. She imagines their reception with buckets of calla lilies, and wonders what her son's expression might be at his wedding, surrounded not by ivory, but hues of yellow and pink—confident, endlessly happy, glowing as if lit from within, the certainty that marrying her was the right thing. Indeed, some people are that way, who live without ever knowing that glint of regret, who find and marry their true love early on, never haunted by all the things that never were. Her parents had loved one another in that unalloyed, unchanging way. Her father saw her mother coming down the steps from somewhere, he said, and by the time she reached the bottom, he knew that he loved her, and that he always would. So, love stories are uncomplicated sometimes. Silently, and for the first time since the engagement was announced, Sally sends a sincere blessing into the air as one sends a wish into the universe with the blowing out of a candle.

She carries the basket to the cash register, pays the bored looking girl behind the counter for the ivory candle and decorations, and steps outside with her bags. It's getting late, people are emptying out of the tall glass buildings and cluttering up the sidewalks. She shivers again, sets the bags down on the pavement, gathers the collar of her coat around her neck, and fastens the top button. She takes a shopping bag in each hand and walks purposefully toward her car on Notre Dame Avenue, feeling neither happy nor unhappy.

Jaime sits on a stool in the garage after dinner. He has occupied himself for more than an hour by changing the tires from summer to winter on both his vehicle and Sally's. Today is only the first day in October, but he's learned that it's better to complete the task sooner rather than later. He had worked under the inefficient glow of two bare bulbs that dangle on strings from the rafters, and curses himself for not installing better fixtures.

He lights a cigarette. His wife is inside, perhaps either washing dishes after another strained, polite dinner, or painting. He's taken note of the new canvases, the still-wet paintings leaning against the wall, the submerged silences from the corner room. Or she may be doing something else entirely. He isn't sure.

It's worsened over the last month or so, this feeling of separateness between them. She scarcely looks at him, and gathers into herself when he touches her. These are the tiring, antiquated roles they play as husband and wife—she the pursued, him the pursuer. Yet those moments when he catches her, when she submits and seems glad not only that she was caught, but that it was him who caught her—those are singularly the most powerful moments of his life. He loves her still, despite himself, despite her woodenness. That her feelings for him during those perfect moments never quite rise to the same prominence seems incidental, a fair price to pay. Until now, that is, for this new brand of separateness has shed light on their peaks and valleys like nothing before. Sally is no longer merely the pursued; she is the fierce resistor whose eyes scream with reproach to leave her alone, and so he has. And here he sits again, in the garage with a cigarette dangling from his lips, seeking out some chore or other. There is always something that needs to be done, always a task to fall back on.

Jaime rises from the stool and moves toward the window, where in the scant moonlight he can scarcely make out the straight lines of the porch. He takes another drag of his cigarette, and his eyes shift toward the lit window of the dining room. The increased tension of late must be linked to something. There must be a motivator, some hidden causation. The change in his wife, Jaime considers as he exhales a thick, greyish cloud of smoke, magnified as Mary's cancer spread, although Mary has always been demanding of Sally's attention for one reason or another.

Jaime plays ponderously with the cigarette between his fingers, then returns to sit on his metal stool. He kicks a wrench to the side by accident and decides to give the garage a more thorough cleaning tomorrow, or the next day. And once this engagement party is behind them, he will consider what sort of lighting to install. He sighs, feeling unable to focus his thoughts on anything other than his wife. They're dissimilar in many ways, but in his mind, they were strengthened by these differences, and were conjoined resolutely; two separate streams merging within the same flow, ebbing and languishing, removed from one another here and there, but ultimately tied together in a forward movement. He thinks back to the moment he proposed, on one knee under the shadow of the Sylvia River oak, as he calls it, his hands red and sweaty, the sweet sound of her voice when she said yes.

Jaime again rises from the stool, suddenly restless and keyed up. He strides back and forth over the cement pad, feeling that his marriage has met a kind of eminence, as if his actions on this night could be emblematic for what follows—a foretelling, for better or worse. He presents to himself what he sees as the unavoidable question: Is it better to avoid her, to hide complacently in the garage for another evening, or to confront this thing head on? Swiftly he decides that the gloomiest thing imaginable is to lose her, to be permanently removed from her in the stream, sent adrift, a man without a wife to battle for or console, wholly impoverished. Thus, he crumbles the butt of his cigarette in a heaped ashtray, and heads with definiteness toward the door.

Enough is enough, he tells himself, certain that once confronted, any obstacles that lie ahead of them may not be as bad as they seem. Maybe the severity of their problems will fade if their authenticity is no longer taken as fact, much like the belief in the existence of heaven or hell started to fade as people over time began to question their merit. And if the conversation goes well, the party tomorrow would be so much the better. Maybe he will kiss her with confidence in the middle of it, and maybe he'll be met with a warm reaction.

Jaime crosses the yard and makes his way up the porch steps. He resolves not to be interrogative, but reasonable and patient. The goal is to clear the way for a calm, controlled discussion, an honest, intimate conversation with his wife; it should be possible. He must ensure, above all else, that she is alright. However, these sort of unpleasant conversations with his wife have seldom been easy. She has an unusual way of withstanding simplicity, stability, predictability, yet it is precisely those things that he craves most within their marriage. Sally is hard, indelible, and he muses that all women who are hardened and indelible would be difficult to live with.

Jaime opens the door and steps into the warm, silent house. As he removes his boots and coat, he hears a shuffle of movement from the room that has unequivocally become her own. He takes a few steps farther down the hall and glances around the corner. Sally, sitting reticently in front of the easel, is intently absorbed in a painting that is already marvellous. He leans against the door frame, watches his wife, elegant and unassuming, almost elegiac, as she dabs the edge of her paintbrush in water, raises her hand, then places the fine tip of the brush delicately against an upper corner of the canvas.

Artists are incredibly sentient beings, Jaime observes. They are the privileged, somewhat strange visionaries who see beauty in all things, who feel everything deeply. Yet it seems exhausting and tragic in a sense to move through life with such a deep way of feeling, as if the creative minds of the world exist as a separate race of unprotected nerves being made to endure constant waves of stimulation. Ostensibly, that was always his interpretation of what it must be like to live as an artist—enthralling, but tiring.

It wasn't until he first watched her set a brush against a canvas that he understood, truly, the beauty that could be found in a woman's movement. Sally is beautiful in all she does, of course, but she is also impenetrable in a way that breaks his heart over and over; every time he looks at her reverently, he's reminded of her elusiveness. Like a glass dome covering an amulet in a museum, he can look but not touch; he knows he has never possessed her heart in its whole. She is, in a word, surreptitious.

Sally turns to him. "How long have you been standing there?"

"Not long. Just a minute or so. That looks great, what you're working on. It's nice to see you painting again." He hopes his compliment will make her smile, but it doesn't.

"If you're still hungry, there's leftovers in the fridge."

"No, not hungry. I just wanted to see what you were doing."

"Oh," Sally says, setting down her paintbrush. A short silence passes.

"The winter tires are on," he says, futilely trying to impress her, though he sees already a tired expression on her face. Tired, or perhaps she feels bothered by him for disrupting her work. "I know it's a bit early for winter tires, but I went ahead with it anyway. Because, you never know."

"That's true," she says, looking back to her painting.

"I didn't mean to disturb you," he says apologetically.

"It's fine. It's getting late. I was going to stop soon anyway."

Jaime considers what to say next. She is still turned away from him, and everything he thought of saying to her as he crossed the yard now seems petty and ineffectual. He realizes that he doesn't want to talk at all, but that he would love nothing more than for her to come to him without a word, wrap her arms around his shoulders as she so often had, years earlier, whenever he stepped through the door. Then he would kiss her, a singular kiss, quick and innocent. It would be easy; no declarations needed. Now, however, Sally remains clear across the room, stiff and straight on the stool under the cone-shaped light of the easel lamp.

"If you're finished painting, maybe we can spend some time together," he suggests. "We can watch a movie."

She hesitates for a moment, then says, "If we put on a movie I probably wouldn't last very long. I think I'll just go to bed early."

"Come on, Sally. When was the last time we curled up together for a movie? Your pick."

"No, I don't think so," she affirms. "Not tonight."

"I know you're tired. I'm tired too. There were a lot of repairs at the shop, we're still behind. Then, I came home and changed eight tires. The point is we haven't spent time together in a while."

"I'm not sure what you mean. We just had dinner an hour ago."

She speaks in a level sort of tone that bothers him, one that seems devoid of energy. He has hit a wall, one perceptible only to himself. She offers no concern, no indication of interest.

"I know that," Jaime presses, "but Jesse was here with us for dinner. We should make time for just the two of us. It will give us a chance to talk."

"I'm too tired. Maybe another night."

"Sally," he begins, then pauses, feeling rather embarrassed at having to plead for some time with his wife. His eyes alternate from her, to the canvas, then back to her. "Please don't be this way."

"What way?" she asks, turning to face him again.

"This way. Saying you're tired whenever I suggest spending time together. You're brushing me off."

"I'm not brushing you off," Sally says offendedly.

"It certainly seems that way sometimes."

"Well, then, you're wrong."

"It's as though you want to avoid being in the same room as me."

"That's not it at all," Sally insists.

Jaime sighs, lets his eyes drift down toward her canvas, then absently up to the shelf beside the window, lined with books. He sees, on the window ledge, the clear vase stuffed with the flowers she came into the house with a day or two earlier. He watched her carry them into the corner room, unwrap them slowly, arrange them in the vase—the vase he bought for her, years ago, because something about its classy yet simple aesthetic reminded him of her. She tidied the room recently, he noticed yesterday, cleared out most of the clutter, and now the room speaks more to what he perceives to be his wife's tastes—tasteful, bare, and bright. Finally, she lowers her wide brown eyes to meet his.

"How about tomorrow?" Sally suggests, though her tone still sounds flat and unaffected.

"Tomorrow?"

"Yes. Tomorrow," she says obstinately. "Once everyone has left."

"Tomorrow night wouldn't make any sense," Jaime says, beginning to sound impatient. "The party can go until who knows what time. We'll be just as tired tomorrow night as we are now, if not more so."

"I know. But we shouldn't stay up late tonight, with all that needs to be done in the morning."

"There won't be much to do. We'll bring up a couple of tables from the basement, set them up in the yard, and put around a few of the chairs."

"Is the firewood ready?" Sally asks.

"There's more than enough."

"Valerie's mom phoned earlier. She's bringing the cake and snacks in the afternoon. I'll just have to get all the plates and cutlery out before everyone else arrives."

"Good. Come on, then. Let's curl up on the couch together. Just for a little while."

"I don't think so. Not tonight. I'm just—"

"No, I know. You're tired. Fine, I won't beg." He steps back from the doorframe, irritated. Pathetically, this is all he will get from his wife tonight—evasiveness and vague, persistent complaints of fatigue, even though during their conversation, there was no hint Sally was at all tired, just bothered. He reaches across to switch the light off in the dining room and, depleted, begins to make his way down the hall.

The anguished expression on her husband's face as he turned away very nearly coaxes her to say, "I love you, please give me some time to figure this out," but instead other words tumble from her mouth. "I'm sorry, Jaime, I just can't."

He stops nearly halfway down the hall when he hears her voice, turns around, returns to the spot he stood a moment ago. He looks absorbedly at his wife, at her grave expression, at her tightly pressed together lips. There is a look of such sadness on her face that he is overcome with an urge to go to her, yet he stops himself. There are times, he has learned, when she would rather not be touched. He crosses his arms and again rests his shoulder against the door frame. "You can't what?"

Sally takes a breath, deliberating over which of her thoughts are better to share, and which are better to keep. Her muscles tighten, for even she has grown frazzled by their pull back, push forward, pull away again dynamic. It's a long, abstruse tug of war. She considers telling him what she has done, to purge the poison, to kill the slithering thing, for since she passed through the market on McGill Street the notion of confessing to her husband has been lingering in her mind like soft music from another room.

"I know something is bothering you," Jaime says, with a softness in his voice that surprises her. She meets his pained eyes, lowers her glance, but his eyes, now, are fixed. "I know you," he continues. "You're my wife. I can sense when something is bothering you, and I know you well enough to know that I shouldn't press you to say anything. But something's wrong, I know it is." A short silence passes, then Jaime adds, "You seem so far away."

"I know," is all Sally can manage to say at first. She was naïve to think he wouldn't have a sense of there being something amiss. She knew all the while that he probably did have some sense of it, but still, she had hoped he wouldn't. She chastises his concern, then quickly chastises herself for chastising such a wonderful thing.

"I just wish you would tell me what's been upsetting you," he says, looking at her expectantly, but knows he probably won't get very far. Her eyes are vague and wandering. "Is it your mother?"

"I don't know," Sally sighs dully. "No. Well, yes, maybe that is part of it."

"Is it me?"

"No. It isn't you."

He feels himself relax a little bit, for she said it convincingly. "Is it Jesse? The wedding?"

"No."

"Yes. It's the engagement. You're worried about him."

"No," Sally says. "I've made peace with it, for the most part."

"Well, then, what is it?" he asks her calmly, discerning as he has so many times before that being married to her gives him a feeling of living within a varicoloured mirage, with Sally as the mirage and him merely struggling toward her in a feeble, solitary path.

"It isn't any one thing," Sally confirms emphatically, feeling a few tears well up unexpectedly. She shields her face, and Jaime worries that he is, perhaps, encroaching too far too fast. He can see that she is near tears. Still, it's worth a try.

"You can say it all then," Jaime pleads. "If it isn't me, and it isn't any one thing, fine, then it's a lot of little things, and you can tell me about all of them."

As he says this, Sally finds it difficult to keep her eyes on him. She has shared one vestige of truth, that her miseries do not stem from only one thing, but a calamity of things; the misty, shapeless mess of mournful thoughts about unsatisfied artistic ambitions, the illness eating cruelly away at her mother, the embarrassment of being trapped and useless in a life that disappoints her when the logical part of her mind professes daily and adamantly that she ought to be grateful for every moment. She can't think of any words that would do. Yet she needs to say something. Jaime is watching her, rather more furtively than patiently.

"Look, Jaime," Sally begins, rising from the stool, and the narrow stretch of silvery moonlight that falls in from the window and across the floor reminds of her of the way the stars sometimes light up the area by the ravine, where her and Jaime had strolled happily one evening, a few years ago, after mourning the end of another raspberry season. They had picked only a few to eat, and stood there for a while unexpectedly, taking in the fields and the end of the summer, everything blue-lit and vivid.

It's through the mixed light of the lamp and silvery light from the window that Jaime sees Sally taking a single step toward him.

"It isn't any one thing, and it isn't you," Sally repeats, "and it isn't anyone's fault. Only I'm just not sure what to do."

"What aren't you sure about?" Jaime asks, making his voice very soft, as though trying to soothe an upset child. He hears in her voice some allusion of tragedy, the hint of some devastation unknown to him. The whole of her personality can be described in this way, as something perpetually hidden just below the surface, faintly visible, and constantly under the pressure of a long-held emotion, waiting to jump out.

Sally begins, "I feel that I've reached a place where I need to start thinking about things differently. I feel stagnant, I guess you could say. I haven't been productive enough. I've just let the time get away from me."

Jaime frowns in a struggle to decipher what his wife is saying. He shifts his feet slightly. "So, you're not happy with the way you've been spending your time, is what you're telling me. You're bored with things the way they are."

"Yes, I suppose that's it, essentially. I've been doing the same things for years. I've been living my life idly in a way, just going through the motions without considering whether or not it was enough. And now I'm just starting to realize how much time I've wasted being idle."

Jaime crinkles his forehead. "Wasted?"

"Yes."

"Idleness and boredom, I can understand," Jaime says after a pause. "Most people feel bored at one point or another in their lives. I'm just a bit surprised to hear you say that you've been wasting your time, as if you feel your time here has been misspent."

"Well, that feels like both the right way and the wrong way to explain it," she says, feeling that the word 'misspent' is both overly pessimistic and true. To put it more aptly would be to say that she wouldn't necessarily trade away this life, but wishes she could have lived another life alongside it. She glances at her damp canvas, feeling her mind as split in two, half existing in this blue-lit room, her husband staring pained and impatiently, the other still flittering somewhere beyond that searing threshold. Just a matter of minutes ago she was there, in the parallel world, where poetry, tragedy, and beauty touch all who inhabit it, where sculptures with seeing eyes look about, where the long strident sound of a bow against a cello issues from one window while a woman's cries over an unrequited love issues from another, where the brightness of tulips and wildflowers are noticed keenly instead of passively, where one hears divine messages in the swaying of trees.

"I wanted to be a painter, Jaime. I wanted to finish school."

"I know that," Jaime says, clearing his throat. "So, this is about school."

"Partly, yes."

"What else?"

"I'm not sure. It's hard to say what I would have accomplished if I hadn't, you know, had Jesse so young. If we didn't get married. But I know I would have finished school. Probably, I would have moved away. I might have had a better chance at a career."

"It isn't Jesse's fault that we had him so young," Jaime says, bitterly. "Things happen. It also isn't his fault that you had to stop school. I, or rather we, were trying to start a business. We couldn't afford it."

"I know that."

"And it certainly isn't my fault if you're bored. Or that you don't have a career, whatever career it is you're referring to."

"I know," Sally says, lowering her eyes. Her thoughts now are moving quickly, shooting this way and that, as if misfiring, pulling her mind in multiple directions at once. "I'm sorry. I'm not trying to place blame."

"And if going back to school at this point is what you feel you need, then all you have to do is say so," Jaime says, still sensing that there's more to it. He watches her steadily, hoping to read more into her expression, which now seems drained of something indefinable that it held in its grasp a moment ago, as if she were wanting to say something, hoping to say something, but the moment had passed. Her eyes seem suddenly more vacant.

"We can afford for you to take some online courses," he continues, "or for you to drive to the city one or two days a week. You have your own vehicle, after all, something you didn't have last time you were in school."

"Yes, that's true."

"And I'm sure we can find someone else to help at the shop, if you'd rather quit. As for a career, again I'm not sure what sort of career you're thinking of, but I'm sure you can find something other than managing invoices and payroll. Which I know is not your passion, by the way. There's an art gallery here in town, and an arts council."

"Yes, I suppose I would have to work somewhere nearby," Sally says despondently.

"Well, where were you thinking? It doesn't make sense to drive almost an hour and a half into the city. At least, it wouldn't be practical to do five days a week. Part time, maybe, and even then—"

"No. It isn't at all practical," she says, though in a rather rote and distracted way, and now regrets allowing the conversation to wrap itself around them in a way that implies her sorrows can be absolved in a school course or a new job. Each would help, significantly as a matter of fact, but they would not inherently change how she feels about herself, about this concealment, about having made such a decision, as a mother, as a daughter, as a wife, as a woman. And so her attempts to protect the secret of her procedure tonight suddenly evoke the image of defending a ship already wrecked and crumbled to the abyss.

"You're right," she says wearily. "There's the arts council, the schools, and the art gallery. And it's a nice gallery."

"There's the museum as well, which might interest you. There might be something there for you." Jaime searches his wife's face for reassurance, a sign that they've reached some kind of common ground, but sees none. Still she seems unsatisfied, sombre, miles away.

"You'd rather find something in the city, is that it?" he asks.

"No. I mean, yes, I do think I could find more interesting work in the city, only ..." Sally trails off as she meets his eyes, this man who loves her openly yet wears such a depressing scowl. She longs desperately, unexpectedly, for her husband's smile. She would be sated by such a sight, could reconcile the facts to him more easily somehow, the fall of words resolving into some wonderful new prose of their marriage, of their life, and settling everything into place. Yes, Sally thinks wishfully, rather naïvely; his smile would rouse in her soul such a willingness to surrender.

"Only what?" Jaime asks stonily.

"Even if I drove to the city for work, even if I took some courses that interested me, somehow it just wouldn't be enough. There's so little worthwhile to experience here," she says negligently, and in a very sad, distant tone, the words falling out of her before she can prepare them properly, before considering the effect they might have on a man who means only to help. He doesn't immediately respond, and something about his expression now seems altered and grave, as though the moment she uttered those last words, so aloofly, he had arrived at some sobering understanding about their marriage. He seems far from her now, withdrawn in a way she hasn't quite seen before.

Again, Jaime is envisaging her as the mirage he perpetually sees, but cannot reach. Yet for perhaps the first time he has no interest in continuing the trek. He feels his own tears plumbing upward. There will be no moment of intimacy between them, for it seems that the only way to please her is to somehow capture the uncapturable, to lasso the moon, to grasp firmly in his palm an intangible wisp of smoke. He feels, also, a sting of failure; he adores his wife, but has failed. She is unhappy, fully dissatisfied.

"I have no idea what you expect me to do," Jaime says dejectedly, breaking the silence, and the sadness in his voice prompts her to say something more optimistic. She's never seen him looking so bleak.

"I don't expect anything more from you than what you already do," Sally says quickly, taking another step toward him. When he doesn't answer, she continues, "I couldn't have found a better man, and I couldn't love our son any more than I do. We've made a good life together."

"I never doubted that. You're the one who seems to doubt that."

"But I don't doubt it. I know it's a good life. There's so many more things I love about living here than things I don't."

Jaime feels a hint of common ground. "I hope you mean that."

"I do," she says frankly, and they settle into another silence. Within that silence, and with him still wearing that gloomy expression, the idea of confessing, the soft, persistent music that has been emanating from another room, plays more clearly now, more alluringly. Yet the borders of the melody are coated in fear of what will happen once she confesses—once she allows the melody to move from the next room into this room. Yes, she admits quietly to herself, the struggle is less about what is right or wrong, and more about fear. If she tells him, she might lose him, or even if he stays, there is the fear that she will be as sullied in his eyes, as she is in her own. Despite this quiet admittance of fear, she begins to pursue this melody in her conscience with an extreme seriousness, trying to transform the musical notes into the words she might use and the tones in which she will speak them. She considers how wonderful it would be for them to recover together, rather than her alone. Not to blot out what she's done, but to soften it. To have some assurance, maybe, her that her fears were hollow from the start, and that he isn't going anywhere.

"Sally, I'll be as supportive as I can with whatever you want to do," Jaime says gently. "I want you to do whatever it is you need to do, if it means seeing you as happy as you were when I walked in and saw you at the easel, with a brush in your hand. You deserve that."

Sally takes the final two steps toward him, wraps her arms around his shoulders and rests her head against his chest. She inhales the soothing mixed scents of his sweat and cigarette smoke, and of something else that captures his essence more than those two things—the smell of freshly chopped wood, mixed birch and pine. Jaime wraps his arms snugly around her waist, pulls her close, rests his own head against the top of hers. Sally closes her eyes, listens to the steady quiet beating of his heart, his heart that binds together the varying strings and threads of his being, and somewhere between those threads, she imagines, little specks of light that jump or fall whenever he thinks of her.

"Thank you," she whispers, but says nothing more. The moment now feels too precious to break. An old warmth spreads through her, and through Jaime as well, for the way she is resting her head against his chest so calmly is enough to assure him that there has been some kind of breakthrough. The feel of this moment is all he needs, all he will allow to matter. He closes his eyes. They stand together for nearly a full minute, comfortably and silently, listening to the wind running through the poplar leaves and the wind chime outside, making its hollow sound.

"I know you worry about things," he says, then adds after a few moments of silence, "I just want you to be okay. I want us both to be okay."

"I want that too."

"I love you."

"And I love you," she says, resting her head deeper into his chest, and allowing a few more moments to pass before speaking again. "I've been thinking of having another exhibit. The same gallery where I used to hold exhibits. The one on Ripon Way. Remember?"

"Yes, I remember," Jaime says softly. "That's a good idea."

"Yes, I think it might be good for me."

Jaime draws a deep breath and says, though in a dispirited-sounding whisper, "Me too. I can't wait to see it."

They continue standing together for a long time, each with their head resting against the other, both feeling tired but full of thought, reassured by their physical closeness. But the longer they stand, the more Jaime begins to feel constricted in a way he never has while in her arms. Some kind of breakthrough may have happened, but it's not enough. It's arid and lacking. Yet he has no more questions than those he has already asked and nothing more to say to her, either in understanding or acrimony, than what has already been said. Words seem all at once like useless things, ineffectual strings of letters incapable of representing anything worthwhile. An essential part of his wife will remain as the proverbial mirage in the desert, the amulet hidden behind glass, stubbornly elusive, denying him something tactile and beautiful. Internally, he gives up the fight, as much out of despair as fatigue. He pulls her in closer.

It occurs to Sally that she can't quite enjoy in full the safe feeling that comes with being in his arms. She opens her eyes. Today, if not for her weakness, for she can think of no other word, she would be two and a half months into carrying their second child. He deserves to know this. It was his child too. But if she had carried the pregnancy through all the way, she would explain, some living part of her would have been impeded, halted, damned, and forever caged, like clear, free-flowing water running in a sinuous stream through trees and light, then unexpectedly into a high dam.

Sally closes her eyes again, inhales the scent of sweat, the cigarette smoke, the faint woodiness. She has no idea what he's thinking; nothing in the way he holds her reveals any definiteness about his thoughts. His hands on her back asseverated nothing. She feels suddenly emptied and rundown by having just compared the notion of a child in her womb to some kind of detrimental water dam. Her thoughts return to the disordered, mixed anxiousness that she often finds herself in when she's with her husband—wanting him to go, wanting him to stay. Yet to Sally's surprise and disappointment it is he who withdraws from their embrace first, and she looks up at him enquiringly, the man so effortlessly capable, it seems, of unending devotion and all the weight it carries. Delicately, he cups her chin in his hand and kisses the top of her forehead. He whispers, simply, "Good night."

"Good night," she replies, and simultaneously their arms fall to their sides and the tender moment slides to the floor between them. With his back turned, the guilt of her treachery and cowardice sweeps all through her. She stands motionless for several minutes as he disappears down the hall, as the bedroom door closes, as her corner room falls silent again. Not knowing what else to do, she returns to the easel and switches on the lamp. Feeling wide awake, she stands behind the stool instead of sitting on it, looking distractedly at her nearly completed painting. It's a vibrant canvas, a colourful image of still-damp brush strokes, the top third of the canvas filled from edge to edge with yellow flower petals.

She had drawn inspiration from the little cup-shaped petals of lady's slippers earlier this morning, traipsing with her cup of coffee through the dew drenched grass, for the yellowness of their petals was beginning to dwindle in a way that depressed her. She longed for a return of the brightness their petals held a few days earlier, and so it occurred to her, then, to simply paint them that way. It was something that had never really appealed to her before; to paint things not precisely as they are, but rather, a little differently, a little brighter, more upbeat, more spirited. She sipped her coffee and smiled as visions of a dense, concentrated group of gleaming lady's slippers came rushing toward her. Through these visions she felt herself physically expanded in a way, as if something were swelling inside of her, a feeling she could only explain as a love for this landscape and a gratitude that the artful feeling had been returned to her, this dilation of the soul, this glittering, indescribable need to paint. And as these vivid yellow flower petals played around in her mind, she marvelled at some of the other sights around her as well—the neighbour's golden hayfield, lit up perfectly by the still-rising sun, and made even more spectacular now that the farmer had lifted away the round bales, returning the prairie to a perfect, undisturbed flatness. The broad illumination of the sunrise over the horizon was such that, if she purposefully blurred her eyes, she could not quite tell where the colours of the sky ended and those of the earth began. It was speckled gold layered upon speckled gold. And then after finishing her coffee, she spent a few hours at the shop, then a few hours with her mother, all the while making outlines in her mind of how she would begin the flowery painting once she returned home. And the moment she arrived, had searched for and found a tube of cadmium yellow, the best choice for the flower tips, she thought, an opaque shade that finishes off any painting with the perfect splash of light. And in the spirit of wanting to make some paintings that were more upbeat and spirited, she decided to paint not only the bright yellow petals dancing around in her mind's eye, but also, on another canvas, the neighbour's golden hayfield below the equally golden sunrise. For both paintings, she will take what's there, then embellish their colours, brighten it all up. It had seemed suddenly like the most exciting thing to do; brighten things up, embellish, add a lot of light.

Standing now in the quiet of her room, Sally fathoms differently a kind of truth that she had long-held in her subconscious, that while the old, illusory place in her mind, the parallel world, is a world wreathed in beautiful things, there are also things wreathed within her life here, in this town, in this home, on this side of the threshold, that are very nearly as beautiful; things that matter, things that in the end, mean more to her than the sculptures with seeing eyes, pink lilies that never wilt, cello music issuing from windows. The feelings she had this morning, the love for this landscape, the love for her life here despite its disappointments and faults, swells inside of her again. In this moment, that love feels suddenly more like faith, and she clings to this unexpected dapple of faith as she picks up her thin-tipped brush, imbues it in black paint, brings it forward, and completes her signature on the bottom right corner of the canvas. This painting, of which she had earlier ideas on how to improve, now appears finished.

Sally looks affectionately at the damp, luminous painting, and glimpsing the pretty glass vase that bears the flowers, the simple, classic-looking vase made more beautiful because it was an unexpected gift from her husband, she instinctively sets the brush in the cup of water and heads down the hall with only two thoughts in her mind. The first is that her husband bought her this vase for the best possible reason—because he merely saw its beauty in a store one day, and thought of her. The second is more of a hope, a hope that all the things etched in the memory of that day in the clinic will become etched as well, or more so, with the memory of this moment, this day, when she painted a luminous painting of flower petals and watched a sunrise of speckled gold, then, quietly, a little late perhaps, found the strength to be honest, to let him know about the innocent life that never really was, and never will be.

Sally steps slowly, yet purposefully, clinging to hope, hope being that mysterious glinting feeling, that pure speck of radiance in the dark, and she thinks somewhat amusedly, as she reaches the end of the hall, that it seems somehow to be the fleeting glimpse of a vase that compelled her intuitively to confess.

She opens the door to the bedroom and steps inside. Jaime is sitting on the side of the bed, slumped forward with his elbows against his thighs, his hands clasped. She thought, when she opened the door, that he might appear irritated, or critical, but instead, as she met his eyes, he smiled.

Mary

The large bow window looks out over the front yard, and when the curtains are pulled back, the view goes all the way to the horizon. A small finch is perched happily on the porch rail, dancing and making weird sounds. It looks around, cocks its head mischievously, then flies off. A single grey feather floats downward and lands on the pointed tips of the overgrown grass. A quiet settles through the yard, broken every few minutes by a breeze that stirs the leaves of the surrounding poplars.

Having sat in her armchair by the bow window since dawn, Mary is now attempting to do something silly, something her daughter would rightly scold her for. Standing in front of the open door of the linen closet in the bathroom, she tries to reach two things from the top shelf: her mother's pearl necklace, stored in its original wooden box, and a small, round, two-sided mirror. One side of the glass reflects with exactness the way most mirrors do, whereas the other side offers a magnified image. She uses her cane to pull the desired items to the edge of the shelf, then stretches her fingers upward to clutch each item. She takes the mirror first and tucks it under her opposite arm, then grasps the wooden box. Though no one else is around, her movements are stealthy and quiet, as though fearful of getting caught. She is not supposed to leave the sunken living room without help. Yet, as she reminds herself, this is still her home by rights, this is her bathroom closet, these are her own things inside of it. As she turns from the linen closet, clutching the wooden box protectively, she smiles a frail yet jubilant smile. On her own, she has solved the problem of having nothing to do, and not wanting to spend yet another full morning in front of the bow window seemed to merit the task. She makes her way back down the hall with slow, thoughtful movements.

The difficulty of movement still surprises her at times. To

simply keep herself upright and move forward is cumbersome—lift one leg, lower it, rest, then lift the other—and no less laborious than if her legs were weighted to the floor. Indeed, they are weighted, for in her refusal to wear compression stockings, an excess of fluid sits immovably within the tissues. The joined effects of arthritis and tense swelling have rendered her legs to feel less now like limbs of warm muscle and flesh, and more like steel cords binding two blocks of wood. Sometimes it is the degree of physical decline that shocks her. Other times it is the degree to which she feels that her body has not so much declined, but that the body of her youth has been snatched and substituted with another, one she does not recognize or possess in full. It does not listen well to her commands; it has strange moods and exists as its own entity, with an agenda apart from her own. Mary admits quietly to her own human frailty, her own pathetic destiny between these slumbering walls. Everything involves more process, more of a challenge. There are terrible moments when she hasn't any strength, better moments when she does, and back and forth it goes.

Mary stops at the edge of the linoleum, and feels the pain that stabs wildly from beneath her rib cage whenever she grows short of breath. She knows she can't stand still for much longer. Her legs, especially the left knee, won't tolerate it. She looks fearfully down at the step, the only obstacle remaining between her and the living room. She regains most of her breath, turns her body slightly aslant, and leans all her weight against the cane. Very cautiously, she lowers her right foot onto the stair, then repeats the move with the left leg. Only now does she recognize the difficulty in manoeuvring this step without someone to hold her arm and guide her. It's been several weeks, months perhaps, since she has attempted to do so without anyone next to her. She argued to the caregivers, and to her daughter, that it wasn't necessary, that she wasn't helpless, that they shouldn't fuss. Some days she's sincere, others she argues out of habit while clenching tightly to their arm for fear of falling.

Mary slowly but surely makes her way to the armchair facing the window. Her moss-green afghan remains tossed along the side of it. She briefly admires from an upright vantage point the contents of a vase in the centre of the small round table on the other side of her chair. The cream-coloured roses have opened in earnest, bursting from prickly green stems with the kind of fullness that flowers put on display for a day or two at most, before they begin to wilt. They stem from the glass in variegated positions, their petals leaning this way and that. All flowers are beautiful, each distinctive in their own way, but there's something uniquely special about a rose. The collective shape of their petals is absolutely stunning, bold and timeless, mystical yet familiar, their sweet, musky scent somehow the most calming, yet vivid. Roses, Mary reflects, are almost otherworldly in their perfection.

She leans forward, takes hold of the arm of the chair, and very carefully lowers herself into the seat. She sighs with relief. Mercifully, she accomplished her little task unscathed. As she sits calm and still to catch her breath, she glances once again at the roses, smiles at them, for it's been more than a few weeks, it seems, since she's had a bouquet in the room. The sight of them complements the room the way only fresh flowers can, heightens the mood of any surroundings, for it seems in some small way that the lively presence of these roses is what encouraged her to seek out her mother's pearls, her mother having also been a woman with a great love of flowers—lilac especially—but all flowers, she said, had their place. Mary thinks absently that there are so many lovely things in life that people are too silly and too busy to appreciate, then sets the mirror down on her lap and carefully opens the wooden box that bears the necklace.

At first, she only stares at the antique strand of pearls, inhales their nostalgia, breathes in the slight musty smell. It's a round, clasped thread of yellowing beads set against a soft, navy blue film. She lifts her hand and gently runs her fingers along the line of pearls, pausing on each one as if within their rounded surface she might touch on some preserved essence of her mother. Oh, that the sensation of her might have been kept available in this necklace somehow, the way the presence of a person attaches itself to a thing they owned for a long time. Mary stops when she reaches the final pearl, then starts again in the opposite direction, slowly, for she is slow in all her movements. The days of rushing long passed. Her younger self's habit of checking the clock, wondering how much time they have until they need to be at this place or that, is gone. The hours cease to matter now, for they are all the same, blurred incidentally as one. Mary pays no notice to the clock unless it chimes, and otherwise she merely lets the time tick away without much acknowledgement. Whole days come and go without much care or notice. It's a unique kind of passivity that belongs only to the very old, to those who have already gathered a lifetime of mortal experiences, some less dispiriting than others, and who now, as the days pass, take ease in shabby armchairs, feeling sentimentally thoughtful and wishing for little more than some degree of continuance. Of course, one only wishes for continuance that falls within reason and within certain parameters, for there always comes a time when enough is enough.

With some difficulty, uncertain of the dexterity of her fingers, Mary unclasps the pearl necklace. She lifts it around her neck, and after a few failed attempts, resets the clasp. She lifts the round mirror from her lap and turns it to the side that will enlarge her reflection. The shapes and intricacies of her features appear to her with a shock in the small circle. It has been several months since she's had a clear look at herself. Yes, she catches glimpses in household mirrors from time to time, but they're from farther away and the views are always brief and muddied, her vision being less than it once was. She's taken aback now by the hollowness of her cheeks, the topsy-turvy profusions of steely white hair like pulpits along her scalp, entirely longer and thicker than she thought it was. It drifts down in tangles and lands over each of her shoulders in a mangled flop. Mary looks with a kind of complacency at the rest—the cruelly crinkled skin, the sallow eye sockets, the dry, pale lips. She appears within the glinting surface of the glass slightly elegiac, a strange, startling figure, who now with the string of opulence resting against the sagging skin of her neck, looks like a very old woman indeed, grandly unkempt, half insane. And so, the isolation has made her a little bit odd, perhaps, an odd and ineffectual old woman reft by lung cancer and, she supposes, some form of senility.

Mary and her daughter question to what degree her recent memory problems are the result of age, and to what end the issues have been exacerbated by the hydromorphone tablets, blessed things. Mary is more inclined to believe it is the tablets, rather than age, that have fogged her mind and taken a kind of half-possession of her thoughts. The number of pills she takes is not healthy in the long term, of course, but she will continue to insist on them, for they are at least fleetingly curative in allowing some respite from the pain.

Pain. Her daughter, Sally, continually fails to wrap her still-young mind around the spasms of hurt this illness sends so exquisitely through the runnel of her back, along her shoulders and into her hips. The agony in certain moments is indescribable. On top of this, each morning, and sometimes throughout the day, she must inhale then exhale a series of breaths that feel as though little shards of glass are quivering along the insides of her chest. At night the breathing worsens, and she lies awake, envisaging her lungs being filled up then swallowed by the fluid. In addition to all this, a mysterious new ache announces itself each morning in her left hip. It feels like a stiff vice that stays latched until midday at least, or until she moves around enough to loosen it a little. And so, a month or so ago, rather tired of all this, Mary did something she knew she wasn't supposed to, something that seemed to alter the course of things. She drastically over-medicated herself.

That morning brought an unusually harsh spasm of pain through her back, and she knew that the usual two milligrams wouldn't suffice. In her mind the only thought was to do whatever she could to find respite from the pain, which was unbearable, as seething as ever. Her heart thumped as she made her way into the kitchen in an appallingly slow, cautious tread. It seemed half an hour had passed before she reached the far end of the counter where the pills were stored in a little reed-woven basket. To remove the lid of the bottle was no small task; she turned it, winced, turned it again. After ten minutes or so, it popped off. She removed each pill from the bottle very carefully, methodically, for she would have had no means to retrieve them from the floor if they dropped. Three or four extra pills, that was all she wanted, was all she needed to mitigate the discomfort, to absolve her body for at least a short while from the unruly suffering. Otherwise she might very well have vomited from the pain, and wouldn't that have been an attractive scene for one of those damnable caregivers to stumble upon. The pills had an almost immediate sedative effect, and after making her way from kitchen to living room, she fell into her armchair and into a deepened sleep.

Though she's been more than slightly depressed, ending her life, or harming herself in some way, was never the intent. One enlightened doctor referred to the incident as a lapse in judgement brought on by physical desperation, which Mary found fitting. It would have been false to diagnose her with some unusual form of melancholy, to imply that the act was brought on by the profound loss of spirit that sends scores of others running for the pills. Nevertheless, once Sally found her invalid mother lying crooked and lethargic in the armchair, she went into a bit of a frenzy. An ambulance was called, unnecessarily in Mary's opinion, and from that day forward she was deemed unfit to manage her own medication. Twice a day, in addition to the home care already in place, a nurse enters her home to retrieve the medication from a metal box in the kitchen, locked by combination, all arranged by her own meddling daughter. Mary knows it's somewhat unjust to describe her daughter in such a way, yet oh, how deeply she resents their help, their unconscious, cheerful degradation. The presence of paid staff entering her home without her formal consent implies, rather it screams, of her own futility. Decisions about very basic things have been culled from her hands.

So quickly life changes. So quickly it happens.

Mary coils her mother's pearls around an arthritic finger, and gazes again into the small round mirror. She can scarcely accept this as her own reflection, yet at the same time the reflection seems accurate, and in consonance with what she feels—emptied, exhausted, abandoned to this life for a few years longer than necessary. It's a drawn-out process, a sense that life has already stripped her bare, yet continues to demand more. Life, she muses, is a curious kind of metamorphosis. It begins with the impressionable years of youth, and all the innocence and dream-filled fantasies that marked her early years on her father's farm. Her innocence was ended, partly, by her father's own hand, who drank excessively and had a habit of hitting her, regardless of whether she'd done wrong. Regardless, by one route or another, cynicism seeps into one's mind by degrees as they grow out of childhood. Things seen in dreams are inevitably set against what is true. Then one marries, perhaps, and the family of one's childhood splinters off, older members pass away while new members are born and grow, miraculously, into independent beings. The figures of her past have become, in her memory over time, amplified versions of themselves, more symbolic than human. Mary's mother and father, for example, have come to symbolize warmth and steel furtiveness, respectively. Her husband, John, is love. Her daughter is challenge. Her sons, loss.

Mary releases the pearls and lays the mirror flat on her lap. Though there is nothing but light coming in from the window, she feels suddenly unsure of the time of day, whether this is morning or late afternoon, and wonders whether someone is coming to see her, or if they have already been. She hopes they have already been; that way she will not be bothered. Her eyes rest upon her hands, half unrecognizable, thin and starting to curl in on themselves, almost claw-like. They're stained with liver spots, under which are long pointed bones and ugly blue veins that bulge over top. The knuckles swell always with a cruel inflammation, so much so that she can no longer knit, cook, or write a letter. Here, then, is the final phase of the metamorphosis, where one is useless, forgotten, frightened. If not taken swiftly during a deep sleep as her husband was, bless him, or by something quick, then one is left in the suspense of something long. Hers is a disease that lives month after month in an ominously stagnant sort of way until one day it will capitulate suddenly to death. And so, until then she will sit quietly in her armchair by the bow window, remembering and wondering, and she'll let death shadow over her in its subtle way, sly and deliberate, like a slow ticking metronome, watching, waiting.

This house and yard are already deathly quiet. It's a quietness that bothered her until recently, but now she doesn't mind. She has fallen in love with silence.

As Mary sits in her armchair with the mirror on her lap, Beth, the caregiver, is walking up Elnor Road. The walk to Mary's house normally takes about twenty minutes, but given that the sun is falling in a more thorough way than it has in days, she decided this morning to leave a little earlier than usual, and to stretch the walk by taking a longer route. The day is warm, and there's something about bodily movement that helps to settle her thoughts, and to brighten her spirits. And so, three or four mornings each week, she makes her way to Mary, a client she looks forward to seeing, more perhaps than any other.

Last night Beth was in her apartment, and in a mood that has become depressingly common. Sometimes she is comfortable with the loneliness, as one becomes comfortable with a daily routine, whatever it may be. But more and more the solitary nature of her life bothers her. On one hand, living alone means that she is not held to anything the way other women her age, who are wives and mothers, have been when it comes to upholding a family's happiness. In that way, loneliness can feel like a privilege.

There is a luxury in having no one to disappoint. On the other hand, there is a real sadness that comes with unlocking the door at night, stepping inside, and finding that no one has been up waiting, or wondering. There's a perpetual feeling of being untied from other people, dissevered, at odds with everything, for it seems sometimes that if a woman does not have a man in her life, or a child, then she somehow matters less than a woman who has those things, and is less needed.

Life has some nuanced ways of communicating this, which, in Beth's experience, usually comes in the way of pitying or consolatory looks; thinly veiled looks she did not receive four years ago when she had a fiancé, plans for a small wedding, a feeling not just of house but of home. He left unexpectedly, and she has been imbued ever since in a kind of teeming, unremitting sadness, a sadness so tenacious and long-term that she has come to claim it as much a part of herself as her clothes, her furniture, her unpainted nails, her long brown hair. Yet the persistent melancholy seems less and less to do with his leaving and more to do with something indefinable, something more subtle and quietly injurious. She cries for reasons she doesn't understand, for a sorrow she can't identify or link to any clear cause. The seeds of it planted, perhaps, long ago. It is, seemingly, an impressionable kind of sadness, one so flimsy and sensitive that even the little yellowish-brown leaf that now falls to the damp pavement in front of her depresses her unreasonably.

Lately she has been referring to her sadness—this indefinable thing that follows her around—as white noise, for it seems impossible to otherwise define this prolonged state of gloominess. Perhaps, she muses, because there are no right words to describe such an abstract thing, no sure classification. To describe the white noise in full would be as complex as trying to illustrate for someone a skewed and ominous sight seen only once in a flash through the darkness. For unless someone has seen this singular flash of sight, they cannot understand the weight of it, the feel of it, the power it has to forevermore haunt by degrees whomever sees it.

There has been one bright spot in all of this, something that fills her with gratitude many times during the week, and that is her work. Providing care is the only work she's had, the only work she's wanted, the distraction that shields her mind from depression the way a prayer protects a believer from disaster. The provision helps, if only for a while. On a morning such as this she can set the sadness aside, perform her duties, and offer herself something to look forward to.

Beth reaches the stretch of Elnor Road where the pavement gives way to gravel, past the bordered-up corner store, past the sign for flax bales. Mary's house is already in sight. The old homestead, because of its age and lack of upkeep, carries a sense of being a separate entity altogether from the rest of town, which is in a state of rampant development. The wet leaves pinned against chipped siding, the clothesline with nothing hung, the tattered sandbox beside a garden overgrown with weeds all say the same thing—this was once an animated place with many moving parts to keep it all aflow, like an enchanted house from a fable that, once the spell broke, devolved into a shack-like dwelling deserted at the edge of a poplar bush. As Beth turns onto the driveway, she sees the raised, failing shingles on the roof and the wrap-around porch that leans a little to the west. Yet the bones of the house are in good shape, if antiquated, in the way that reminds her of the old school desks with little unused wells for ink and feather quills—technically functional, but slowly grandfathered out of the system to make way for the new.

Beth ascends the worn steps of the wooden porch, passes a

set of garden trimmers resting inside an empty flowerpot, and lets herself inside. She hangs her coat, then quietly goes to the kitchen to check the logbook where notes and reminders are communicated between caregivers. She reads the entries that were recorded since her last visit and makes her way to the front of the house, and as she crosses the linoleum, can already see Mary through the dining room that opens into the sunken living room.

The curtains are drawn back and the room is unusually bright, alternating the usual tints of objects and making them more vivid than usual. Beth muses that the shades of colour in any room are always painted differently given the time of day and the movement of the sun and the clouds. Today, the shabbiness of the furniture is fully exposed, as is the scarred surface of the coffee table and Mary's old armchair, facing the broad window at an angle. Beth stands quietly for a moment at the edge of the dining room, looking at Mary in her armchair, half crouched, bathed in sunlight. A small mirror rests mysteriously upon her lap. At first glance she has the appearance of someone in a deep, contemplative trance, her head bowed reticently and her eyes staring downward in a sort of dreamy gaze. Mary has yet to give notice to her arrival.

"Hi, Mary," Beth says in a loud whisper. When there is no response, Beth moves slowly, hoping to warn Mary as gently as possible of her presence. However, as she descends into the living room, the creak of the wooden step causes Mary to startle and shoot an alarmed, angry look her way. Beth sighs, knows already by Mary's expression that she has found her in an irritable state, not in a mood for company.

"I'm sorry I startled you," Beth says apologetically. "How are you this morning?"

"Wonderful," Mary replies dryly, though her expression

begins to soften somewhat.

"How is your pain today?"

"Not too bad. The less I move, the better."

"Can I fix you some breakfast?"

"No," she says tiredly. "Not yet."

"Okay," Beth says. She takes her usual position on the floral sofa, next to the small round table that today holds a vase of fully blossomed cream roses, roses which were just beginning to flourish three days earlier, their petals still angled slightly upward instead of outward. She hadn't asked that day who the flowers were from, assuming it was Sally, as she often brings fresh ones for her mother. Nevertheless, hoping to keep her visit with Mary on a lighter note, she asks who brought her the roses.

"My daughter, of course." Mary responds, looking at the creamy petals with a glint of happiness before a more befuddled expression takes over. "She brought them a day or two ago, or it might have been earlier in the week, I'm not sure."

Mary yawns and a pained look comes over her face as she takes in the air. It seemed that her whole torso tightened and retracted inward, slightly, in derision.

"I am tired after yesterday," Mary says. "You won't convince me to do much walking today."

"What happened yesterday?" Beth inquires. She notices, now, a string of pearls around Mary's neck.

"There was a gathering at my daughter's house. It was a gathering in honour of my grandson, who is engaged. I had no interest in going. I'd just as soon have him pay me a visit here on his own. It was too much for me, all that noise, all those people."

"I see," Beth says. "I didn't know he was engaged."

"Yes, very recently. I don't remember her name." Mary draws a deep, wet sounding breath.

"Your pearls are nice."

"Hmm?"

"Your pearls," Beth says, pointing. "The necklace you're wearing. It's pretty."

Mary lifts her hand, rests her palm against the necklace. "My mother's pearls," she says inattentively, as though her mind is occupied elsewhere.

A silence passes. Beth watches Mary fall back into the same watery-eyed trance she found her in, her head bowed forward, half conscious, her face drooped and languid. Beth knows her medication intake is closely monitored, so it must be as Mary says, that she is tired from the gathering. The lucidity of Mary's mind is a bit tricky, though, and like many palliative clients, she seems to inhabit two separate realms simultaneously—one being the realm of the dying, or the realm of ending hopes, and the other more indicative of the indelible woman Mary has always been. Beth first knew her in childhood, the mother of a friend who drove them to school after a sleepover, who spent hours behind the wooden garden troughs, planting and picking. The woman in front of her now, with a frail hand resting on a pearl necklace, is very changed, a gaunt half-ghost of the woman who once moved about the house and yard purposefully, and if memory serves, loudly. She was very unlike Sally's father, who scarcely said a word.

"Mary?" Beth says concernedly.

Mary seems unusually lethargic. She shudders awake, looks at the skinny woman sitting placidly on her chesterfield.

"Are you alright?"

"Of course I'm alright," Mary says churlishly, then quickly regrets the churlishness. She's not very pleasant to deal with in the mornings, she knows, always a little grumpy, as though all her frustrations gather when she wakes and dissipate slowly, but never completely, as the day goes on.

"I was only checking," Beth says, averting her eyes.

Checking on what, Mary wonders. She leers at Beth, but only for a moment, for hers is a genial little face, mild and meek, one that seems filled to the brim with benevolent thoughts. She is pretty, yet dowdy. Mary recognizes her now as the caregiver who compares favourably with the others, but despite the familiarity of her face, hers is a name that never seems to keep still in her mind from one moment to the next. Today, the name eludes her once again.

"Remind me of your name."

"It's Beth."

"Sally's friend."

"Once upon a time, yes."

Mary, whose palm still rests against the pearl necklace, lowers her hand to her stomach and winces.

"Mary," Beth begins carefully, knowing she is about to encroach on a delicate subject. "Have you had a movement today?"

"A movement?" Mary reclaims her scowl.

"Yes, Mary, a movement," Beth presses. According to the logbook, it's been four days. "I can bring you some prune juice otherwise."

"You people have no problem being crass," Mary says shrilly, finally understanding. "You say and ask anything you like." She turns away, more out of anger than embarrassment. This girl, Mary recalls, is more rabid than the others about discussing movements and prune juice, although all the caregivers give rise to the same feeling; the offending feeling of being pinned down and stripped of her dignity in a slew of subtle ways she never imagined. Unable to escape the woman's presence in her home, she can only sit with a scowl, fully exposed by the light of the window, and endure the rest of this little harangue. These people, these paid staff, how they love to harangue.

"That prune juice is awful," Mary adds. "It was Sally who brought it, I'm sure."

"Yes, Sally brought it for you," Beth confirms. "But it's alright, I won't force you to have anything."

"You won't force me. Aren't you kind."

"I only offered as I believe it's been more than a few days," Beth says somewhat wearily, knowing that any argument with Mary usually proves futile. No matter what is suggested, Mary argues for the other, and no amount of good intentions will suffice.

"A few days?" Mary snaps. "Who told you this?"

"It's in our logbook," Beth says, but quickly realizes the logbook shouldn't be mentioned, as it tends to upset her.

"Logbook?"

"It's good to keep track of these things, such as how often you've gone, how well you've slept, or what your pain levels are. That sort of thing."

"A national bestseller once I'm gone, I imagine."

"Maybe so," Beth says, smiling subtly.

Mary, growing irritated, faces the window. She admits, quietly in her own mind, to feeling somewhat bloated and heavy. Her stomach this morning is in some dimly perceptible state of nausea, though none of this is new. Vague feelings of discomfort move around her body at their leisure, settling this place or that before travelling faintly elsewhere. These vague, faint, difficult to describe feelings of sickness—is that what is meant by generalized malaise?

"If this is a recurrent issue," Mary begins, "then someone should bring me milk of magnesia. It would taste far better than prune juice, that I can say."

"Mary," Beth resumes cautiously. "Sally brought you milk of magnesia a few weeks ago, but unfortunately you didn't like the taste."

"I've never once had it in this house, stupid woman," Mary says crossly, though she knows it wouldn't be untypical for her to forget such a thing. Only, her forgetfulness frightens her, angers her, for the loss of a clear mind makes her easy prey for pity, and surely there is nothing on this earth lower than pity.

She is so unlike her mother at times, Mary concedes, a whispery-soft woman who never raised her voice beyond the neglectable chirps of a purple finch, whose words always held some sympathetic meaning or other. Regrettably, Mary inherited the fragile temperament of her father, whose composure was coated only with the thinnest of veneers, marred over time with cracks and tears, out of which careless words float up, unbidden. She, like him, knows that it's a wonderful alleviation of pressure, however shameful.

All in all, Mary reflects, she isn't as unreasonably frustrated with life as she used to be. Weakened by illness, perhaps, her frustration has started to thaw, as though something once deep and hard is finally allowed to rise and soften. Even now, the release of anger fails to satisfy her. The poor woman on the chesterfield only means to help, and is doing her level best to reason with the shrill old woman in pearls before her, the cruel-tongued convalescent whom, as was so cordially put to her, hasn't had a proper movement in several days.

"Fine," Mary announces grudgingly. "I'll have a small glass of prune juice. A very small one. A thimbleful will do."

Beth assumes an air of relief, and Mary watches her rise from the chesterfield before she has a chance to change her mind. She listens, a moment later, to the quick footsteps making their way across the linoleum, and Mary dreads already the taste of the black, purplish swill.

In the kitchen, Beth opens the fridge and finds the prune juice. She always feels disposed toward Mary, however caustic her mood. Why Mary suddenly agreed to the juice, she isn't sure. She seems increasingly irritable these days, more argumentative, so submitting to the juice seems uncharacteristic. Beth retrieves a small glass from the cupboard.

One of the psychological effects of aging, she recalls while filling the glass to three quarters, particularly of those whose cognitive abilities become impaired for whatever reason, is that one after the other, the fundamental aspects of their personality become increasingly magnified. If one is anxious throughout their life, their anxiousness increases with cognitive decline. If one is naturally quiet, they grow steadily silent. In a sense, the core of the self is reduced to its primary colours, overpowering other traits, filtering out adjacent shades. The traits that remain are more indicative of the true self. Yet in Beth's experience, that assessment seems too rigid, even improbable, because humans are too complex to be reduced to anything definitive. Personality traits, like moods, are affected by what's around them, and can be very fluid, changing shape all the time. It's a multi-factorial thing. She returns the carton of juice to the fridge.

While Mary waits for Beth to return from the kitchen, she runs her fingers along her cotton nightgown. The material against her skin feels clingy and slightly damp, as though she's been sweating in it for days. Perhaps she smells of sweat, or of something more fetid, something more akin to the foulness of old age, if indeed there is such an odour. The woman in her house, whose name she forgets again, arrives with a dubious smile. That horrid glassful of syrupy fluid being placed in her hands will run right through her. Surely once it has, the woman will put a gold star sticker in the logbook, and go home feeling like she's conquered Goliath in the valley.

"It's more than a thimbleful, but here you are," Beth says encouragingly. She is surprised to see Mary drink all the prune juice in one full, uninterrupted effort. Mary's expression afterward is indicative of complete disgust, to the point where Beth thought she might cry or bring it all back to the surface. Instead Mary draws a deep breath and defiantly places the glass on the table beside the roses.

Beth feels somewhat remorseful for inciting the juice, but also gratified. These are the mandatory ministrations after all—prune juice, meal preparation, dressing, and encouraging exercise. Keep day-to-day life running as smoothly as possible, for as long as possible. However well-meaning the ministrations, there's often a nagging feeling in this line of work, one of repentance, an uneasy sense that you're not doing it right. Again, Mary looks as though she might throw up.

"Are you alright?" Beth asks despite herself, knowing how it might be received.

"Yes," Mary replies derisively. "I'm perfectly alright. Do something for me and do not ask again."

"Okay, I won't ask."

They fall into another silence. Beth reclaims her spot on the chesterfield, and to Mary she appears bored the way Sally often appears bored, with a dull, unreflecting expression. Perhaps she herself inspires boredom in anyone who enters this house of late, and now they all have the same impression of her—a drab, plaintive old woman who lives too long and bores others to stone. Perhaps the final scenes of her life are a considerably dull thing to witness. Nevertheless, a pertinent question continues to nag her.

"Can you tell me, when was my last shower?"

"Thursday morning."

"What day is today?"

"Sunday. I was hoping to help you with one this morning, as a matter of fact."

"I see," Mary says ponderously, knowing the word help is added only for decoration, for this woman is about to undertake all the work herself.

"Only if you're willing," Beth adds hastily.

To her surprise, Mary agrees. She lifts the mirror from her lap and places it gently on the small table, then allows Beth to reach supportively underneath her armpit as she hoists herself from the chair. For the next few minutes, they're absorbed in the routine of maneuvering up the step to the linoleum, then across the hall and into the bathroom. Beth runs the warm water, and Mary passively allows her to remove the nightgown and undergarments. Mary is both relieved and embarrassed when the clothes are pulled from her body. In the fog-wreathed mirror, she catches a glimpse of herself, a pallor mass of skin, wizened and rough looking like shoe leather, topped by white hair and a string of pearls. Instinctively, she looks away. Her withering naked body is a disheartening sight against the beauty of her mother's necklace.

"Take my mother's necklace off," Mary says, in a slightly grieved tone.

"Good idea," Beth consents. She undoes the clasp, then lays them on a dry towel. "We don't want them tarnished by the soap."

Holding Beth's hand for stability, Mary lurches herself one leg at a time into the tub and sits heavily on the raised shower chair. Water a touch too warm falls on her head, and the rough-ness of cloth is felt immediately down her back, then across her front—the simple and delicate washing routine one is accustomed to doing themselves, until they can't. It's taken for granted that the routine is conducted alone, until one has no choice but to allow an audience. Mary usually consents to this woman, whose name she now remembers as Beth, because there is something trustful and kind about her, which makes the whole unfortunate process a little more tolerable. A little.

"There, we're just about finished," Beth assures after washing and rinsing Mary's hair. Mary savours the last moments of warm water running along her shoulders and down her back.

The water is turned off and Mary rises, shivering, from the shower chair as Beth drapes a towel around her. Clutching Beth's arm, she coaxes each of her legs over the side of the tub. When one leg falters, the sore left leg, Mary is on the verge of falling backward until Beth rights her forward. The abrupt correcting of her posture, however, sends a sharp wave of pain across her lower back, and the intensity causes her to shriek. Beth, otherwise help-less, can only soothe by rubbing the small of Mary's back. She stands beside Beth, dripping.

"Let's dry off so you can get a clean nightgown on," Beth says, taking a towel from the closet. She starts with the hair, but stops for a moment when Mary coughs several times; the steam from the shower always helps to loosen things. Her deepest coughs always resemble a sort of unearthly growl, powerful yet ravaged.

Beth does a quick pat down of Mary's hair before moving to the rest of her body. Strangely, as though by religious rite, this part of the routine is always completed in silence; none of the caregivers speak as they dry her off. Maybe it's a dreary task for them, as much as it's disagreeable for her.

"When does the nurse come?" Mary asks in a tired, gravelly voice as the nightgown is slipped over her head. She feels short of air, but when she tries to take another deep breath, she can't. She is seldom able to inhale a full breath; it always feels interrupted somehow, never a good, strong chestful.

"There won't be another until evening."

"I'll need something before then."

"Sally can get the hydromorphone. She'll be here in a little while. She's bringing some lunch for you."

Mary and Beth make their way cumbersomely to the front room of the house, the southerly room, still pleasantly full of light. It's the exaggerated light of midday when everything is so lit with sun that they give off an intensified shade of white. The sky is clear, all glimmering and uniform, like polished glass. Little shards of glass are pushing their way out of the lungs, Mary thinks to herself as they come into the room, then is surprised a moment later when she realizes the words were said aloud.

"That sounds awful," Beth says.

"What sounds awful?"

"The feeling of glass shards in your lungs. Sounds very painful."

Beth leaves Mary in the armchair and comes back after a minute with a glass of water and two regular Tylenol.

"Here," Beth says. "This is all I'm allowed to give you."

Mary takes the pills and sips the water gratefully. One of her medications, a mystery as to which one, always leaves her feeling parched. Beth sits on the sofa with her arms clasped around her knees, watching Mary, who sets the glass down so unsteadily that Beth is almost inclined to rush toward her, but Mary manages to set the glass down without spilling. Mary takes a few deep breaths, and they are both still and quiet for several minutes as the slow steady sound of a train approaches, lingers, then passes well beyond the tree line. Each had similar thoughts about the distant sound of it grumbling along the tracks; Mary found the sound to be melancholic yet stirring, and Beth found it to be eerie, poignant, and haunting, for the unique sound of it has an odd way of clinging to the mind. After a few more minutes of quietness, Mary peers at the roses.

"Roses, roses, roses," Mary says wistfully, feeling very refreshed after her shower. "I wish there were buckets of roses around me at all times. I wish they were brought to me in armloads, fresh ones every day."

"They are pretty," Beth agrees. "I haven't had flowers in my home for a long time. My ex-fiancé said anything that wilts so quickly wasn't worth the money. He said I should buy artificial flowers if I wanted some, or a cactus, like a succulent, something that lasts and doesn't need much watering. He only bought me flowers once."

"Sounds like a dummy."

"Well—" Beth begins uncertainly before Mary interposes.

"I have been thinking of lilac. As pretty as I find this bouquet, I'd trade it in an instant for lilac."

"You prefer lilac over roses?"

"No, not normally, but lilac was my mother's flower. She loved those flowers, my mother and her lilacs," Mary says dreamily, her voice falling in a way that Beth perceives as sorrow, not necessarily for her mother or lilacs individually, but for the memories conjured when those two elements are considered together at the same time.

"My mother told me something once about lilacs, something I'd forgotten until now," Mary says, then grimaces as she takes another deep breath. She continues, "They mark the remains of homesteads. She said lilacs aren't native to the prairie and don't grow well in the wild, and so every lilac bush you see on the prairie was planted purposefully. If a lilac bush seems out of place, not obviously in someone's yard, then you will probably also find, somewhere around it, remnants of a doorsill or an old foundation wall."

"That sounds sad," Beth says thoughtfully.

"Yes," Mary says, for the image of this depresses her as well. There is something grim about the thought of a young home-steader planting things around his home, only for him and the home to grow old, deteriorate, eventually giving way to that dete-rioration and crumbling like dust to the earth, the story of the place soon forgotten, grown over with burdock weeds and thistles. It magnifies a truth that, to some degree, one must grow old to understand. No matter what seeds are planted, whatever stones are laid, life does end, and whatever was cultivated or assembled with those seeds and stones ultimately falls into decline, or at the very least are changed. Mary thinks of her gardens, rather the vestiges of her gardens, and the strife to maintain them all those years. It was a joyful strife, but a strife nevertheless; a wonderful pursuit, a passion of hers, very fulfilling, yet so quickly turned to a pit of barren wet mud and weedy squalor.

A car passes along the gravel road, and the house settles once again into silence. Yes, she understands the essence of it now—the futility, the utter oblivion, the world snatched from old hands—and she accepts that in the moment she passes, her life in this house, each of those gardens, one for vegetables, one for flowers, and the myriad seeds of moments and memories planted here will all blow away in the wind like the remnant spurs of a dead dandelion. There will be someone else nipping at her heels, ready to move in and plant their own. Then another, and another. She understands it in her bones.

Her husband's handmade wicker chairs sit on the front porch, carved from willow, if memory serves, and Mary wonders now what will happen to them once she's gone. Like the gardens, is it nearby, yet already seems further away. It already belongs, somehow, to whomever will live here next, or to whomever will see fit to take it, perhaps Sally. She feels herself already dispossessed of many things—the beautiful wicker chairs, handcrafted by her husband, the green-shaded lamp in her bedroom that was her own mother's, the wide velvet painting of orange-leaved trees hanging above the red-brick fireplace. Good riddance to that hideous painting—it's an ugly sight, but it was John's, and so she couldn't bring herself to throw it in the burn pile after he passed. She has never seen the fireplace without it.

Her mind returns once again to the willow wicker chairs on the porch, and the hours her husband spent on the weaving, simply because Mary once mentioned liking the look of wicker furniture. John built many things—an oak easel for Sally one year, who was thrilled at the first sight of it—but in Mary's heart those picturesque chairs, and the memory of his rough, capable hands bending and tying the strips of wood into place, hit the highest mark.

"There," he said, setting it down on the porch with a proud grin. "Now you'll have something better to have coffee on and watch your sunrises from than that old lawn chair." Mary recalls the moment clearly, his grin, her coral-coloured housedress, and when she wrapped her arms around him, the feel of a thousand sprinkles of shaved wood caught against his denim shirt, like rough sand on her palm. She remembers that afternoon in flashes—the beating hammer, the whine of the table saw as it lowered through one of the bigger pieces of wood, the smell of sawdust, the clear sky behind him as he finally set the first of the chairs down on the porch. Another day, some years later, she recalls sitting with John in the evening, crickets chirping, their sons running in the yard, the song of a meadowlark or chickadee emitting here and there from the poplars. They had sat on two wicker chairs pushed snuggly together on the porch, her right hand held softly by his left. She is grateful for all the moments that she can still envisage with some degree of clarity, for while some of the scenes in her life are recalled more vividly, others, for whatever reason, are more splintered, whole years of her life either forgotten or reduced to a series of fragmented images floating muddily through her mind. She sees most of her life as if walking backward through a thin fog, everything blurred and wistful.

Mary shuts her eyes, recalls an evening long ago, when a friend of her mother's, a French speaking woman, paid them a visit. Mary would have been about 15 or so, and she, her mother, and the French woman, sat comfortably around the kitchen table with each a fresh cup of tea. It was mid-summer, for Mary remembers the humidity affecting the air around them and the beads of sweat on the visiting woman's brow. The woman's name, alas, she can no longer recall, though she was known to her mother through church, and often wore floral, floor length dresses, and was much more heavy-set than her own delicately-framed mother. The three of them spoke of simple things for a while, the crops and the gardens and the weather, until the conversation moved at some point to the topic of childhood memories, and why some things are remembered easily while others are all but forgotten. The French woman proceeded to explain, in tattered English, her straightforward belief on the subject.

"I think, me, if something is still in the mind after several years then that maybe is how it should be, and if it disappears from the mind, well, then, maybe is how it should be too," she said, then shrugged dismissively and wiped her brow with an off-white handkerchief.

It had greatly intrigued Mary that evening to be presented with the notion that everything meant to be remembered is naturally remembered, and all that is meant to be forgotten is naturally forgotten. If one can only recall a particular person in a jumbled way, or if one experience is recalled clearly while the memory of another experience evades the mind completely, then it is meant to be so. It seemed comforting, this simple concept of allowing things to fall out of the mind organically, and to trust one's memory to keep only what it should. Indeed Mary still finds, especially now, a great comfort in this, for it bids a romantic idea that her mind is not broken or diseased, but instead working actively with rather than against the passing of time, in a kind of balance or harmony that keeps some memories close while leaving others to fall away into an abyss, just as they are intended. And so how marvellous after all she's forgotten to still cling to the memory of her husband in the garage, an image that warms her spirit, for it's an image that speaks somehow to their happiness—her in the garden after breakfast and him nearby, sawing and carving, finalizing the details of whatever he was working on. He took a craftsman's pride in his projects, whether the wicker chairs for the porch or benches and birdhouses to sell locally. Yet he did little about the depreciation of the house itself—the curled linoleum, the uneven, holed pavement of the front walkway, the winter drafts coming in through the windows. He frustrated her because of this, and they each became irritated if the subject came up, which she made sure to do.

"That's enough, Mary," John said to her sullenly that day in the garage, not looking up from his measuring. Little pieces of wood shavings were trapped in his thin black beard and lay in sheets on the ground. Small heaps gathered around the legs of the table saw.

"It isn't enough until you agree that it needs to be done."

"It will get done."

"Yes, so you keep saying," Mary sighed, finding laziness to be the most unattractive quality in a man. But she knew he was never lazy; at worst he was just choosy about his projects. It was a dark morning, she remembers, early spring, the grass still tawny and morbid looking. She glanced over her shoulder at the holed sidewalk, starting to cave. "I suppose I may have to do it myself somehow," she said, rather more to herself than to him.

"You wouldn't know the first thing."

"Granted. So, do it yourself instead of wasting so many hours on this junk no one asks for," she said sharply. Often she spoke sharply with him when some task or other needed to be done, and when asking more softly the first time hadn't cut any ice.

With those words, her husband slowed his movements, but did not respond. Say anything to light a fire, she thought, anything at all, but he kept his focus on the piece of wood. He made a careful measurement, went around to the other side, and measured it again to be sure. He drew a line with a pencil. It was just his way; far less likely to respond in an argument than to brood and be silent, though by his eyes anyone could see that he was thinking all the time, weighing one thing against the other. John's eyes were deep, dark, mysterious under black brows, and initially she loved the look of absorbed thought that went on behind them. It's interesting that what a woman finds endearing at first about a man can lend itself over time to becoming one of the most maddening; the more annoyed with him she grew, the quieter he became. Indeed, he would drive her half insane with these drawn-out silences, so much so that at times she could have throttled him. But she steeped her own sins in the marriage, and now what bothers her most is that she never let him know how much she appreciated those handmade willow-wicker chairs, the prettiest outdoor decor. She thanked him, but not properly. Regrets about a lot of things lie heavy on her heart, and all the regret in her marriage is symbolized, somehow, by those wicker chairs, creaky in places and weather worn, maybe rampant with rot by now, for they were never properly varnished.

"Mary?"

A warm hand touches her arm, and she opens her eyes.

"I thought you'd gone," Mary says, noting with embarrassment the garbled sound of her voice.

"I'm leaving right away. Your daughter will be here in an hour or so."

"Fine," Mary says sleepily. "Why don't you buy yourself some flowers."

"Flowers?"

"You mentioned not having flowers in your home. Buy yourself some. You'll see what they do to a room."

"Okay, maybe I will. And I'll see you again tomorrow morning," Beth says in a kind whisper, before withdrawing her hand.

"Fine," Mary says again, and now finds her eyes so irritated by the sunlight pouring in through the bow window that she tells Beth to close the curtains before she leaves. Mary squints as the curtains are drawn across the metal rod, and after another minute of light footsteps across the linoleum, the door closes briskly. She is alone again, but not lonely, a differentiation that anyone content with their own company are enlightened to understand. The pain is tolerable at the moment, so she's content to be by herself.

Let the voices fade, let them all go away, let this room be her noiseless haven, her squat and silent sanctuary.

There are, Mary muses, both rewards and punishments for growing old, long stretches of time alone often one of them. Leave it to the individual to discern whether the solitude falls under the category of reward or punishment.

On the table next to the roses, Mary sees the small wooden box, and realizes she'd forgotten to ask Beth for her mother's pearl necklace. Likely it is still beside the bathroom sink, a lavish little heap of beautiful bijoux, as her mother's French acquaintance might have said. When Sally arrives, she'll tell her to put them away properly; a foolish request since it will almost certainly raise the question of how the pearls found their way from shelf to sink in the first place.

Carefully, Mary takes back the mirror. She looks with intent upon the reflection, a reflection now absent of pearls, but cleaner looking, less like that of a mad widow. Of course, the liver spots remain, as do the lines around her lips and the web of wrinkles stemming from her eyes. Old age has not merely brushed against her, she thinks; it has whipped her crudely across the face with a wet towel. The loss of her looks hasn't bothered her as much as it seems to bother other old or ageing women, nor does it bother her that she will soon die, likely right here in this shabby armchair, quietly and unheralded. Along with her illness, and in consideration of the prognosis, she is drawn to dwelling more on her life, to lose herself in lamentations, as though the disease itself is telling her that the time has come to find some sort of prophecy in all its scenes and shapes, people and places, words and sights. Living under the close shadow of death makes a prophet of many, she imagines, as it forces one to scrounge for a last-minute meaning to it all. Yet despite her pondering, she knows she will never be able to understand the purpose of her existence on earth in any more depth than a leaf can understand what its purpose has been on the branch of a tree, just before it falls off. For like the inherent leaves, we stem from branches, we grow, expose ourselves to the battering of north winds in exchange for a few days here and there of brilliant sunlight until we wither and crumble to dust. The unsympathetic universe never reveals why.

Nevertheless, she tries to place some kind of order to her memories, some kind of balance or centre point. But she remains perplexed, unable to link the moments of her life in a coherent or continuous way, as in one after the other, in the same way her mother's pearls succeed one another perfectly on the string. Rather she is compelled to recall her life by a series of fragments and scattered parts, as if a black drape fell over her mind, one punctured throughout with a multitude of little holes, and each little hole a memory set alight. Together they form a pattern of brightly lit particles, and everything else, all the memories behind the drape, are forever blackened, blotted out, lost, cut to cinders as if burned by fire. Gone.

For all that she has forgotten, all that escapes her, she is not embittered; rather she's thankful for having at least this much command of consciousness following her into these final days, this final refrain. And the remaining memories, the brightly lit particles, are each one cherished and distinguished, albeit imperfectly. Indeed all her reminiscing of late has each of these moments laced with a kind of poetic conceit, and, gratefully, more of an understanding.

Every beautiful and innocent element of her childhood, of her entire life, in fact, seems crystallized within the sound of her mother's humming. That voice, though she took it for granted then, was of unbelievable comfort, a palliating sound, a soft, smooth mezzo-soprano. If only Mary could have gripped that voice in her palm, sealed it in a jar, and carried it with her all these years, she is certain there would have been times it would have stilled her. Even as a child she would stop what she was do-ing to listen. Her mother hummed in the kitchen, whisking a creamy batter, padding and rolling dough, and the radiant sound issued from her in the same easy way the cheerful melodies issued from the meadowlarks that sat along the branches every summer. Her mother was never a woman Mary wanted to resemble in any way; she was weak, too servile and submissive, a feathery form gliding from room to room. Yet Mary admired her warmth, her devout attention to all of them, and it is only in hindsight that she appreciates these qualities that as a child she saw as weaknesses. Strange how a woman can give birth to another woman so in-comparable to themselves.

Somewhere in her mind remains a singular image of those isolated acres, and of a particularly vivid sunset. It was the evening of her eighth birthday, and her mother was about to offer a rosary as a gift. Mary sat on the porch steps surveying the sky, and just above the brightness of the sun on the horizon were tremendous pigments of coloured light—a strikingly lucid crim-son that, as the colours rose, softened into pink, orange, then yel-lowish white. She would sometimes imagine that the skies across the prairie were inhabited by spirits of some kind, floating around in an ephemeral borderland, deciding and implementing the weather. She imagined that it was a herd of tinselly spirits and not clouds she saw that evening, dancing in crimson waves across the sky. Between two of the brightest crimson waves appeared a long thin thread of glittering white radiating above the still-gleaming sun—the gate, she imagined, to the borderland. She used to imagine a lot of things about skies.

Below all of that was the brassy look of the earth, bleak and cheerless when compared with the magnificent sky. The evening was warm and dry, well advanced into a summer of drought, and her father's farm looked as though a layer of tan-coloured dust had settled over everything, like a monochrome shadow. Crickets chirped vehemently from all around. There were long muddy rows in the garden and clean clothes on the line, blowing and flapping. To the south were the sun-scorched wood of the granaries, the red auger and, next to that, her father, leaning against a picket fence post and staring apprehensively at the sky, scanning for uncertainties. She fixed her eyes on him for a while. It was the stare all farmers share—hopeless and hopeful all at once, timorous yet patient.

The year earlier saw the fields illuminated with canola, and the sight was a marvel to her, brilliant yellow against mid-morning blue. To this day she's never seen anything more beautiful.

Mary rose from the porch steps and turned toward the house, away from her father's fervent stare and the spirits dancing in the sunset, and stepped inside. Immediately through the suffused light of the kitchen she saw her mother at the table, praying. She prayed in a whisper with her eyes closed, looking very peaceful. Mary stood still for a moment, watching curiously, until her mother, perhaps, felt she was being watched. Her expression softened as she met her daughter's eyes, becoming less serious.

"Come here," she said, patting the seat of the chair next to her. "Come sit beside me."

Mary quickly obliged, feeling a little bit excited, because she loved having talks with her mother. Her mother was greatly concerned with religion, and so many of her thoughts, and thus her words, were tinged with this. When settling her children into bed she often rehashed sermons and parables from the Presbyterian church, some geared toward children and some not, but all read with the intent of imparting some saintly moral. Her mother was not a woman educated by formal means, but simply by reading and thinking, and like many devout parents, had likely assumed her children would grow equally devout simply as a matter of course. Most people who adopt a religion, after all, adopt those of their parents. Sitting with her mother had a very different feeling than being around her father, who was more detached, intrinsically more in love with working alone out of doors than spending time with his children. To Mary, her parents' marriage held a feeling of indifference, as though they were going through the motions in an almost mechanical way, each tolerating the other. They existed somewhere between respect and dislike, committed to one another in a way that was unloving, but polite.

"I have something for you," her mother said, as a glow came into her eyes. It was the glow an angel might have, Mary thought at the time, for she was often sentimental about her mother. She lifted a rosary and showed it to Mary, red beaded and ancient looking, glinting and majestic, beautiful in a slightly sinister way, as are many objects to do with religion.

"Perfect for a birthday present," her mother said, before laying it across Mary's palm. "You're old enough to have your own."

A rosary was like a talisman to her mother, a holy guardian, a thing that promised protection from whatever sinister undertones were lurking all around. The string of beads stood for more than a simple prayer; it was magnificent assurance from above. How beautiful, Mary thought, to believe in that sort of protection.

"It's pretty," Mary said, and that was true, though she was never compelled to believe that a rosary was anything more than that—a pretty object.

"You remember the prayer," her mother prompted. "The Apostle's Creed, Our Father—"

"Then three Hail Mary's. Yes, Mom. I remember." Fumbling her fingers along the red beads, Mary had then peered out the window, listened respectfully to her mother's pious words, and wondered if her father was still by the fence post, watching the sky.

"And Glory be," her mother said.

"Glory be. I remember the rest."

"Good. It's important to remember. And Mary," she cautioned, perhaps interpreting her daughter's restlessness as taking the rosary less seriously than she should, "God knows what's in your heart. He knows if you are praying, and he knows if you're not praying."

Mary raised her eyes. That was, in her innocent mind, the first time she considered God as an unseeable, yet all-seeing entity. Her father, she had thought, would have scoffed at the idea had he been in the room. Though he was raised in the church, then married by the church, somewhere along the way he must have lost interest, changed his mind, or realized his mind had never properly aligned with its dogmas to begin with. Mary was never sure of his reasons. He attended the Sunday sermons less and less until he stopped going altogether.

Mary, sitting next to her mother at the kitchen table,

continued to ponder the notion of God as an all-seeing, ever-lurking, ever-watching thing. It seemed an idea too strange, too foreign, difficult to touch.

"Mom," Mary began, "if we can't see God, how do you know he sees me?"

"Well, there's a lot of things we cannot see, but we know they are there," her mother said, tenderly. "Can you think of any?"

Mary thought about it for a moment, then shook her head.

"Remember when you were afraid to go for a ride on the horse with Dad?"

"Yes," Mary replied, recalling the day her father tried to lure her onto the massive animal. Her father became disappointed at the failed effort, and rode off.

"How did you know you were afraid, if you could not see your fright?"

Mary understood immediately. "I just knew."

"Some people might say they don't believe in God because he can't be seen," her mother explained, and Mary, for one fleeting moment, succumbed to the notion of this ever-lurking entity. "They think they need evidence the way a scientist needs evidence before he can say something is true. But even if science can show the way something works, it doesn't disprove that it wasn't the Lord himself who designed it to work exactly that way. So never mind what you can and can't see. Your fear was real because you felt it inside of you. That's proof enough."

Mary looked at the rosary again. It was beautiful to her, but in the end, nothing more than beads on a string, as much without divine power as the chair she sat on. Nevertheless, she was not raised without manners, and when one is offered a gift, it comes with an obligation to be thankful.

"Thank you, Mom," Mary said, as sincerely as she knew was expected.

"The Lord forgives our doubt," her mother responded absently, but in a way that showed she was very serious.

As she passes from one memory to another, Mary recalls doing a lot of childhood daydreaming in the pews of the Eleanor Hicks Presbyterian Church on Main Street. They were odd daydreams, but she decided, resolutely, that the church was an odd place to be. Gazing up at high windows painted with the glimmering saints who said nothing yet stared back with sightless eyes, made her mind wander to strange places.

She sat subserviently on Sundays between her mother and brother, was present for all the hymns and readings, but listened with only a half comprehension of the words, and thus was only half interested. She was young, and could not qualify the passages she heard against what she had thus far seen and felt. It sounded like gibberish, expired sayings, depressing myths. Between daydreams, her eyes wandered quizzically around the great inner hall, a high room filled from floor to ceiling with wood columns and stained glass. It felt damp and murky, as though the place were at the bottom of a lake, and the wooden beams of the vaulted ceiling were like dense seaweed arching overhead, knotting their ends together. Everything was gloaming, mysterious, full of meaning. The sculpture of Christ bleeding on a crucifix above the echoing choir haunts her to this day. What struck her most, though, was that there was something juxtaposing about it, oxymoron-like, as though things were not quite as they seemed. There was a cheerful misery around the great room, dark lit shrines, known secrets, meretricious salutations, stiff rustlings. It was a world somehow as hushed and reserved as it was abrasive and loud. In other daydreams, she believed herself to be subversive to this holy world, her consciousness infected somehow by the malevolent reptile from the stories about Eden. Hers was a foul, resistant spirit, an unenrichable soul. Maybe, because of her disbelief, she was sullying the sacred place by her presence; perhaps, then, this world and everyone in it would be strengthened by her absence. It frightened her as a little girl to think of what could happen to an errant soul. She imagined herself being cast to the underground, thrown into a great fire, and forgotten.

Cutting into her daydreaming would be the gentle hand of her mother, coaxing her to stand. If Sam didn't follow suit quickly, Mary nudged him with her elbow. With the congregation all standing, a closing prayer would be read, heaven praised, and a final amen shared emphatically by the faithful. Everyone left in polite clusters from the pews. If the weather was fine Mary found this time of day exciting, and would have been anxious to get home to do other things. But she first had to wait, always near the edge of the stone steps, for her mother who wanted to thank the priest. She seemed so much under his influence, so eagerly penitent. Maybe he blessed her or offered encouragements for the week ahead; Mary never really heard them beyond a whisper. Whatever was said, her mother, just as she had complete elucidation in King James' version of the Bible, listened to the robed man's words as though he were King James himself. Still, her mother had a charming way of interacting with others at the church. These were her people, her like-minded contemporaries. When she spoke, they understood, and vice versa. It is the singular bond shared by those who believe in the sanctity of the trinity as much as they believe in the ground on which they stand, and who believe in heaven as incontestably as if they'd already been.

As one memory succeeds another, Mary is out in the yard, examining a fuzzy caterpillar as it weaved through the blades of twitch grass. Growing bored, she looked up at her mother in the nearby lilac bushes, trimming the excess bits. A bundle of lilacs had already been cut and set aside. She took great care of her lilac bushes, endearingly sentimental about their scent and colour, and the way Mother's Day just so happened to fall around their quick season. She let the trimmers fall to her side and turned to Mary.

"Want to help me bring the flowers inside?" she asked, and together they gathered the cut lilacs from the grass and brought them into the kitchen.

"I'll get the vase!" Mary said excitedly, knowing precisely which one her mother would want for her precious purple flowers. The pottery amphora vase was heavy and had once belonged to her mother's aunt, she recalled, a cheery and biblical woman who sometimes visited for tea on Sunday afternoons. Using a small step stool in front of the counter, Mary filled the pretty vase, pale green with white scalloping along the top, with fresh water.

"Sometimes I think I should just leave them in the shrub," her mother said rather dreamily, lifting the vase from the sink and resting it on a round white doily at the centre of the kitchen table. "The scent of lilac is stronger in full sun, and in here, they'll have less of it."

Mary quietly and lovingly stood by the sink watching her mother, who seemed oblivious to everything else, humming beautifully and arranging the elegant stems just so. The purple blooms rose for the next week or so from the centre of the table, taking in the light of the window, and since then Mary cannot take in their sight or their sweet, heady scent without coming back to this lovely little moment.

Her mother died young, after a cruel illness of her own, though hers was at least rather quick. After a stay in the hospital her father brought her home, to die in her bedroom, among her things. She died far outside of lilac season, which seemed unjust, as if her death would have been more bearable, and more tranquil, had Mary been able to trim some lilacs from the high panicle in the yard and place them in a vase by the bed. The scent of them in the room would have made a difference, somehow. She recalls sitting by the bed with her mother, stroking her hand in quietness, wishing for a vase of lilacs. Mary scarcely remembers the moment she passed, yet still feels the sadness that came with knowing she would never again hear her mother's voice. And so now it is these three elements that stand out about her mother— the humming, the rosary, the lilacs.

Over time, the magic of some childhood moments either magnify or dissipate.

One day, she took a walk with Sam. It was nearing the end of August after another dry summer, a year or two after she received the rosary. It was late morning, and hot, everything scarred yellow from drought. She stayed a few paces behind Sam in the grass, which was brittle and made crunching sounds beneath their feet as they walked the half mile toward the tracks. The heat made their movements more languid, and she keenly remembers the sight of him, a ruddy little boy in little-boy overalls, sun-burned, the pretty scattered stems of dropseed and long grass drooping inward, brushing his elbows.

Each summer they went on these aimless expeditions. One year they went on a search for grasshoppers and caterpillars, the year before they make-believed at having to escape an evil monster lurking in the corn stalks, one that would pull you beneath the mud if you didn't run fast enough through the rows. In the year of this memory, Sam's newfound interest in trains led them along the path beside the ditch toward the tracks. Mary was older, the sibling in charge, and dotingly proud of his new love of moving things. Trains, trucks, bicycles; they all seemed to fascinate him unreasonably, and he understood the way those things worked more thoroughly than she ever cared to.

When they reached the clearing, Mary took a stern hold of Sam's hand. She was protective of him, as proprietary as a mother perhaps, because she was left to care for him much of the time. They were a few feet from the rails.

"Mary, I brought a penny for the track!" Sam exclaimed, unaware of the pennies-can-derail-trains myth, but well aware that a train would flatten them.

"That's silly."

"Please, Mary," he said, looking at her almost desperately, and Mary knew there was no dissuading him. It was too hot to argue anyway.

"Go on, then."

Mary let go of his hand. Sam pulled the penny from his pocket, eager to begin the experiment. He knelt his little body over the tracks and placed the penny on the steel rail, very absorbed in his task. Mary watched indolently, feeling equally annoyed at him and the scorching sun; though still a child herself, Mary thought of him as much more childlike. In hindsight, she may have been too grave and serious for her age, having quickly grown beyond the play of small children, of magic and make-believe, and the thrill of putting pennies on tracks. Nonetheless there was a common feeling between them when they went off together, a kind of complicity, a sense that it was the two of them existing happily in a bubble, with everyone else outside.

When Sam was satisfied with the penny's placement he ran back over to Mary and the two of them crouched in the grass, concealing themselves from view like two thieves in the night.

Nettie Marie Magnan

They didn't have to wait long.

"There!" Sam shouted. "There it is, Mary! It's coming!"

They concentrated their eyes on the oncoming locomotive, the sound of it growing more and more massive until it exploded past them like the roar of an angry creature. Sam's eyes were wide with fascination, whereas Mary found it frightening to be so close to a moving train. They seemed so tumultuous and powerful, shockingly loud, and the air swirled all around them as though they were caught in the eye of a storm droning furiously across the plain. There were the scents of smoke and oil as it passed, the mournful sound of the whistle, pulled twice by the driver, as it approached the next crossing. As quickly as they started, the swirls of air settled, and Sam immediately set about retrieving the penny.

"It worked!" he announced.

"Let me see," Mary said, holding her dress down against the breeze as she emerged from the long grass.

"Look! You can still see 1941 and the nada part of Canada!" He examined the altered penny, completely delighted, as children are when everything seen for the first time is momentous. Mary looked down at the flat penny indifferently.

"Keep it for luck," she told him.

"Mom says there's no such thing as luck," he said, squinting against the sun.

"There might be," she said sharply, then resigned not to argue with him. He looked too happy to argue with, she decided, so she repeated the words more softly. "There might be, Sam."

"I'll keep it forever and ever, even if there's no such thing as luck," Sam declared, putting the newly flattened coin in his pocket.

The sound of the train moved farther and farther away, and in its place rose another furious sound—that of someone angrily

158

shouting her name. Brother and sister immediately drew together, their eyes widened in paternal fear. Instinctively she looked toward the house, and though he was out of view, she knew where he was shouting from—the edge of the yard, behind the row of granaries, where the grass dips into a ditch of tangled bulrushes. Mary took Sam's hand again and they made their way compliantly toward the house. She knew why he was angry. She'd left the baby unattended. Her sister might have cried, and the cries might have been heard all the way to the barn stalls, or she soiled herself and was found lying in it. Mary walked along the ditch slowly, in procrastination, in defiance, but also so Sam would have no trouble keeping pace with her.

Her father came into view, and he was just where she imagined, between the granary and bulrushes, waiting.

"Sammy wanted to go to the tracks," Mary said weakly. "He wanted to see the train."

Her father didn't reply, and she had no right to press him. Where Sam disappeared to, she doesn't recall; he might have hidden somewhere, or run into the house. Her father clenched her arm toward the porch without another word.

It seemed to Mary, that as a child, any show of his being proud brought such a jovial feeling to the surface, yet any show of his disapproval pulled her into despair. If he smiled, then all was well in the world; if he scowled or ignored her, she fell into a depression for the rest of the day. No one other than her father inspired that kind of alternation of feeling. She felt his hand that afternoon, huge and rough, wrapped around her like a brace as he pulled her along, a fierce grip that communicated the height of his anger. She'd gone to the tracks after being told to stay in the house and mind her baby sister. She imagined baby Millie crying in the crib, not knowing where her protector had gone.

Once they climbed the porch steps, he turned suddenly, and when he raised his hand, she knew what would come. He'd struck her before, but the moment she felt the blow to the side of her head that day she burst immediately into tears. She would have done anything to keep from crying in front of him, but the pain overthrew her, as if a dozen hot arrows had pierced suddenly through her temple. He struck her a second time, something he'd never done, then a third, and all she remembers now is the aversion in his face, and the smell of him, putrid, like layers of sweat. He hadn't been drinking; it was too early in the day. Yet something about his eyes was different that day, something unfeeling, unsympathetic, something mean.

The mind does strange things during difficult moments. Landing awkwardly on the porch after the back of his hand met her face a fourth time, her mind emptied, swept itself clear, and she could focus on only one thing—clouds. As his heavy boots descended the porch steps, she recalls only the feeling of uneven wood beneath her dress, a ringing in her ear, and a sky of beautiful billowy clouds. She began to make shapes with them; one cloud was the swirling silver mane of a horse, a large horse, a Clydesdale she imagined, and the cloud next to it, more of a wisp, were the reins. She lay curled on the cool wood of the porch for a long time, her arms wrapped round her bent knees. She watched the swirling mane and the white reins, and envisioned the sky spirits riding the horse, with a hidden carriage pulled behind. The carriage would be lined with jewels the colour of sunsets—yellow, orange, pink, gold. She loved the skies when some part of it held that deep vivid crimson, but there was none of it tonight. She imagined, then, that the crimson colour was the colour of the borderland, where the tinselly spirits dance, and the Clydesdale was on his way there. He would reach the gate, pull the carriage through, and disappear into the brilliant, mystical place. Maybe there are high willows to sit under, she thought absently.

Eventually her mother gathered her little girl in a dress from the porch, kissed her on the forehead without a word, and laid her into bed. Sounds floated in from the kitchen, cupboard doors opening and closing, prayers in a whisper, then, at one point, sobbing. Mary fell asleep to her mother's sobs and dreamed that night of silver Clydesdales pulling carriages through clouds.

Mary dwells sombrely on this memory in her armchair, for it seemed to be a day that altered her insides more effectively than anything else. There is respect out of love and respect out of fear, and her father managed to extract from Mary a mix of both. His violent fits became less common as she grew and he became an old man. Yet as she reached her teenage years, feelings of imprisonment and unhappiness became more potent, and by the age of 20 she was more than restless. Sam, on the other hand, though wanting to leave behind the fierce hand of their father, had no intention of leaving farm life behind. And it suited him. He was simple, but in the best way. He craved nothing more from life than what humble farmers craved—good food and good weather, full growing seasons, to live and die as a steward of his land. He hoped to one day find a wife, to raise a family of his own. Millie at that time was still just a girl, still rather directionless, difficult to say either way what sort of ambitions, if any, would grow inside of her.

Other women Mary's age were already married, or if they weren't, were well on their way down that road, as though no other natural course was open to them. They had ambition only to secure a husband and bear his children, and were content to live without ambition from then on. They had fanciful daydreams about things like modern white ovens in crisp clean kitchens, floral aprons and brass finishings, fresh pies and a few children trotting across the lawn. What bothered Mary about married or engaged women was the way they held themselves above her, as though by marriage they'd attained some sort of supremacy. She in turn felt more enlightened than them for not settling too young into a dull marriage. Married and unmarried women never saw themselves as equals, still to this day, each with a life too foreign for the other to understand. And like all private thoughts and judgements, nothing is ever said outright on either side.

Looking back, it was not marriage that disinterested her necessarily, rather most men. The ones she knew and went driving with bored her, inspiring no emotion from her at all, which gave rise to an antipathy toward the notion of staying in town with nothing more to do than act as a subservient wife to a plain husband. There seemed to be something inadequate about that sort of life. It was impersonal, a one-size-fits-all sort of existence. Yet she judged those young men, she now believes, too severely. She expected too much from them on first impression, as though the burden of having to impress rested solely on the male. People often judge one another much too harshly, apply judgements too quickly. They gather impressions, filter them through their own bias, then privately draw their own conclusions.

Nevertheless, Mary set a plan into motion as soon as she was able—to flee for any college or university that would accept her. If the plan was not to marry, then an education was necessary, and would offer some originality over the other women her age. But an otherwise ordinary evening, a harvest dance at the community hall, changed all of that.

Sally is standing in the living room, fumbling with the oxygen tubes. An oxygen tank sits next to Mary, not the metal cylinder she was used to seeing, but a large blue suitcase-looking apparatus with wheels on the bottom and dials on the top. The long clear tubing flows from the side of the blue suitcase, and Sally is attaching the end of it to a circular tube that, Mary presumes, will go around her ears.

"I feel alright today, I don't need it," she says.

"Yes, you do," Sally refutes. "We discussed this with the doctor, remember? Your oxygen level is too low. If you don't use it, you'll wind up in the hospital again. We already agreed to this."

"I wouldn't have agreed to this ugly thing in my house," Mary says, though she does remember agreeing to it, faintly. For them to let her out of the hospital, she would have made any bargain. And after Sally found her lethargic in the armchair after too many pills, that's one of the three bargains she made in order to be set free—a lockbox for her medication, daily home care for washing and dressing, and an oxygen tank. Sally approaches her, the clear tubes ready in her hands.

"You need more oxygen and that's that," Sally says odiously, as though she relishes the situation. Though Mary knows shouldn't think of her own daughter this way, as unsympathetic, even as she wraps the plastic tubing around her ears impatiently and pushes the plastic prongs into her nostrils. Mary takes a few breaths, and after several moments can already feel her cells and lungs expressing some degree of relief.

"It pinches my nose."

"Well, I'm sorry about that," Sally says irritably. "The prongs can't be adjusted. I'm sure you'll get used to it after a while."

"Perhaps," Mary groans, sensing her agitation. She seems a bit gruff today, a bit brusque. Problems at home perhaps, her husband being difficult the way all men tend to be, selfish and aloof, leaving their women saddened and licking fresh wounds in a corner, their heart rent in twain, to use one of her mother's expressions. But there's no basis for her way of thinking; men are imperfect creatures, but both she and Sally managed to snag two of the better ones. Mary looks at her daughter and thinks, as she has many times before, that Sally is much more beautiful than she has a right to be, given the commonplace features of her parents. She's beautiful in the way only an artist can be beautiful—lit from within, incandescent. The one commonality Mary feels she has with her daughter is that they've inherited very little from their mothers.

Mary watches Sally wheel the large oxygen-holding apparatus near the armchair where she sits, then catches her in a smile, a flighty, distant sort-of smile. Once the ugly blue thing is parked, she observes Sally stepping calmly toward the window, where she folds her arms and tilts her head slightly while gazing intently, it seems, at nothing in particular, then after a minute or so, turns around rather gracefully.

"You're in an odd mood," Mary remarks. "Cross with me one minute then dreamy-eyed in the next."

"I'm sorry, I didn't mean to seem impatient. I've had a couple late nights."

"And the smile?"

"What smile?"

"You had a smile on your face as if you'd swallowed a cardinal."

"Canary, Mom," Sally says, her expression brightening in a much more expansive way than usual. "Something happened the other night that made me feel better about things. I'd rather not tell you about it now, I'm just so tired. Another day, maybe, okay?"

"Well, I suppose in exchange for seeing your smile I can wait for the details."

"Speaking of losing sleep, you look exhausted, Mom," Sally remarks, sitting on the chesterfield, and Mary perceives that the lighter moment has passed, and her daughter will resume this nagging trend of hers. "I'm guessing you slept in your armchair. I wish you would let the staff help you to your bed at night instead of sleeping in that ratty old chair all the time. You should try to have a good sleep once in a while."

"I have never once aimed for a bad sleep, I assure you," Mary scoffs, trying to adjust the prongs and feeling a sudden, sharp wave of heat pulsating then cleaving its way up her back then splitting through her shoulders.

Sally sighs and steps toward Mary, tries to help her reposition the thin tubes.

"Oh, just leave it! There's no use in fiddling with it," Mary sneers.

"I wish you didn't feel a need to argue all the time," Sally sighs. "I really do."

"My dear, I don't enjoy arguing with you either. But the onus is on you. The disagreements always start on your end."

"How do you figure that?"

"You don't know how to leave well enough alone. You're never satisfied."

"You have that backward."

Mary doesn't reply, knowing it is herself being unreasonable, not her daughter, whose brightened expression is expectedly long gone. The wave of pain has receded, for now, but is still perceptible. She touches the tube that now runs along the tops of her ears and across her cheekbones, feeling strangely depressed. The plastic feels cool and rigid inside her nostrils. She gazes out the bow window, a view so ingrained and familiar that everything on the other side of the glass recalls an innumerable number of memories of her life on this property. So many ghosts of so many moments, she reflects, and the sight of certain things at certain times can conjure a specific scene. She can look at the branches of the willow during the winter without thinking anything in particular, yet the sight of its dangling leaves in the height of summer is so strongly associated with Sally as a young girl, who would sit for hours beneath the shade of it, reading or drawing or painting, dreaming all the things that a young artist dreams about. Sally painted the leaves of that willow one summer. To this day the canvas hangs at the end of the hall, twenty inches by twenty inches, a bright bough of green foliage with just enough space in between to let through a dramatic blue sky. She loves her daughter's paintings, astonished to have given birth to a being who can paint so well, especially without any in-depth training. That she more or less taught herself to paint, then, was perhaps the most astonishing thing of all. Mary turns away from the window, suddenly conscious of her daughter looking at her, awaiting a response to a question she doesn't remember hearing.

"What did you ask?"

"I just asked if you were okay," Sally says.

"I'm fine."

"You're breathing easier. I can tell."

Mary, not responding, leans toward the vase of flowers. But she leans a bit too far and a tinge of pain enters her left hip and angers the previous wave, so she leans back in her chair to relieve the discomfort. The left hip has always been the bad hip, yet today, for whatever reason, it aches and twinges and pesters her like the devil. She won't mention it to her daughter, who fusses over these things. Yet it seems that Sally may have noticed her leaning, then wincing, for she gently glides the vase over to her. Mary leans only slightly this time, smells them, admires them, strokes one of the petals tenderly.

"They're doing well," Sally remarks.

"They are. The petals are good and strong."

They gaze absently at the bouquet of roses, absorbing their tranquility. Mary silently acknowledges a second commonality between them—each is able to lose themselves completely in the beauty of a flower. Mary looks over at her daughter, who appears a little dreamy-eyed again, as if the simple sight of the flowers returned her mind to this mysterious good news of hers, this fresh, allegedly favourable change in her life, whatever it is. The satisfied look on her face is, quite simply, a nice thing for a mother to see. Sally visits this house nearly every day, and usually comes and goes with the same disheartened, tired expression, but right now her daughter seems content, despite their little tiff, and so, as her mother, she allows herself to relax into a contented state as well.

They sit quietly for a few more minutes, under this warm coverlet of temporary tranquility, then Sally rises from the chesterfield. Her expression is still somewhat soft, but by her eyes Mary sees that her daughter's mind is busy again, her thoughts shifting from one direction to another. A person's mind seldom has a chance to dwell on one thing for too long before something else comes along, whether good or bad, to intervene.

"I'm going to tidy up for a while," Sally says before turning to leave the room. "Let me know if you need anything, alright?"

"Fine," Mary says, then returns her gaze idly toward the flowers. She lifts her hand and is about to stroke one of the petals again when a bird, one that approaches the house too suddenly for Mary to see which kind, swoops toward the bow window and slams squarely into the glass. The sound is awful, and Mary sees its little brown-feathered body fall from view, then hears the soft thud as it lands on the porch. It might have been a meadowlark, she thinks, though it's rather late in the year for them to be around.

Already gone from the room, Mary presumes Sally did not hear the bird, or there would have been some kind of response. It really is an awful sound, that heart-stopping wallop against the glass. Heartbreaking as well, for there's nothing to be done. One can only hope its death was quick. It happens on average once a year, the wide windows acting as a kind of inauspicious death trap for them, like a bright light for insects.

She hears Sally moving about in the laundry room, shuffling and trifling, closing the lid of the washing machine, turning the dial. The water begins to trickle. Despite her daughter's flighty smile and lightened expression when looking at the roses, Mary concedes that she is probably worn-out, as anyone might be in having to care for their mother, and their father before that. Mary considers whether she would have had the heart to care for her own mother, had she been called to do it. Sally, nevertheless, continues to find strength from somewhere. She speaks to doctors, arranges any changes to medication, delivers the oxygen tank herself. She scurries around the house once or twice a week, scrubbing and washing as though driven by a whip.

Mary has often suspected that Sally's concern with cleanliness was merely a way to distract her herself, a busy habit that momentarily wards off the subtle cruelties of unhappiness. And maybe this is true today as well, for a dash of good news and a fleeting moment of contentedness by a vase of pretty flowers says nothing in the end of one's overall happiness. Some cook or bake, others do this or that to bestir themselves. Everyone hires their own therapists, as it were. Mary had her gardening. That was the thing she loved. Somewhere within the flowerbed in the front yard and rows of vegetables in the trough out the back, she found peace. There was a predictability to it, and an order. She could beat up and down the rows and forget everything else, culturing the ground and letting flowers rise along trellises until they surrounded the porch in an earthly pavilion. And there in that earthly pavilion is where Mary spent much of her mornings, particularly during the years when her two boys had left for school, sipping coffee and daydreaming about this or that, similarly to her days now, but thinking about life is a different experience when there is much of it still ahead. In the middle part of one's life, thoughts can move obliquely forward or backward, one can reminisce over things that happened twenty years ago or make vague plans for twenty years ahead. One is somewhat cushioned, Mary reflects, between layers of time, not pinned to an outer edge. For along those unpadded outer edges, one is less in command of themselves, more exposed and susceptible, more dependent.

Mary hasn't properly tended to either of her gardens in at least four years, and is saddened whenever she catches a glimpse of their muddy ruins. It seemed, when she last caught a good look at the wooden troughs, they were fully rotted, and also flimsy, as if the long planks of wood had disintegrated into delicate threads of ash that would collapse to the ground if touched. She misses her gardens so much it's better not to think of them at all.

Sally fleetingly comes into view, sweeping the dining room floor before heading upstairs to vacuum the bedrooms. After a while she is back in the laundry where telltale sounds confirm she is placing the washed clothes into the dryer and has switched it on. Mary thinks absently that doing all these chores is a thing she both misses and doesn't miss at the same time.

"Are you alright?" Sally asks, coming back into the room.

"Yes, for heaven's sake. You don't need to ask me every ten minutes." Mary is again embarrassed by the sound of her own voice, which seems more and more like that of a weak, wimpling old woman.

"Fine, I won't," Sally says dismissively. "But I've been meaning to talk to you about the pathway between the driveway to the back door. It's in rough shape, and with all the rain, it's getting pretty sloppy. I'm going to have Jaime come and lay down a few planks of wood over the ground so the caregivers don't slip or get mud all over their shoes. We'll have to think of a better solution later, but it'll do for now."

"Very well."

"Other than that, there's nothing else to do for now," Sally says as she looks around the room.

"You don't have to leave."

"I know," Sally replies. "But I should go soon to Jaime's shop. I don't usually go in on Sundays, but I'm behind on the paperwork."

"I see," Mary says solemnly.

"I'll be back in the morning," Sally says reassuringly, sensing her mother's disappointment.

"It's fine, I understand," Mary says with little conviction. She typically loves the silence, craves it, but suddenly, for whatever reason, the thought of Sally leaving depresses her. She wants noise and movement, the feeling of life around her. Her eyes begin to water at the thought of long hours ahead in a private world with nothing to do but think and reminisce, a world that feels so separated from everything else, as if her house were behind some great and ominous moat, one that keeps the away the warmth and clings to grief, wintriness, and anything bleak.

Quietness, she thinks, holds more weight when one lives alone. For when one lives with others, the quietness is temporary, an interim thing that never has a chance to fully settle or make its way through the creaks and crannies of the mind before people are heard coming in and out of rooms again. When one is alone for long stretches, as she is, the quietness is free to steadily make its way, like a slow flood, into those crannies, then settle, and even if a visitor comes occasionally through the door, it never quite recedes. She thinks absently of the sounds of John in the yard, or in the garage, starting up the lawnmower or sawing through a plank of wood. Those were the sort of day-to day sounds that kept the flood waters at bay.

"Please, before you leave," she says, "at least tell me how the party went."

"The party?" Sally says, looking at her quizzically.

"The engagement party."

"Mom, it was yesterday. You were there, remember? It rained a little in the afternoon, then the sun came out. You giggled at Jaime struggling to start a fire with damp wood."

"Oh, yes, that's right, I do remember," Mary says, feeling slightly thrown, recalling in a thin wave certain details of the party. "Jesse sat with me. He brought me a piece of cake."

Sally smiles benignly. "Yes, he did."

"He's a handsome young man."

"Yes, he is," Sally says, then shares a few other details about the party.

Mary lowers her head and gathers into herself solemnly, in a way she doesn't often do. She is both listening and not listening. She looks down at her hands, the swollen knuckles, the dry, tissue-like skin, the yellowing nails in need of a trim.

"Mom?"

"Yes?" Mary says, meeting her daughter's eyes.

"Did you hear me? I said one of the caregivers will be here in a few hours."

"Which one? That Beth girl?"

"No, she was here this morning already."

"Oh, yes. That's right."

"And I'll trim your nails tomorrow," Sally says, as if reading Mary's thoughts. "I see they're getting long again."

"Fine," Mary says, then breathes deep through the nasal prongs.

"Okay, well, I'll just heat a bowl of beef stew before I go. Promise me you'll try to eat some of it."

"What about a piece of toast, with some jam. I think I have some left."

"Which jam?"

"Your raspberry jam. I keep it in the door of the fridge," Mary says, thinking it has been months or years since she last spent time at her daughter's home, even for a few minutes or to take a little walk by the ravine where their raspberries grow. Her grandson would come along when he was very young, she remembers, to help pick some of the raspberries and chatter away about this or that. He once fell into Sally's arms in tears, Mary faintly recalls, for in his innocent mind he believed that once the raspberries was picked, others would never grow in their place. Mary watched curiously as her daughter wiped his cheek, held him, soothed him, kissed his forehead. So endearingly peculiar sometimes are those innocent little minds.

"No, Mom," Sally says. "You finished off the last jar a while ago."

"Oh, did I?"

"Yes. I didn't get around to making any this year,

unfortunately. I'm out of it too. But I can make you some toast. There might still be some marmalade or something."

"No, no, the stew is enough, whatever it is."

Sally disappears into the kitchen, returning after a few minutes with the warmed stew. Steam floats up from the bowl. It looks well enough, but the scent of beef nauseates her unexpectedly. Sally lays down a napkin, and hands her mother a spoon.

"Have a bite. Let me know if it's warm enough."

"I'm sure it's fine," Mary says.

"Well, just try it anyway," Sally encourages, with gentle, yet somewhat feral eyes, coaxing her mother's hand into taking a spoonful. "I want to make sure you have at least one spoonful before I go."

Mary lifts the spoon and brings to her mouth a slice of carrot in beef broth. She purses her lips at first, then opens her mouth compliantly, like a child placating a parent. Such an indignation to be coaxed in this way. Her daughter, like many, won't understand the condescension until her own body begins to fail her. Then she'll know it well. Mary puts the spoon in her mouth, chews the lumps of food loudly, and swallows. Immediately it feels as though her stomach resents the forced process as much as her mind.

"Good," Sally says. "Have a little more. As much as you can." She leans over and kisses her mother lovingly on the forehead. "I'll see you in the morning."

"Wait," Mary says with a start, remembering. "A bird hit the window. It must be on the porch."

"Oh. Alright, I'll look for it on my way out."

Sally leaves the living room, and Mary hears a brief shuffling in the back foyer before the door opens and closes firmly. She feels right away the effects of being left alone in this house again, the settled flood water in the creaks and crannies, rippling quietly, reminding her of the sounds that are no longer hers to hear; a saw working its way through wood, children arguing over some inconsequential thing, like a toy or how to play a game, her husband creeping into bed just as she started to doze off. A moment later through the bow window, she sees Sally step onto the front porch and quickly scoop up the unfortunate creature in both hands to inspect it. Mary watches her daughter inspect the bird in a reverent way, and she tips her hands toward the window so that Mary can also see some of its smashed body, the pretty feathers, its compact wings turned backward. Both Mary and Sally gaze mournfully at the stiff, beautiful little thing, offering the dead bird a moment of silence, a speedy funeral, and Mary wonders with unanticipated sadness whether she will ever again be so physically close to a bird. Nevertheless, there is nothing to be done for the creature, and Mary can see for certain that it is not a meadowlark, but a barn swallow. She watches Sally cross the lawn and toss the swallow gently into the bush, and a few minutes later Mary watches her car pull sharply out of the driveway, past the elms, and out of sight.

After a few moments in the ensuing quiet, Mary glances at the bowl of beef and vegetables and decides, with some misgivings, that she's put enough effort into eating for the day. The spoon makes a little echoing clink against the side of the bowl as she sets it down. One thing's for sure—Sally's homemade stew tastes far better than the slop served at the hospital. But hers was only a four-night stay, thank heaven.

The town's hospital is as old as Mary. With twenty-one beds and a greyish overlay to everything, it's a realm of strange noises, prodding eyes, and pain both flaunted and hidden. Things beep and clang, depressing moans inhabit the halls, and a whole litany of dismal sounds and smells echo the misfortunes of the patients. There are drawn curtains, superstitious practices surrounding deaths and births, days punctuated by plastic meal trays, medication rounds, and a visit, if requested, from a priest.

How absurd she must have appeared when she arrived by ambulance, how crazed and unhinged, flailing pathetically, shouting and wresting against the paramedics as the drugs wore off, absolutely run out of breath and panting like a dog by the end of it. She was incorrigible, but it stands in her mind that the staff were worse. She bore witness to the villainies of doctors who spoke with Sally about various symptoms and treatment plans as though she weren't within earshot. Along with old age comes a decreased relevancy, it seems, to the value of one's opinions, and now that she's been around long enough to gain some perspective about life and the world, she's too old to use it, and has no one to impart it to either. The young, who think they know better, see the old as they would an endearing yet ignorant child. The baby-faced doctor, with a thought process as thin as oxygen, hears her complaints more out of obligation than sympathy. Insensitivity made flesh, given a court to hold. Without a word to her, he pushed a salving potion through an intravenous line, and she remembers with unfortunate vividness the specks of dandruff along his collar and the swollen row of knuckles, smooth and symmetrical in a way that reminded her of bird's eggs.

An unwelcome face poked through the grey curtains the next morning, and the quick squealing of their rings along the metal track woke her with a bit of a shock.

"Just checking," whispered the prodding face. "Need anything?"

"Did you not see that I was asleep?"

"I did," the woman said. "Of course, I—"

"Then get out."

The nurse, a tall, stooped figure, a hunchback Florence Nightingale who limped and appeared on the brink of illness herself, left in a huff. On the second night, or it may have been the third, Mary struggled her way out of the bed and made her way down the long grey hall, clutching the banister that lined it, and seeking, if memory serves, someone on whom to take out her anger. She came upon a timid looking girl behind the nursing station. She'll do, she thought, this chesty little wren-like woman. Yet the girl only looked at her dubiously as she unleashed a string of threats and demands to be set free of the place. The hunchback Florence Nightingale must have heard, for she came stomping around the corner like a hick with a shotgun eyeing an irritant squirrel. After a few more minutes of arguing, they negotiated Mary into a wheelchair and wheeled her back down the hall, a weary prisoner denied her release.

They passed a white-haired patient, a man, staring intently at a painting on the wall. It was one of those strange paintings, an oily mess, as though the artist blindly threw paint across the canvas, then tried to pass it off as art, when anyone with sense would be just as quick to dismiss it as trash. A person who creates such a thing must have bizarre, vagabond-like imaginations, while Sally, at least, has a genuine talent. The white-haired patient was either holidaying from his right mind or sanely enamoured with the image, for there he stood, hands clasped behind his back, gazing at the splashes of paint as would a tourist in an art gallery.

There were cries from the next room on the final night of her stay. They were wet screams, as though the man's mouth was filled with bile or spit, and all Mary gathered from the commotion was that the man had soiled his sheets. It was insufferable to listen to until the staff calmed him down. They were the same awful sounds of her own father in his final days, anguished shouts of different men at different times, though one and the same.

"Your father's wet," the aide at the nursing home had told her. "We don't like to leave him that way, but sometimes when we go to change him, he becomes very combative. If we wait until he's tired, he's usually more compliant."

"I understand," Mary nodded, before stepping into her father's room, which was clean and dull. The rooms of a nursing home are usually furnished similarly to those inside a hospital—a single chair, a single bed, a single window—yet while a hospital carries a sense of transiency, a nursing home carries an air of finality. Hospitals want to heal, to lead their patients to better health, whereas nursing homes have a feeling of powerlessness and acceptance, of death in suspense. She sat at the edge of the bed and held his hand, and when her father met her eyes, she turned to the window. His eyes were too pained, too full of emotion, too reflective of her own.

"Mary, take me home," he whispered in a sorrowful way she still remembers, and although he lasted several more weeks, that was her last visit to him, and the last words she heard him say. She considered returning once more to his bedside, but stopped herself intuitively from seeing him again, and to this day she doesn't quite know the reason. We don't always understand ourselves, Mary muses; we simply do what we do. Perhaps she wanted nothing more from him than some words of sympathy about the past, an acknowledgement of wrongdoing, and knew that none would be forthcoming. It would have to be enough, she decided, that she had held his hand for a while in that unfeeling room, that she had stroked his crude skin tenderly. The perfect smile he once gave her as a child, when he was pleased by something small she'd done, a dozen raspberry muffins baked fluffy with brown sugar on his birthday. It would have to be enough.

Life is a mysterious affair, a strange and layered gift, though it's a gift no one asks for. It is depressing and stultifying in some ways and an absolute miracle in others. It is so rich, so thick. One is born, completely by chance, and set out ahead of them is a flurry succession of moments, some happy, some sad, though most moments sit passively somewhere in the middle. Finally, we ascend to a point, as if having reached the tip of a climbed mountain to look over a cliff, at which point one realizes, well, that's just about it, here is the summit, there are no more adventures ahead. The mystery of life, or the strange beauty of it, lies in why certain moments are remembered while others curl up and disappear like pieces of paper lit on fire. Why does she remember so clearly that the lace on Sam's baptismal gown was torn at the fringe, yet cannot remember whether or not he cried as the watery blessing was poured along his head? Why does she forget so many of the Bible verses her mother read to them at night, yet vividly recalls the sound of her voice as she read from the Book of Ruth, "… whither thou goest I will go; and where thou lodgest I will lodge; thy people shall be my people, and thy God my God …" Why does she remember glancing out the kitchen window at her oldest son who, in a curious movement, drew a blade of grass, examined it, then set it down again, yet she cannot remember the seconds that followed or preceded this? Why are some memories unreachable?

Mary considers once again what the French woman said at her mother's kitchen table—all that is meant to be remembered is naturally remembered, all that is meant to be forgotten is naturally forgotten. She was once again consoled by this, and the memories in her mind again became the precious, brightly lit particles poking through the drape that obscures her mind.

The clock chimes one o'clock. Mary raises her hands slightly and feels the pain of her rheumatic joints. Before the hassle with the oxygen tubes, Sally had given her the allotted amount of hydromorphone, and Mary thinks in an absentminded way about its chemical mechanisms, dissolving through her insides and working its way, too slowly, in inches, to the centre of her pain. She listens to the annoying whistling sounds of the oxygen tube and thinks of how much she wishes her daughter could have stayed a bit longer, and of the little brown-feathered bird, already forgotten by the world, beginning its slow rot in the bush.

Every year in mid to late October, a harvest dance was held at the Kruchak community hall. Mary had never gone, though her plans to leave for college and the encouragement of a cousin convinced her to go to the dance as a kind of celebratory send off. The inside of the hall was dark, the dance floor lit only by long strings of light that hung loosely over the room. A trio of navy-suited musicians, a fiddler, a bassist, and guitarist, crooned and plucked their strings from a corner stage. The women wore smart skirts and blouses or dresses adorned with flowers, their hair pinned in billowy curls. The men, who often gave no more care to their appearance than combed hair and a clean shirt, were less formal, but still spruce. Mary glanced down at her own dress, a pale solid yellow, thinking that although she was not dressed well enough, she liked the way the colour enhanced the darkness of her hair, which fell loosely along her shoulders.

They found an empty table, and Mary slung her black-wool sweater over the back of the chair. No sooner had they sat down when her cousin, a blonde, lithe little thing, was asked by a man to dance; the two of them disappeared into a haze of coupled dancers. For a while Mary sat quietly with little more to do than look gloomily around the loud, overcrowded room. She watched the dancers, middle-aged husbands and wives and lonely or single men with arms around lonely or single women.

Nearby, a man stumbled awkwardly as he got up from his table, knocking over a chair and spilling some of his drink on the floor. Immediately the man headed straight toward her, looking at her in a lascivious sort of way, very fixed. Unamused by his lack of composure, she hoped that her irritated expression would be enough to deter him.

"Would you care for a dance?" the man asked in a murmuring way that was difficult to understand. In his defence, however, the music would have drowned out anyone's voice. He stumbled even as he stood and was unconscious of spilling drops of his drink here and there, which made him appear all the more foolish. Mary merely shook her head and tried to amplify the harshness of her expression, hoping that would be the end of it. But the gruff-looking man furrowed his brow and started to explain something to her, never reaching a point nor making a great deal of sense, speaking and gesturing as inarticulately as any drunk she'd known. She diverted her eyes. What he was trying to say, she didn't care a fig. She ignored him until he contemptuously turned away.

Mary scanned the crowd for her deserter of a cousin, yet found no sign of her. Soon another man came over and asked her to dance, one rather attractive and gentlemanly, and still she snubbed him for no reason she could name.

She sat quietly for a little while longer, until the air began to feel very low and hot, almost unbearably so. She decided to leave, feeling suddenly annoyed at the jumbling place and the smiling faces of strangers, the braying laughter, the loudness, the trampling and stomping of feet. Such an overheated scene was never to her taste.

Mary made her way through the hot room, blasphemed her silly cousin, then pushed open the door and stepped into the coolness of the night. No sooner had the cold hit her than she realized she'd forgotten her sweater. Frustrated with herself, she returned to the main room, passed the swaying pairs of waltzers and the sedentary others sitting at tables, some of whom were yelling at each other, struggling to be heard over the music. There was a break between songs and the couples on the dance floor paused to applaud the band. She found the sweater where she'd left it, but a thread had caught a sliver of wood on the back of the chair, so she carefully loosened it free. Heading to the door, she averted her eyes by examining the pulled thread.

Life is not without coincidences, its strange perversity of timing. Had she not forgotten her sweater, she might not have met the man who may have otherwise passed through the night unnoticed. She observed him dismissively at first, as she would any stranger, merely a man leaning against the iron rail, tall, quite thin, about 30 or so. Slowly, Mary descended the last step until she was next to him on the grass, this alluring man who had not been there when she had first stepped outside a few minutes earlier. She felt herself fixed in his gaze.

"Mary, right? I thought I recognized you."

She looked at him, perplexed. "We've met?"

"No, but I've seen you around. I know your father. My brother owns the farm to the west of your family."

"Oh, yes. Bachelor Bruce."

"Bachelor Bruce," he scoffed. "I didn't realize he had a nickname."

"It's what my siblings and I have come to call him."

"I see," he said. "In any case, I'm John."

"Hi, John," Mary said, her mind rapidly comparing his features with the burly bachelor she'd seen come and go for years by her parent's farm. John's features were darker, and more delicate, with black hair and thick stubble on his cheeks and chin and above his thin lips.

"You don't resemble your brother," Mary remarked.

"That's what everyone tells me. My brother inherited his looks from the Irish side of the family, I think."

"Do you farm as well?"

"No. I did, but recently sold off the field and kept the house and four acres. That's enough for me."

John watched as Mary wrapped her sweater around her shoulders. "You're leaving I see."

"Yes," she quickly replied. "It's too noisy and hot in there."

She started to turn away, but when he asked her to take a short walk, she found herself saying yes. They walked on, not too far from the community hall, just until no one else was in sight and the sounds and voices wafted through the air as one would hear a steady thrashing of waters from a nearby river. They spoke for a while about their families, the recent dry weather, then John explained that the community hall was named after a kind Ukrainian farmer who had owned then donated the land, a sturdy and stoic well-read man who once said to him, "if you can't find it on the farm, you probably don't need it."

"Well, I appreciate the sentiment, even if I don't agree," Mary said.

"I've never known a better man," John remarked, and as they walked further, Mary listened to his observations about the dryness of the soil and the lack of birch trees around them. He bent over to examine the leaves and bark of a tree bathed in the full moonlight, as intently and carefully as a botanist. Mary remembers thinking to herself how he touched and looked at them with such consideration. She also couldn't help but notice, as the conversation went on, that his eyes became either more or less lit depending on what he was saying.

"Look," John said, running his fingers across a bare part of the trunk, where a length of bark had been purposefully stripped away. "It will probably die now, slowly. Tearing away the bark kills the tree."

"Yes, I know that," she replied somewhat defensively. She thought it was somewhat haughty of him to assume she wouldn't have known this fact about trees, a fact anyone around there should know. He either didn't notice her irritation or was ignoring it, and went on inspecting the tree bark.

"I see one birch over there, and another over there," John said, pointing. "But this area is mostly poplar."

Mary was more or less aware of that as well. Though when she looked around at the trees, spread out all around them in an array of mostly white, slightly crooked columns with speckled lines of black, they all looked the same.

"How do you tell birch from poplar?" she asked, confessing aloud that she never noticed much of a difference. Until then she looked at trees absently, knowing the two were different, but never seeing the distinction.

John looked as though he were holding in a laugh, out of politeness maybe, or perhaps because he already understood her well enough to know how bothered she would be if he let it out.

"There's a few differences," he began, then went on to inform her that birch is usually whiter on the trunk, and described the processes by which they adapt themselves to the seasons.

He spoke about these things with an ardour that endeared him to her even more, so much so that she only heard half of what he was saying. She followed his eyes as he walked from tree to tree. She could have listened to him forever. He seemed so comfortable in his words and movements, so unrestrained yet calm, full of solicitude, and she had the thought that he was probably this comfortable with everyone, as are most people in complete confidence with themselves. He also seemed completely unconscious of the effect he was having on her. She knew he probably wouldn't be able to see her face flushed with colour in the near darkness, yet she scorned herself, hard. She drew a deep breath. John had just finished with his monologue about the differences between birch and poplar and was looking at her curiously.

"You should have been a botanist," she remarked.

"No, I don't think so," he said seriously. "I don't think that sort of thing was right for me."

"What sort of thing?"

"Studying at a university somewhere, which is what I'd have do to become a botanist. I was never interested."

"Was it university that disinterested you, or the thought of leaving?"

"The thought of leaving."

"Well, the college I've been accepted to in the city is the right thing for me," she said quickly. "I'm looking forward to it, really."

"What sort of course do you have in mind?"

"I'm going to take a secretarial course, for starters, and once I've completed that, it will open the door to other things."

"Secretarial?"

"Yes."

"Well, good for you, if that's what interests you," he said ironically. He also looked, to her surprise, somewhat disappointed.

"Of course it interests me," Mary sternly replied. "And as I said, it will open the door to other things. And there are other courses I can take while I'm there. I'll learn to speak French properly, and I'll take some poetry. There's a course in sewing, but I know enough about that already and could teach the course myself."

John grinned, then nodded. "I'm sure you could, which tells me there's not many things you can do there that you can't do just as well here."

"Such as?"

"Well, for instance, there are plenty of French speakers around here to learn from if you want to get by conversationally, which is all anyone needs anyway. As for poetry, that sort of thing is everywhere. There's enough here to get by on." His words conveyed a confidence that unnerved her slightly.

"It's about more than just getting by," Mary replied, feeling a need to justify herself. "There's nothing wrong in wanting to be more formally educated, and there's nothing wrong with being more articulate than someone who can't put a sentence together without an impermissible word. There's also nothing wrong with wanting to leave."

"Impermissible," John repeated at length. "There's a good scholarly word."

"Some people think they're better than those who want to be more educated or professionally trained in something. My father is one of them."

"I don't think I'm better than anyone," he said firmly. "I

don't think in those terms at all, and I don't have anything against educated people. In fact, I might have liked the chance to be more educated than I am."

"Then what do you find so wrong about my going away to college?" Mary demanded, though becoming less aggravated with him. Indeed, she was surprised at herself for being so outwardly annoyed when inwardly she was feeling just the opposite. Her usual good senses had deserted her, just like her harebrained cousin, and she found herself moved by nearly everything he said. His face as he spoke implied a certain unique and charming quality, a quality conveyed by the subtle changes in expression, no big movements, just a myriad of slights. She felt herself in a kind of blissful, anticipatory state, a state she had never quite felt before or since, on tenterhooks in the most wonderful way for what he might say, or do, next.

"I love living here, impermissible words and all," he said satirically. "But as I said, good for you, if that's the sort of thing that interests you."

To Mary he seemed almost antagonistic, but playfully so, as though he enjoyed provoking her. She later learned that it was his way of getting her to arrive more quickly to the truth of what she meant.

"What interests me, John, is having the means to take care of myself."

"Ah, there it is," he said, looking gratified, as though he'd won an argument. "You're the independent sort."

"Yes, I am," she said emphatically.

"I think you should stay here and marry me instead," he announced.

The words came out of his mouth plainly, uninhibitedly, as though it were an expected thing to say. Mary couldn't help but smile and turn red again, scorning herself a second time. It was not like her to be so girlishly smitten, to be won over so easily. But then he smiled, and somewhere inside, there was a rush of new feelings, a silent explosion, as though something in her heart had been lit by gunpowder and no one else had heard. It's a moment that still sits pendent in her mind several decades later. As the evening went on, she started to understand what it meant to disappear into another person, to stand alone in the world with them, a world flipped upside down, where everything seems new and infinitely better.

At one moment he edged closer; no man had ever come that close. It was a private enthusiasm at first, but when he kissed her, she knew that he felt the same way. Miraculously, he already loved her back. And that's how it unfolded between them, very easily, very naturally. No grand declarations were needed. One thing Mary has learned, one thing that stands out, is that love flows easily from one person to another without either having to say a word.

It might seem unbelievable to others that they met and immediately felt this way. It's an improbable story, this uncomplicated meeting of hearts, but that's how it happened. She didn't formally accept his proposal until the next day. Merely she wanted to ensure that a night's sleep wouldn't change his mind, and it hadn't, nor had it altered hers. Her spirit rises, still, at the mere thought of him, and her mind sometimes drifts back to their first few meetings, those first few impressions. A beautiful memory time hasn't yet pilfered from her is that first time she saw him smile, a little shyly and slightly ironical, his brown eyes peering straight into hers, giving her a previously unknown sense of self-assurance. She remembers the cool air and moonlight reflecting off the silver snap buttons on his denim shirt, and the roughness of her black wool sweater against her arms. How clearly some moments come to mind, even now.

Another memory comes to her, one that closely followed their wedding. They were sitting on a blanket in their front lawn after dinner, near dusk, watching the trees and sky meditatively. Their shoulders brushed as they talked, and here and there the first stars of the night were starting to peek through. They were in a discussion about the history of wedding vows, which put Mary in rare form, as it inevitably led to a discussion about religion.

"The church makes people rotten with intolerance," Mary said plainly. "I've known people from the church who are some of the most intolerant people I've ever met. They seem so cold, some of them."

"Yes, but people are not so simple," he replied reflectively. "They might seem to be one thing, when really they are something else. I don't think anyone is inherently cold or intolerant, to use your words."

"But it's the intolerant teachings that lead to decent people being so harshly judged."

"I don't know if religion can be blamed for all that," John responded. "Like I said, people are not so simple. They generally mean well and can think for themselves. They can make up their own minds about those teachings, then change their minds again if they want to. I'd say the way people treat one another is more to do with free will than anything."

"But their free will is influenced by the cruelties of their religion."

"Not really."

"Yes, really," Mary countered.

"Alright, I'll give you an example. By all accounts your mother was a wonderful woman, a devout Catholic. She died a year or so before we met, right?"

"Right, but why is that important?"

"Well, if we'd met earlier, I might have had the chance to meet her. And now I wish I could have met her. But the reason I'm bringing her up is to give an example of someone who was by all accounts a kind woman, yet also happened to be religious in a strict way. She raised you, and influenced you with her own beliefs. And look at you. You're wonderful. You were exposed to the same teachings as those you now dismiss as intolerant."

"You say I'm wonderful, but if she could see me now, she might describe me as lost or unenlightened because I don't go to church, and neither do you, so, there's the intolerance. And by the way, my mother was Presbyterian, not Catholic."

"I thought it was the same thing, more or less."

"No, Catholicism is a separate denomination, as is Presbyterian or Baptist. They're all under the Christian umbrella, though."

"I find it interesting that you know about all of this," John said after a pause.

"One thing you have to agree with," Mary continued, "is that religion is to blame for the oppression of women."

John smirked at her. "In some ways, I suppose, but I don't know a lot about it. My instincts tell me that's also a matter of free will."

"But it's because of religion that the word 'obey' entered the vows," she pressed.

"You never had to say that at our service."

"No, not in a Presbyterian ceremony. But a lot of women are still obligated to announce in a crowded church that they'll obey their husband. Right before they martyr their father's name in favour of the husband's."

"Martyr?"

"Essentially, yes. I'm Mary Mattern now. Legally, I think, it's a proprietary thing."

"Okay, but you don't have to take everything so seriously," he grinned. "Things are different now. Marriages, at least in this corner of the world, aren't necessarily run the same way they once were. Men can't govern women. Or they shouldn't, if they know what's good for them, and if they consider their wives' happiness of any importance. I guess some of the vows just haven't caught up with the times."

"I assumed …" Mary started, then trailed off.

"You assumed what?"

"I assumed you would be, more or less, the boss of things. Not of everything, of course, but most things. That's how a marriage works. I knew that when I agreed to marry you. You're a good man, so I know you'll treat me well, but I assumed some of my opinions about the general running of things, like financial for instance, would always be at least a little, you know, subsidiary to yours." Mary was referring to observations of her father and the other farmers, rather her observations of farmers' wives, who seemed little more than subservient cooks with babies in their arms and children at their feet, who heeded to their husband's demands the way a criminal heeds to the demands of a magistrate. They assembled on the afternoons when their men were occupied elsewhere, to chat mindlessly on porches with tea while their children played on the grass. She had no intention on being one of those women, yet her love for John made her look at them in an altered, more sympathetic light. Those women she observed through her childhood weren't all weak, subservient child-minders. They were just like her, rather she was just like them; she simply fell in love, and was changed by it. She was softened.

John was looking at her intently. "You really believe that I won't consider your feelings as much as I consider my own? Why? Because I'm a man?"

Mary thought about this for a moment, then absently again about some of the farmer's wives, those obedient women who polished and scrubbed and saw little reward, seemingly.

"Well, yes," she said.

John snickered and shook his head. She was about to say something else when, from the corner of her eye, a deer started to creep very slowly and tentatively from the edge of the poplars. The deer, suddenly aware of them, arched its neck and delicately cocked its head to one side. John and Mary watched the deer in absolute silence for another minute or so until something spooked it, and the deer leaped back into the bush.

"It's a funny thing about deer," John remarked quietly, after a long pause where neither of them had spoken. "All they have to do is run through the trees, and they're home."

Mary fell, in that moment, deeper in love with him. She smiled to herself and gazed at him as he kept his eyes fixed on the poplars. He looked so strong, so thoughtful.

"I hadn't thought of it that way," she said, enraptured with him. They fell silent again, and sat on the lawn together until dark, content as children. A kind of peace gathered around them that night, as though the weight of everything that came before, and all that was ahead, their past and their future, had fallen away, and nothing had ever existed in a way that mattered more to Mary than the blanket on the grass, the poplars, the deer, the first glimmering stars. If only she could have kept that evening, crystallized it, held it, for it somehow encompassed everything that could ever matter. John, the trees, the sky at dusk, and complete solitude; life held no greater value than when those things were given to her.

And that was the happiest time, those first years of marriage without children. Their lives were joined together as the binding of a book or threads of a necklace are carefully woven, by degrees, one day after another. Her mind flutters through the little treasure trove of memories that came with those years—the two-car garage that John built after the wedding; the two of them painting it together in the fall; the way he hung his tools on the pegboard and arranged screws and nails in old coffee cans; the garden troughs in the back yard for vegetables, then trellises along the front of the house for flowers; him waking her from afternoon naps, always by kissing the nape of her neck; those cooler evenings when he wore his heavy beige cardigan, never buttoned, as he stared indolently into the fireplace, deep in thought, saying nothing; the metal fire pick he occasionally used to nudge the wood to grow the flame, despite her nags to leave well enough alone.

There's something quietly cathartic about getting to know the intricacies of a man, in learning by heart all his quirks and moods, his movements and sounds. And John, in turn, seemed to find a peculiar interest in learning her qualities as well. She thought of them as lost in a loving dance, refined over time. And he had been right; Mary learned enough conversational French locally, merely by listening and speaking, here and there, in small amounts. As for poetry, John bought her a book of poems for their first anniversary, a selection by the Irish William Allingham. 'See how a seed, which autumn flung down,' was the first line of a poem that became her favourite, and for years it was propped with magnets against the side of the refrigerator. There is something hopeful about this poem, something pure and innocent, something that points to the indelible beauty of her small mornings on these acres, sipping coffee, reading poetry, watching the leaves, often from the wicker furniture John made for her with his own two hands.

Perhaps the cruellest thing life does, Mary muses, is provide people for us to love, only to suffer through their loss later on. "The Lord giveth and the Lord taketh away," her mother would simply say, a divine warning not to get attached to what's given to you, for all of life's gifts are temporary, fleeting, not quite yours to keep. And there isn't anyone who can argue against its truth. "God never closes one door without opening another," her mother would also say. And that is also a difficult concept to argue with, though neither saying has ever managed to afford any relief. If anything, these old biblical sayings caused her to feel somewhat dejected, ill at ease, for the more she heard them, the less meaning they held. They were fruitless, ineffective, hollow as a reed, useless in their inability to change the course of anything, or to bring a person back once lost.

Mary was at home the day Samuel died, nearly seven months pregnant with twins. Bachelor Bruce had been in his yard that afternoon, mending a chicken coop or something else, when he witnessed a tractor overturning and heard the horrific scream that followed. She didn't believe in its truth at first, when her father arrived at her door with the news, as though her brother's death were an impossibility, a cruel bit of fiction too terrible to accept. Though she never shared her mother's faith, Mary immediately longed for her, wished her alive to impart some words of comfort. Life, her mother proclaimed, even at its worst, is a beautiful thing, full of gifts, a rich blessing on the part of God, and Mary craved that dyed-in-the-wool optimism. Indeed, it was the warmth of her mother's presence, rather than anything biblical, that would have offered the kind of solace none other than she could render.

The church still carried for Mary that juxtaposing feeling of housing two opposing forces, a world that seemed kind and inclusive on one hand, yet cold and uncompromising on the other, a world somehow as incapable of truth as it is incapable of untruth.

Everything about church and prayer and all that was contained in the Bible felt too grave, too grim, too opposite of Sam, who was decency and light. Religion had always seemed too closely tied with death, and death is nothing, certainly not an antechamber to everlasting life as so many insisted. So, for good and for always, she consigned that precious book to perdition, turned her back, and let the door shut firmly behind her. Her brother was dead, and so there is no God. She felt this clearly, simply, as though her disbelief in God required no further explanation. And because she never explained this argument aloud, it gathered weight, for in keeping it to herself no one was given a chance to contradict.

Sam's death also gave rise to the thinking that nothing is pre-ordained, that nothing of human condition is part of a preset design, rather everything is random, happenstance, occurring for no reason at all. And as disappointing as some may find this idea to be, Mary found a kind of freedom in the idea of a Godless world of self-authority and self-government. It ascribed a way to perceive the world and its people in true proportions, to see things plainly. It made the order of the world somehow easier to swallow. Better to follow this more secular way of thinking, one based around sober facts, than to vex oneself over what is essentially folklore about a divine being in the sky working in mysterious ways. Sam's death, somehow more than her mother's, cemented this rather stiff way of thinking. We are alone, our bodies do not shell our immortal souls, they shell only blood and organs, and in the end our lives portend to nothing more than their dust.

Yet she can't help but feel that somewhere along this path of thought, she made a misstep. Keeping her company now as she sits in her armchair in a silent room, is a nagging uncertainty about the reasons that brought her to that level of cynicism, cynical being what she now considers these perspectives to be. And so now at the end of her life she can't help but wonder whether this secularism, that is to say, living her life outside the belief in anything spiritual, has been in any way for the better.

Mary wakes from a nap, thinking at first that it's the middle of the night, until she sees the colours in the sky. Layers of greyish white are churning in a rather ominous way, as though at the beginning or end of a storm. Her mouth is dry, so she reaches carefully for the glass of water on the side table, and takes a few sips. The water runs down her parched throat, relieving the dryness as it seeps into the embroidery of veins. She looks at the clock on the wall. It's six o'clock, an inauspicious hour to be waking from a nap, she thinks, then humours herself by concluding that she's fortunate to be alive and awake at any hour, inauspicious or not.

She returns the glass to the table, then gazes again at the sky outside the bow window. It seems buzzing in some way, quite unsettled, to the point that she might describe the clouds as vibrant, as though a violent paroxysm of some kind is gathering overhead, moving in waves, rising and falling, then finally letting out a loud crash of thunder somewhere in the distance. The room falls a shade darker and raindrops begin to lightly tap, here and there, against the windowpane. Mary sits motionless in her armchair, watching the sky unfold, listening to the sombre, deepening wind and the rain that soon starts falling in heavy sheets, rattling against the roof and windows. She hears a heavy trickling sound; the eaves are running over. The thunder claps again, still sounding distant, and the air, even indoors, carries a feeling of uneasi-ness, but also the kind of anticipation and wonder that accompa-nies the first few minutes of a storm.

Mary takes a deep, sharp breath, in and out. What Sally said is true, though it pains her to admit. The oxygen does relieve the shortness of breath, and the clear tubes running around her ears and along her cheeks are less of a bother when she is sitting still. She has even grown accustomed to the rougher prongs that still pinch her nose, if slightly less so. Even with that first sip of water, her mouth and throat still feel quite parched, somewhat scorched, so she again reaches for the water and takes a few more sips. Then a silent bolt of lightning brightens the room so unexpected-ly that she nearly topples the glass as she replaces it on the table. In the split second the lightning struck, she caught a glimpse of the poplars bending in the wind and the tattered clouds in a low-hanging mosaic of deep and mournful colours, moving swiftly toward the east. The sky, she muses arbitrarily, always has so many things to say. Yet what it has to say is heard differently de-pending on the listener, for while her mother likely heard the magisterial work of God Himself, her farming father, with each uneasy sound the sky made, probably heard either a rising or fall-ing in the price of wheat. Mary considers the condition of the surrounding fields after such a rainy season, for although she was never a farmer herself, merely being the daughter of a farmer is enough to instil an annual concern for the crops.

A concern for something else stirs inside her, one far more personal and meaningful to her than any crop—her mother's pearl necklace. She meant to ask Sally to get it for her, or at least to put it away properly, but she'd forgotten. Maybe the care work-er placed them carefully somewhere, she doesn't remember, or maybe that care worker's concern about the soap tarnishing the pearls was feigned and they were left on the counter in a damp heap. That the necklace may have been left in a careless way concerns her now to the point almost of bereavement, as though nothing would be more unbearable than their mistreatment. She resolves to find them, as she had before. Yet she knows that like an infirm, or rather like a child, she's supposed to wait where she's told and not go about the house on her own. She can move around the room if she needs to stretch her legs, but is not to attempt the single step that leads out of it. In that moment, she resents the restriction, but in her heart, she knows Sally was right to limit her. Her limbs grow weaker by the day, as though her physical strengths are sliced away bit by bit, leaving her less and less capable.

Thunder claps again, closer than before. The sheets of rain, which had been falling for some time in a monotonous way, increase in strength and make such a noise that if someone else were in the room, they would have to shout to be heard above it. She looks out the window again. Just as the sky swept everything in darkness earlier, the lightning and rain have grown so furious that the sky looks a luminous white, almost ethereally so, like an upside-down field of freshly fallen snow with streaks of light mingling and dancing all over it. The brightness strains her eyes, and with each strike her eyelids flicker. But the storm isn't enough to distract from her resolve. She wants the pearl necklace, can think of nothing else, and there is nothing to do but relent.

She slides her bottom to the edge of the seat, places both hands firmly on the arms, and hoists herself upward. The act of rising from a chair is still easy enough to do; the issue is how well she's able to steady herself once she's upright. Mary stretches for her cane, which leans against the small table next to the armchair. The stiffness in her lower limbs is complete, for she can scarcely bend her knees, and the muscles from her knees to her feet are inhabited with such numbness and lassitude that she feels only half aware of them. Her heels balk and quiver. She presses the end of the cane into the carpet, takes the first uncertain step, then another, shuffling along until she reaches the stair. She is careful not to trip on the oxygen line that follows her, yet the fear of losing her footing is more palpable now that the armchair is several feet away. She pushes fear aside, and when she lifts her leg onto the step, she is surprised by the ease in which her legs cooperate with the manoeuvre. She feels faint for a moment as she reaches the top, so she stands motionless for a full minute, gathering her bearings, listening to the battering of wind against the walls of the house. There's another clap of thunder, this one louder and closer, and the flashes of lightning are more frequent. Mary looks with curiosity over her shoulder and through the window, sees the poplar trees bending and swaying in a rush of hysterical wind, their trunks half stooped to the earth. The rain swishes and falls in such a thick and wicked way that it looks as though a foamy mist is building between the house and the tree line, which is barely visible.

Tonight is a rare, intense sort of storm, so terrific that it makes one's house, indeed one's own self, seem so much smaller than their true dimensions, for what's happening outside is so high and powerful that one can't help but be reminded of their own mortality, their own primal vulnerabilities. There is nothing to do but wait for its mercy, and for the sense of relief that will come when it passes.

The feeling of faintness has lessened somewhat, and knowing that her legs will only hold her upright for so long, Mary continues across the dining room toward the hall. The length of the oxygen tube, which she hadn't considered properly, reaches its limit and she feels the slight tug against her ears and nose, preventing her from forward movement. She considers foregoing this mission of hers, to return responsibly to the living room where she can rest and breathe with ease through the nasal prongs. Instead she tears the thin plastic tubes from around her nose and ears determinedly with one hand, and continues on her way. She moves slowly and methodically, using the cane to keep balance at each step, like a skier using their poles to balance each stride. Finally, she reaches the threshold of the hallway, but something stunts her leg from moving forward. She gasps, and knows she's going to fall. She releases her cane as her muscles tighten in anticipation of meeting the floor, and the moment she hits the floorboards, she is immediately blindsided by an absolute rush of pain to her left hip. She hears the quavering scream come out of her mouth, one that matches the volume of pounding rain as it echoes through the house.

For the first few minutes the pain is so bad it takes her breath, and she feels almost suffocated. The pain burns like an acid leaking from her hip through to the surrounding nerves. It spreads quickly, infiltrates more of her, cloaking her waist and lower back like a chrysalis. Mary clutches her left side. It's a horrible, seething pain, one she's never experienced. She knows her hip is broken. Her heart beats frantically beneath her rib cage, still shocked by the jolt of the fall. She takes several slow, deep breaths, wishing for her oxygen tubes that would have made breathing easier. She tries to detach her mind from the pain and set her focus to something else, anything. She listens to the clock, hanging nearby on the dining room wall, ticking away the seconds. The only light with which to see is the diffused light pouring in from the dining room window, draped with thin curtains. It's an unsteady, intermittent light, for the moment the lightning sends its strike of blinding whiteness into the atmosphere, the brightness is caught then carried to and fro by the assailant wind.

Mary lies on the floorboards for a long time, helpless and still, listening to the storm outside, her pain ignored somewhat as her mind stays fixed on the clock. The less she tries to move the better, for if she lifts her head or turns in any way, her left hip knows of it, and throbs and squeezes in unbearable contractions. She feels the tears welling in her eyes, but doesn't want to let them out, tears gathering as much from pain as out of chagrin. She is trapped on the floor in a heavy, immovable heap with nothing to do but wait.

Really, if not for the pain, and if she had a pillow to place beneath her head, it would be a very peaceful thing to lie quietly for a long time. She closes her eyes and listens to the falling buckets of rain, hoping to sleep. A moment later she feels something warm press against her from behind, and for a second thinks John is huddling up next to her, for she had decades of that sensation, thousands of nights, yet knows in the next second that it isn't so. She herself saw his lifeless body in their bed the morning he passed, and had laid next to him for a long while before they took him. It was an act that never seemed at all gruesome when she thought of it afterward, yet she kept it to herself, knowing others might have perceived it that way—others, perhaps, who'd never lost a man they loved so deeply. John's death arrived far too suddenly for the slow, soft reality of their bedroom that morning, and some part of her felt, foolishly, that the truth of his death would only pierce through the walls if she left him there alone, that her presence might somehow shield him from death's arrival the way a levy holds back the floodwater, protecting all that remain inside. And because it was still her husband, the man in the bed still John, she sank beside him in the sheets, rested her head against his chest, stroked his still-warm arm.

"John?" she whispered to him at one point, and when he didn't answer or move, the water passed silently through the walls of their bedroom, and when it rose high enough to touch her, wrapped her in a kind of acceptance. She kissed him a very gentle goodbye on his forehead, and that was that. John was gone, and the rooms became quiet in a depressing way that still lingers through the house, even now as she lies on its floor.

All of Mary's selves have lived in this house at one point or another, first as a young woman, a joyful newlywed relieved of a mostly unhappy childhood, then a mother, then a drunk, then a sad old widow, and now, an invalid with a smashed hip, lying helpless on the floor after all other selves have left. She thinks absently of an old trunk that sits upstairs among the clutter, containing only old photo albums, ones that hold so much of the evidence of these former selves between their pages. Her life is well catalogued there, to a degree, yet in another way not at all, for none but her will ever know the whole of her life, and once she has passed, everything she has felt and thought and remembered, all that was accumulated and built and cherished privately within her core, will be cauterized along with her. Sympathize and empathize with others as we may, no one will ever really know the depths of another, that private version of ourselves that remains enchained, exiled to the inscrutable corners of our minds and hearts in the dark, with none to know of it. Inside every person one knows is another person they don't. People are nothing but ghosts of the version they put forward.

Cancer, Mary muses, kills many things, yet gives birth to many depressing thoughts she never would have had otherwise. Or maybe it's just old age.

She hears the refrigerator as it shakes and clicks into a steady, competent hum. It's an old refrigerator, encased in olive green, as was the style at the time. Magnets still cover it, mostly plastic fruit-shaped ones—bananas, oranges, a bundle of purple grapes with a brown stem at the top. Sally would take those magnets, trace the outline of them on a piece of paper, and colour the insides. Then there would be colourful drawings of fruit pinned to the refrigerator with fruit magnets, a thing that always seemed to make Sally laugh.

Mary tries to move her head into a more comfortable position just as a crash of thunder falls so violently that her body shakes in consonance with the sound, and when she shook, the pain in her hip was incredible. The rain and wind pummel against the walls and windows so fiercely that the very bones of the house shudder, as though it, too, were whimpering in fear of something far greater than itself. Mary imagines that if another similar wave of wind passes, the whole house will crumble on top of her. And just as well, she thinks; they'll find her in the morning with two legs sticking out of the rubble like the Wicked Witch of the East after the cyclone.

If only she'd thought to bring the phone along for this foolhardy expedition. It's a failed expedition, to add insult to injury, for her mother's pearl necklace still sits vulnerable somewhere near the bathroom sink. Quietly, she wishes the necklace well, as though it were a living thing. She has a sudden thought then, a sinking feeling, a vague memory of Sally mentioning the necklace, but the memory fades and now she feels uncertain. Had Sally found the pearls by the bathroom sink? Had she found the wooden box, and put them away? She can't remember. Her mind is too scrambled, the pain too great.

She closes her eyes again and tries to ignore the dull throbbing, to compartmentalize it in such a way that she might be able to rest. She soon falls into a kind of half-sleep, but then a sound drifts in, one louder and closer than the wind. The back door of the house opens, sending a cool rush of air laden with the remnants of angry rain across the linoleum. She hears the door close and a clamouring of feet heading toward her, and then sees a long shadow in the shape of a woman draw over her. Mary squints up. The shadow says something in an alarmed, high-pitched sounding voice that echoes and hurts her ears, but in her pained, helpless state on the floor, it also has the sound of a savant voice, radiant and full of hope.

Shortly before they turned 20, there was an evening that fractured an already unstable relationship between Mary and her sons. It was September, the end of a long, humid summer, but some of the meadowlarks had yet to fly south, and her flowers, still without the arrival of a heavy frost, were bloomed in full along the trellises that stood around the front porch, making up what she called her earthly pavilion. The boys had their minds set on leaving the next morning, to head west like so many before them, where winters are milder, and well-paying jobs, they insisted, were easier to come by. For Mary, their decision to leave caused an interchange of emotion; she was happy for them one moment, miserable and resentful the next.

She was drinking heavily that evening, something she'd been doing with increased frequency once Sally came along, the beautiful yet unexpected child. Mary's younger sister, Millie, who had grown into a prying, lonely spinster, was also there for a farewell dinner. The table was clothed and set, everyone was seated, except Mary, who was still in the kitchen. The chicken was ready to be pulled from the oven, but first she wanted to fill her glass. She clenched the bottle with both hands, rather than hold the bottle with one hand and a glass in the other, for if one is inclined to shake, there is less risk of the tell-tale sound of glass against glass. She'd adopted the insidious habit of holding the bottle with both hands whenever anyone else was in the house. At the time she didn't think of herself as an alcoholic, merely that she was teetering on the border of it, not yet crossed over, and still believed that things weren't as soap operatic as her sister made them out to be.

With her glass filled and another sip of wine taken, Mary slipped on the matching oven mitts bearing faded images of roosters, and pulled the roaster from the oven. She moved the chicken to the platter, took a carving knife from the drawer, and carried them to the dining room for John to cut and serve. She snuck quickly back into the kitchen to retrieve her glass of wine before joining them.

"They have blue boats that carry people across the harbour," Robert was saying as she sat down at the table. He was sifting through a stack of pamphlets detailing various attractions on the west coast. Mary sighed at the sight of his elbows on the table and filthy plaid shirt; he dressed the same way no matter the occasion, and would have worn plaid if standing in line to meet the Queen. He sipped his drink and opened another pamphlet. "They're called sea boats," he explained. "I can't wait to see them crossing through the ocean."

"Honey, they cross the harbour, not the ocean," Millie corrected.

"Still, it's ocean water," he said, looking from his aunt to his brochure. "Besides, according to this, it's not really a harbour at all. It's an inlet." Turning another page in the brochure, he looked to his father across the table and asked, "What's the difference between a harbour and an inlet?"

"No idea," John said dully.

John Junior, or Jack as he was more often called, listened quietly. A similar man to his father, Mary thought absently—very serious and only speaking when there was something to say. They are the sharp-eyed brand of men who observe the behaviour of others more often than joining in, who are subtly wise, subtly dependable, yet unmistakably charismatic. She smiled vacantly at Jack, then sipped her wine and shifted her eyes toward John who, Mary observed, even sliced through the chicken in an enigmatic sort of way. One by one they passed around their plates and John divided the meat between them.

"I'm sure your father would agree," Millie said confidently, "that riding across such a big body of water would be frightening. Like your mother and I, your father never learned to swim well. Wouldn't a sea boat ride be frightening, John?"

John kept his eyes on his plate and shrugged dismissively. Mary smiled at him, not necessarily because he wasn't giving Millie's comments any attention, but merely because he was so stubborn in his habit of wanting to enjoy his meals in peace. At dinner one should only ask a few necessary questions, expect a brief response, then return to silence. Yet in Mary's stupor, it hadn't quite occurred to her that the reason for his aloofness that evening was not due to Millie, but that he was equally heartbroken by his sons' decision to flee. He spooned some potatoes from the earthenware dish and passed it to his left.

"Children these days can learn to swim properly," Millie continued. "It's a good thing too."

"I guess so," Robert said. He turned to Sally, who would have been about 6 years old or so at the time. She was mostly playing with her food, taking a small bite here and there, but seemed un-interested in the meal. She seemed misty-eyed, Mary observed, then was distracted by the earthenware dish of potatoes passed to her. She absently spooned out a heavy glob and dumped them on her plate. Though like Sally, she only played with them, for the more she sipped her wine, the smaller her appetite.

"Aren't you hungry, Sally?" Jack asked in the sort of soothing voice with which one speaks to children, before helping her cut the rest of her chicken into small pieces. "There you go. Eat as much as you can, then we'll have dessert."

Sally does seem a little withdrawn, Millie thought, too sullen-looking for a little girl. She watched concernedly as her niece re-leased one hand from the cabbage-patch doll in her arms, lifted the fork, ate a tiny piece of chicken, then laid her fork next to her plate. Millie shifted her eyes to Mary, who was predictably sipping away once again at her gosh-darn glass of red wine. Millie knew her sister would be in a low mood tonight, what with her sons moving across the country, yet her concern was more with her niece, who was eyeing her mother in a strange way. Between bites, the lithe little girl was clinging tightly to the funny looking doll with hair as whitish-blonde as hers. All evening she was the quietest of all.

Mary tried a piece of chicken, found it to be a little overdone, then laid her fork back down. She sipped her wine quietly for a few minutes, yet was deeply thoughtful, for over the last few weeks an unpleasant feeling had begun to boil up inside her. Her boys were leaving, fleeing to the west coast, possibly where they would spend the rest of their lives. But what really grated at her is that neither of them bothered to ask what she felt about it. They seemed entirely uninterested in her opinion, oblivious, maybe, to her suffering on their behalf. But they were not boys any longer, she reminded herself. They were men. She held no dominion, no vote, had no power over them in any way. She tried, reluctantly, another piece of the overdone chicken.

"Instead of construction, maybe I'll get a job driving one of those sea boats," Robert said, taking a bite of his potatoes. "I'm not sure what it pays, but riding around on the water all day sounds good to me. It's probably an easy job too."

"For you, Robert, a job like that sounds really delightful," Millie said, a little too cheerfully, only she was already beginning to feel somewhat desperate to keep a positive air in the room. She glanced at her sister, who clung to her glass of wine and was beginning to make peculiar movements with her face, movements that may not be as easily interpreted by others, but easily interpreted by those who knew her well. Millie knew these to be the odd, tick-like movements her sister made when she'd had enough to drink. Mary would blink repeatedly, but it was a hard, exaggerated blink, so that both her cheeks lifted for a moment. It was the squint of someone trying to look directly into the sun. And it meant, sometimes, that Mary's mood was about to shift.

"So, you plan to go after a low paying job simply because it's an easy job," Mary groaned, annoyed by her son's slipshod way of thinking. It sounded lazy to her. She was used to the men in her life working all the time—harrowing and tilling, odd repairs or running a combine, whatever needed to be done. Even John, a man without a farm, usually found a way to keep himself busy. It was her belief that a man, indeed both men and women, should always be useful, never work-shy. "Don't you want to work toward something? Don't you have an interest in being challenged?"

Robert swallowed the potatoes. "Don't tell me you're in a bad mood already."

"She's going to miss you, that's all it is," Millie interposed. "If you find work that you enjoy and pays enough for you to take care of yourself, well then, that's all that matters."

Mary was tempted to snap at both of them, but she checked herself, took a breath, then a bite of potato. It was their last dinner together until who knew when. Yet looking back on it, she had no real intent of letting them go with grace. She was hurt, spoiling for a fight. And the questions that had plagued her that night are similar to the questions that plague her to this day. Were her sons so damaged by the drinking and cheap parenting through their teenage years that they wanted her out of their lives? Did they forgive her for it, but out of pride, kept this forgiveness to themselves? How often did she pass through their minds in a sentimental way? A million times less than they passed through hers, she presumes, but she'll never know one way or the other.

"I'm only saying that you've never known what it's like to be short of money, and if you're going to live in a more costly place, you'd better have a plan," Mary rationalized.

"I plan to find a job when I arrive, and the rest will figure itself out. If I don't like the first job, I'll look for another, so you don't need to worry about it," Robert said, tearing into his bread and avoiding her gaze.

"It seems exciting, to start off on an adventure," Millie said, and once again heard her voice as coming off a little too buoyant. She noted Mary's sour expression, and felt the hairs on the back of her neck stand up for a moment, for she appeared grave and vaguely threatening, just like their father. Yet while their father, after a few drinks, hid for the rest of the evening in the barn and only made his way into the house when it was time to sleep, Mary seemed to crave their company, or an audience on which to unleash her slurred and noisome thoughts. Their father was a solemn, quiet drunk; Mary wanted attention. Millie was quietly growing more annoyed that her sister was focusing more on her wine than her young daughter's impressionability. The droopy-eyed behaviour repulsed her, and although she usually had no qualms in telling her sister off, Millie only held her tongue at the table that night for the sake of the children.

"That doesn't sound like much of a plan," Mary said to Robert. "You're not thinking enough about money."

"I'm thinking of it quite a bit," Robert said emphatically. "You've just decided unfairly, once again, that we don't know what we're doing."

"Well, I can't help it," Mary said, "I've never seen you manage anything."

"No, you haven't," Robert said tersely.

"Meaning what?"

"Meaning nothing," Robert said, then encouraged Sally to take a few more bites.

Mary sipped her wine acrimoniously and envisaged her sons in rags somewhere on the west coast, tattered and hungry, poor as church mice. They weren't too young to take off on their own, rather they were foolish and unprepared. She thought of her father, after four years of bad crops, layering corn husks in the holed soles of his work boots to make them last, and of her mother, weeping one morning over batches of tomatoes that were spoiled overnight by an unexpected killer frost. Her mother had draped a thick blanket over the plants, but it hadn't been enough, and they would be short of preserves for the winter. Her mother was a sensitive woman, but as Mary later understood more thoroughly, she was also a woman raising a family with not a lot of money to spare. Mary assisted as a child with the gardening and canning, but took for granted all the jars of vegetables that seemed to last indefinitely.

"I'm sure it will all work out, but I'll admit that it isn't fun to go without money," Millie said, then added, as if reading Mary's mind, "You boys should have seen what our father put into his work boots to make them last another year."

"Well, anyway, working on a sea boat is just an idea," Robert professed. "I'll be fine. Nothing is decided yet."

"You're an intelligent young man," Mary continued calmly, fixing her eyes on Robert. "You were always lazy about school, but now is the time to work hard at something. If you don't now, you'll regret it later. It won't be fun to be broke and to wish you'd done something worthwhile when you were young."

"I think they'll be some degree of challenge and regret no matter what route I choose."

"All creatures have their challenges," Millie agreed resolutely.

"Well, of course," Mary said, rolling her eyes at Millie, then looking back to Robert. "There will be challenges. That's life. But if you don't put your back or mind into something when you're young, you're in for a unique kind of hardship later on."

Robert shrugged. "Not if I'm paid well. If I can find a job that pays well and doesn't make my life more difficult than it needs to be, so much the better."

"Oh, you sound ridiculous!" Mary snapped. To heck with being calm, she thought, for these idle comments were hare-brained and begging for some kind of correction. "You've never had to work for anything yet! You were given everything, that's the problem."

Mary's tone shocked the room into silence, a silence that was brief yet clearly marked, for the room seemed much livelier a moment ago. She was oddly pleased that everyone had stopped eating. Now, perhaps, she would be listened to; here was the fight she wanted, yet in her heart knew she had already lost, and as such, had nothing to lose.

Robert sighed deeply and leaned back in his chair. "Yes," he said dryly, "I've heard your hard-knock, uphill-both-ways speech before."

"You've never been grateful," Mary said, becoming more irritated. "You and your brother, but you especially. Take, take, take, with no thought to where it came from."

"That's a damn lie and you know it. I'm grateful to you and Dad."

"I'm sure they're both grateful for the start in life they've been given," Millie said to Mary, still hoping to lighten the mood, yet protecting her niece from having to witness yet another one of Mary's arguments with her sons seemed hopeless. Millie looked at Sally, who watched inquisitively as her mother continued with those harsh, exaggerated blinks. Millie continued, "I think that driving a ferry boat is just fine, and besides, I'm sure it can lead to other things down the road."

"If I had ever, even once, sworn at my mother," Mary said, ignoring Millie and pointing straight at Robert, "my father would have smacked me to the ground."

Millie glanced nervously at John, who predictably said nothing to help things; damn his eyes. The man merely ate his meat and potatoes and kept to himself. Millie took his silence almost personally, as she felt it was a man's duty, not a woman's, to step in rather than leave things to get out of hand.

"Times have changed for the better, if you ask me," Millie said, somewhat halfheartedly. "Most children today have more than their parents had. I think it's a positive thing. Now, we should all try to relax and enjoy our dinner."

Mary had already caught on to her sister's none-too-subtle attempts to soften the feeling in the room. She took a few more sips of her red wine, then gently spun the stem of the glass between her fingers.

Dear Millie, she thinks, ready always with supplication. Her sister veiled her words a little differently each time, but over the years the same pronouncements had been made—Jack was too flippant, Robert was too impulsive, their house isn't clean enough, Sally was strange and never spoke, John was too uninvolved, and Mary drank far more that any woman with any degree of self-respect should. Millie's chirpy criticisms were like the buzzings of a trapped insect, thumping persistently against the window-pane—of no consequence but impossible to ignore. In hindsight, Mary should have been more sympathetic to those well-meaning buzzings, as they stemmed, probably, from the loneliness of not having a family of her own to nurture or be concerned about. Only now can Mary see how deeply her little sister had cared for them all.

"It's selfish to move so far away without caring what I have to say about it," Mary muttered, breaking a few moments of tranquility. Millie glanced at her niece, who was in her own world, building a castle with mashed potatoes.

"I'm sorry I didn't talk to you about it," Robert said. "I figured there was no sense in talking to you about it when I already knew what you would say."

"It's not that we don't care," Jack offered, finally with something to add. "Maybe I was wrong to think you'd be happy for us."

"Mary, why don't we go to the kitchen for a minute," Millie suggested, hoping to convince her sister privately to lay off the wine, for her children's sake if not for hers. Though suffering her ill-tempered sister, in the spirit of trying to rescue her, had long ago shown itself as a useless sort of martyrdom. When Mary had a glass of wine in her hand, the conversation wandered sooner or later into the weeds, and any attempt to stop it was all for naught. Yet she didn't know how to stop herself from making these overtures.

"Even if you think you know what I will say, I still have a right to say it," Mary said. She sipped her wine, and in her mind, sipped it gingerly.

Robert, who had set down his fork, lifted it again. "Go ahead, then. I'll eat and listen at the same time, if you don't mind."

"What you boys don't understand," Mary started, before spilling wine on her blouse.

"Oh, Mary," Millie sighed despairingly.

"It's fine," Mary told her. "With this material, it shouldn't stain."

"Right, and saving the blouse is what's important," Robert said sarcastically. "Ooh, look at that. Your glass is almost empty. What a shame. Why don't you pour yourself another?"

"I just might," Mary sneered.

"Maybe you should both be quiet," Jack said wearily.

"Or, maybe we can talk about something else," Millie suggested.

"Yes. Talk about something else," John said seriously, stunning the room to silence a second time. The wind had started to pick up outside, and Millie briefly considered stepping outside, knowing a few seconds of cool air would be soothing, though a moment spent alone in any fashion usually soothed her.

Mary stopped wiping her blouse and looked at her husband, who characteristically prefers a meal of calm and regularity over one of brazen truth. Easier, for some, to ignore the elephant and sweep all negative thoughts under the carpet. Yet there was nothing truthful or useful in the things she said, and Mary wishes, in retrospect, she could have been more that way. Kind people are happier for being kind, calmer people are happier for being calm, or so it seems. She should have been kinder to her sons. She should have been a better mother, a better wife.

Clasping the empty glass in her hand, Mary rose from the table and went into the kitchen. Millie did not follow, perhaps perceiving its futility. The bottle on the counter was nearly empty, so she found another in the lazy Susan. She uncorked it, and again using both hands, poured herself another glass. She sipped her wine, leaned against the counter, and fixed her eyes on the darkening sky and leafy summer trees outside, which hung languid and joyless in the humid air. In the dining room the family continued their dinner without her, with Millie enticing the boys to tell her more about the west coast. A little more was said about sea boats, then a shorter discussion about how awestruck the boys will surely be when seeing the mountain range for the first time. If Mary remembers correctly, it was Jack in particular who developed an interest in seeing the mountains, though she could be wrong; her drinking ensured their teenage years were seen through a blurred lens.

At first the wine was an occasional bad habit, something she would do now and again to pass the time and relieve the stress of two increasingly headstrong boys and one upstaging daughter. For the unanticipated addition of that little girl robbed her of an inner element difficult to pinpoint, stripped her life of a certain detail, altered the family dynamic permanently. Mary and the boys, that is, John, Robert, and Jack, had been content for years as a well-oiled unit, a perfectly imperfect encompassment of an ordinary family. Sally's birth somehow gave her the feeling of stepping off a train while the boys continued happily and unrestrained along the tracks, spending their time as they pleased and helping Bachelor Bruce more and more on his farm as he aged, while for the most part she was trapped at home caring for a sweet, enigmatic, unwanted daughter.

It was cruel and wasteful, in hindsight, to have thought about Sally's birth in such a dreary way—as a trap—for she was the one who cheated herself, cheated her family, out of far better moments than they had. Nevertheless, as Sally grew, the cravings deepened, maneuvering their way into her mind to such an extent that the value of a bottle of wine soon supplanted that of her marriage, her children, her sister, her garden; everything was incidental to having a drink. It would have been awful for the children to see their mother stumbling through the rooms of the house, sneering, repulsive, like some wicked villain from a fairy tale, lurking around darkened corners with a hooked nose and menacing eyes. Even on her sober days she was both present and not present as a mother. They came to her for affection, and she gave it, but she rarely went to them. She loved them, but ignored them. She cared for her children more robotically than lovingly, tending to their needs as one cares to the needs of a crop—out of necessity. Children have strange ways about them—silly complaints, tears that fall unreasonably, little heads full of big, mystifying thoughts. They stare at things solemnly, then curiously. They take forever to grow, and their needs go on and on. Mary had little patience for disobedience, but learned to bribe them into submission, which they fell prey to as predictably as fish to lowered bait.

Her children were fairly well behaved, despite her, simply because they were inherently good. And there was one thing Mary never did—she never hit her children, not once. She could at least be proud of that as a mother.

When she finally returned to the dining room, Robert was speaking to Millie, though in a hushed way that seemed unaccustomed. Mary took her seat and recalled what she was about to say before she spilled the wine. Tonight, she would speak the words plainly, seeing no reason to varnish them, least of all in front of her own family, who should be aware of her feelings in full.

"There's something you have to understand," Mary began abruptly and very loudly. She'd interrupted Millie in the middle of a sentence and was looking critically at Robert.

John had finished his meal, and stood up in a sudden way before Mary could continue. His chair scraped loudly against the floor as he pushed it back from the table, and then he promptly left the house, slamming the door behind him. Such a show of anger was atypical, and at the time Mary foolishly dismissed his anger as fleeting and not necessarily to do with her.

Millie, however, was pleased that John had finally offered a display of emotion instead of sitting there all evening like a gloomy owl on a tree branch. Clearly, he'd reached his limit. She found him to be a somewhat cagy, standoffish man, but very decent, and Millie often marvelled at how he could remain so devoted to his wife. And it occurred to Millie that perhaps she should have followed her sister into the kitchen a few minutes ago, tried to reason with her, despite the inevitable futility of it.

"Mary," she said firmly. "You'll lose that man if you're not careful."

Mary scowled at Millie, blinking those hard blinks, noting that her sister's crinkled expression amplified the lines along her forehead. Somehow, Mary observed, the more wrinkles she gathers on her face, the more frizzled her hair and the more wimpling her voice.

"Mind your own business," Mary cautioned.

"I'm your sister. I'm here because I care for you and your family."

"You're here because it intrigues you, and because living in an empty house gives you nothing better to do," Mary said vehemently, as though she found some pleasure in the narrative. She had unkindly observed over the years that her sister was drawn to silence whenever her lack of a husband and children were remarked on. Predictably, Millie's face sagged, and she became quiet, perhaps, as Mary hoped, even somewhat embarrassed.

On this occasion, however, Millie felt something worse than embarrassment. She felt unneeded. She glanced at the empty chair between the boys and gathered that Sally had slithered out of her chair at some point, and was now probably hiding in her room. Millie drew a breath, summoned strength, then turned to her sister.

"You're wrong, and it is my business," she said. "Please, Mary, you need to quit drinking from that glass and listen for once."

"Please, Millie, you need to wet a comb to tame that frizz."

"Oh, Mary," she said at length.

"Oh, Millie."

"It's no use," Jack said directly to Millie.

Millie opened her mouth as if ready to speak again, then seemed to withdraw her thoughts as though she'd decided, as she had many times prior, that any conciliation was beyond her reach, or beyond her power. Mary, on the other hand, wasn't through.

"How long will you be gone?" Mary asked, painfully aware of the slurring of her words. "One year? Two years? Twenty?"

"We'll see," Robert replied dismissively.

"You must have some idea," Mary pressed.

"No, I don't. If I like it, I'll stay. If I don't, I'll go elsewhere."

"Will you come home?"

"At some point for a visit, yes. But not to stay."

"You can find work here," Mary implored, hearing a ring of plea in her voice. "You can find work in the city, for the railway. At least it's close by. Or buy some acreage around here, find work in town. There's not a lot of work, but there is still work. I've never met anyone who couldn't find work."

"It's not about that," Robert insisted. "I've been here long enough."

"Long enough!?" Mary spat the words across the table.

"Let me put it to you this way," Robert said, in as calm a voice as he could muster. He glanced at his aunt in a way that seemed to exclude her from what he was about to say, and saw fresh tears glistening in her eyes. "As much as my grandparents and great grandparents wanted to work and live around here, I want just as much to be away from it."

"Life isn't always about what you want."

"Of course it is. It's a simple choice."

"You're spoiled," she told Robert, who appeared to her for the first time as a stranger, an arrogant young man. It was still surprising when either of her sons spoke to her as adult to adult, rather than child to mother, and yet there they were, grown, fully formed beings, brimming with thoughts and wants and opinions she couldn't guide or control. Though she was similarly restless at their age, wanting more than this place could offer, she couldn't help but look at them with disappointment. While she had wanted to attend college as a means to an end—to educate herself and be self-supportive—Robert seemed snobbish, as though staying would only lower himself. If her father felt that way when she applied to college, he never mentioned it.

"Are you so special that you can't listen to what your own mother has to say?" Mary continued. "If you want to leave, fine, but if you're leaving because you think you're better, or because you think you're gifted in some way, then you're in for a shock."

"If by gifted, you mean pounding back a bottle of wine every night, I've never been that gifted, but I could certainly try."

"You're a fool."

"You're a drunk," Robert sneered, then remarked quietly to Jack. "I won't miss any of this."

"No, I imagine you won't," Mary said disdainfully. "You'll be too busy earning money in the easiest way possible. You're thick-headed like me and lazy like your father. You're the worst of us put together."

Mary took a sip of her wine, and the quiet sense of something lost in that moment permeated the room. Robert fixed his eyes on the table.

"I think I'll go check on Sally," Millie said, and without meeting anyone's eyes, quickly rose from the table. She dashed out of the dining room, hearing Mary muttering something from the table, and brushed away the tears that had finally fallen.

Mary will lose John, Millie thought again as she headed down the hall. She will lose him and everyone around her, barring some miracle. It's peculiar, Millie mused, and somewhat depressing the ways in which genetics govern one's life, because whomever one shares genetics with are hopelessly more difficult to abandon. She had genetics in common with Mary and little else, yet because they are related, there is a need to be forgiving, while in the absence of relation, she wouldn't need to worry about Mary or engage with her at all. It's a long series of mutual yet somewhat inauthentic involvements. They have, however, had their share of good moments, she thought sentimentally, strings of petty arguments followed by good days together. Families are complicated webs of good and bad, each member their own double-edged gift. Sadly, Millie thought as she started up the stairs, in the paradigm of her own family, the good has tapered, and the bad is swallowing whatever is left. And the thread that held her to Mary was starting to feel somewhat inauthentic.

"Millie," Mary whispered loudly. Millie jumped and turned quickly around on the second step. Mary was there, standing unsteadily, looking suddenly very weak and unimposing in the half-light of the hall.

"What is it?"

"Didn't you hear what I said?"

"No."

"I said I don't need you to check on my daughter for me," Mary said offendedly, for in her mind at the time, while she was indeed worried about Sally's handling of her drinking, she felt threatened for whatever reason at the notion of consolation coming from anyone other than her. Those were the muddled years when Mary half-tricked herself into believing that a perfectly placed kiss on a child's forehead in the morning and a perfectly prepared breakfast were reconciliation for the night before. "Sally is fine, and I don't need your help."

"Oh, for heaven's sake," Millie said, descending the second step briskly. She irritably began heading down the hall toward the dining room, stopping halfway and turning to confront her sister. "I'll get myself out of here then, seeing as you have everything well under control."

"Stay as long as you like," Mary slurred. "Just don't coddle her as if she doesn't already have a mother to do it."

"You're wrong, Mary, if you think she isn't affected by all this nonsense."

"And if she were affected more by you than by me, then my oh my, wouldn't she wind up lonely," Mary said, regretting the words immediately, yet she knew they had hit their mark when there was no response. Of course, Millie, at times and in her own way, could make Mary feel just as small. Each took their turn in highlighting the imperfections of the other, each magnifying somehow their collective flaws as a microscope expands the lines on a stone or the intricacies of a blade of grass. Maybe it's a sister thing; one points out the flaws of the other, the other points out the flaw of the one that said it first, and so forth. It's the pot addressing the kettle, in a sense, for no one is faultless.

Millie turned on her heels and returned to the dining room, with Mary in tow. She retrieved her navy-blue cloche hat and matching purse, which was flung around the back of her chair. Robert and Jack were bringing the earthenware dish and some of the plates into the kitchen to be washed. Something about Millie's movements, the way she deliberately shielded her face, caused Mary to conclude that their relationship had now been damaged for so long that it seemed they'd both given up and agreed to its insurmountability. And even if healing their relationship was a surmountable thing to do, neither of them was in any mood that night to mend the gap. Mary returned to her seat at the far end of the table, and reclaimed her glass of red wine.

I shouldn't have said it, Mary said silently to herself. I shouldn't have said that Sally would be better affected by me than by you. Millie continued to shield her face as she went from the dining room to the kitchen without another word to her sister, and Mary, alone in the dining room, felt the old anger churn inside of her, the unreasonable frustration with life. She sipped her wine, thinking absently of Sally, the gentle kiss she will place on her innocent forehead, the breakfast she will make, the flowers that have a few more weeks yet to bloom along the trellises, and her sons, fallen through her fingers like water.

"I hope to hear from you boys once in a while," Millie said in the kitchen, and while they spoke for a few more minutes within earshot of Mary, she kept her breathing relaxed, her voice calm and steady. She wanted to leave the house as soon as possible, and get home as soon as possible, yet did not want to forego a proper farewell to her nephews.

Millie lamented that with her sister's drinking, she now had only herself to count upon, and would need to make reconciliations for that. Already, being a single woman, she's made herself stronger, less in need of others. The world, she mused, still had a way of shaming women for being unmarried, and in her younger years she bought into that narrative fully. The older she got, however, the more that narrative faded and settled into a kind of peace, and within that peace, slowly, came a gratitude for having a life carved out entirely for herself, however small, however quiet, however insignificant to a world that might passive aggressively shame her for it; a world that never bothers to consider whether a solitary life, for a woman, is not only a choice, but a preference.

"I wish you boys all the best."

"Take care, Aunt Millie," Robert said amiably.

"I'll miss you," Jack said, and offered a quick embrace.

Millie turned from them and made her way out of the house, and as she pushed open the screen door, noticed the light on in the garage. She briefly considered speaking with John before heading to the refuge of her car, if only to see if he was alright, but quickly decided against it. As usual it would be seen as meddling instead of love, and she'd had enough of being seen that way. Millie stepped out onto the porch, and the further her steps took her from Mary's house, and the more she felt the cool evening air against her skin, the less volatile her thoughts, and she found herself thinking that the most wonderful thing in life is the quietness of her little home just a few miles away, and the peace that awaits her there.

As the screen door closed, Robert and Jack made their way back to the dining room to collect more dishes. Mary can't quite remember how, or for what reason precisely, things escalated to the height that they did, or who said what first, but soon she and Robert were raising their voices in a fight that ensued for quite a while. Mary recalls a shattered glass, a thrown plate, Robert shouting in a manner she'd never seen, and herself, shouting in a manner she never had before or since. The anger in the room twisted their faces unnaturally as they spewed hateful words across the table, releasing a pressure that lived between them for some time. They drew weapons and opened old wounds. Robert called her to task on her drinking, she raked him up and down with her eyes while shaming him for any weakness she could think of.

Jack, waiting for it to end, reclaimed his seat at the table and pressed his lips together in restraint. He was surprised by how long the shouting lasted; it just went on and on. Then Robert clenched his fist and slammed it down hard, twice, against the table. The remaining dishes and cutlery rattled and they all went silent. For a few moments the only sounds were the throes of wind that hissed and hollered through the trees, a sound somehow both soothing and dreadful.

After a few quiet moments of everyone finding their bearings, Mary, sobbing, cut through the profound silence by whispering to Robert, "My life was better before you, so it will be better once you're gone."

It was said only once, but echoed through the years more than anything else, and it wouldn't matter that she later told him that nothing could be further from the truth. It was said, and couldn't be undone.

Robert raised his hand to cover his mouth, slowly lowered it, then fixed his eyes on the spot of wine on his mother's blouse.

"You're pathetic," he said.

"Don't speak to her that way," Jack said, and Mary could tell by Robert's expression that he was as surprised as she was by his protection of her. Dear Jack, she thought, advocating for his mother when anyone observant would see she didn't deserve it in the least. And somehow, with that, their warfare had ended. The wine was starting to wear off and she was more aware of her heart beating, of the slow breaths moving in and out.

The years of heavy drinking—and there were about five or six of them—were demoralizing, and she can't imagine that anyone who has been through anything similar would be unfamiliar with the dark place that follows. They'll understand shame, and if they recovered at all, the feeling of relief when they finally surfaced the murky water and breathed fresh. In that fresh air, she acknowledged it was with her own actions that she stabbed herself and bled, and made others bleed. She could not blame her sons, nor her daughter, nor her father, though she bemoaned for a time the vile, sinister gene passed from him to her—the drinking gene, as she referred to it in her mind—yet her father experienced the gene in somewhat of a contrast. He wept or sulked quietly in the barn, she became irritable beyond measure and angry beyond reason.

Their plan was to leave the next morning, but Robert and Jack left that night. The car was mostly packed anyway and John helped them with the last of it. Jack came into the house to say goodbye to his mother, who'd stayed inside, cowering in the dining room amidst the broken glass, sobbing, feeling the gravity of her love for her children, and cursing whatever it was inside of her that assailed her show of it. She hoped Robert would say goodbye as well, but she misjudged the seriousness of his pain. In the murky water it was all too easy to misjudge things.

"I'll call when we get there, I promise," Jack said reassuringly, and he knelt down so they could hold one another. She would have liked to say something warm, something motherly and sympathetic, but she said nothing. Instead she held onto him for a long time, for as long as he let her, with a feeling that letting go would wreck some part of her, and shred her soul to rags. In hindsight, a stupid reason stopped her from telling him how much she loved him—that it might have embarrassed them both. Jack kept his promise; he phoned as soon as they arrived. Robert eventually phoned a few times too, though through the years each of her sons phoned steadily less and less.

When John finally came inside, Mary listened as his heavy footsteps moved straight into the kitchen. It sounded as if he lifted something from the counter, and a moment later she heard the sound of liquid being poured down the sink. She knew then that he was pouring out what was left of her wine. It was something he'd never done. He then did something else he'd never done, by disregarding her entirely as he made his way through the dining area and into the living room to start a fire. Still staring absently at the ruins of her wine glass, she listened calmly for a while as he raked the cold cinders away, added kindling, then methodically stacked the wood along the grate, for she knew so well the way he ordered things—rake, kindling, a few small pieces of birch, topped with a wider piece of pine. She heard him crinkle a piece of newspaper, which he would have placed at the base of the heap under the grate, then the rough quick sound of a long match being lit.

Finally, her desire to be near him, whatever his feelings, prompted her to rise from the chair. As she stepped into the fire-lit room, John rose from his crouched position in front of the fire, and without a word, they sat together on the chesterfield. They watched the fire, burning and flickering, a silent and calmative postscript to all that happened that evening. She knew, though, without him offering an inkling to his inner feeling, that he thought her heartless, and she herself felt heartless. Yet he forgave her everything, and it was a thing she loved about him, that he seemed to have no facility for resentment.

Soon after, starting to doze, she was roused by the sound of a small voice.

"Mommy?"

Mary turned to see Sally standing at the edge of the living room, arms wrapped tightly around her doll. By her eyes Mary could see she was bewildered, even frightened. She would have heard the pounding fist against the table, the shouting, the shattering of glass, car doors slamming, and the unnerving silence when it was finally through. Immediately Mary held out her arms and encouraged Sally toward her. Sally obliged, wiped her small cheek with the back of her hand, then quickly curled up on her mother's lap.

Something about the innocence of that movement makes Mary smile and remember the moment all these years on.

She wrapped her arms around her daughter, thinking affectionately about the day she was born, when she held Sally in her arms much the same way. Yes, she was an unwanted child, and at first Mary didn't fully understand the challenges that would come with a third child in the home, but all of that, the future and the past, in that pure, singularly perfect moment in time, was neither here nor there. Between the four white walls of that hospital room, the disappointment surrounding the pregnancy melted away completely, lifted and cleared off like the tail end of an oppressive dream, leading, then, to a vast clearing of a fresh, radiant, unspoiled meadow, a perfect sight. Mary was lost, simply, in her daughter's endearing little face, her skin as soft as a rose petal, her hair like spun silk. From the start, Sally was an endearing spate of life. She cooed and slept, had wistful eyes, and everything she did was perfect. Loving the child was unavoidable from the beginning. Despite the difficulties, she couldn't help but love her.

Occasionally John rose from the chesterfield to shift the wood or add another piece, doing little things to stretch the fire out for the rest of the evening. The pine crackled, the clock ticked, and the wind howled, but the three of them were silent and comfortable. Sally fell asleep, and Mary turned at one point to see John dozing with his chin against his collar bone. She watched as the light from the fire flickered and mingled with the shadows along his skin. He looked perfectly serene, and handsome. As the only one awake, Mary considered moving Sally off her lap so she could add wood to the fire, but decided not to break the moment, a moment printed on her mind for all its warmth and simplicity. It was a moment of clarity, a breath of fresh air, a soft blanket. Never again did a drop of alcohol pass her lips. And looking back on that night, it seemed, maybe, that Robert was right. Maybe she was pathetic, because she didn't realize until she was an old woman what she would have been better off realizing in her youth—that if she set her heart on being content, she could achieve it quite easily.

Mary is no longer lying on the floor. Her hip still pains, but not as much. She's in an uncomfortable bed, weaved into it like a cater- pillar in a cocoon of sheets. There is a strange sound from some- where nearby, metal dragging across metal. The air is dry and horrible. She tries to swallow, but her throat is bone dry and it stings. She begins to understand, with a touch of her gown and the sight of the bed railing, that she's been brought to the hospi- tal. She recognizes the smells, the incessant beeps, the narrow window that can't be opened, and the high grey curtains sur- rounding her bed like an ugly canopy. The metal dragged across metal sound, then, was one of these curtains being dragged by its rings across the bar in a nearby room. She has some recollection now, as she wakens further, of being carted into this room in the middle of the night and left to wait, just another grey-haired con- valescent parked in a corner by the window. It's a private room, at least. She recalls, vaguely, something about a cancelled surgery, her daughter whispering in her ear although she couldn't make out the words, a skinny woman in a hospital gown praying loudly in a thick Polish or Russian accent. But that wasn't here, not in this room; there was another room, a shared room, with two or three other beds. There was the Polish or Russian woman, an empty bed, and a scrawny old man who slept and slept. She was there for a day, maybe two, but surely it can't have been that long. One day, perhaps, but no more.

Mary tries to turn in the bed from her back to her side, but can scarcely move. The sheets are wrapped with such tautness that she suddenly feels anxious, unwillfully trapped, like a rabbit in a snare. She pleads for someone to relieve the tightness, but when a woman approaches her bed, she tugs too gently and takes too long to loosen the sheets. Mary furrows her brows and begins to struggle against the tightness herself, until a jolt of pain shoots through her hip.

"Watch it!" Mary scowls.

"I'm sorry, but if you'd just hold still a moment—"

"Get out of here, silly witch."

Mary instantly regrets her boorishness, but what's at issue is that she is growing tired of being a burden, of not having the strength to untuck her own bedsheets. If only she wasn't so quick to anger, but she can't help it, she's unchangeable, and she'll not bother changing now. People never change at their core anyway.

Lying there alone, slightly calmer and more comfortable in the loosened sheets, Mary takes better stock of her surroundings. The hall outside is a misty white with a wood railing, and above her bed on a post is one of those square machines with a little screen displaying green numbers and letters. This machine followed her from the shared room to this one. It gurgles strangely every few seconds and has a long thin tube running through it. Her eyes follow the tube from the machine all the way to the top of her hand where it connects to her vein, held in place by a thin bandage. She thinks back to the fall, the storm, the shadow of a woman hovering over her, and suddenly, the most depressing thing of all—not knowing what has happened to her mother's pearl necklace. She knows somehow that she'll never return home to find it, that she'll never again hold it in her hands. After all she has lived through, the children and marriage, the long battles and quiet days, it will end here. If only she could convince someone to take her to her own home, to her own bed, to die in simple peace. Instead someone found it more suitable for her to spend her fading moments as a prisoner, caged as she may as well be by the impassable raised rails of the bed.

In her mind, she begins shouting, trying to get someone's attention again, pleading for them to take her home, but all she hears is her own hoarse, broken whimpering rising to the ceiling. She tries to lower the bed rail, but finds she is not coordinated enough in her movements; she reaches for the rail, misses it, tries again. The more she struggles for the rail, the more she slides down in the bed. The pain in her hip comes back, and although her cries internally grow louder, all she can hear is a voice that sounds devastatingly small, faint and half imagined, the illusion of a voice. She is conscious now of a new pain rising from deep beneath her rib cage and settling in her chest. It's a beating, heavy pain, just beneath the surface of her skin, and the more she scuffles in the bed, the greater the pain in both her chest and hip, yet she continues to move about. There's a desperation to it, as if she must free herself from the bed this very moment or be imprisoned behind a grey curtain forevermore. Then she starts to feel dizzy, her head lighter than the rest, as if it gently broke free of her shoulders to linger just above her neckline. There is something wrong, she knows. She feels strange, half asleep, befuddled; she's both present and not present, moving about in the bed, yet perfectly still. Finally, her fingers clamp onto the metal rail, and she begins shaking it with what's left of her might. Then three new figures surround the bed, their faces grey and stone-like, gawking and perched above her like gargoyles breathing steam.

"Hi there, it's alright," one of them says gently, but Mary wrestles furiously with the bed rail, rattling it back and forth. "Just relax. You're in the hospital."

The grey, stone-like woman somehow pushes a fluid of some kind into the long thin tube. The potion swims into her veins, then like magic the pain starts to lessen. She lets go of the bed rail, feels her body flatten and calm, and turns her head to the window. It's impossible to know whether this is day or night, for the sky is not a telling blue or black, but a bright, unearthly crimson. A lightness comes over her, such a lightness that she worries she might up and float away, and when she senses herself rising to the ceiling, she grips the sheets in fear and slowly sinks, gratefully, back onto the bed. She blinks against the brightness of the crimson sky, hears a light trampling of collective footsteps as the three gawking figures walk away.

She is comfortable now, and other than the odd gurgling of the square machine, the room is quiet. She starts to doze, drifting in and around the margins of sleep, unsure at times whether she is dreaming or awake. She tries to recall where she lives, but can't, thinks of little moments in her life that may or may not have happened. Her father hammering a nail through rotten wood, the wood splitting, and Samuel, nearby, laughing at the accidentally split wood in his boyish, teasing way. Robert in a cloth diaper, jabbering and crawling through the grass, then crying when a wasp bites him. The great willow in the yard on a windy summer day, and Sally nestled down on the grass in its shade, painting something beautiful, her hair so blonde it seems to light up the shadow around her, the strands billowing up and down in the breeze like the long drifting sails of a ship. Jack, the sweet sound of his voice over the phone, telling her about a horse ride through Stanley Park; it was a restless horse, a sprightly thoroughbred, and he had to manage a good grip on the reins to keep her from breaking through the trees in a full gallop. She thinks, finally, of her greatest love, John, not in any specific way, just the feeling of being around him, which was a better feeling than any other. There are more people, so many more people, and so many more moments, but they're drifting away now, quietly, almost tranquilly, each one like a raindrop that gathers with other raindrops to compose a nearby river she can hear, but no longer see, no longer touch. She wonders absently about things she's never seen, places she never really cared to visit, like the Sahara desert or the Pacific Ocean. She considers the smaller things she's never seen, like a polar bear or a fully bloomed rosebush. That she adores roses yet will die having never seen a rosebush in full bloom suddenly seems significant. Mary mourns never seeing a rosebush as another wave of lightness comes over her, stronger than before.

The sky continues its crimson shine, and Mary stares through the window thinking odd, languid, roiling thoughts. She imagines death as a cloaked visitor, prowling and stalking outside her window, waiting for the right moment, the moment when it will float toward the window, parting the crimson the way a wizard from a parable waves his arms to part a path through the sea. The tree branches outside are moving strangely, wringing themselves together one minute, then quivering and twisting apart in the next. They do this over and over, knotting then unfurling then knotting again. Though she can't see them, she knows that the long white tree roots beneath her are moving in tandem with their branches above, a choreographed dance stretching from one end of the tree to the other. She struggles to envision the depth of the ground as it descends from the base of each tree, the invisible miles beneath the grass, with millions, perhaps billions of pieces of soil and minerals, and how fascinating it might be if each speck of earth was unique in some way from the next, like snowflakes. She feels suddenly that this is the most overwhelming thought one could have, as wondrous as trying to contemplate all the stars within all the galaxies floating inside the depths and lengths of all of space.

Mary hears a low, faint flow of voices wafting in from the hall, but can't make out what they're saying. When she turns her head toward the hall, she sees that their voices have become physical things, their words taking the form of luminous beads that dance on the tiles, bouncing this way and that at random, upward then downward, backward then forward, to then fro, until they fall through the floor, out of sight. It's a salving thing to watch, these dancing beads as they leave the room, for they don't fall through the floor quickly, but instead spiral downward in a very measured and satisfying way through little gravity wells covering the floor. When the beads are gone, the gravity wells remain, round and spinning like grey parasols. The curtains are doing funny things too, for they are threaded through with vines, and from the high tips of those vines are ripe fruit. There are water-logged tomatoes and crab apples, bright pink, flamingo coloured, reflecting the crimson sky. Then the fruit starts to melt quickly, causing the apples and tomatoes to droop in downward pieces like balls of plastic held too close to a flame. They shrivel and drip bright red drops. Without their fruit, the vines become wispy, re-leasing themselves from the curtains and moving in ribbon-like waves of air through the room, each their own gust of earthy incense. A woodpecker begins its busy work, punching its beak into the bed rail, tap, tap, tap; strange, she hasn't heard that sound in years. The woodpecker flies away, unnaturally quick, into the hall.

Then comes a sudden wave of clarity, where everything drops into place, and she starts to understand that there are no dancing beads, no gravity wells, and the curtain draped along one side of the bed is just a curtain. It will be alright; she is safe, she is cared for, an elderly newborn well looked after. She is aware of people coming and going, conglomerating around her bed, then dispersing into other rooms, sometimes a doctor, sometimes a nurse, and Mary feels all at once grateful that they are keeping her free from pain. In her last hospital stay she rejected the po-tions, blasphemed the dithering nurse who injected her with them. This time she'll consent to whatever they wish to give. And if the pills addle away what's left of her good senses, so be it. Arguing seems too heavy a task, too costly of her energy. She'll let it go, let them lull her away. What a relief it is to let go, to give in, let come what may.

Mary hears more voices, murmurs, and whispers, and then a new sight, a shadowy figure moving toward her and pulling up a chair. She knows intuitively that it is her daughter when the shadow gives way to dim light, and Sally's hand is entwined with her own. Mary looks in awe at the beautiful features, a stunningly lit face wearing a sullen mask. Sally presses her mother's hand against her cheek.

Mary tries to speak, to tell her daughter for the first and last time that she loves her, but when she opens her mouth it seems there is no longer a voice in her throat, yet there must be, for a moment later Sally whispers, softly, "I love you too."

Mary shuts her eyes again for a while. The pain in her chest returns, a hot, tight wave, then after a moment it begins to subside, but not completely. The nature of it has changed somehow, lowered from a harsh pointed thorn in her shoe to a soft pebble that rubs only every third or fourth step. It's a persistent annoyance, a frail assault. So frail and so diminished that it almost ceases to matter. And just as she felt tightly cocooned in the beginning, she now feels the opposite. Completely free, unconfined, less aware of her feet, her lower legs, her thighs. She feels herself become very light, almost feather-like. And as quickly as Sally arrived, Mary knows somehow that she is gone, and in her place is a familiar sound, the most beautiful sound she has ever heard. Someone is humming a song. The song comes into the room unexpectedly, yet at the perfect moment, as when a needle is set down unexpectedly on a phonograph record in a room that was far too quiet. The voice is haunting, graceful, sorrowful in some notes while joyful in others, exactly as Mary remembers. It echoes and swells and wraps around her body in solacing waves. The melody is all she can feel, all she can hear. She loses sense of everything other than the soothing sound of her mother's savant voice. There is no more bed, no more pain, no more crimson sky.

Beth

*B*eth is outside, barefoot, finding her way along a narrow path of grass. The path is full of unexpected turns, winding before her like a serpent. With each step, she is conscious of the crackling and snapping sounds of dry leaves and twigs underfoot. It's early dawn, and very cold. There are animals and insects calling and murmuring all around her, but because there is no wind, their sounds seem amplified. The trees are high and still, not a single leaf stirs. There is the feeling of having fled a horrible place, some vague suffering place she can't quite see in her mind's eye. She continues along the narrow path, through the stagnant trees, searching for a place to rest, a place to hide, until suddenly she stops and turns around. There is always a sense of something behind her, but never the vision of it. There is only the path of grass winding through the eerily still woodland, and herself, alone, a single figure against a vast, darkening sky.

Beth awakens abruptly from the unsettling dream, slightly disoriented at first, but quickly consoled by the warmth of sunlight spread across the room. She's not in her bed, but on the sofa, where she often falls asleep late in the evening with an open book on her lap. Her eyes wander for a moment, finding reassurance in the sight of her belongings, the worn, chestnut coffee table, the black wool sweater tossed over the back of her blue upholstered chair. She closes her book and places it on the table next to a still-lit lamp, and glances at the clock that sits atop the piano. It's after nine.

She slept late again. Soon, she'll need to get ready, but not yet. She still has time, and this is the sort of time she is careful with; it's a calm mid-morning, she's alone, comfortable in her apartment, the casement windows are letting in a lot of light, and the heavy sadness hasn't yet started to churn inside of her. But the uneasy feeling brought on by the dream, the strange recurring dream, stays with her for a few minutes. She still feels herself shadowed, followed, not quite alone. The heavy sadness has been with her for several months, or years, maybe; it's hard to say exactly. She only knows that it has worsened lately, deepened in a way that is difficult to describe, but the dream manifests the feeling aptly—haunted by where you've been, fearful of where you are, of where you'll go, unquestionably alone, and a sense of being pursued. Not by a person or animal, but by something far less distinct, something ghostly, even supernatural. She can never get a clear glimpse of it, this invisible predator. As she starts her day, she knows that the vague sense of a threat will pass, that soon it will begin to lift like an ominous fog that finds strength in the night, then weakens little by little as morning approaches with its all-embracing sunlight, until it clears.

She rises from the sofa and sets a kettle on the stove, listening passively to the harsh gusts of wind as she waits for the water to boil. She regrets having agreed to meet him for coffee, but he caught her off guard when he phoned, and she couldn't at that moment think of a reason not to. His voice sounded so sincere, so polite, and after all, they haven't seen each other in years, this old friend of hers who fled like many others, like she, perhaps, should have. Yet it would be so much easier to linger the day away in the living room, under her plum-coloured afghan and the warm yellow light of the windows, reading. Here, she can do as she chooses; alone, she is the unguarded version of herself, the admittedly odd, quiet woman, the incessant loner who always shuts herself inside a cluttered little apartment, to sleep or try to sleep, to think, to languish on the sofa with a book. She sighs. Her days feel parcelled—shower, work, errands, home, dinner, read on the sofa or blue upholstered chair—and the energy to do anything more has drained out of her. It's an anesthetized existence, but a manageable one.

When the water comes to a boil, Beth sprinkles tea leaves on the loose leaf strainer, then pours the water through. She leans against the counter with her cup and looks out over the small, open space of her apartment, at the row of casement windows on the opposite wall, and the millions of tiny specks of dust floating listlessly in the sunlight. On the coffee table sits a pot of wilting daisies, having been prompted a few days earlier by Mary Mattern to buy flowers, suggesting it would improve or brighten the room. And it had brightened things, if fleetingly so, with their pretty white and pink-tinged rosettes. She hadn't watered them properly, or they're dying prematurely for some other reason, for she knows little about flowers. Or perhaps she felt there was little sense in watering a thing that was already plucked from the ground, clear of its nutrients, and would die anyway. She sips her tea, which she prefers without milk, thinking, isn't that the essence of despair? To feel that caring for a plant is useless and hollow? To abandon all hope and purpose because it will die anyway? She feels saddened unreasonably now by the wilting petals, a few of which already having given up and fallen helplessly against the wood of the table.

For a while she continues sipping her tea against the counter, feeling acutely responsible for the dead and dying petals, and absently gazing outside as the elm trees that line her street withstand the wind. Autumn has begun to strip away their leaves. From where she stands, she can see some of these leaves as they're pulled away from the branch, some orange, some yellow, some still green, thin slices of colour blowing this way and that before falling listlessly to the ground, below the windowpane, beyond sight.

She sips the last of her tea and turns to check the time. It's nearly ten. She sets her cup on the counter and heads to the washroom, thinking that the calm, hushed quality of her apartment seems almost subversive to the bursts of noise that now fall from the apartment above. She hears them from time to time, the abrupt, hurried little footsteps of children across the floor, the muffled voices of parents, doors closing. She conjures up images in her mind once in a while of this family on an ordinary morning, sights that might match some of their sounds; little hands playing with wooden blocks that sometimes tumble, coffee being poured, a husband tiredly wishing his wife a good morning while she offers, perhaps, a drowsy, tender glance. Beth removes her nightgown, steps into the shower, and imagines these two people, this husband and wife, falling cozily asleep in their bed together each night, having tucked in their children, and laments her own nights on the sofa, which is too short for her long legs and not all that comfortable. Yet from the sofa, it seems she can pretend in some way that he hasn't left, that Tom is nearby, that he is merely in the next room, just beginning to doze, and she is merely reading on the sofa temporarily so as not to bother him with the light of the lamp. But to lay in bed alone, with no one temporarily in another room, Beth muses, can be a loud feeling.

Beth steps out of the shower and catches a quick, foggy glimpse of herself in the mirror, a too-tall, too-thin woman with long, stringy brown hair, and skin far too pale. She brushes her teeth, rinses the brush under the tap, and returns it to the drawer. From the bedroom closet she chooses, after a moment's hesitation, a long, green cotton dress, then tugs a brush through her hair. She leaves it loose around her shoulders, then clips it up, then loosens it again. She returns to the washroom, applies a stroke of blush before quickly rubbing it away, detesting the colour, then stares in dismay at her reflection in the oval mirror above the sink.

"You're so unusual sometimes," Beth's sister, Holly, said to her once, long ago. "Why do you keep your hair so long and buy makeup when you can't manage any of it?" Holly gathered clips from the drawer. "Here. I'll do your hair for you."

Though 'unusual' was used only once, Beth has grown to hate the word because she has become, slowly and irrefutably, everything the word seems to imply about the lives of spinsters, about repressed expectations and quiet rooms. Meanwhile Holly is anything but unusual, embellished with their mother's beautiful auburn hair, and graced with enough writing talent that she's able to make a career of it. Given that their communications are scarce, Beth can only conceive of her sister's daily life in that great French city of hers, and like the family in the apartment above, Beth envisages little things about her sister to go along with the breadcrumbs. Dinners in dimly lit restaurants with other writers and editors, somewhere off a cobblestone lane maybe, weekend trips with her family to a lake where her daughter might pick stones from the beach and glance adoringly, as children do, at her mother. She wonders absently if Holly still keeps her hair so often in a long auburn braid.

Beth grabs her purse and the black wool sweater off the blue chair, locks the door, descends the worn carpeted staircase, and steps into the sunlight. The air is cool, and she shudders, but the wind has died some. Copper and ochre-toned leaves are predictably scattered along the heavily treed Rosewood Road. She turns onto Main Street, past the bakery, the one-room theatre, and the high stone walls of the Presbyterian church and the eerie cemetery behind it. She's heard the church-like sounds at times in passing, her attention always drawn by the organ music playing loudly and in an arcane, echoing way, like preternatural sounds emanating from another realm.

She has strange, fearful thoughts about this church sometimes, about religion, perhaps from only stepping inside once or twice as a child. There is something terrible about this cemetery, something affecting her on a primal level when she passes, with its high tombstones locked behind pointed iron gates, as if to guard non-believers from this foreboding, shadowy realm. She thinks morbidly of their ritualistic funerals, of being laid forever in the dirt, cold and covered in layers of earth while everyone above weeps and lays flowers before turning their backs and disappearing quietly beyond the hedge, back into what might be called the ordinary, everyday realm. There, they return to ordinary lives, to the warmth of ordinary homes where plants are watered and clocks strike an evening hour, where kisses good night are offered and received and bed covers wrapped around children. They're free to fall asleep with thoughts of another day, perhaps already starting to forget about the one they left behind in the mud of a different realm.

There is so much sadness in the world, Beth muses, so many people abandoned in one way or another.

She takes a deep breath, inhales the cool air, and tries to think of something else. She wasn't always so dreary and pessimistic. Yet she can easily fall into this mood lately if she isn't careful, a dark, detached mood where the tale-bearing stabs and cuts of her flaws, and all she has done wrong or lost, pains too greatly. She tries to align her mood with more optimistic thoughts, as a satisfied woman passing her days here in this ordinary, everyday realm, who is meeting an old friend for coffee, who does take some pleasure in the sight of autumn leaves scattered thick and pretty along the pavement.

Beth approaches the restaurant, crosses the parking lot, and pulls the door open. The place is quiet with only a few patrons. Quickly, she finds James' face on the other side of the room, waiting in a booth. She'd nearly forgotten the dark, deep-set eyes that always looked at her in a way she could only define as sharp, almost knife-like. He waves her toward him, and she makes her way across the plain, sanitized room—it has the scent of being freshly scrubbed following a bustling breakfast crowd. The tabletops are damp as if recently wiped down with a cloth. She's struck suddenly by a sense of nervousness, of unease, as it has been a while since she's had a prolonged social interaction with anyone outside of work. It's a vague sense of unpreparedness, one similar to what a performer might feel before stepping onto a stage, she imagines, overcome by stage-fright.

"Well," James says to her. "It's been a long time."

"Yes, it has," Beth says, taking a seat in the booth. He appears more or less the same, only slightly heavier and a little more wrinkled around the eyes. She wonders how she might appear to him after so many years, but quickly recognizes the futility of wondering. No one can ever really know, with any definiteness, how they appear to others.

"When did you get into town?" she asks.

"Last week. My dad hasn't been doing well, and coming home was long overdue, anyway. I don't think I'll be leaving again anytime soon."

"I'm sorry to hear about your dad."

"Thank you. I guess we'll have to see how it goes. He may get better, we're not sure. I'll help out any way I can, but soon enough he'll move to the new assisted living home. It's about time they built something like that around here."

A lithe young waitress approaches the table to pour coffee,

then sets down two spoons and a small bowl of creamers before retreating into the kitchen. The odd feeling of sitting across from someone she was once close to, yet is no longer close to, keeps Beth silent for a few moments. She pulls the warm coffee toward her, feeling unacclimatized, the vague sense of stage-fright pressing her every nerve. She sips her coffee, which is bitter despite adding milk. She should have ordered tea.

James watches her nervous movements. She was always a shy, tremulous type of woman, resplendent despite being awkward, simple but still interesting; somehow, she is still all of those things.

"It's nice to come home to some familiar faces," James says, stirring a healthy dose of cream and sugar into his coffee.

"You must find that the town has changed since you were last home."

"In some ways, yes, and in other ways, not at all. The tone of the town hasn't changed." He pauses, then adds, "I have missed it here, more than I ever thought I would, and yet if this town wasn't my home, I can't see why I would ever want to come."

Beth shrugs. "A lot of people feel that way about where they're from. At least, I imagine they do. I think someone's feelings about their hometown can be complicated."

"I suppose."

"It's a courageous thing for someone to do, to move so far away from home."

"You think so?" James replies with a smile that shows he is flattered.

"Of course," she says impetuously, feeling slightly more at ease. She has a passing thought that socializing is a kind of life skill, something one learns to do then perfects over time, like baking their own bread or driving a car. It needs practice. It's a thing that develops mechanically, without thought, by repetitive exchanges. And so she relaxes her mind to a degree, fills herself with an air of being well rehearsed, unconcerned, alongside this long-gone yet familiar man with piercing eyes and the somewhat contradictory look, still, of a debonair farmer.

"Sometimes I think I was an idiot for leaving."

"No, you weren't. It's brave to follow through on something you want to do."

"Well, I was a brave idiot, then."

Beth offers a hint of a smile, then peers around the room, noting that indeed nothing about the restaurant had changed since she'd last been inside. Like most places in town, it clings to a set of constant qualities; the black and white checkered floor tiles, the beige curtains, the framed colourless photos that line the lacquered walls depicting the early days and denizens of the town. She finds it both reassuring and depressing that the macrame plant holder next to the cashier still hangs with the same plastic stems of eucalyptus.

Beth has, James observes, managed to stay quite pretty, though in a rather plain, understated kind of way. He recalls a distinct, indiscernible quality that drew him to her years ago; something disarming, something delicate, something he still can't put his finger on, knowing only that he hasn't encountered this quality elsewhere. She is, seemingly, as polite and self-contained as ever, almost infuriatingly so. He was never quite able to know her as well as he wanted to. She was long engaged to his cousin, after all.

"Are you still working for the care agency, Beth?"

"Yes, I am," she says, and he watches her tuck a strand of hair behind her ear.

"Do you enjoy it?"

"Yes, I really do," she replies modestly. "Actually, I am working tomorrow at Mary Mattern's."

"Ah, Sally's mom. I remember her well. I hear about her from time to time, from my parents. I'm surprised she's managed to stay in her house for this long."

"I don't think she will be able to for much longer. It's day by day with Mary."

"I see. And how is Sally? Is she still painting?"

"I'm not sure."

"You haven't stayed close?" he asks in a way that shows his surprise.

"No, we haven't," Beth says, considering the sadness of the friendship that dissolved, as so many do, despite effort and time and whatever magnetism brought them together. All those years with Sally as a sister, of sharing and mulling over together the minutia and little feats in life and first moments with men, of sitting quietly together in the comfortable way two people only can when they know one another so well. Beth recalls the great oak tree by Sylvia River, the one they would sit under, and then her mind shifts to Mary, and the effort it now takes her to move from one room to another. Beth recalls the pretty pearls strung around her neck, the ones she had laid on a towel before the shower, and the way she looked so lovingly at those cream-coloured roses in a glass vase.

"I see her in passing," Beth adds rather numbly, "but that's about all."

"I'm sorry to hear that," he says absently, recalling the last time he saw Sally, many years earlier. She was beautiful, probably still is, but they were never very close. He glances at the framed row of old photos lining the wall, the blacksmith shop, the fire-hall, the hardware store, a business opened by his grandfather and operated, now, by his father. "I like these old photos. I like that I know enough about the area to remember what some of the old buildings were used for, or where certain businesses once stood. My roots are here. My family has farmed here for four generations. And now I've become sentimental about moving back into the house I grew up in, and of growing old in those rooms. I even romanticize the thought of dying in one of those rooms, or out the field somewhere, old and stinking of sweat and hay. I like the thought of my ashes being scattered on the farm."

"Well, that's very poetic." As Beth watches James, she begins to recall the finer detail of his mannerisms, the way he rubs the bristle of hair along his jaw with the back of his fingers. It depresses her to recall the similarities between him and Tom.

"I don't sound too morbid?" he asks, raising his eyebrows.

"Not at all. It's nice to know where you belong."

"I suppose so. I'm not old, but time goes fast, so I'm starting to think about these things, like what I really want to do with my time before I die in that field."

"It sounds to me like you've just missed the feeling of being home," Beth says empathetically, and James has a thought that her empathy was one of the things his cousin loved about her.

Beth sips her coffee judiciously and notices a lone, urbanely dressed older man at one of the tables near the window. He appears somewhat removed from the unremarkable scene of the restaurant, quite unsuited to it, to these crackled vinyl booths and glass ketchup bottles, as if he were an actor or semi-famous writer who had wandered into the room accidentally and decided it wouldn't be such a bad thing to sit and read quietly for a while. He focuses only on the pages, frowning at some of the words. He nudges his wire-rimmed glasses a bit further up his nose, pushes his empty plate to the side, passively places his finger along one of the passages. She briefly regards him, unaccountably, as a sorrowful man, a lonely man, a man unwilling to return to the cold quiet rooms of his home. Maybe he's escaping; maybe he's afraid of the silence. All human loneliness can be filtered down in one way or another to the singular, tragic element of silence; one is merely a euphemism for the other. No wonder he might prefer the unemotional setting of a restaurant at mid-morning, where the transactions are measured and predictable, where the voices and movements blend like a steady hum.

James has absorbed himself in his coffee, thinking briefly of his father's untiring wish for him to take over the hardware store, an idea he once deplored by now thinks of merely with a kind of mild disregard. He could do worse in life than run a hardware store. He shifts his eyes to Beth, who appears distracted, looking oddly around the room. Such a solemn, easily distracted creature, he thinks sentimentally.

"Beth, do you mind if I say something?"

She redirects her attention. "Not at all," she says, meeting his eyes.

"I only want to say that I was genuinely surprised to hear that you and Tom decided to end things. I know three or four years have passed, but I have to admit it was surprising."

"Yes." Beth taps her fingers against the side of the cup. "But maybe it was for the best."

Of course, no part of her believes it was for the best, only she has scant idea of what else to say. The waitress stops to refill their cups, yet James continues to look at her expectantly, as if hoping for a few more details, so she relents.

"I think we wanted our relationship to be something that it never really was," Beth offers. And this is, she justifies, a truthful remark. "We were happy for a long time, really happy. But for him, well, for both of us, but mostly for him, the feelings slowly went away. I'm not sure how else to explain it. No one did anything wrong."

"I'm sorry to hear that." James pauses briefly to tear open a sugar packet, then adds, "It's depressing, the way relationships end. It happens all the time, but that doesn't make it any less difficult."

Beth nods without responding.

"He's living in the city," he continues. "I'm sure you know he's engaged again."

"Yes, I know," Beth answers quickly, then glances again at the lone, sorrowful man. She knows that James might be hoping for her to say more about it. She hears a steady clattering of dishes from the kitchen, as if they are being roughly washed, then roughly stacked. The sounds remind her of Mary's sister, Millie, a kindly yet quick moving woman who visits her ailing sister frequently and often seems ready to tackle any minor mess in the kitchen. Beth finds herself hoping Millie might emerge at some point tomorrow, for she adds a certain warmth and, momentously, some help in dealing with Mary during some of her more difficult moments.

"Maybe I shouldn't have brought it up," James says remorsefully.

"It's fine," she says, then leans forward a little in the booth. Tell me a bit more about what you've been doing for all these years."

"Well, I don't want to talk about my job, it's too depressing. I could talk about some of the trips I've taken, mostly to the mountains, the mountains that bore me."

"I'd love to see the mountains."

"They're beautiful at first, but not enough to keep me there. I suppose it's true, the old adage, that you can take the boy out of the prairie but not the prairie out of the boy. There's something in the air here, that gets lost somewhere around the foothills. And the end of my own drawn out relationship made it much easier to leave."

"Drawn out?"

"She works for a theatre, mostly with props, set design, that sort of thing. She's also somewhat of an environmentalist, attending various conventions. Her goal was, or still is, to merge her two passions by writing a play about 'the ailing natural resources.' I found her passion remarkable at first. I've never had that sort of passion for anything."

"She sounds interesting," Beth says resignedly, still somewhat struck by the notion that a person could ever be brought to boredom by mountains.

"She was," James says, absently rubbing the bristle of hair along his jaw. "The thing is, I never saw her write or do anything substantial. It became obvious over the last few years that she didn't have a passion for anything, really. She demanded a lot from others, mostly from me, but didn't contribute much herself. She reminded me too much of every other relationship I've been in."

"How do you mean?"

"Well, the ignorant lust and hope at the beginning followed by just a gap."

"A gap, meaning love and the expectations adding up to nothing," Beth acquiesces, sipping her bitter coffee gingerly and feeling, despite the agonizing gap that so often replaces love, quite envious of James for having more recently experienced the joys and miseries of it—the love making, the first pangs of disappointment, the forgiving and the fighting, the slamming doors. She can't imagine having the energy for any of it, both missing it terribly on one hand while feeling repelled by the hurt and the poverties left behind by the gap, by the nothingness. She adds, vaguely, "A small nothing, a long nothing."

"She never would have been happy living here anyway," James says with a small wave of his hand, and easily resolves that the end of his relationship was well worth being able to live once again on the vastness of his father's farm, to wake every day with the dry sun and the thundering prairie wind, to experience three hundred and ninety acres of golden rows of wheat under an uncertain sky. It will be a beautiful thing; he will impel himself through one harvest season, then another, and another. It's what he was always meant to do. Sure, he thinks. I'll take over that old hardware store if it can afford me those things.

"You asked me earlier," Beth begins, "if I enjoyed being a caregiver."

"Yes, and you said you did."

"I do, and some of the things you're saying reminds me why I enjoy it."

"How so?"

"It's comforting, the way the work distracts you," Beth explains, recalling the mornings when she would leave Tom alone in the apartment, thus leaving the unravelling aspects of her relationship behind for the day. "I guess a lot of jobs have the power to force you out of your head for a while. It pulls me out of myself. And when you consider all that people go through, like physical pain or sickness and dying, then the problems outside of that don't seem as relevant, do they?"

"No, compared with a lot of things, I guess they don't," James says, listening intently.

Beth quietly considers the aspect of her work that is perhaps the hardest to deal with, that being the elderly who despondently, yet understandably, pray aloud for death. Yet, it is the softer moments, the holding of hands, the draping of a warm blanket, that carry the essence of why she loves her work, needs it, she would say, to steady her own self-worth. Her work as a caregiver alone cannot offer or maintain happiness, but it is at least gratifying, a good and worthwhile endeavour, a cord to help shepherd her through.

Beth sips her coffee, decides she's sipped enough of it, then looks contemplatively around the room. At some point, without her noticing, the sorrowful man slipped away, back to the dank silent rooms of his home or, she briefly envisages, to some great theatre where he auditions for the part of a redemptive man, a mysterious but driven man, one who ends the play by leaving the high mountains to farm his father's flat land, as James now has. And then the vision of a great theatre is gone and she imagines the man in a silent room, alone after all is lost, and how her own silent rooms are waiting for her. They always wait for her, those walls, that sofa and lamp, that gap, that silence.

"We all need to find our own thing, a thing that manages to distract us and fulfill us at the same time," James says, again envisioning the golden rows of wheat under a prairie sky, himself living there, himself dying there.

"We do, and I think for the most part I have that," Beth nods, and feels her mind pulled from the small rooms of her apartment and immediately to Mary Mattern, and all the moments where her taxing personality gave way to glimpses of something completely endearing and vulnerable.

Beth stops the waitress from warming her coffee, while James has his filled. He then talks for a while about some of the trips he's taken—various drives and excursions through the northern mountains, hiking through hills along the Athabasca River. Beth listens somewhat curiously for a while, politely, yet soon feels restless. Her mind now wanders to thoughts of how she will spend the rest of the day. It's better to keep busy, she decides; to distract herself with provisions. There is still the whole of the afternoon ahead. Quickly, she decides to spend time with her mother.

James stretches his shoulders back in the booth, sees Beth glance around the room for the waitress, as if getting ready to leave. Wanting to extend their time together, and because it's a brisk autumn day, he decides to offer her a ride in his antiquated truck, a beaten-down remnant of his second year out west. It's rusted and worn, but functional.

"I can drive you home," he offers. "It's a bit cool out there."

"No, I'd like to visit my mom for a while before going home. It's not far. I'll walk."

"At the nursing home? I heard about that also. It must be difficult for you."

"It is, but she's more settled now."

"Good, I'm glad," he says gently, remembering Susan, the kindly red-haired woman he saw on occasion yet met in person only two or three times. His own mother is hosting a dinner tomorrow, a thing he looks forward to only passively, for though he enjoys their company, even small gatherings seem to wear him out these days. Maybe it's age; when he was younger, he wanted to be around people almost all the time. Regardless he invites Beth to the gathering. The thought of her being there with him would make his homecoming feel more meaningful, and more complete.

"That sounds nice," Beth replies slowly, both wanting to attend the dinner and not wanting to attend the dinner.

"I suppose my parents need to have my siblings and I under the same roof for a few hours now that I'm home. It's not a formal gathering, just a small dinner, around six or so. And don't worry about the coffee, I'll take care of it."

"Thank you," she replies, then conquers an urge to whine a little further about the scarcities of love, about anticipations followed by a key left on a counter.

"You're welcome. Oh, and Beth?"

"Yes?"

"I have no doubt that you do good things in your work."

To his surprise, she smiles, if diffidently, and he notes the thin wrinkles starting around her eyes. Those eyes say something to him both tragic and mirthful, each eye its own epic verse about the harshness and beauty of life, of routine and growing old, of the drabness of middle age.

"Thank you," Beth says more sincerely, before rising from the booth. "I should be going."

"Let me know if you'd like a ride tomorrow. It's a far walk otherwise."

"I will," Beth says, and heads for the door.

James watches resignedly as Beth makes her way through the restaurant. He feels unexpectedly saddened, and vaguely unsatisfied with the way things have gone. He feels as though he has both succeeded and failed; the connection between them remains both present and lacking, as if the ingredient necessary to form a better connection with her was somewhere nearby, well within his grasp, if only he could unearth it, whatever it is. He sighs deeply; he knows she is unlikely to appear at his parent's house tomorrow evening. She remains too stubbornly elusive, too cagey. It is as equally unsurprising as it is astonishing that she is still alone. He resolves, however, because of her meek, fragile qualities, that this wavering feeling for her over the years has merely been one of concern, a feeling that stems more from wanting to protect her than out of any romantic conceit. Nonetheless he can't help but sit in the booth for a while and think of her with a sort of vague, exhausted interest. Finally, he sips the last of his coffee, which has gone cold, and pulls the wallet from his coat.

Shuddering from the frigid wind along the sidewalk, Beth is nevertheless grateful for the abrupt infusion of clean scents and wet grass. The air since earlier in the morning had altered slightly; it feels cooler, and more animated because the wind fiercely spins some of the fallen leaves into little autumn-coloured funnels along the pavement. She pauses at the corner, looks to the right, looks to the left, then crosses Main Street and moves purposefully along the broad sidewalk of the tree-lined Weiser Crescent. She is conscious for the first time that there are fewer birds around, most having already flown south. On one of the branches she sees, finally, a sparrow, sitting noiselessly, its beady black eyes looking both sharply vigilant and blank minded. The restaurant already seems like a faraway world with all its stage-fright and clattering of dishes and cutlery from the kitchen, a world antecedent to this one with its singularly quiet and charming street, where there is hardly anyone else around and the town park extending from the corner of Main and Weiser appears particularly tranquil and still.

She may go to the dinner tomorrow evening, she may not. She feels indifferent about either possibility. It was nice to see him, and in another way felt backward, as if the chapter in her life in which she was meant to know him had long since ended. Beth continues along the leafy pavement with her head slightly lowered, thinking of the morning's details in a distracted, affectionate way—the man of sorrow, the plastic leaves of the hanging eucalyptus, James' salient eyes and the bitter coffee, the grandeur of the Presbyterian church and the frighteningly preternatural-looking cemetery, and the wretched dream, directly preceding the wretched feeling of waking alone.

She thinks unwontedly of Tom, her abandoning knight, the

simplicity of her life when they were together. It's a thwarted simplicity, a thwarted future, and everything since then seems essentially like a long and dreary postscript. It seems so faint now, so far
away, as if those glowing years had been lived by another woman.
Yet it was irrefutably her. She remembers, still, the smell of his
skin, his sleepy quietness in the mornings, a vase of yellow roses
on a windowsill. She recalls, with perfect clarity, a ring slipped
onto her finger.

The rooms when he closed the door were the same, yet different, every colour a slightly dulled pigment, the configuration of
everything in the apartment—the tattered reading chair, the
plum-coloured afghan, the sheet music on the piano bracket—
altered in some imperceptible way, as if even these inanimate
things were affected, meaningful possessions transformed into
cheap, miserable remnants of her favourite years.

As Beth nears the end of Weiser Crescent, she feels, now that
she's alone again, the slow return of the white noise—what she
calls the sad, heavy feeling that lurks perpetually nearby, hovering
behind a wall, beyond a clipped hedge, waiting to carry the hopeful part of her away in a coalescing wave of taunts and shadows.
It's the best way she knows how to define such an indefinable
thing, a thing that others might refer to as depression. Yet that
word also fails to define properly the coalescing waves that are so
cold and barbarous, and like the shifting tide, draw near at certain
moments, recede to some degree in the next. She struggles, always, against its relapse.

She wondered, when the sadness gained strength, when the
quiet nights were torturous and she couldn't sleep, if she was suffering the beginnings of some kind of insanity. Not the loud in-
sanities seen in movies, with padded walls and screams that echo
down the hall like sirens from a cave, but instead something that

harms in the gap, in the nothingness. She once read of a young woman who saw horrible things, shifting swarms of shadows just beyond the corner of her eye, or fizzling, bird-shaped flocks of light moving across her bedroom wall before heading in a flash of intent toward her face. She claimed her depression would take on a liquid form, and she would lie helplessly on her bed as the sadness slithered under doorways and through keyholes. The demon liquid was hiding behind the bathroom wall, the woman insisted, the way river water becomes hidden from sight by a green mass of grass and trees rising out of the embankment—unseeable, but whole and unimpaired.

Beth doesn't suffer hallucinations or have unreasonable thoughts. Yet the white noise has caused a slow dimming of spirit, a spirit that hasn't been extinguished, but greatly quieted. But maybe that's how things started with the young woman who saw horrible things. Maybe she had an ordinary sadness at first, spending far too much time alone and concerning herself too much with the sort of thoughts and questions that more optimistic and busy people would have less time for, like who am I, and what am I doing here? Why have I ended up alone when others haven't? Is that man over there in the corner giving me a funny look, or is it a trick of my eye? Does he see that I am beaten by this? And, finally, is the amount of care and observance I give to daily things, like flowers and mud on graves or the blank expression of a sparrow on a branch, normal or abnormal? Maybe that other woman started out this way before something more sinister took hold of her world.

Beth turns the corner and winces against a fresh gust of wind. She gathers the collar of her wool sweater around her neck as the whirlwind sends another small, swirling torrent of yellow leaves up into the air.

The nursing home has a crisp, clean smell to it, an aggressive combination of pine-scented cleansers and floor wax. Two large potted ficus trees stand guard at the point where the foyer opens into the main hall. Inside the hall, glimmering white floor tiles change their colour in consonance with the time of day and the weather outside.

As Beth passes the main dining area with its trussed vaulted ceiling, she sees an elderly woman sitting under the skylight, quietly working on a puzzle, while a male resident sitting nearby looks on. Beth knows the man as Norman, the man who erupts occasionally in a fit of wails and shouts, prompting nurses to emerge from the nursing station in an effort to calm him. His episodes are common, yet unpredictable; he is calm one moment, triggered by something in the next. Norman is non-verbal, and cannot express what upsets him, though the staff correlate it either to a sudden movement made by another resident, or a loud, unpleasant noise, two rather unavoidable things in a care home.

Another resident in her wheelchair near the hall is Alice, with coarse white hair the appearance, as always, of being half lethargic, caught somewhere between this world and the next. On the wall across from Alice is a whiteboard with the date and the day's planned activities written in blue marker—chair exercises with music at three, Bingo in the main dining area at seven.

The air in the building carries, as all nursing homes do, Beth presumes, a sense of long, orderly bereavement. The messy war against death is being fought here, and each numbered door leads to a room that has been used over and over for the same things—final kisses on foreheads, tired eyelids helped shut, tearful losses for some while polite acceptance for others. But there are many good things to say about the home. Hopes are nurtured continually behind these doors, weakened hands are held, reassuring things are said to family members by caring staff.

At the end of the hall, her mother's room is unusually bright and clean, a watered-down version of what it once was. The crooked shadows of cedar branches swaying outside the window leave a ghostly image on the sheer, ivory-coloured curtain. The bed is made.

"Hi, Mom," Beth says, kneeling next to her mother, who is resting in a rocking chair and facing the curtain, an afghan tucked around her lap. A folded towel is placed behind the right side of her back because she has a tendency to lean too detrimentally over to that side. Susan's reddish-white hair and peach-coloured dressing gown, along with her stillness in the dull light from the window, make her appear almost decorative, sculpture-like, a diminutive figure hewn out of brilliant pink marble. Beth takes her mother's hand and strokes gently along the thin, fragile bones. Slowly, Susan shifts her head toward her.

"Have you seen my daughters?"

"I'm Beth," she tells her gently. "I'm your daughter."

"Yes, but I have another daughter," Susan says anxiously. "I'm sure I have two daughters."

"You do. You're thinking of Holly." The bewildered, grief-ridden look in her mother's eyes gradually sharpens into something more keenly aware. These transitions in her focus always seem like a painful effort.

"That's right," Susan whispers. "She couldn't wait to run away."

"That's true," Beth agrees, and notices, beneath the dressing gown, that the maidenly nightgown her mother is wearing is not her own. There is always a confusion here with clothing, a confusion helped along partly because some of the staff seem indifferent to which bit of clothing belongs to whom, and also because many residents cannot recognize their own clothing. This one is a yellow and white polka-dot nightgown, something her mother would never have worn. Beth considers this sort of mix-up undignified, almost crude, and, despite her past complaints, ongoing.

"You girls have always been so different," Susan reminisces, directing her smile to an old photo of Beth and Holly, standing side by side against a poplar in the yard. "You were different, but always managed to get along."

"Yes, I suppose we did," Beth says resignedly, glancing at the framed photo. She sighs. One sister is auburn and bright-eyed, the other brown-haired and melancholy.

Her mother takes a deep breath, is quiet for a moment, then turns to Beth. "Your father will be home soon," she says casually. "I should get dinner ready."

"It's too early, Mom. We've only just had lunch. He won't be home for a while." Beth usually plays along, an act often necessary to prevent an anxious episode. Moreover, it wouldn't do any good to remind her about the wintry accident, decades earlier, when Beth's father didn't see the train coming, or if he had, the ice likely swept him into it. And she, Beth, a little girl, had drearily imagined it, the utter stillness of his torso slung over the wheel, his eyes frozen wide with fear and aimed at the tiny glistening shards of glass that had rained around him.

"We can at least check what's in the fridge and have something ready," her mother insists, then clasps the arms of the rocking chair as if getting ready to stand.

"He'll be late today, won't be home until later tonight," Beth lies. "I'll help you make supper later."

"You're sure he said that?"

"Yes," Beth replies decisively, then sighs. "It's still early in the afternoon. We don't need to worry about dinner yet. But we have time for a walk outside, if you'd like."

"No, I'd rather not," her mother says wearily, then diverts her attention back toward the window, where the ghostly tree branches sway relentlessly in the breeze, and the shadow of a bird passes swiftly and elegantly across the ivory curtain. Something about its quick movement, there one moment and gone the next, reminds her of her dream, the sense of something prowling just beyond her range of vision, and a thought comes to her; the prowling thing is her mother's disease lying in wait. It will happen to her too, very young as it did her mother. An involuntary loss, occurring slowly, perniciously, like grains of sand through the glass, until all that remains is a beating heart and eyes so desperately mystified. It's an old fear, acquiring this disease, but unlike the dream, she cannot wake from it.

"Alright," Beth whispers, then laments her mother's weak hands, her mild, trusting eyes, all the way back to the innocence of a child. "It's a bit cold today anyway."

"Better to stay inside then," her mother says, and her eyes seem to droop. "We can relax together while we wait."

"Yes, we can relax for a while," Beth softly agrees, and after a few moments, her mother's head begins to lower. As Beth often does on these undisturbed afternoons with her mother, she lies down on the bed, letting her mother rest. There's a surprising relief in the clasped hands on her lap, her head bowed slightly forward as though in careful prayer. She is asleep; she is not anxious, not wondering. And Beth, despite her fear of the disease, is consoled by her mother's presence as well, feeling the kind of safeness she knew only as a child, as if together they are cushioned from the leaden world in a haven made warm with sunlight and a cleanly made bed. Beth again expresses a private gratitude that her mother's room is at the end of the hall, where it is usually quiet, where the noises from Norman and the nursing station are easily overlooked.

The move to the nursing home was an event that Beth fought against, much more so than her sister, or her mother, whose memory had already dissolved to the degree that her house and relics of the past meant nothing. There were, in the beginning, scattered notes throughout the house serving as odd reminders, announcing in red felt marker where to find her car keys, the dishcloths, the ironing board. Another on the front door reminding her to lock it when she left.

"She forgot my number."

"What?"

"Mom forgot my number," Beth sobbed to Holly over the phone, hoping to inspire some care and interest from her sister on behalf of their mother, some confirmation that their cries were still received from far away on the other end. Holly was her reflection in the glass of sorts, a thing to prove she exists, is heeded, and validated.

"Maybe she just doesn't want to call," Holly quipped. "I don't hear from her either."

Sometimes it was hard to tell if Holly's belittlements were made consciously or unconsciously; other times, she didn't even try to veil herself. Holly was a woman who could seem soft and entrancing in one moment, and malicious in the next.

"You know how clean she is," Beth goes on. "Or how clean she used to be. There's food left all over the counters and bugs everywhere, and she put her sweater in the fridge."

"What are you talking about?"

"One of her sweaters. She folded it and put it in the fridge," Beth said, her voice trembling. It was a demeaning condition for a retired English teacher who managed the details of her life carefully, an astute organizer who went from arranging her cookbooks alphabetically to forgetting to eat. Her sense of reason, the sentience of her being, sliced thinly away, layer by layer by the skulking disease.

"I didn't realize it was this bad," Holly assented after a pause.

"And she phoned the police, Holly."

"Again?"

"She demanded they go out looking for Dad," Beth said, thinking something about her mother that she thought so many times previously as a caregiver; there are symptoms worse than death itself, battles not meriting a struggle, misfortunes not worth living through.

"Well, I don't know what you want me to say right now," said the sister who found little reason to bother with the family of her past, the one she never assimilated with, the one that bored her. And after she left, their conversations went this way, futile, circular, nothing between them was ever swept open, nothing relinquished then laid bare for the other.

Beth watches her mother breathe in and out, an elegant woman robbed of most of her memory and banished to a little white room, the former English teacher, a long-dying sovereign, a disregarded angel.

Something about the moving branches, swaying oddly from behind the thin curtain, where the bird had so quickly swooped then disappeared, evokes once again the images of her dream, and thoughts about the origin of dreams, if such a thing could ever be known. They're sometimes dismissed as some kind of automated, reflexive operation of the body, throwaway nerve molecules flung meaninglessly through the brain, firing randomly and without aim. Others believe profoundly in their magnitude, as if there is an important message attached. They examine the minute details of a dream the same way another might analyze the pattern of tea leaves settled at the bottom of a cup. Others, still, say that a dream is an answer to a question we aren't ready to ask, and the question will continue to torment the dreamer until its significance is acknowledged, understood, then resolved. And so, gravitating for whatever reason toward this final explanation, Beth tries to think of a question, one that relates the dream to the white noise, perhaps, or to her mother's cruel disease, lying in wait, but soon grows tired. Trying to apply some great meaning to anything seems too wearisome right now; she's tired of thinking, tired of analyzing, tired of trying to find some deep meaning in her worsening sadness and coming up empty.

She looks at her mother, still asleep in her chair. With her illness, there must be such a sense not only of loss, but of being lost, of walking alone down a narrow path, as in her own dream, through a foreign, hostile landscape. Beth pretends for a moment that her mother sometimes has dreams with visions very similar to her own—the snapping twigs, the cold ground, the tormenting sense of something malicious lurking from behind. Maybe it is a shared dream, a kind of nocturnal *folie-à deux*.

"Maybe we're both lost, in our own way," Beth says aloud to her mother.

Beth closes her eyes. She decides to spend the rest of the afternoon in this crisp quiet room, where there still lives some beautifully soothing fragment of her mother, as if her mother were the only speck of colour in a landscape otherwise barren of colour, the lone purple plume growing on the ground aside a blackened river. She knows that when she returns to her apartment, the plume colour will fade and the sadness will spread itself over her spirit like a heavy cloak. Outside the apartment her spirit can rise slightly from the sadness, if only for a while. Distractions are powerful, pleasing, fleetingly medicinal. On difficult days, this clean corner room with her disregarded angel asleep in a rocking chair by the window speaks to security the way the phases of the moon speaks to the tide, and here, in this place, in this moment, Beth imagines an altered version of the dream, one where they find shelter in the end, beneath the glowy moon, having been received by a savant and offered a place by the fire.

A month or so ago, Beth ran into Millie on Mary's porch. Beth had settled Mary in for an afternoon nap in her armchair when Millie pulled in, and when she met Millie on her way out, they had surveyed together the remnants left scattered across the yard by the overnight lashings of rain and wind. It had been a good prairie wind, high and harrowing, yet short-lived, a late-August assail that snatched then flung some of the leaves and weaker twigs to the ground. And as Beth and Millie mulled over the corpses of small branches, they sat on two of the old wicker chairs that cluttered parts of the porch, while Beth had pondered two things. The first was that everything is a shed remnant of something else, herself a shed remnant of a family of three others that steadily left her, either unwillingly or of their own accord, and of the failed engagement with a charismatic man who bought her yellow roses, only once. The second thing that came to mind was the stable impression of Millie herself, as another shed remnant, and the qualities of a lonely womanhood as they water down into old age. Water down, perhaps, because when a woman is still young enough to hold out hope, the spinster-like qualities feel somehow more noticeable, more threatening, while when one finally passes the age of hope, the threat and fear can dilute into a duller, more passive acceptance. And so Beth often feels, on one hand, kindred by Millie's presence, for there is an understanding there, yet on the other hand, she feels a bit uncomfortable, reproachful, as if the cursed sediments of a woman who never married or had children will tumble onto her if she gets too close. For she, Beth, is still in the age of hope.

Millie was visiting her sister more often, Beth had noticed, and so Beth found herself speaking with her more often in passing. Yet it was this brief conversation on the creaky wicker chairs, among the casualties of wind, that they spoke more unambiguously. Millie had an air of warmth and motherliness that made it easy to do so. They'd communed a few times already about the advantages and pitfalls of living alone, over which they'd exchanged a few synergistic glances, and on this day Millie was trying to find a word that best defined, in this day and age, the general perception of a woman who chooses to live life on her own.

"Scandalous?" Beth had suggested, half-jokingly.

"Perhaps, but not very seriously."

"Radical?"

"Yes, but quietly," Millie said at length, and after a pause where she seemed to measure the weight of the word carefully. She clasped her hands in her lap, then added, "I have relished my years of solitude."

"I can't tell sometimes if I enjoy the solitariness or if I've just grown used to it."

"Maybe both."

"Maybe."

"I find the quietness comfortable more often than not."

"So do I," Beth replied quickly, yet the words uttered aloud that afternoon rang suddenly false. No, she did not quite relish the solitude the way Millie, sitting upright and dignified, had frequently proclaimed to. At least, not usually. Seclusion was a mixed bag, sundry in an immeasurable way, perfectly agreeable to her at one hour while inflicting an almost etherealized helplessness in the next. It's a double-edged, paradoxical, limitless thing.

"When I was young," Millie continued, "I was worried about meeting someone and being tied to them for eternity. Women can more easily untie themselves now, if need be, which is a good thing, if you ask me." Then she added, rather emphatically, "I would never want to be married in a society where divorce was not acceptable."

Beth did not respond, yet greatly admired the self-assuredness with which this poised, elderly woman spoke, a woman who had endured Mary for all of her life, who wore her hair neatly in a bun and seemed so wonderfully fastened in her thoughts. Absently, Beth followed the deepest wrinkle emitting outward from Millie's left eye, down toward the pale sunken cheeks, toward the thin, fragile skin of the neck. She, Millie, could have been a bird in this moment, blithely perched, lingering on a willow branch, an assertive yet motherly presence, assuring Beth without a word that the winds have passed, the leaves have fallen into place, the solitary women of the world will triumph.

Beth turned away from Millie, from her bird-like dignity, and her eyes wandered solemnly around the yard, to the abandoned garden, the overgrown grass, the shed remnants. The white noise had gained strength in that moment, became more persuasive, for everything in sight seemed unusually stricken with melancholy; the long wrinkle, the thin skin of Millie's clasped hands, the stubborn greyness of the sky, the chipped porch wood, and the look of her own hands, already starting to age, for when she stretched her fingers outward the back of her hand resembled parchment paper.

"Don't let anyone shoot you full of holes," Millie continued with a smile. "That's something Mary told me, once or twice, when I was younger and worrying too often about how others would perceive me, a woman who never married. My sister sure took turns shooting me full of holes over the years, but she does have those kinder moments."

"She does."

"Mary once told me that I wasn't a spinster. She said I was a distinctly brave, unaccompanied woman. A lone wolf. I liked those definitions, but maybe your word is better."

"Radical?"

"Yes. It implies wonderful things, like strength and resilience and forging paths."

"I suppose," Beth said quietly, yet felt wholly unconvinced and unmoved. Nothing about her life spoke of any radicalized movement or sentiment. The casement windows in the apartment, the blue chair, the dust on piano keys, the unevenness of the sidewalks around town, and her outstretched, parchment-like hand, all spoke of something opposite to radical; inessential, hollow, forgettable. And it occurred to Beth that Millie's viewpoint was merely part of a façade. Maybe Millie, sitting quaint and very ladylike in the rickety wicker chair, was thinking of the aspects and items in her own life and regarding them, too, as hollow, bereft of meaning. Yet it's a frightening place for a lonely woman's mind to go, to let the high and harrowing gusts of wind flow throw the window and let fall this carefully coiffed house of cards. The crumbling of cards, the corroded façade, is not without some uniquely terrorizing aftereffects. It makes the steady ticking of a clock sound cruel instead of innocuous, the sight of a child or an exchanged kiss on the street between lovers seem demoralizing instead of commonplace. Such moments add up essentially to a kind of maceration of the soul. Beth glanced at a yellow leaf, still wet enough from the rain to cling immovably against the porch rail.

"I wonder sometimes," Beth began unsteadily, "why some women become lonely."

"You shouldn't wonder such things."

She glanced at Millie, then back to the yellow leaf, and after a few tongue-tied moments, found herself asking instead, "Do you ever think, Millie, that unhappily married women are envious of our quiet lives?"

"Yes, I do," she said unhesitatingly, and they fell into a comfortable silence.

Beth thought sympathetically about Mary during that silence, the wilting woman sleeping nearby under an afghan. Mary has her kind, more tender moments, as Millie mentioned, yet Beth was more tolerant than some of the other caregivers when it came to Mary's fluctuating moods which, truthfully, could be difficult to deal with. Though anger is merely sadness rising in another form, Beth had once read, or heard, and when they are sitting comfortably together, Beth feels that they are somewhat alike. Each lives in relative seclusion, even if their dispositions don't match. Mary's isolation is the end result of widowhood and old age and distance from most of her children; Beth's is the result of circumstances she can only blame on her unusualness, a quality that probably emits from her mutely the way qualities like confidence or composedness visibly emit from others, the way poise and maternal warmth emit from Millie. At the thought of this exposed quality of unusualness Beth had gathered into herself, looked at the skin of both her and Millie's hands again a little self-consciously. She felt generally sad, and restless.

"Don't worry about me. It's a nice day, I think I'll sit here until she wakes up, then she and I can have a nice visit," Millie had said, as if cued into Beth's restlessness. "I brought a pie for her, as well. Made from the apples of my own apple tree. She likes those."

"Sounds nice," Beth says, warmed by the sweetly pure and bright image of an apple tree in one's yard, of plucking its fruit and baking fresh pies. It seems almost fable-like.

"I won't have my sister to share pies with for much longer, I suspect."

"It's hard to say."

"I think she's ready."

"Me too," Beth acquiesced, and they exchanged their usual quick, kind-hearted farewells. Mary, Beth had thought, was very fortunate to have this woman, this patient sister in a wicker chair on a porch, wanting nothing more than a nice visit.

Beth thinks back to this brief meeting with Millie as she makes her way this morning around a corner and past the library, where a few yellowy wet leaves cling to its stucco siding in much the same way they did to Mary's porch rails. The overnight rain had mostly ceased as she left her apartment, and now only an intermittent drizzle remains as she makes her way to the agency building. A staff meeting is an ordinary situation, but she knows they will be looking at her inquiringly when she arrives. She overslept; the meeting started ten minutes ago. It may not be worth going at all.

Nonetheless, she's grateful to be on her way to work, and to walk alone shortly after the rain passes, when its earthy smells still linger above the ground, is something she derives a simple pleasure from. Yet by the looks of the sky, one fall of rain has passed while another is on its way. These days of rain go on and on it seems, without much respite. When she arrives at the agency building, she will endure the staff meeting, whatever is left of it, and then, unless there has been some change to the schedule, which does happen, she will be with Mary Mattern in another hour or so.

Once again at the corner of Weiser Crescent and Main Street, Beth waits for the light that will allow her to cross. There's little traffic, but she waits for the light anyway. The freshness of the autumn air usually carries at least a slight feeling of assurance and sanguinity—a promise of colour and movement, of a crisp, evolving beauty. A burst of wind sends her hair streaming across her face, and a man entering the park across from her holds his hat against his scalp. A few raindrops land surreptitiously on the pavement by her feet. The season's beauty is somehow both here and elsewhere, close but removed, as if it exists for all others in this town, the lone occupant of a passing car, the man with the hat, but not quite her. She is suddenly the lone greyscale figure in an image of otherwise vividly yellow, orange, and reddened tones. The white noise has increased its occupancy somehow on this corner, drifting invisibly along the dripped-on pavement, and there, in the fluttering then falling leaves of an ancient elm, and in another dwelling place she cannot see or even perceive properly, the fastnesses of her mind, where a significant part of it waits whole and undissolved, like an antagonizing demon in an alcove.

As her mother's skulking disease slices away at her reason and memory, so this demonic white noise slices at her will, her faith, for it stifles the blood flow somehow to those parts, the good and gentle parts, the part of her that still loves and wants happiness. As usual, it will rise into full prominence at night when the day comes to an end along with all the stimuli that accompanies it— car doors opening and closing, people moving in and out of rooms, lights being switched on and off.

It would be nice in a way to flee this town as Holly did, or as James had, to start over, to give in to the human desire to escape and see one's life anew as it opens broadly ahead into wonderful things, like the speckled lights of a modern city or the mountains in the west, the balcony of an apartment overlooking a completely foreign place that will take months to explore in full. And she could leave her sadness behind as one leaves unwanted furniture behind, decorate this new balconied apartment with attractive things that are harmonious with sentiments like optimism, sanguinity, and brightness, for in this new apartment she envisions some great glass standing lamps reflecting and mirroring at all hours the varying sunlight and moonlight. There would be no sadness there, her sadness is here, in her apartment, lingering in the dust on the piano bench, along the dry petals of the unwatered daisies, on the tattered fabric of the old blue chair. It is tempting to believe for the moment that sadness can be left behind so easily, as if it were an object, just another thing to throw in a closet and forget about. Yet some part of her does think it to be possible, for the prowling white noise seems attached to things the way her happiness once attached itself to things. Some objects have one or more memories attached to it, whether good or bad. And the more days in a row that begin and end in this same lonely way, this unendurable white noise that at some points make her want to tear the skin from her bones so that she can be somehow let out of it, the more enticing the thought of escaping, in any way possible, becomes.

It rises potently in her mind now, the word 'escape,' a word that seems all at once to calm her. It does not seem strange, or foreign, this idea of escape.

Beth glances upward, sees that the light has already changed. She crosses the intersection and heads down Main Street, her muscles relaxing somewhat as she steps onto the curb. She thinks again of Holly, the escaped sister, the one she continues to admire with a kind of asperity from afar; her life seemingly better, more established, full of good things and recompense, which leads her vaguely to thoughts of their poor mother. She has probably finished her breakfast by now and is sitting quietly in the dining room, having a morning of mild confusion, for her confusion tends to start off as mild before deepening considerably by the evening. Sundowning, it's called; a strange and depressing phenomenon attributed to many things and seems, at least in her mother's case, to involve a panicky need to go home. What a horrible thing it must be to feel a desperate need to return home, only to have an unfamiliar face approach you and proclaim, bafflingly, that you already are. Beth sighs mournfully, and reaches the agency building just as the raindrops are starting to fall more heavily. The drops hit the pavement then bounce an inch above the ground like a thousand little glass-white marbles.

Beth pushes the door open, steps onto the crisp tile floor. The foyer leads to a single hall, clean and verdant, with rows of offices behind doors, except for the first door on the right, which opens to the conference room. She glances at the iron metal clock on the foyer wall. She is now more than half an hour late, and silently reaffirms her earlier thought that it's probably not worth going at all. Better to turn and leave than to make an undignified entrance into a full room. But before she makes a move either way, Beth hears an assertive, familiar voice echoing from the conference room, calling the meeting to a close. Carol is the manager of the care agency, 53-years old but appearing slightly older, and as she steps out of the conference room, something about her limp, wrinkled eyes remind her of the way a woman can sail through her youth without a thought of old age, until one day she might look into a mirror in a certain light, aghast, and think, well, here it is, the cruel deterioration, the slow loss of shine.

"Good morning," Carol says, peering above her glasses, as if not entirely surprised to see the latecomer.

"Good morning," Beth says meekly. "I apologize for being so late."

"Beth, I need to quickly drop off a few papers with someone, but I'd like you to meet me in my office," Carol says peremptorily, turning toward the hall of offices. "I won't keep you long, only there's something you should know."

"I'll be right there," Beth replies uncertainly, then sees Angela approaching, a kind and feathery woman who has been with the care agency for as long as Beth. Alison, one of the newer staff members, walks along with her.

"I'm sorry I was late," Beth says again, even more meekly than before, though Angela is in no more of a dominant position at the agency than herself, nor would it matter to her anyway. Her blonde hair and bursts of freckles seem especially vivid in the bright light of the foyer, and Beth always envisages her as the sort of woman whose disposition can brighten anyone's mood and make everything in a room seem more florid. Some women, rather some people, have that effortless way about them, succeeding with their easy composure in drawing others to them. Beth has often felt vaguely guilty around Angela, for she has rejected her invitations for after work dinner or drinks so often that she no longer asks.

"Don't worry about that," Angela says airily. "I only wanted to tell you about the meeting. That Assisted Living building on the west side of town? It's all ready and finished."

"Is it?" Beth says, feigning interest in the new building. She inexplicably resents most of the new buildings and houses going up on the north and west ends of town, just as she inexplicably resents most things to do with change. Yet many seem to watch the urban expansion with anticipation.

Alison, who is nodding, eagerly adds, "From what we heard, it's much better than the old senior home. Everything is brand new, of course; there's big paintings on the walls, and the suites and hallways are incredibly spacious."

"I'm sure it's very nice," Beth assents. "It should be. They've been working on it for a long time."

"We already have a new client there," Alison says, "so I'm sure you'll get a chance to go inside soon."

"Is that what the meeting was about?" Beth asks, with a degree of solicitude, given that Carol did seem slightly more rigid than usual when asking her into her office.

"It was mostly about our payroll," Angela replies. "They're making some changes to the pay slips. We all have to fill out a new form."

"I see."

"Are you working today?" Alison inquires. She is nearly as jovial as Angela, and equally innocuous; no wonder they are friends.

"Yes," Beth replies. "I am on my way to Mary Mattern's."

Angela and Alison quickly exchange a knowing glance, and

Beth looks at them furtively.

"I'm surprised no one told you," Angela begins at length, as if wanting to make the words very clear. "Mary Mattern passed away in hospital. It was yesterday I think, or the day before, I'm not sure. You'll have to ask Carol. I'm sorry, Beth, I know you cared about her."

Beth doesn't respond, letting the words settle into her consciousness. Mary was old, weak, palliative, yet the news stuns her. A searing, almost blinding sense of grief sweeps through her body, and her thoughts wander suddenly, and vacantly, to the old practice of opening a window when someone passes away to allow their soul to flow out of the room, whether in hospital, or elsewhere. Never before, though; to open the window prior to the death is considered bad taste by some, in the same way completing an obituary or death certificate would be if the person still breathes in the next room. Beth envisages all those tired human souls, unseeable white wisps, floating farther and farther away from beds and circling up to an unimaginable place. Beth pauses in these wandering thoughts for so long that Alison gently asks Beth if she is alright.

"I'm fine," Beth says unconvincingly, feeling oddly detached, nodding her head slowly. As Angela explains what she knows about what happened, Beth envisions Mary as a white wisp, and wonders whether a window had been opened for her, and whether she had danced through the clouds before rising to the tops of the sky and passing out of sight, to the other side, if there is another side.

"Well, I'd better go have a talk with Carol about it," Beth says, her voice wavering. "But thank you for letting me know."

"Take care, Beth," Angela says in concerned sounding tone that Beth appreciates, yet ignores, her thoughts still scattered and consumed with the vision of Mary as an ethereal dancing wisp, and on the slow steady grumble of a train passing through town, sounding its horn, a sound that seems both close and distant, somehow as smooth as it is scathing.

Despite the juxtaposing sound of the whistle, and despite the manner in which she lost her father, she usually finds herself captivated by their sounds in a way that is more positive than negative. Maybe it was because he himself enjoyed trains, Beth muses as she makes her way down the hall, having worked as an engineer for the railway years earlier. Ironic and depressing that the thing he so loved would also bring about his end. As a boy, he told her, he would ride his bike to the tracks on days when the train would be heading through town. He stopped on the gravel, let his bike fall to the ground, and as the train passed, made huge, ecstatic, child-like waves with his arms. Whomever was in the front cab, he said, waved right back. She quite liked that story, and the innocent vision of her father as a little boy, smiling and waving, regarding the world around him in the marvellous and tender ways of a child. He never said either way, but Beth imagines him in those moments as squinting in intense sunlight, the yellow dust blown up wildly by the torrent of wind. Life for him held infinite possibilities, Beth thought wistfully, though children tend to take this for granted. How could they possibly know what it means to lament and regret?

The door to Carol's office is open, yet she knocks gently before stepping inside.

"Come in," Carol says. "Unfortunately, I have some bad news to tell you. Please, have a seat."

Beth sits in the little leatherette chair, wondering if her father was ever one of those little white wisps, flowing up from the place by the tracks where he was hit. Carol sits in the chair opposite with a look of trepidation, and Beth begins to tell her that she already knows. Surely Carol will send her to another client in need. At least, that is what she hopes, and she reflects as she so often has that this particular line of work chose her in some mysterious, unearthly way, rather than her choosing it. She thinks of the nature of giving care, how the holding of hands can be swift, or long, but always distinct, always full of meaning, and how one can feel broken at the end of a day, hardened, pushed beyond their limit. She listens to Carol, feels the sadness settling upon her as dust settles quietly on a windowsill, and thinks of the armchair by the bow window in Mary's home, of the dust already descended there, and of her father's final sight, maybe, a thousand shards of windshield that had fallen around him like glass rain. It might have been somewhat pretty, that final sight, that quick, glimmering conclusion. Off in the distance, the train sends its ghostly whistle through the town a final time.

The news of Mary's death intensifies the peculiar sense of gloom and quietness in her apartment, the combination of which provides ideal conditions for the white noise to perfectly frame itself in Beth's mind. It sifts itself through her thoughts, becomes clearer, more well-defined, and she sees it for what it is—an unyielding presence taking many forms, a shape-shifter manifesting into anything it chooses, a thief in the night, a halo round the head of a sage; the white noise presents itself differently to everyone. At least, she imagines it so. Beth envisions the white noise, usually, as a high flittering of air, an unseeable melody, a flatness of emotion hiding in plain view. It's a thing that is constant and stable, and yet completely varied in its manifestations. For it is there in the shadow of the piano bench, then lingering elegantly somehow within the shape of musical notes resting upon the bracket's open score, and there it is again, hovering in the blue light of the standing lamp. She can touch it in the dry feel of her palm against the cool cotton arm of the chair. She hears it in the voices passing outside along the sidewalk; a woman laughs, a man says something, the woman laughs again. The white noise, the sadness, exists in all these things. And that is why she is inclined to believe, now, that the sadness is an unbeatable thing.

She looks dispassionately at the wilted daisies in the little ceramic pot, now thoroughly dead, and lets her eyes trace the outline of their shadows on the wall. The sight of this dead useless pot of daisies only adds to her sense of melancholy, as if it were itself a taunting emblem of her depression; its dry, enfeebled petals somehow embodying the very spirit of despair.

She thinks of Mary, whether she suffered in the end, if she was in pain or at peace. She thinks, grievously, of her mystified mother in the nursing home nearby, and feels more palpably now the old fear of the skulking disease, as though it might grasp her in the coming hours rather than several years from now, and the terror of this idea interweaves itself so thoroughly with the white noise that she can scarcely tell one from the other. The terrible thoughts are no longer isolated from one another; they are related, allied, no less in pursuance of her than a red fiend or spirit that prowls the landscape for someone to take hold of. And this fiendish spirit, she muses, is the invisible pursuer from her dream, taunting and jeering, relentlessly spiteful.

She turns her head toward the window. The days are getting

shorter, and already, the air has a feeling of wintriness. An hour passes, and the more the windows blacken and the more she thinks of her life as it was in the past, the more she feels the depth of her loneliness. So profound is the loneliness, so close is the sadness tonight, that she feels herself almost disembodied, as if floating, a muted strand of air, a wraith in a slumbering room, her mind so wandered that she is only half aware of her physical presence in it. She is haunted more deeply tonight by thoughts of those she has known and loved, those she feels justly and unjustly abandoned by, and by all the unknown moments and nights ahead of her. Tomorrow morning, she will open her eyes. It will be a morning similar to all other mornings. It will begin, first, with sunlight and the heavy awareness of her solitude. She sees it now, her fate shown to her in plain display, if she would only listen unequivocally to the silence; the unwanted, insignificant, peculiar woman, aging slowly inside a hollow chamber. One day will be followed by another, round and round like a circlet. And it will go on and on and on.

She cannot even claim to be gifted, to have something of value to offer, to find some reassurance in having made the world a more worthwhile place. She is peculiar, but not eccentric. Yes, she has her work, a good deed on its own, but in lieu of her, anyone could be found to take her position. Beth herself, despite all her individualities, doesn't bring anything inherently valuable to the table that another can't. She's not needed. Even Mary, a woman full of foibles and challenging traits, attracted a man who would love her to the end of his life. She was not quite so churlish when she was young—Mary admitted as much to her—and yet her husband stayed, was good to her. It's enviable, romantic; she had a home, a life, three children. Granted two of those children have all but disappeared, but Sally was making great efforts to keep her feeling loved and comfortable. Beth will never have any of that; she will never have a child to leave her, nor one to love her. She will never fathom the blessing of holding a perfect little being in her arms, one born of her own flesh, a tiny innocent soul. She perceives her lack of children as a kind of punishment, a result of having failed at something. The sensible part of her knows this to be untrue, yet to be denied what makes other women happy, to live every day with the unfairness of it, seems nonetheless punishing.

"It's one of the only times I remember feeling nothing but love," Mary told Beth not long ago, during what turned out to be one of their final visits. Mary was in her armchair under her green afghan, refusing to have breakfast and instead talking dreamily about the day her daughter was born.

"It was the first time I felt protective of another person," she continued. "I thought, stupidly, that boys could better manage themselves. Even when they were young, I didn't show the boys very much affection. I didn't think they needed it, or wanted it. And I had little affection to offer them. I see that now. I regret that now. But there was something special about Sally when she was born. She was an angel, pale as milk. I loved her at first sight."

Hearing those words, Beth had looked at Mary, a very old woman under a steely mass of white hair with an oxygen tube wrapped round her cheeks, and perceived her as blessed. Beth savours moments such as those in her work, when there is little actual work to do, leaving her free to listen to the stories and dappled memories that rise to prominence near the end of someone's life, times recited with clarity when life opened up and offered one or two moments of unsullied happiness. The sick and the weak are the beautiful broken, like clipped-winged birds that knew the sky until a greater power pulled them down. And just like those birds, the elderly or the extremely ill struggle with their new, limited, terrestrial cage. Her thoughts shift to Millie, to the sorrow she would be feeling on this night, in her quiet little home with the apple tree. She will visit Millie, she decides. They will have tea, sit on the porch, if she has one, have a discussion about life after Mary and whether she has ever baked something other than pie with those apples.

A sound punctures her thoughts. There is someone outside her door, knocking. The sound shocks her so intensely that she jolts upward in her seat, no less than if a pendulum had swung through the window and sliced through the air in the room.

"Beth?"

She recognizes James' voice immediately. She wonders how he was able to enter the building, yet the residents are often coming and going, knowingly or unknowingly letting others slip in or out. She keeps still, hoping he might go away, but he knocks again, and then she recalls, suddenly, his invitation to dinner. It would have taken place earlier this evening.

"I'll be right there," she rises from the chair, swallows a pang of guilt, and steps torpidly across the living room and onto the cool kitchen tiles. As she passes the small bronze-framed oval mirror near the door, she chides the tired, elegiac woman looking back at her, this half-mad, rather pitiable version of herself who looks older than her age. Her hair is plastered to her scalp on one side, the ends having frayed themselves into separate dry strands along her shoulders. She takes a moment to quickly straighten and smooth her clothes before giving up on the effort and opening the door.

"Hi, Beth," James says, apprehensively, as though some embarrassment came over him when she opened the door. Either he took note of her aura of melancholic discomposure, or she caught him in a moment of regret for visiting her at this late evening hour without notice.

"I'm sorry to come by unexpectedly, but it was a spur-of-the-moment," he tells her. "I was driving around nearby, and I wanted to see … I hope I'm not bothering you."

"No, come in," she says somewhat mechanically, yet softly.

James steps inside, and she offers him a cup of tea. Normally she might be somewhat panicked by an unexpected visit, yet presently, in her detached and mournful mood, a feeling as strong as panic is too weighty, too dense. The usual worries about how to present herself seem frivolous. There is too much awareness tonight of the sadness, of dust on piano keys.

"I haven't had tea in years," James admits.

"I can make coffee, if you'd rather have that. I only have instant, though."

"No, I'll try a cup of tea, if that's what you're having."

She sets the kettle on the stove element before switching it on. She stares blankly at the stove dial for a moment to avoid his glance, then says, apologetically, "I'm sorry for not going to the dinner with your family."

"It's fine. You didn't miss anything except for some loud kids running around, and my father telling a few bad jokes." James sits on one of the stools at the counter.

"Sounds like a typical family gathering," Beth says sardonically, taking the sugar and two cups from the cupboard. She thinks to herself in a vague, distrait way, that people are complex and difficult to count upon, so avoiding them is a negation of complexities.

"I suppose so," he shrugs. The silence hangs rudely between them as James absorbs the general aesthetic of the apartment, which is close to what he'd imagined; tasteful yet drab, minimalist, a bookshelf that spills some of its contents onto the floor and coffee table, everything awash in a dull linen colour. "I ran into Sally on the street today," he tells her. "I hadn't seen her since I got back, so we talked for a few minutes. She told me about her mom."

"Yes, I found out this morning."

"I told her we had lunch. She mentioned that you'd grown close to Mary."

"I had, in a way. We spent a lot of time together."

"So I hear," he says concernedly. "She was wondering how you were."

"That's nice of her," Beth says, for she had faintly wished this morning after leaving the agency building that Sally had reached out herself, despite them being no longer close, despite their exchanges settling over the last few years into something more transactional. It's hard to say whether she herself would have the presence of mind, once her own mother passes away, to reach out personally to her caregivers at the nursing home. There are two nurses in particular who've been exceptional with her mother. Eventually, after a week or two, after some strength of mind was regained, she would thank them for all they've done, though the words 'thank you,' accompanied by some flowers perhaps, hardly seems like enough. Beth goes to the fridge for milk, still thinking sympathetically of Sally for losing her mother in a way that was quick, yet long expected. It seems more favourable, she decides, for the mind to be kept relatively intact as the body deteriorates, rather than watch the mind deteriorate inside a body that is physically well. Sally could at least have meaningful conversations with her mother.

When the kettle finally whistles on the stove, Beth sprinkles the tea leaves on the strainer and pours hot water through to each cup; one for James, one for herself. She hands him a spoon, pulls a second stool around toward her, sits down, and all of this she does without looking directly at him.

"Beth?" he asks in a strange tone, as if he were saddened by something, and she finally meets his eyes. "Do you remember our spot by the water, under the oak?"

She smiles dimly, for she remembers the spot well. They, that is James, Sally, Jaime, Tom, and herself, would gather there, on the embankment at Sylvia River, and she sometimes had the thought that her ashes should eventually be set free and scattered there, for that was the place where she felt her best. She had always felt sated, it seemed, when she could walk to the river spot, sometimes alone, to watch the drifting beneath the shade of the enormous oak tree. It was like holy ground, a perfect place to die, to spread ashes, just as James prefers his ashes to be scattered at the farm, somewhere in a wheat field.

"Of course I do," she replies.

"Before lamentations of the future lost their sheen," James says prophetically, yet with a smile. "The young never know that it really is quite a thing to be young."

She envisions the fork in the river, the water continuing largely in one direction on its way to Sylvia Lake while breaking into a narrow creek in the other, the red covered bridge stretching over the creek, the wood of the inner walls carved with lovers' initials encircled by hearts and a few lyrics and odd sayings. She would run her fingers along the crevices, letting them bestow in her some varied depth of their meaning, something forlorn, something triumphant, something that gives a voice to the many suppressed inflections of being alive.

"I remember some of the words…the beauty, the moonlight, a holy dove, then maybe a blaze of light," Beth begins slowly in a faraway voice, awash in teary nostalgia for the uneven crevices that bore the letters.

"What's that?"

"Lyrics carved in the covered bridge. Those are the only ones I remember." She takes a deep breath then sips her tea. "Why do you ask?"

"It's not important, only when I ran into Sally, she told me the oak tree is gone."

"Oh, I didn't know," she says despondently, yet she should have considered that to be the case, for new condo buildings are visible above the tree line on that end of town.

As Beth sips her tea, James notices that her fingers are quivering, her cheeks colourless and hollow-like. She seems only half conscious of him sitting opposite her. Something about her demeanour cautions him against questioning her in any way.

He felt cynical leaving the family gathering, since spending an hour or so near Sylvia River. A picturesque boardwalk has replaced the rural, rugged area where the oak once stood. The steady light of the streetlamp, for the stars were scarcely visible through their artificial light, were somehow enough to bring about that dismal feeling one sometimes gets when they catch themselves in a moment of feeling so much older than they used to be. The younger version of himself that once loitered around on the couch grass seemed a thousand miles from the here and now; a scoured man who was once too dumb and happy to know that lying ahead of him were a series of failed romantic relationships and an absolute paucity of joy. The current version of himself, who watched the running river long enough to feel, for lack of a better way of saying it, his emotional core, couldn't be more fulfilled at the thought of inheriting that farmland. He got back in his car, the arching elms and pavement along Main Street narrowing like an arrowhead to this little apartment on Rosewood Road.

He peers at Beth, the delicate, pretty, quavering woman. He wants to take her in his arms, hold her until all else vanishes; the intermittent street noise, the now howling wind, their ghosts and weaknesses, the world who convinces us so thoroughly that we are never quite doing enough. Yet whatever told him not to question her hangs in the air. She seems on the verge of tears, not entirely unaccounted for if she cared for Mary, yet it seems to come from something graver than that. She's gathered into herself, staring vaguely past him.

"What do you think it means?" he asks, unsure of what to say, and always feeling uncomfortable in a silence. "The lyric you read."

"Well," Beth sighs, "I think the beauty of it is that you can apply it to anything you've ever read, or any song you've ever heard, even something someone once told you."

"You once told me that you wanted to put life in your pocket like a pebble."

"I did?"

"You did. It felt like an interesting epigraph. I wanted a tattoo of it so I'd never forget."

"Thankfully you didn't."

"I'll remember it anyway," James shrugs.

"It sounds like a thing I would have said as an alternate woman in a foreign life."

"We all have our foreign lives. It's strange. I felt the presence of my alternate life tonight after the dinner, or my foreign self. I went to that spot by Sylvia River, which is now covered by a boardwalk and street lamps by the way, and trying to see the stars through the light of a lamp, I had the thought that every single thing in life is hollow unless you can eventually find at least one other person to talk to who understands exactly what you saw, or felt. It doesn't even matter what that one thing is, or was, so long as you can talk to someone who about it, who can meet your eyes and understand," James says, knowing his words are wandering, his mind unnerved since leaving the boardwalk by a realization that all his relationships, all his romantic exploits, have been unfulfilling. It all seems now like a fruitless project, a doomed quest. And it isn't the grandeur of a relationship that matters, rather just to find, here and there, a connection over something, anything. It doesn't have to last long. A couple minutes, a few words, are sufficient.

"It's the result of moving home, to the farm, and my father, who's getting worse," James continues, for Beth remains silent and dreary, impenetrable, a docile figurine. She could be put behind glass and studied as a woman who inspires frustrated poetry. "All this deconstructing I've been doing lately. It's the harvest. It's the time in the field, the time to move slowly, to think. It seems that if I died tomorrow, heaven itself wouldn't measure up to the feel of it."

"I've said it before, that you're very poetic," Beth replies quietly. She reaches toward him and rubs his back, just for a moment, before returning her hand to the handle on her cup. "I'm sorry that he's getting worse," she says, recalling the skinny farmer seen around the hardware store from time to time. She sighs ruefully and considers that skinny farmer in a deathbed somewhere in town, then her own father and his glimmering glass, and the wind, howling outside and mixed with the sounds of rain. It's mournful, the wind tonight, deep and at times furious, like a heart-rending low note played with excessive force on a piano keyboard, further resonated by the damper pedal.

She listens to the long sounds, distinct and soaring, violently emotive, and somehow harmonious with her feeling tonight. She closes her eyes and muses over the way a sound can so easily strike a nerve and give involuntary rise to a despairing, or, just as easily, a wonderfully saccharine thought. As in a piece of music, notes come together perfectly the same way words come together in a brilliantly written literary composition, setting your mind on a certain course of emotion, capable of either dashing one's spirit or keeping it close. Some words and sounds are so infernally beautiful she could cry. Many things in life are beautiful in that infernal way, she reflects solemnly, like pricking your finger on a rose stem while breathing the scent of its perfume.

James asks, "Do you still play?"

"Play?"

"The piano," he says, nodding absently toward the dusty mass of rosewood, ivory, and copper strings, for he never knows what to say to a woman who says they are fine when clearly, they are not fine at all. Women, he thinks impatiently, are incomprehensible creatures with a slew of odd habits.

"No," Beth whispers, studying the dust laying across the yellowed ivory. "I miss it though. It's right here in front of me, but I miss it. I remember playing all those old classics—Bach, Beethoven, Strauss, Chopin. I knew so many by heart."

"I remember. Your mother played as well."

"Yes. It's a beautiful instrument," Beth says, then drifts into memories of the fanciful childhood daydreams conjured up on that bench, where she was the lead in an orchestra in a cavernous room with gilded balconies and velour seats. Beth takes a sip of her tea, peers longingly at the instrument. This piano could be a prop for a moody musical, lowered on golden vines to a pineplanked stage, a stunning and indestructible embodiment of music, covered in emerald lichen. And she feels all at once like nothing next to this image, that she has failed. She has not touched its keys in months, she has not visited Millie and her apple tree. Yet these things, the keys, the dangling apples, the low and dire sweeps of wind, and the feel of James' shirt against her palm a moment ago, seem suddenly isolated from her, rather herself isolated from them, as if she was not meant to take any part in them. Her presence here is an accident. The steps in the apartment above start, then stop again; little feet like the steady sound rain, like evenly played piano notes, like a heart beating. She senses a tear welling in her eye and sees in her mind a series of strange, disjointed images, long black slopes, sulphur currents, the thread of a savage weed catching in her hair as she tries to breathe. She is exhausted now; to rally against the white noise is as hopeless as quicksand.

"Beth, are you alright?" James asks, watching her a little fretfully as she sips one sip of her tea, then another. She compresses her lips, sighs, sets the cup down unsteadily.

"Yes," she says frailly and without meeting his eyes. She's thinking, still, of emerald lichen, of little feet, of black slopes and the incurable white noise, of Mary and Millie and the scent of roses, some yellow, some cream-coloured.

"I'm happy to listen, if you—"

"I'm fine," she tries again, unconvincingly. "I'm just tired. And…" she breaks off for a moment before continuing, "And I guess I'm not at my best tonight."

"Don't worry about it," he says gently. "I understand. You've had a rough day, finding out about Mary and all. I shouldn't have dropped in on you unexpectedly."

"It's alright," she asks, watching him set his cup down. "How did you enjoy your first cup of tea in years?"

"I'll stick with coffee from now on," he says mockingly, and watches as Beth manages the glint of a smile. She has both an air of fragility and of tenseness, like glass under pressure. The pained look in her eyes, betraying the smile, inspire in him a similar protective feeling that he had for her at the restaurant, only the feeling now takes a step toward something more resounding, and more loving. Something broke her down between when they were young and now. Time sometimes does that to people. He wants to heal it, whatever it is. Again the urge comes to gather her in his arms and not speak at all, or to speak all night, whichever might be the cure, for that, again, is the essence of what this life should be about; that rare link, a union of the hearts or minds, as if meeting one's counterpart, even if the meeting is temporary. It would be better, richer, to join with one's corollary in an interim flash than to sit on an uncomfortable stool sipping bland tea, waiting, wanting to hold a woman who doesn't seem to want to be held, then to head out into the night feeling unsatisfied and weak.

"Thank you anyway, for the tea."

"Thank you for being concerned," she says tenderly.

James rises from the stool. He meets her eyes, surprised again that some rustling quality about her he was once aware of in a more offhand way is now pushed to the forefront as the most appealing thing about her. It is so strange, he muses, how someone's attractiveness can change in one's eyes, or perhaps it's the mind accumulating masses of things over time and thus it is the perceptions of the eyes themselves that change.

Beth stands and takes a few steps toward the door. He follows slowly, already feeling weak, and also overcome with the strange feeling that he might never see her again.

"I hope you can rest, and I hope you feel better tomorrow," he says simply, and without waiting for a reply, he steps out of the apartment.

The moment the door clicks shut, the white noise spreads itself uninhibitedly across the room, like poison water released from a dam. It moves out from the shadow of the piano bench, down from its hovering place above the standing lamp, in through the keyholes like the liquid hallucinations of the insane woman from the article. The footsteps from above have stopped. Beth places her cup unsteadily on the counter and notices that at some point the rain had started, the water trickling nimbly down the windowpane. Something is wrong with her, she feels it clearly, something somehow both subtle and incredibly loud, like a muffled scream, an inner scream that conspires with the sadness to bring her, now, to a slow, somnolent collapse to the kitchen floor. She lays perfectly still with her cheek against the cool tile, her eyes carefully following the raindrops as they land then slide in broken paths, awkwardly meeting the paths of other sliding drops.

She thinks distractedly for a while about the rain, the origin of it, water condensing in clouds before falling in heavy droplets to the ground, then her mind drifts to thoughts of what her sister might be doing at this minute in her French city. Maybe walking along the Saint Laurence River to the south or Rivière-des-Prairies to the north, on cobbled streets and cobbled lanes, of course, with walkways to snack bars and bakeries or Théâtre Maisonneuve. All of these things distinguish themselves in her mind as rare and glittering and wonderful, so much so that she thinks it might be better never to see them in their true pathos, lest they lose their glitter and wonder.

Beth closes her eyes, listens indolently to the rain tapping against the glass, and in her mind sees the dark river water running along the embankment, the covered bridge, and herself, sitting in the tall twitch grass beneath the shadow of the oak. The water laps rhythmically against the shore, and laid over everything is a spectral calm, made prettier by the rose-gold sunlight reflecting across the water and the grass. Behind her, the further one goes from the water, the more the earth rises, and the thicker and wilder are the undergrowth and the pointed stems of new trees. She edges herself forward to immerse her bare legs in the river. With the tips of her toes she can feel the water-washed stones, and knows that this water has been polishing these stones for hundreds of years. She wades steadily further and further into the water, then without resistance, lets the current take her in. Her body flows passively along the centre of the river, her arms dramatically outstretched, angel-like, her eyes fixed on the golden sky. Her hair glides along the surface, long wet ribbons. The current strengthens and pulls her more hurriedly through the river, then under, until all of her body is immersed. From beneath the water she still sees the sky, its golden pink light dappled and frayed, the colours swimming and blending then breaking free of one another, then blending together again. She drifts lower, and she senses the cold riverbed. As she sinks into the earth, the cool soft mud gathers around her, cradling her in sympathy as she descends deeper and deeper into the absolute stillness of her funerary berth, at which point the roots of the oak tree, the rose-gold sky, the rippling water and the swaying weeds all declare her a welcome part of the riverbed.

Soon, sometime next week probably, Mary will be laid to rest in her own muddy funerary bed behind the Presbyterian church. She will be left in the darker realm.

Then, without warning, an idea flows into Beth's mind as she lies on the cool tiles, a silent epiphany, a revelation, a concept she's considered unconsciously yet now illuminates itself quickly, almost like a spark, as when someone strikes a match unexpectedly against the night, and in that moment, one glimpses the landscape ahead in an amended way, the path made perfectly clear.

Soon, she will die; she'll become one of those ethereal white wisps that flow out of windows and through clouds. One part of her rising to the sky, maybe, the other part in the muddy, darker realm, as in the benevolent riverbed, her bones cradled and mingling with the muck and minerals and tree roots. It's not a reckless thing to do, she thinks, but a very rational thing to do. She's nurtured these hopes for long enough, these short, self-imposed rest cures having failed; the chain on the door, the incessant sleeping and reading, the hours spent not speaking to anyone. And so this wind-stirred ripple in the water has grown and grown until this moment, laying utterly still and half-curled into herself on the floor, when it reached a breaking point against the shore, with nowhere left to go.

Only now, her decision sure and definite, can her mind and body work with more ease. Carefully, and with a new resolve, she pulls herself up.

Inside the great inner hall of the Eleanor Hicks Presbyterian Church, the funeral service is about to begin. Two inordinately large vases on either side of the altar hold a mass of cream-coloured roses, and beside each vase are three tall, white, lit candles. Each flame is surrounded by its own gold circle of light. High, stained glass windows illuminate the walls with their interweaving colours, looking both morbid and lovely. An organist sitting below a towering crucifix plays an eerie hymn; indeed, any music that issues from the pipes of an organ sounds eerie to Beth, no matter the song. The sunlight strikes the crucifix directly from top to bottom, as if the funeral had been planned for the hour when it would be lit perfectly. Beth makes her way slowly down the red-carpeted centre aisle, revering the windows and crucifix, then chooses an empty pew about halfway down the rows. A little further ahead, two dark haired men stand in the aisle. One man speaks quietly to the other, whose eyes seem solemnly fixed on the carpet. Beth recognizes them from a photograph in Mary's home as her sons. Angela and Alison are seated a few rows ahead, whispering to one another, while Sally sits very still in the front pew, facing straight ahead, beside her husband and son and a young woman Beth doesn't recognize. Then there is Millie, wearing an olive-green cloche hat that strikes Beth as wonderfully vintage and feminine. The twenty people or so in the cavernous-like room are either congregated more to the front, or scattered somewhat distantly from one another in ones or twos. The open coffin sits front and centre at the head of the aisle, parallel with the pews, and seems placed in the room the way a bouquet is propped perfectly in the middle of a dining room table, for maximum viewing.

This morning when she awoke, feeling restless within the walls of the apartment, Beth decided she would pay a final visit to her mother at the nursing home. She arrived early enough to help her mother change and have breakfast, and then they sat outside in the courtyard for an hour or so. The staff had already given up on maintaining the summer flowers, so from now on they'll be left to their own devices, at the mercy of the elements. Some of the petunias held on stubbornly to their pigments of purples and yellows, while others were already suffused from stem to tip with a dank, earthy brown. Neither of them ever had a green thumb, and so instead of discussing the flower garden, Beth and her mother talked here and there about random things, like the weather, what sort of meals the home would be serving for lunch and dinner. Mostly though, they gazed relaxedly at the withering flowers in wooden troughs, stranded between life and death.

The eerie organ hymn comes to an end, and a suited man near the organ, presumedly one of the church members, quietly drapes the closed half of the coffin in a white pall. The minister, a monastic figure in a white robe, approaches the altar as the few men and women still milling around in the aisle take their seats. A coarse cloth is lifted from a book on the altar, and the minister begins to read aloud.

"What man is he that desireth life, and loveth many days, that he may see good? Keep thy tongue from evil, and thy lips from speaking guile. Depart from evil, and do good; seek peace, and pursue it. The eyes of the Lord are upon the righteous, and his ears are open unto their cry."

Through the reading, her eyes stay fixed on the altar, on its roses and white candles, and on Mary, whose nose and forehead and chin are visible at their tips over the side of the coffin. She resolves that an open coffin is much more depressing than a closed one. Indeed, everything inside the hall, from the stained glass to the mysterious ornaments and cups, seem depressing and foreign. The room has less the feel of a church than it does a sort of crypt—too morbid to be a place of comfort. There's not enough light in the room, not enough movement. There are bowed heads, clasped hands, closed eyes, people who appear precisely like those she imagines gather here every Sunday, seeking reconciliation, praying for those lost and never found. Indeed, the only half-cheerful thing in the room is Millie's vintage olive-green hat and matching dress.

Beth feels suddenly apart from the room, rather like a fish out of water, an intruder, covertly watching the private undertakings of a separate class of people from behind a parted curtain. The ritual proceedings are not as foreboding as she had imagined in all those times passing by the church, not quite as menacing as she'd imagined, yet the fish out of water feeling clings to her. She belongs here only temporarily, only for Mary. For there's still very little to say about the validity of God, and she leans quickly now into the belief that there is nothing more above the ground than the varying shades of blue surrounding the birds, clouds, and stars. No unearthly awards await her on the other side. On the other side, only rest, only peace.

Millie then rises from the pew and steps to the podium and delivers a brief and gracious eulogy, one where anything unflattering is left out, and there were certainly some unflattering things about Mary's life—the estrangement from her sons, and the drinking, just to name two. Beth had come to know about all of it. Lives are reassessed in a more favourable way after death, it often seems, and maybe that's a better way of going about it. It's better to be compassionate and well-meaning. Four or five pews ahead of her, and through the shoulders of others, she observes Sally dabbing her eyes with a tissue.

Beth considers what her own reassessment will be. It's perplexing to consider this day as her last; not waking up in her apartment tomorrow morning still seems like an abstract sentiment. She's left a note, already written and waiting on the nightstand for whomever. She didn't need to stay awake until the small hours writing and re-writing, leaving discarded crumples of papers on the floor. She simply sat on a stool by the kitchen counter and wrote a clear, short note, had a long shower, then slept surprisingly well. She has requested no funeral, and everything in this room gives rise to a feeling that she has made the right choice. The pained figure on the crucifix and the yellow flames wavering and flickering joylessly on the candlewick mean nothing to her, the intended message of the sermon too dim, too unmoving, despite herself being Presbyterian by birth. Although the sightless figures painted in a mosaic across the stained glass windows seem oddly appropriate, given they depict the story, in shimmery colours patterned from one end of the room to the other, of the heavy cross being carried to Calvary along a stone street known appropriately as the Way of Sorrows.

A few more words are said at the podium, then the congregation is asked to stand for a final hymn and benediction. Afterward, the minister steps down from the altar and offers condolences to Sally, her brothers, and the rest of the family seated along the front pew. He returns to the altar and allows a brief pause with everyone still standing, his eyes closed and his head bowed as if in remembrance. Finally, Millie returns to the podium.

"Please join us in the next room for a light lunch and refreshments," she says, smiling genuinely.

The small congregation makes their way with circumspection toward another room at the rear of the hall, feet shuffling hesitantly along the red carpet. Beth joins them in the aisle, uncertain whether she should stay or leave, but a balding man in front of the main exit extends his arms as if directing traffic, and she feels herself steered along with the rest of the mourners into the brightly lit refreshment area. Fine, she thinks, she will stay a little while longer, if only to offer Sally her condolences. When she is gone, there will be no one in need of condolences, and so in that way the act seems like a less shameful or wrong thing to do. Her mother, thankfully, won't miss her. At least this was her thought at first, but as she thinks further on it, her mother might indeed miss her, though not terribly or in a specific sort of way. Rather she might have a vague, far-off sense that some modicum of familiarity—the sound of a voice, an essence of touch—has left her, but she won't quite know what it is. But it won't break her heart, Beth convinces herself; she'll be fine, and well cared for. And then there's Holly, who will initially be very shaken by the news, and maybe she'll lament and become nostalgic about the past for a while, but she shouldn't have her life interrupted for too long. Really, the only one Beth has any sympathy for is whomever finds her in the apartment, after she has done it. She pushes the thought aside, for the unpleasantness of someone finding her is in no way avoidable. Besides, once she loses consciousness it becomes as incidental as everything else. Her absence at work, the disposal of her belongings, how her sister will be notified, or by whom; these things will no longer be her concern. They will not matter. Life will stop, unreservedly. All the trivialities and all the things that have mattered—the dust on piano keys, the sadness and laughing walls, the memories of friends and times past; all of it will simply end, as easily and painlessly as the blowing out of a candle, the cut of a thread, the turn of a page. Quick, seamless, forgotten.

At the centre of the bright room is a long table clothed in white linen. There are trays of fresh fruit and small sandwiches, and a glass bowl of punch sits at the end. Angela and Alison, each with a glass of punch in hand, approach her.

"You made it," Angela says. Under the bright bulbs her skin appears more awash with freckles than usual, her hair an even lighter shade of strawberry-blonde. She wears a green floral-patterned dress. To Beth she looks beautiful, almost decorous.

"Of course," Beth replies, then says with sincerity, "It was important to me."

"It was a nice service," Angela remarks. "And it was nice that her sons were able to come. In the year or so I worked with Mary, she rarely talked about them. I wasn't sure they'd bother, if I'm being honest."

"I didn't know she had sons, but I was only at Mary's house three or four times," Alison admits.

"Oh, they're a lot older than Sally," Angela informs her. "They didn't all get along, but I don't really know the reasons for it. Only that they didn't talk often. It was right for them to come to their mother's funeral, though, whether or not they were close."

"Now I wish I'd had the chance to know her better," Alison says.

"It'll take time, but you'll get to know the other clients. I'm sure you'll develop good relationships with them," Beth gently reassures her, though she is beginning to feel a little on edge. It's too warm in this room, too bright, and the small amount of people seem like too many.

"Poor Sally, I hope she is alright," Alison says diffidently, emphatically, and the three of them turn to look at Sally and her husband, who are standing next to a bowl of punch and the olive-green Millie, the presumably lonely woman she failed to visit, who appears as an embellished leaf holding a crochet purse. By her expressions, Beth is reminded of her kindness, her clean essence, as if she were not a leaf, but once again a bird perched blithely on a branch, motherly, whisperingly, assuring the congregates with certainty, you are safe, everything is as it should be, it is enough to have survived such a day.

"I hope so too," Angela replies, "It's a shame when one sibling is left to handle everything on their own. By the way, Beth, how is Susan doing? Has she settled in okay?"

Initially startled by the question, Beth remembers that Angela had looked in on her mother a few times before she was moved to the care home, so it was obvious she would ask today, albeit today of all days. "She's doing okay, she's well cared for."

"I'm glad," Angela says compassionately, then takes a sip of her punch and looks out the window. "At least the rain has stopped for the day."

"Yes, it turned out to be a nice day," Alison concurs. "We haven't had many of those."

"I don't remember a fall with this much rain," Angela adds.

"Yes, so much rain after such a dry summer."

Beth hears the words, but they seem too far away, too immaterial. The other things in her mind are much more potent—the note on the nightstand, the irrecoverable mother in a nursing home, the open coffin in the next room, the white candles still ablaze.

"Yes, it's a lovely day," Beth says unsteadily, and a bit too cheerfully. The two women meet her eyes; she gathers into herself. Their glances are tender, benign, too traitorous somehow to the belief that all good is lost. "I should be going."

"Sure," Angela says after a slight pause. "It was nice to see you."

"You too," Beth replies. Politely, but quickly, she says goodbye to Alison, then takes a few steps toward Sally. She is still standing with her aunt, the motherly bird, who rubs Sally's shoulder gently and whispers something in her ear. Beth watches them for a moment. She is overcome with a sense of remoteness, a foreigner among strangers, yet at the same time she is overcome with affection for Sally. She wants to go somewhere with her, pull her away from the wreckage and set off somewhere airy and unspoiled, like that spot by the river, where they would reveal their broken parts, sift through the pieces, make sense of them in a way they aren't able to do on their own. They would reassure one another that possibility is a thing that exists, as true and sheltering as the shade of the oak. It seems suddenly possible that they can be that way again.

Yet she knows she will not go with Sally to the river, nor will she visit Millie on her porch with a view of the fable-like apple tree. She will turn toward the door then hurry alone to her apartment. She will leave this, all this, and she will go to sleep. Sleep is the most peaceful reward at the end of a day, this day more than any other. Beth pauses at the doorway to look back briefly into the brightly lit room. She watches the others sip punch, sees Angela and Alison speaking lightly and easily with one another, feeling all at once resentful. It's so careless, so forbidding that they will continue about their day while she is at home, facing her own demise. She pleads quietly for one of them to see, to approach her and say no, wait, there are good days ahead. But no one approaches her; no one conceives that the woman in a funereal dress in the doorway has been privately plotting her escape. They sip, they stand, they whisper, they do not see.

Beth steps out of the bright room and re-enters the dark one, the great inner hall lit only by the variegated light emanating from the stained glass windows and the barely flickering flames on the white candles. The empty room is atmospheric and beautiful. She steps reservedly back along the red aisle that traverses the church behind the velvet-lined pews, looking around, feeling strangely enraptured with the place. Perhaps because she now has the space to herself. When her eyes come to rest on the casket at the head of the main aisle, waiting, as per the program, for a private burial with the family, morbid curiosity takes hold of her.

She approaches the altar, timorously, and glances somewhat

nervously into the open casket. Mary is yellow and opaque, arms gently folded across her stomach, her thin lips painted an exaggerated crimson. She looks somehow both elegant and repulsive, her body presented as a sentimentalized attempt to convey a state of peace and rest, but Beth sees none of that. She's shocked instead by how unlike Mary this body appears. She is surprised, also, not only by the lack of peace, but merely by the utter lack of anything. There is a peculiar hollowness in the casket, and in consonance, a peculiar blankness sweeps through her mind. Mary is gone, having probably flown in a white wisp out of a hospital window. She is gone, and only Beth is left standing alone on this altar, exposed to the bleak inference that death is.

And she, too, is already gone, or nearly gone, herself a bleak inference, a ghost, a white wisp caught between the sky and ground, the light and the mud. She has been moving steadily further and further away from herself, in subtle ways, giving in to this sadness, day by day, until the pure centre light of her being has become a distant, glimmering thing she can no longer touch. And yet, standing here, looking at what was once Mary, where the flame is clearly completely extinguished, Beth suspects that perhaps for her, it's still there, simply hidden, the hint of a flame that hasn't gone out—small and tapered, but not yet quelled. Beth glances at the high white candles burning assuredly above the roses, and follows their reach. Some of the more hidden, shadowy areas of the room are untouched by the candlelight, but not all. Many parts are illuminated by it, and despite those darker areas, the light paints in front of her a warm image of golden effulgence, and added to it are the metallic reds and blues and yellows from the windows. Thus despite the darkness, light still breaks in from all around.

Beth looks at Mary's closed eyes and trembles, a visceral reaction not entirely distressing, yet carries elements of distress, as well as a glint of something being rinsed or driven out of her mind, expelled in this moment from her body as much as Mary's soul, or being, had been expelled invisibly from her own. Beth gives her one final glance, a knowing glance, as if sharing an understanding with this immobile version of Mary, then turns to leave. She moves quickly, making her way down the red aisle between the pews, then pushes one of the heavy wooden doors open with both hands. With a stunning burst of sunlight and traffic noise, Beth rejoins the land of the living. She descends the stone steps and makes her way down the sidewalk, unsure of where she is headed but moving swiftly nonetheless, letting the wind brush away the residue of the afternoon. A car sounds its horn nearby, inadvertently drawing her attention to a woman on the stooped entrance of the bakery bending down to scold a disobedient child as the sweet scents of scones and croissants unfurl around them, and an older man wearing a fedora on the street corner trying to light a cigarette while waiting to cross, turning halfway from the wind and using his upper body to protect the flame. Beth considers going to the nursing home, but quickly decides against it, thinking anywhere indoors would be too close and confining for her wandering frame of mind. She feels instinctively a need to spend the rest of the afternoon outside, despite the frigid weather, with the trees and falling leaves and whatever birds haven't yet flown south. It seems, as she turns the corner and heads north on Richland Road, that she'd left the church and entered directly into a kind of fog, where the sounds seem muffled and the sights blurred, a miasma reminiscent of the detachment that directly follows a time of fiercely absorbed reading on the sofa, when a few minutes are needed to gather herself and believe in her surroundings. It's a reverent, almost preternatural turn of mind. The man in the hat and the scolding woman on the bakery stoop were faceless, half-perceived, and she was thus only half among them, a tall, lithe figure dressed in mourning black flowing silently past, unheeded.

After an hour of walking aimlessly along residential streets, Beth returns to the centre of town. Not wanting to go home and still wanting to be outdoors, she heads to the park. The streets are getting busier, people coming home from work, children walking home from school. She steps onto the grass, slips off her shoes, and gingerly walks to a wooden bench, taking her place in the worn centre. The grass is cold against her bare skin, which incites a kind of physical vigilance, or a hyper-awareness of senses, one which makes her mind feel suddenly more sharpened than it had been while wandering through town. She keeps her eyes sternly fixed on the circular fountain in the middle of the park and the water that falls in weak, measured streams along its four sides.

The fresh air has done little to clear her mind, though it seems her attention is being directed away from vaguer thoughts of death and more toward things that are directly visible—the stone fountain, the green and yellow leaves tossed by the wind, the tawny stems of dying flowers lining the gravel path that runs from one end of the park to the other. But even those secular things are tinged with an element of unreality. She imagines that everyone from the funeral has left by now, the lights switched off, the half-empty trays of sandwiches and fruit covered with plastic and placed in the fridge. And while Mary waits to be laid forever in peace and covered with flowers, those who mourn her have departed the dual realms of the church, one of faith and light and the other of serpents and shadows, and returned to the ordinary, everyday realm.

After sitting for what seems like an eternity on the wooden bench, the cold wind starts to bother her. Even so, she is not yet ready to leave. She is glad to be here, inhaling and exhaling, listening to the sounds the town makes at the end of an ordinary, everyday afternoon. It's only the third week of fall, but the sky is already struggling to fight the dusk. There are more shades of orange and pink above now than white and blue. It seems acutely unjust, somehow, that Mary is not seeing this day, not seeing this sky, not seeing the wind blow this leaf off this branch, not hearing the fluttering sounds of this bird's wings as it flies from that branch of its own accord. And suddenly, Beth is intensely aware of her own fortune of seeing this sky, this leaf, this branch, this bird. And after having envisioned death as a very desirable thing, she is fully aware that she is, in fact, much more content being out here in the trees than she was while in the same room as a coffin, a cross, an organ issuing its sad tremolo while tears are dabbed away below stained glass windows.

Though it's hard not to regard death as emblematic of peace, it's also hard to deny that for her to actively seek death, to end one's life willfully, is emblematic of many other things—surrendering, quitting, renouncing this gift of life, whatever it is. Maybe life's mysteriousness is why she can't put this subtle, unexpected change of spirit into words. It's an individual sensation, a restorative feeling, a singular shift in the air. She thinks once more of the horrific sight of Mary, her yellowed face blended with the flickering candlelight, before her mind drifts to an older, prettier memory, that of her mother sitting next to her at the piano, a simple and beautiful prelude by Bach resting upon the bracket. A prelude, she said, is a hopeful thing. It's a declarative introduction, an opening to a larger movement. They're usually brief, yet long enough for the listener to pull from the melodic motifs a sense of what's to come through the piece, while remaining elusive enough to allow for unexpected bursts of notes that provide so much more than whatever was anticipated; an extravagance overflowing from a quick, humble cadence. Like Mary's beloved flowers, Beth ruminates, the cream-coloured petals that grew plush and lovely from the cool mud of the earth.

The cold is less bearable now, having worked its way steadily through her thin dress coat and permeated her bones. Beth shudders, slips on her shoes, rises from the bench, and exits the park. The streets have grown quiet, the children have all gone home. The sign in the florist's window has been flipped from open to closed, and in the second-storey window of an apartment building, a lamp is lit. Beth takes a step forward. The sun is setting on this ordinary autumn day. There will be another, tomorrow, if she chooses.

With a mutual love for literature, they've had their share of arguments. Beth had a deep love for Margaret Laurence, while her mother had an equally deep love for Margaret Atwood. During their breakfasts at Le Beau Café, their disputes over which of the Margarets was the more talented storyteller became so overwrought, so recurring, that sometimes the discussions became almost less about them intellectually exploring a variety of angles and avenues, and more of a fun, irrational hobby, where neither needed to make sense of their opinions. They were referred to as The Margaret Arguments.

Beth took only a small amount of milk in her tea, while Susan preferred a sugary coffee. On the table between them were torn sugar packets, teaspoons, and empty plates pushed aside, all evidence of a deep discussion. The walls of the café, with its lime green colour made more pale by years of sun, seemed to give the place a feeling of embedded calm; just outside was the bustling world, and inside, a green, well-lit retreat, a clean room in which to feel safe and catch your breath. In the light of the window they sat across from one another, each with their apparent certainty that the Margaret they loved was the Margaret more deserving. It wouldn't have mattered if one had changed their mind; they argued for mere pleasure.

"Atwood is a wonderful poet," Susan said during one of their more serious discussions. It was a bright June morning at the café, and her preference for poetry over novels was on full display. "Yes, she's also a novelist, but in my eyes she's a poet first and a novelist second, which is why her novels feel so poetic. It's what makes her far and away the better writer."

"You always say that, Mom, as though poetic writing would definitely make for better writing."

"Of course it does," Susan replied impulsively. She often pulled at this thread during their discussions, her belief being that the beauty of writing depended on the elusiveness of the plot and characterization. She argued that if a novel held on to an element of mysteriousness, then it deserved more respect.

"I don't think so," Beth countered. "I think a little mystery or mysticism is fine, but I don't believe it's necessary for a good novel. Novels can be different. One way of writing doesn't have to be regarded as better or worse than another."

"For the most part, yes, of course. But it never seems as special reading the imagery in a novel when it's written in more of a novelistic way."

"Novelistic?"

"As in, less poetic, more rhetorical, like an exposition," Susan explained thoughtfully while tearing open another sugar packet.

Beth sat quietly for a moment, mulling that over, gently tapping her fingers against her lips. "I suppose I prefer a more straightforward style of writing. I love imagery, but I also like having the writer tell me what the imagery means, and to be informed of which dots I'm supposed to be connecting."

"It's more powerful when the writer lets the reader form their own connections." Susan stirred her coffee before continuing. "It's more powerful to show the reader what's happening, rather than simply tell them. Telling the reader what's happening implies the writer doesn't trust that they're bright enough to figure it out for themselves."

"Show, don't tell."

"Exactly."

"I think that's an overrated theory," Beth remarked confidently, sipping her tea. "I think it's bolder to tell, openly, rather than gesture." During these breakfasts in which Beth was going up against a former English teacher, it behooved her to remain confident in all her arguments.

"We'll just have to agree to disagree," her mother shrugged. She raised her coffee and took another sip.

"For today," Beth said, lifting her tea, and from over their cups they smiled at one another knowingly.

Though they spoke of many other things during their time together, their discussions on books and writers is what Beth misses most. And so, after passing Le Beau Café on her way home from the park last night, she became consumed with thoughts of her mother. By the time she unlocked her door and stepped into the apartment, she was consumed further by thoughts of all the literary characters she'd read about and loved, and how words, put together in the right order, can jump off the page and make the world seem beautiful. Her conceptions were shaped early on by the stories her mother read to her, then by the novels and short stories she chose herself. Those stories painted a world in her mind that seemed mesmerizing and boundless.

Which is why she is not surprised to find herself now at Grape Lane's New and Used Bookstore, doing what was always among her favourite things to do—walking through the aisles, running her fingers along a row of novels, sifting through pages, reading passages, and like an eager child picking out a pet, trying to decide which of them to rescue and take home. The main room, where the new books are kept, is high, wooden, and inadequately lit, but the dim lighting adds to its charm. The floors creak and moan, and browsing in the non-fiction section gives the feeling of standing at a slight tilt; if she were to put a marble on the floor here, it would roll directly toward the large sunken area at the back, where the used books are stored, and where textbooks and encyclopedias, which probably no one will ever buy, line the walls. Both rooms smell musty, and from anywhere in the store the swinging bell above the door can be heard.

A visit to the bookstore is not an unusual or surprising way to spend a morning, but to her it feels like an extravagance. There's an antiquated sense of lavishness here, a kind of forgotten opulence, or of something opulent being taken for granted, like dust settling on a majestic heirloom. The store almost has the feel of a temple with its high walls and reserved silence, but also its offer of enlightenment. So many things in the world that have been known or imagined can be found within these walls. And yet, above all else, this place offers a sense of pause and remove from the ongoing world.

The previous evening when she arrived home from the park, she closed the door and removed her black dress coat. Without hesitation, as though it were the most obvious thing to do, she retrieved the note from her nightstand, returned to the kitchen, and threw it away in the same impassive manner in which she'd written it the night before. The note landed on top of the garbage heap, exposed, so she shuffled the other papers and wrappers around until it was fully hidden. Then she grabbed the dead daisies and tossed them, pot and all, into the trash. The pot of wilted white, pink-tinged daisies, which had stood out as a symbol of her sadness, her loss, her failures, her destiny, was instantly defeated by a thoroughly cleansing act. Her mind wandered rapidly as she stared for a few moments at the dry, discarded petals, yet in another way, she felt cooler and more self-possessed. Now I can breathe, she thought simply, now I can start over.

She awoke uncharacteristically early, still on the sofa, still in her funerary dress, the morning already having drawn a pale and whimsical light across the walls, piano, and bookshelf. She could think of only one place to go. She showered and dressed quickly, feeling exalted by this very simple idea—the unremarkable plan to go to Grape Lane's New and Used Bookstore and buy herself a book.

She left the apartment without checking the time and found herself having to wait twenty minutes at the entrance before the doors were unlocked. With nothing to do but wait, she paced back and forth on the pavement in the cool air, ruminating over the day before. She thought about how the emotions of the afternoon, which altered as they ran late into the evening, had affected her in such a way that she became, surprisingly, more assured than she had in an awfully long time. The more she ruminated in front of the entrance, and even after they unlocked the door and let her inside, the more certain she became that she didn't dislike her life, she only disliked the sadness that surrounded it. Life, at its core, is a thing she loves, and apprehending this thought painted the walls of her mind a completely different colour. This brighter, clearer colour prompted her to think that it wasn't necessary for her to like everything about life in order to love it. She didn't have to love every last stitch of every last thread of every fibre. She didn't need to know for certain whether the sadness would always be around to taint her life, or if happiness would always seem as elusive as it does now. Maybe all she needs is to wake up each morning with one good thing in mind to look forward to. Today, she is sifting through books in an abundant, ambient bookstore, and later on she might visit her mother, her beautiful friend. Those are two perfectly wonderful things.

And so there would have been a purpose to watering her daisies even though it would eventually die, just as there is purpose in building a castle in the sand despite the rising tide, just as there is purpose in gathering wood and kindle for a fire only for the wood to crumble to the grate and leave the room cold again. The flower, the castle, the fire; each raises the spirit, calms the spirit, adds a bit of joy, a bit of warmth and pleasantness, for as long as it lasts. Then, you do it again. Go back to the florist, buy another flower, build another sandcastle, gather some more wood. There's a coherence to these things; they let shine through what matters most, which is indeed an indefinable thing, but is best described, perhaps, as life itself, a string of sentimental and un-sentimental elegies, some of them quick, some prolonged. We love, then endure, then love again, a series of affecting moments. Watering a pot of daisies, smelling their musk, enjoying the way a bouquet brightens the room; that's a moment. Holding her mother's hand, comforting her; another moment. And they add up, these moments. They should be acknowledged, harnessed, held in the palm and cherished like a rare stone. A thing within this rare and precious stone is what matters most, the thing that makes the day worth living through and offers a reason to carry on with the next.

On the shelf with last names of authors beginning at 'L', she finds Margaret Laurence's memoir, *Dance on the Earth*. It's a book she's always wanted to read, but surprisingly never has. On her way to the cash register she passes a shelf of journals. It's been years since she's kept a journal, yet almost instinctively she picks up a dark purple one with the word 'Journal' etched in yellow print on the cover. She buys a two-pack of pens along with it, pays the woman behind the counter, and returns to the street with her purchases in a brown paper bag with handles. She already knows where she will go next. Le Beau Café is close by, so she makes her way through blowing leaves to the corner of Grape Lane and Pine Street. Clean, bright, and usually quiet, it's the perfect place to read or write, or read and write. It's also a good, comfortable place to think, and she feels there are a lot of things to think about. Mainly, what she has to look forward to tomorrow, and the next day, and how to keep herself from falling back into the abyss.

She arrives at the café, pushes the glass door open and steps inside. Here there is also a bell above the door and it sounds loudly in the small space, which is inhabited by only two other patrons. Beth orders a tea at the counter, then seats herself at the same table where she used to sit with her mother, near the back of the room, the one often most brightly lit by the sun. Yet even now, with the sun hidden behind the clouds, this table feels the most hospitable. Near the napkin dispenser is a small empty jam jar, cleaned out and used as a vase, in which sits two tall, obviously fake orchids—one white, one yellow.

She sips her tea, takes the journal and pens from the bag. There was a time when putting her thoughts down in a journal helped to make sense of them, and so with that purpose in mind she'll start doing it again. She opens the journal to a fresh page and begins writing the date.

"Hi, Beth."

Beth glances up to see Sally approaching her table. She holds a cup of takeout coffee in her hand and looks quite pale, almost ashen, as though any colour that was still present in her face at the funeral has now been completely drained from her skin. Almost immediately, Beth reminds herself that she was never very close to her at the funeral, so she could be mistaken about that.

"Hi, Sally, how are you doing?"

"I'm fine," she shrugs. "Are you here alone?"

"Yes," Beth says, closing the journal. "I was at the bookstore. I felt like getting out for a while."

"I had the same instinct. I have an appointment at the bank in an hour, just to finalize some of my mom's things, but I left early because I wanted to get out of the house." She pauses to wistfully acknowledge the outside. "I've just been walking around."

Beth nods in understanding, then says, "You can join me if you want."

"Are you sure? I'd like that."

Before Beth can make the invitation more official, Sally slips off her coat, hangs it around the back of the chair and sits down. Though she looks pale and tired, she still looks very pretty. Her skin appears clear and firm, semilucent, only a little timeworn, and all of these qualities somehow combine to make her seem even more dignified, like an old jewel. Beth never admitted it aloud, but she was often envious of Sally's beauty, envious of Sally for so many things. And then she notices the string of pearls around Sally's neck.

"Were those your mom's pearls?"

"Yes, they were," Sally says, placing her palm against the necklace protectively. "How did you know?"

"She was wearing them on Sunday," Beth grimaces slightly, remembering it as the day Mary had her fall. "I took them off for her when I helped her shower, then left them on a towel to keep them dry."

"That's where I found them when I was cleaning that afternoon."

Sally is still touching the pearls, gently twirling them between her fingers. "I hadn't seen this necklace in years. I don't know where she dug it up from, which means she probably roamed the house on her own. Which she shouldn't have done. Anyway, I knew she kept them in a wooden box, so when I found that on the table beside her chair, I put them away in one of her drawers, but after she passed, I took them out again. They were my grandmother's pearls, before they were Mom's."

"They look nice on you."

"Do you think so?" Sally says, smiling, and glancing at the fake, but pretty, orchids in a jam jar. "I think she would be happy that I kept them."

"I'm sure she would be. And I'm sorry I didn't say this to you at the funeral, but I'm truly sorry about Mary, about your mom."

"Thank you. And I'm sorry for you too."

"Why?"

"Well, I know how well you two got along. Probably a lot better than she and I did. Mom never held back in complaining to me about the care staff, believe me, but she never complained about you."

"That's so nice to hear." Beth smiles to herself. "I was never sure whether she liked me."

"My mother was only verbal about the things she disliked," Sally says soberly.

"So, a lack of compliment should be taken as a compliment?" Beth asks mockingly.

"Exactly. Still, I know she wasn't the easiest person to deal with. I hope she didn't give you a hard time."

"No, most of the time she was perfectly pleasant with me. And I took everything with a grain of salt when she wasn't."

"Probably the right approach," Sally says, before gazing out the window again.

Beth follows her gaze and sees a stray white cat tottering along Pine Street, smelling things, chasing leaves. For a few moments the two women sit quietly, sipping their warm drinks, watching the white cat, each self-consciously waiting for the other to speak. Beth stirs more milk into her tea. She thinks of her own mother and how her death likely, because of her age, remains far away, although it can be hard to say. Some live far longer than expected while others slip away suddenly, only to be found by a shocked staff member the next morning. It's only a half-life her mother is living, when the mind has mostly fled but the heart keeps beating just the same. It's a cruel and maniac disease.

"I suppose it's a blessing, my mother being gone," Sally says reflectively, still watching the white cat. "At least, that's what Jaime says, that it's better this way, because she's no longer in pain, and because she would rather have died than go to a nursing home."

Beth, uncertain of how to respond at first, decides to side with Jaime. "I would agree that it's a blessing, even if it doesn't seem that way."

"She was so confused in the end. You should have seen her in the hospital, Beth, crying out for my dad, then for her mom. We were able to calm her down eventually, but even so, it was horrible."

"Yes, I noticed a few times when she was confused, or just coming out of sleep, that she'd ask for her mom. I heard once that the older a person gets, the more their mind gravitates toward people from their past. The reason being, when there's nothing really in life ahead of them, their mind starts to wander increasingly backward."

"That's an interesting perspective."

"It's just something I heard," Beth says, and then when she sees Sally's grave expression, adds, "I hope it wasn't too morbid a thing to say."

"No, not at all. It's fine. Everything is fine, fine, fine." Sally trails off, speaking, it seems, more to herself than to anyone in particular. To Beth, she also seems very preoccupied, or rather like someone who has been preoccupied for so long that they are now emptied. She appears weakened, like a woman who has been fighting and losing a succession of small battles, and could think of nothing better to do than take temporary leave in a small café. It then occurs to Beth that they have both come here for the very same reason, and so she muses that perhaps Sally has also grown into a woman of sorrow, a woman who goes about her day competently enough, all the while waging a silent, secret war against the white noise.

"It's been a too long since we've done this," Beth remarks in order to break the silence and say out loud what she now sincerely believes.

"What do you mean?"

"It's been too long since you and I have sat together like this. In fact, it's been ages since we've even talked, outside of when we briefly ran into one another in town or at your mom's house."

"Yes, except the topic of conversation was still my mother," Sally says plaintively.

"Then we can always talk about something else. Like your paintings. Do you still paint?"

"Yes, I do," Sally begins slowly, "but for a long time I didn't. For a long time, I put it aside almost entirely, and for years I started paintings without ever finishing them. Lately, though, I've been painting more often."

Sally thinks of the exhibit, the booked gallery, the sent invitations. She was being modest when she said she is painting more often; the truth is, she's been painting like a mad woman. There are now more canvases than she can fit on The Ochre Gallery walls, and all of them sufficiently emblematic of the state of mind she now finds herself in—more optimistic, enlivened, hopeful, like the common cliché of a lowly caterpillar that breaks affectedly from its cocoon to spread its wings as a butterfly. She feels that way; sprung from a drab place, having shed some invisible yet dense outer casing, and emerging into a place that feels far better, even though much of it remains unknown. She feels, physically and figuratively, lighter and freer than before.

"You always painted so beautifully. I used to love going to your exhibits, especially the ones in the city, in that Ochre gallery with the high ceiling. I don't know why I remember that place so clearly. Maybe because your canvases were so big, they went from floor to ceiling." Beth then surprises herself by adding, "I envied you then."

"You did?" Sally's eyes widen.

"Of course I did. You were talented. Everyone thought so. You seemed to have all these good things in front of you."

In saying that, something in Sally seems to surface, something Beth interprets as sanguine, before just as quickly sinking back down to the bottom.

"I had no idea you felt that way," Sally says, looking at the woman opposite her and feeling a long-lost need to confide. "To be honest, for the last ten or fifteen years, I've just felt so down about painting. Maybe disheartened is a better word. It didn't seem to have a purpose in my life anymore. When I was young, I thought painting would take me somewhere. I don't know where. Essentially, I abandoned it because it wasn't bringing to my life what I wanted it to bring to my life."

"You mean money?"

"Well, yes, but that's only a small part of it," Sally says vaguely. "Money would have been nice, and I did manage to make some, but even if money was the only return I got out of painting, it wouldn't have made any difference. I mean, money wouldn't have fulfilled me. It wouldn't have given me purpose."

"What did you want?" Beth asks contemplatively, though she has a glimmering idea of what Sally intends to say. Something about life and the elusiveness of what it means, maybe, something that refers to the intangible things that we want, that we believe will make us happy if only we had them, a light emanating wanly, too vaporous and obscure to wrap your hand around. Beth again follows her gaze across the street and sees that the stray cat is no longer there. There are only mounds of wet leaves, so clumped and high along the curbs that they threaten to clog the storm drains.

"You'll only laugh."

"I will not," Beth states obstinately, wrinkling her forehead. "We used to talk about this sort of thing all the time, remember? You tell me about your paintings and the life you dream about, I tell you about whatever book I've been reading and the life I dream about. We'd go back and forth."

"Yes, but we were younger then. Nothing in our lives seemed set. It's depressing now."

"Maybe, or maybe it's just more important now than it was then."

"I don't believe that for a second," Sally sighs. "But you look so sincere, which you always were. So, fine, I'll tell you about my dream life."

"Good."

"But I warn you, it's just a silly fantasy."

"I'm sure it is," Beth says wryly.

"It's hard to explain, probably because it's so unrealistic," Sally begins hesitantly, for she has learned in her life that these whimsical brands of thought are often kept prettier when they remain absolutely private. Only when they have remained fully hidden in a separate room in her mind, quarantined off in a sense, do they hold onto their integrity as the glittery clouds of inspiration that so exquisitely light up the walls of her insides. Though the clouds, for whatever reason, tend to lose some of their glitter once spoken aloud, she feels herself caught up in the moment, this moment with her friend. Spilling out her private visions of the parallel world seems suddenly like the right thing, the best thing, as if a window had temporarily opened into a chance to share all she wanted about the clouds without worrying that they will lose any of their light.

"At least, that's what Jaime might call it," Sally continues more confidently, "unrealistic or impractical or any other related synonym. Anyway, never mind that, it's a fantasy life, so it doesn't need to be realistic. In this life, I would surround myself with other artists. And I mean to use the word 'artist' in a very loose way. It can mean a lot of things. Painters or sculptors or writers or musicians, so long as they were free-thinkers capable of having

wide open conversations about poetry or photography or literature or music, or even history. About anything in the world, really.
I had vague ideas about living in this unknown, faraway place, a
tragic and romantic place, somewhere in Europe, where I would
easily find those kinds of people. We would share a unique vision
for our lives, individually and collectively, and we would live our
lives in a way that was apart from anything mundane or routine
or expected. We wouldn't be run down by things like money or
errands or illness, and when you look out of any window there
would always be cobblestones, cafés, someone on a corner drawing a bow across a cello, maybe some low-hanging fog, all the
things I associate in my mind with ancient Europe. The artists
would exist together in this higher, more interesting plane of life,
a life that I would be rewarded with and fully welcomed into because I had been marked for it, or because I was special. But I
think I've been too hard on myself for a long time, for not living
up to what I essentially knew all along was a fantasy, even if I
didn't want to admit it, even if it took years for that realization to
move from my subconscious to my higher conscience. And anyway, those words, marked and special, don't really mean anything
to me anymore. Or, maybe it's better to say that their meanings
have changed. I mean, we're all special in some fashion, if only
because we're all different, and we all fill our roles in ways others
simply cannot. And someone can be marked for something, but
have false assumptions of what that might look like, so they fail to
notice and appreciate the life in front of them that they were actually marked for, because they're waiting for whatever they
wrongly assumed they would have. These are the things I've started to tell myself. I repeat these things more repetitively lately, like
cognitive therapy, to assert these new meanings of 'special' and
'marked,' and it makes me feel more optimistic somehow. It might

sound strange, I know, but it does make me feel better, and more self-assured. It's incredibly comforting to finally know that this is the life I was marked for. It's a good feeling, to stop wanting and waiting for something else."

"Interesting," Beth says, stretching the word at length.

"Gosh, that was an earful."

"No. I mean yes, it was, but I'm just ruminating a bit over how sad it sounds, to miss one life because you're waiting for another. I do that. We all do that, or a lot of people do, I guess. But it's just very sad and very true, and also wasteful. Depressingly wasteful. But I'm curious about something else you said too."

"And what's that?"

"Well, you said that part of you hoped all of this was just a transient phase before you moved on to better things. In the dream life you described, did Jaime and Jesse come along with you?"

"I never really thought about it. But no, I don't think they did, because the only way I could enjoy that sort of life is if I found it on my own." Sally says, reflecting as she has so many times before, that it's the most depressing thing in the world to spend the whole of your life around those who are not your kind, knowing that your own kind it out there, somewhere, probably. But even if her husband isn't her own kind in one way, then he's proven to be her kind in another, as her paramour, an ally, a supporter, for he's forgiven her for what she feared he might not forgive her for. That evening, once the shock wore off, it seemed what he was most upset about was that she'd suffered through it alone. More than resenting the act, he resented her faithlessness in his ability to support her. And now, that was the thing that needed to be worked on from her side of the marriage—faith. Faith that he is more open-minded than she gave him credit for, that he will support her, faith that she can be a better supporter to him as well.

It wasn't just that he took her in his arms so easily that night that convinced her, but the manner in which he touched her; she tearfully released the words, he wrapped his arms around her waist in a full, long, stunning embrace. They laid in the bed, then he kissed her forehead and linked her body with his. They didn't talk about all the things that needed to be talked about because such a thing can't be done in one night; the roots go too far back, the hours in a marriage are too old and obscure to be traced. Instead, they opened a long-shut gate, stepped in, unsealed themselves slightly, let their words flow more liberally. He asked if it was a girl or boy, she said she didn't know. She asked if he would truly have wanted another baby, and he said seriously, to her surprise, that he didn't. She looked at him, transfixed, feeling for the first time in a long time like a sanctified woman, a woman who thoroughly shattered herself but still has a chance to fasten the pieces in a new, improved way. Sally looks at Beth, sipping her tea.

"Is it awful of me to say that I wouldn't want my son and husband with me in my dream life?" Sally asks. Despite the renewed love for her husband, that fantasy life, the impossible dream that takes a constant space in her mind and heart, is a place that somehow only exists if she were to find it alone.

"No, you shouldn't feel bad about it at all," Beth asserts. "You're allowed to have a private fantasy. And to me, you're special in the way you originally wanted to be. I think all artists are, because if they're able to see things in their mind's eye that the rest of us can't, then that's a special thing. It also makes perfect sense that you'd want to be around people who share your talent, or your vision. Anyone can appreciate wanting to have a sense of belonging. That's a very human thing."

"Interesting," she replies, mirroring her friend's enunciation and making them both smile. "But I'll be okay without it, I've decided, at least as much as I can be for someone whose dream hasn't come true, because now I've been able to replace that dream with another dream. Or, maybe it's less of a dream that I have now and more of a goal, which is to paint more often and to hold exhibits. I can channel everything into that. And painting feels better, somehow, than it used to. It used to be about what painting could bring me, as I mentioned, always thinking or hoping it would be a portal to that fantasy life, but now the simple act of painting is enough. It's all I need. There's a feeling of complete calmness to it now that wasn't there in quite the same way when I was younger."

"I get that feeling too sometimes, but more through reading. And walking. There's always been something healing about taking a walk," Beth says, then recalls a third activity that would always satiate her, yet had been neglected: her piano. Suddenly the old instrument comes alive in her mind and she intrinsically knows that tonight, she will scavenge the small storage space within the piano bench that holds her sheet music. She will absolutely do this. She will start playing again. She will learn one song, then another. It is something to look forward to.

"Yes," Sally says, "I remember your love of reading, and walking. Those things were always your therapy."

"And my piano."

"And your piano, I remember that too. You were wonderful. Do you still play?"

"No, but I'm going to start again."

"Whichever art fulfills us is what we should do," Sally says thoughtfully. She glances at the fake orchids and adds, more quietly, "Still, I know that some part of me will always wonder about that other life. Daydreaming about it had become a kind of habit. Like a dyed-in-the-wool fantasy. Some little part of my heart broke a long time ago for not having it, and I can't unbreak it. But I have such a good life, a good husband, an amazing son, and my painting. Things these days feel a bit easier. Lighter. Besides, complaining at my age about lost ambitions or the trials of an ordinary life is wasteful, and almost trite. I don't want to be trite. I hate trite."

"Some things become trite only because they're true in such a prevalent way," Beth says emphatically. "A lot of people are dissatisfied with their lives, trite as they may be. I thought I would be married by now. I thought I'd have a home and a husband and kids. Instead I'm alone in the same apartment I've been in for years." She points out the window in a quirky way. "Not even a cat."

Sally laughs for the first time since she arrived. "Do you still want to have a baby?"

Beth sips her tea as she meditates again over the choking sadness that comes with wanting but not having a baby, and her neighbours from the floor above who have, as far as she's concerned, the ideal life. She ruminates over how easy it is to see others as having an ideal life, while knowing at the same time that there is, essentially, no such thing. Her mind drifts to the town's sorority of sorts that she'll never be a part of—the haughty band of motherhood, crossing the street with strollers and meeting in parks for playdates, feigning exasperation over the plights of raising their children. Though maybe it's the chafed envy that makes them seem haughty when really, they are merely as happy as they've ever been.

"Yes, I really do want a baby. I took for granted that it would eventually happen, somehow. But it hasn't happened, and at this point I don't see how it ever will. So, yes, I would have loved to have had a child. When you haven't had a baby by a certain age, there's a feeling that the world is leaving you behind."

"You make it sound isolating."

"It is," Beth says sadly, and with those words, the lightness she felt since she awoke that morning became heavier, more laden, like a clear stream of water suddenly pierced on one side with something noxious, compromising the water's viability. And because anything too downbeat makes that wonderful feeling of lightness less viable, she becomes very aware that the feeling might not last, or that she might not be able to hold onto it for long.

"There are a lot of women who would be envious of your freedom."

"Those women don't understand what they're envious of," Beth says decisively. "Like you, in a way, I think I've been able to accept that my fantasy life may not happen. I remind myself that not all women are meant to find a husband, or have a baby, but that doesn't comfort me. If anything, it only makes me feel worse. Not everyone has what you have. I never thought I'd be alone at my age, and I'm still having a hard time trying to figure out what else there is."

Sally listens intently, but finds herself uncomfortable with Beth's slight change in tone. It's a suffering tone, and she always feels uncomfortable in any position where reassurance seems necessary. At one time she may have been better at dispensing advice or offering comfort, but now with an absence of close friends, she has no faculty for it; she's barely fit to process her own emotions. Some words of reassurance come to mind, and though they're banal and rather plain, she dispenses them anyway.

"Your dream life doesn't have to be a dream though," Sally says apprehensively. "There's still time for you to have a baby."

Beth smiles wanly. "I'd need to find a man first."

"Maybe, but there are other ways," Sally offers vaguely.

Beth averts her eyes. No married woman with a child could understand the devastating loss of a child that never was. But she forgives Sally for her consolatory, slightly placating tone; she means well, and spoke the only encouraging words that any kind person would think to say. She peers out the window, and something about the sight of a single yellow leaf blowing peaceably against the pavement returns her earlier feeling of lightness somewhat. The leaf flings itself upward and seems to her now like an emblem, rather affirmation that there is beauty all around. It's odd, she muses, how quickly that feeling of lightness became weighted a moment ago, yet after a few minutes and the unexpected sight of a leaf dancing on the other side of a window, the lightness finds its way back.

It seems, in life, that it is almost as easy to weep from the pain of perfect moments as from the pain of complete misery. But that is, she supposes, an unignorable thing about life, the ups and downs, the wrinkles and curves, the good days and bad. Gazing at the yellow leaf, tapping her fingers against the teacup, Beth considers something else to say to her friend, this dear friend whom she'd drifted from but had never forgotten.

"I wonder if I would fit into your fantasy place," Beth inquires. "Like I said, I'm not an artist."

"Well, I think that just depends on how we define the word 'artist,'" Sally says with a slight smile, grateful for the change of subject. "I think to be an artist you just have to have a wide-open mind, which you do. You'd fit right in with all the poets and musicians and deep thinkers. Both of us would."

"Maybe so. You and I could sit in those far-away cafés, drinking wine from pretty glasses and reflecting on art and politics and history and poetry and life. We can discuss literature, mull over all the old quotes from great novels."

"You would say that," Sally adds teasingly. "We'd laugh and talk late into the night before wandering back out into the foggy streets of whatever beautiful ancient city we're in."

"It sounds very enticing," Beth says, and it occurs to her that the reason why some of the beautiful things about life are hard to define is because their beauty lives in their indefinability, or, sadly, in their unattainability. "Enticing, even if it is a bit nebulous."

"Nebulous?"

"Yes, but in a beautiful way. It sounds almost mythical."

"Yes, I know," Sally agrees solemnly, as if she were disappointed at having to yield and concede that this vision of hers was just that, a vision, a myth, an untouchable thing.

"Why does this dream life take place in Europe?"

"I'm not sure, except that when it comes to art, it seems like the centre of the world. Probably because I studied mostly the art from Europe. I never fantasized about going anywhere else."

"We're talking as though it is a fantasy, but I'm sure there's something like that going on somewhere in the world right now. Somewhere there's a group of artists and free-thinkers drinking wine in some ancient city, discussing all the interesting things that artists and free-thinkers discuss. Take right now, for example, or better still, take us. We're in a café, having an interesting and reflective conversation, only we're not in Europe."

"And it isn't foggy, and there's no cobblestones."

"No, but if I think about it for a few moments, hopefully I can ponder up an old literary quote relevant to this conversation," Beth says jocularly.

They smile at one another, thinking it a great relief to be sitting across from someone who not only holds, at least partly, a similar feeling about life, but also is comfortable discussing it. Even if it is fleeting, they are each grateful for the other.

"You know, Beth, a long time ago, when I was still in school, the professor told us a story. I think the class was Post-War American Literature, but that's not important. What is important is that he was a cellist with a deep love of classical music, and for whatever reason was particularly fond of eighteenth and nineteenth century music—Beethoven, Handel, Hayden. He had this idea to go to all the great ancient cities where those musicians had lived and performed, believing that once he arrived in each of those places, he would easily stumble upon like-minded people. He was most excited for the last part of his travels, the Carinthian Gate Theatre in Vienna. But when he got there, it looked duller than the image he had in his mind, not to mention the building was half covered in scaffolding. He did meet other musicians, but meeting them and surrounding himself with these ancient stones and statuary and great ruins wasn't as cathartic or transcendent as his heart wanted it to be."

"So, it is a myth," Beth says, letting her shoulders slump as the mystical image of the Carinthian Theatre dissolves in her mind, as if she herself had stood in Vienna and was disappointed by the high scaffolds.

"What's a myth?"

"Well, the idea of a higher plane. Of artists and fog and cobblestones, and all that."

"That's what I gathered at the time. At first I convinced myself that he simply wasn't grateful or open-minded enough to appreciate the beauty of what he was seeing. But I understand it more clearly now. I see a lot of things more clearly lately, especially since Mom passed away. I'm not sure why that changed the way I see things, but somehow it has." Sally pauses for a moment to watch two patrons, a man and woman, rise from their table and leave the café. When the sound of the little metal bell above the door has completely faded away, she resumes slowly, peering down at her cup. "I concluded that people are the same everywhere, when you get down to it. Some just live in prettier cities with amazing architecture around them. That's all."

"Maybe, but I don't disagree with what you felt about the story the first time around."

Beth acquiesces, and sees that the stray cat is no longer in sight. However, beyond where it had been walking, against the weathered brick of another building, sits what she had thought of at first as tall weeds ,now unveiling themselves as dropseed, mostly green but tipped at the top with droopy gold-coloured seed heads. And she can't help but marvel at these golden tips, for there is something eloquent and rather anticipative about them. They could be the golden vines in her mind that had lowered her emerald-laden piano onto the pine-planked stage, but instead of a moody musical she now imagines more of an upbeat production, where the golden seed heads have shed their nuclei all over the place and now, instead of theatre seats and onlookers, there lies in their place a full garden of these things, huge expansions of emerald stems with their golden seeds which will continue to shed then drop, then grow and grow. She looks to Sally, who seems also to be gazing at these pretty golden tips.

"You said that maybe he wasn't open-minded enough to appreciate the beauty of the place," Beth continues, "and I guess it could be true. We're all affected by our pre-conceived notions of things, whether positive or negative. Some might see what he saw and not only appreciate it, but find that it exceeded their expectations."

"Perception is reality, you mean."

"Something like that, yes."

"Or maybe some people simply expect too much. I expected too much. I have heard it said that art is just a reflection of someone's dreams, like a captured apparition, something that is technically impossible. I don't know if I believe it or not, but the thought pops up in my mind sometimes. And I guess it would mean that whatever we see on a canvas or read in a good novel, for instance, isn't something we're meant to base our lives on."

"Maybe I'm too practical," Beth shrugs, "I never thought otherwise. I never once entertained the idea that my life was meant to resemble art."

"Then you're lucky."

"But I've still had my own disappointments."

"You're right, everyone has." Sally looks furtively at Beth, quietly admitting that she knows very little about what her friend has been through since they drifted apart, and likewise, Beth knows very little about her. Yet it would be rather nice to restore that bond, to make these meetings regular. Beth is familiar, disarming, slightly gauche though in a delightful way, and so Sally can speak openly in front of her without having to worry about strange looks or rolling eyes; that's an invaluable thing. There's a commonality here, an understanding, a symbiotic back and forth. It's tempting, now, to open those doors, to let Beth in on all that's happened in the years since they've drifted, but for whatever reason she has no desire to revisit those years right now. Although she intuits that if they meet like this again, she probably will.

"I suppose we want what we want out of life," Beth says vaguely.

"And I suppose everyone has their own expectations," Sally responds, equally vaguely, and wishing, still, that she could have said something more consoling to Beth on the subject of having no husband and no child. She, herself, has no right to presume that she understands what it means to spend several years living alone, for she herself has scarcely spent a day alone. Sally resists the urge to convince Beth, emphatically, to be contented with the openness of a blank slate, with having a life to herself. It always seems easier, Sally muses, to point out the brighter sides of someone's life rather than your own.

The lull in activity in the café affords a moment of reflection on their individual struggles with unhappiness, and while Beth stares outside and thinks inadvertently about the way Tom's reluctant smile on the day he left made her think something about the scarcities of love, Sally reflects on the conversation she had with her mother on the day she trimmed the willow branches in the front yard, the ones that scarped against the window and seemed to remind them both of their own brand of depression.

"Mom said something to me shortly before she passed away," Sally says, ending their silence, and wondering whether her mother, in the end, could see in her daughter's eyes a slightly more mended woman, if not an entirely happy one. "She said that, in part, a lot of her miseries in life were her own fault, and she told me, in not so many words, that I was too self-indulgent and self-involved. She told me my life would be easier if I chose to be more grateful. She said that happiness was a choice she wishes she'd made."

"I've heard that before, that happiness is a choice, but then I think, if only it were that easy."

"I always thought of Mom as unhappy, so it felt backward to take any of her advice seriously. But I think she saw herself in me, to some degree. She could tell I wasn't happy."

"Well, she was your mother."

"She was."

"Maybe she was trying, in her own way, to warn you against the damage that comes with dwelling on things," Beth suggests. "I spent a lot of time with her over the last year, and I hope you don't mind me pointing it out, but she tended to dwell on the past a lot. Your brothers, and especially your dad. She missed him."

Sally recalls her father, the stable force in a childhood spent with a distant, at times unreliable mother. She felt safe around him. The day he passed, she spent the night at the farmhouse, and in the morning, an unusually vivid mist was hovering above the grass. She stood motionless for a few minutes, considering the mist aesthetically—a thick mist equally radiant and dark, obscuring the trees so thoroughly that their outlines were scarcely visible. She mourned as she gazed at the lovely yet foreboding scene, the loss of that safe feeling, until, that is, she went home and was comforted by a man who shared similar qualities; her husband, it dawned on her, also made her feel safe, consistently, dependably, yet she seldom acknowledged it. He was her constant, her companion, the man who loved her more than enough to let her destroy the carpet in the corner room with spilled watercolours.

"I could be more grateful," Sally says quietly and thoughtfully, more to herself than to Beth, her head bent slightly toward the table.

"So could I." Beth says, surprised by the small epiphany these words seemed to provoke. She leans back in her chair, sips the lukewarm tea, stares fixedly out the window. Sunlight falls in random bursts onto the pavement through the branches of elms lining the street, adding to the morning's already translucent glow, which seems brighter than usual after so many days of rain. She considers that this depression has caused her to not only lose focus on the good in life—depression, of course, being a kind of debilitating, all-encompassing condition that forces one to become very distracted and self-involved—but it also makes it nearly impossible to be grateful for anything. Yet there are so many things to be grateful for, which easily ties into the earlier thought of finding something to look forward to each day. Gratitude for the present, instead of fear of what will be, is a sentiment easier said than done, but is still a good sentiment.

"I should get going," Sally says resignedly, glancing at her watch. "My appointment is in ten minutes."

"Okay, I understand," Beth says, wishing the time hadn't passed so quickly. "It was really nice to see you, and to talk."

"You too. It was great to spend time with you like this again."

Sally rises from the table and lifts her coat from the back of the chair. Once her coat is on, she pauses, furtively, and meets Beth's eyes.

"What is it?"

"I'm holding an exhibit in two weeks," Sally says, her smile somewhat stealth, and the sanguine expression that had surfaced on her face a while ago, when Beth admitted to feeling at one point envious of her talent, resurfaced.

"That's great," Beth says, equally sanguine. "Why didn't you mention it earlier?"

"I'm not sure. Maybe it seemed too showy a thing to say at the beginning of a conversation long overdue."

"Then you've changed. You used to shout those things from the rooftops."

"You're right, I did. I haven't invited many people, other than Jaime and Jesse, of course, and his fiancée. The gallery always has its own guests on an exhibit's opening night, so there will be others. Jaime invited James, I think, now that he's back in town. I'd love for you to come. It's at The Ochre Gallery. The one you mentioned before, with the high walls."

"I'd love to," Beth replies sincerely.

"Good," Sally says, her own stealth smile turning into one that is unfeigned and openly elated. "The gallery doors open at six. I know you don't drive, so you can come with us, if you'd like, but we'll have to leave early."

"Thank you, and yes, I'd love to go with you."

"Is your number still the same?"

"Yes, same one as always."

"Great, we'll talk soon then," Sally says, then turns to leave before turning back one more time. "Bye, Beth."

"Bye," she replies, and watches Sally step out of the café, the ring of the little metal bell above the door sounding surprisingly hollow despite the tone of their farewells. She has, as the room quiets again, a vague feeling of being left behind. There goes the artist, she thinks, who sees spectacular things in her mind's eye, who has a husband and child, who will have an exhibit, and it seems, despite some moments in their conversation, a full life. So, what sort of life awaits a woman without those things, with no one waiting at home, and nothing to make her remarkable? How does she reconcile what she wants to have with what she already has? She opens the journal again, to the page where the date is partly written, but before she picks up her pen, she considers whether the turn of mind that prevented her from following through with her original plan was one of courage or of cowardice. She doesn't think about this very long before deciding it was an act of courage. It was not weakness that prompted her to throw away the note, or the dead daisies; it was strength. Thoughts of dying, after all, never presented themselves in her mind in a way that burned steadily, rather it was a distant, intermittent flickering, without form or continuity, always reminding her of its presence while never achieving its purpose or coming to full strength.

Sally had reflected that people are the end result of their own lazy decisions, and for Beth, a person slowly reconnecting with a love of life and the opportunity to live it well, that would have been a lazy decision indeed. Following through with such an extreme act cannot come from something that merely flickers in the distance; there is nothing arbitrary about such an act, so ambivalence has no place in the undertaking of it. Death by choice, rather than by a natural progression of disease or time, requires an organized, steady approach. One has to be certain, firm in their intent. She had been wavering. Indeed, she has been wavering between life and death, between this world and the next, for far too long. It's the ultimate kind of stagnancy. One must choose one path or the other, not stand motionless at the fork.

And so, she thinks, if her recurring dream about the cruelly angled trees and lonely narrow path is some sort of answer, then maybe she has found a question to apply to it: Should she give up, or keep walking? Is her life finished, or unfinished? Has her experience of life so far been enough, or not enough? No, she thinks, it hasn't been enough. Not nearly enough. She wants more. More time; more life. An occasion to not let life run through her fingers like water, but to hold some of it in her hands, to look at it anew, admire it and thank it for what it can bring. Despite not having a husband, or a child, or anyone to welcome her when she comes home, maybe she can find other ways to be happy, or nearly happy some of the time; where one thing in life is absent, maybe another can be found to take its place. If she looks at her life through this more optimistic lens, then the sadness seems to lose a bit more of its power, and the melancholy aspects of her dream seem somehow less weighty, and less worrying. And maybe, as Sally says, she should accept not being marked for one life, and embrace being marked for another. For the only alternative, it now occurs to her, would be to take for granted all that presently surrounds her, at great expense to her spirit.

Like her disease-stricken mother, she has been living a sort of half-life, yet very unlike her mother, she still has a choice. And so, she will reject the darker path, and make her way with tentative faith down the other. She will try again; she will not linger at the fork. She may eventually lose herself to the skulking disease, the half-life, but that time has not yet come, and in fact may never come, so she chooses, here and now, to be more grateful for the years between now and whenever.

Instead of writing these things down, Beth only thinks the words, as though her thoughts are too turbulent for an act as calm as sitting down to write. She closes the journal, leaving the date unfinished. Feeling restless, she decides to leave the café, the desire to sit in a clean, well-lit place having left her.

Sally approaches the bank a few minutes before the appointment. She steps inside, presents herself to the woman at the desk, then sits in the waiting area. On the table at the centre of the room is a bridal magazine, and she immediately thinks of Valerie, who is still scouring the bridal shops for the perfect dress. Valerie has gone to the city with Linda, twice, with no success at finding a gown that measures up to whatever image in is her mind. Sally hypothesizes, however, that at least some of the difficulty in finding a gown has been caused by Linda's criticisms.

The engagement party had gone as smoothly as could be expected. The day was warm, the guests enjoyed themselves, and the decorations closely matched the colour of the icing on the cake; Linda was thrilled. Sally herself was gracious and accommodating, a perfect hostess, acting very agreeable with men and women she scarcely knew, discussing at length a series of things she had no interest in discussing but that seemed of absorbing interest to them; as she had anticipated, her part in the event was full of all the usual forms of domestic impersonation.

At one moment in particular, once the slices of cake had been served to the guests on little pink plates, she felt suddenly depleted by the whole event. She glanced at Jesse, tossing a few pieces of wood into the fire, and knew infallibly by his eyes that he was happy; he smiled, he wrapped his arm around Valerie, kissed her cheek, laughed at something she said. Quickly in her mind, her annoyance with the day flipped, for in seeing his happiness, all the things around her seemed to make a greater effort to display the depths of their colour and drive any negative thoughts out of her head. She felt again, as she had with Jaime after her confession, like a sanctified woman.

When she looked around for Jaime, she found him by the porch in what appeared to be an upbeat conversation with Valerie's father, and she thought vainly, maybe a little immaturely, that he had the most impressive qualities of all the other husbands at the party. He was, to her, a rare grain or pearl nestled on a riverbed, a diamond in the sand, shining brighter than the others, for there he was, the man who loves her, the man who forgave her without hesitation. She sat with her mother under the shade of a tree, watching her husband, her family, the fire, their hands locked together, saying very little. It was peaceful to be with her, and Sally knew, somehow, by some indistinguishable look in her eyes, that her mother would never again have the strength to visit her home, that the morning was coming when she would wake to a world without her mother.

Sally recalls the moments in the hospital before she passed, one tender moment in particular, so perfect and unexpected that she has felt grateful for it every day since. Sally was holding her mother's hand, stroking it gently, when she peered up from the bed and met her eyes directly, and whispered, simply, "I love you."

"I love you too," Sally whispered back, naturally, without hesitation, the words shared easily, as if through habit, as though they had already been exchanged a thousand times.

And now that she's passed, the job of sorting through everything in the house has begun in earnest. Yesterday, after packing up some of her clothes, she asked Jaime to bring his truck for two of the least weather-worn wicker chairs from the porch. They set them down by the ravine, next to the raspberry bush, and had sat there for a while, looking over the mottled yellow shades of the neighbour's hayfield. She had felt, sitting quietly with him beneath the poplars, a kind of mournful gratitude, and in that gratitude, a sense of reconciliation between two things—the parallel world, that fictitious, glittering place, and the here and now, with Jaime, with her canvas and paints. The two places are closer together than she had previously fathomed; they are touching, interweaving at times, allowing her to relax and itinerate easily between both. She can cross the threshold, admire the tragedy and poetry, the cello notes issuing from windows and the pink lilies that never wilt, then return to this side of the threshold and, like all artists with an eye, remain sharp and vigilant for all things equally beautiful—the glimmer of snowfall across an otherwise barren field, a flower that holds on to its colour while the rest have turned brown, a rotting wooden fence still in place except for one post that has half-fallen into weeds.

For it occurred to her, gazing at the pretty golden field, that while she had pined for a far-away place that in many ways resembled the parallel world, hadn't she always been more in love with the vastness of the surrounding prairies than she ever could be with a paved street in Europe? Wasn't it the things around her, and not the things far away, that inspired her art? And wasn't her life the real art just waiting to free itself from within the confines she herself had imagined, or determined, were steering her course?

The fault of her languid unhappiness had stemmed partly from a failure to be careful with her life, to treat it like the important, temporary thing that it is. It's so easy to do. Jaime's ability to forgive her had affected her, softened her thinking, illuminated the chamber where her feelings of unworthiness and uncleanliness were kept hidden, and by illuminating it had all but killed off the slithering thing—the nefarious thing that embodied the guilt. There will always be some traces of guilt, of course, some speckled bits of uncleanliness; they linger on her hands, her heart, pop up when she she's watching a sunset or doing the dishes, and always will. While there may always be some degree of guilt and disappointment in her heart, there is also grace and decency. And so, she has arrived at a conclusion about the act that has filled her with varying degrees of shame from that fateful day.

In the moments before the procedure, a voice told her to leave that place, to pull the intravenous line from her wrist so she could go home to her husband, and together they would make the best of what was coming. But just as the procedure was beginning, the moment she closed her eyes, a new voice came along and silenced the other. It whispered very clearly and sympathetically that for her, it was the right choice. For another woman, another voice may have risen louder and said something else entirely, but for her, that singular voice, emanating from her heart perhaps, which she now believes is good, kept her from wrenching herself from the stirrups. It's the same mysterious voice that inspired her, after Jaime's show of forgiveness, to finally forgive herself. And so, she has.

"Sally?"

A woman in a navy dress and blazer steps into the waiting area, and gestures her toward an office at the opposite end of reception. Sally rises from the chair, follows the woman into her office, where a sepia image of a willow tree hangs on the wall. It reminds her instantly of the willow of her childhood, the one that shaded her while she painted, while she dozed and coloured, where she dreamed of all that could be. The woman closes the door behind them, and Sally seats herself in yet another chair.

Sally painted ecstatically last night, finishing yet another canvas. A birch tree depicted so close that only the bark was visible. She fixated on capturing the exactness of the bark, each fissure and knot, every thin line of shadow. Capturing those specifics has always been a style signature of hers, though what has changed about her work is that she now incorporates a fun, reckless use of colour. From her usual earthy, temporal-like colours that illustrated the images in the most realistic way possible, she has, for whatever reason, jumped completely in another direction. What should be blue is pink, what is usually black is now the brightest yellow. Sally envisages herself in a long gown on opening night, standing in the middle of the wide white room like a seasoned performer on a familiar stage, the whiteness of the room interrupted every forty inches or so by a blazing, brilliant, dramatic celebration of watercolour. Her paintings are so flashy and theatrical that they border on ostentatious, and Sally can't wait to be surrounded by them all.

As the woman in the navy dress pulls her mother's records up on the computer screen, Sally lifts her hand and rests it against the string of pearls. The pearls, she thinks, will pair beautifully with her long gown.

As Beth leaves the café, she thinks of her time with Sally and the day ahead. She moves steadily through the centre of town, toward the park, letting the paper bag holding the book and pens and journal swing at her side. She feels abnormally awake and aware, more keenly alert to her surroundings than usual; all her senses are attuned to the floury scents from the bakery, the stiffness of a woman's beige alpaca coat, the webbed cracks in the pavement, the greenness of the grass sprouting through, the bright, pale, aurora-like sky. A long wisp of brown hair blows across her face, then the wind draws it away again. She came very close to not seeing this day, a day that in many ways is just another day, an ordinary, un-remarkable day, and yet, because she came so close to missing it, everything strikes her differently; the sights a bit clearer, a bit more animated, haloed in light. Autumn is the most exhilarating time of year, she reflects, for the prairie seems rekindled somehow, lively and fresh, allaying the town and its surrounding fields with one more vehement splash of sunlight before the snow falls and blan-kets everything for months in a frozen silvery-white. It all carries the feeling, somehow, of a backward spring.

She knows it won't last, this keen enjoyment of a backward spring, this feeling of lightness, this as yet untrampled sense of optimism. These moments are singular and rare, and should be appreciated, not only because they're rare, but because they seem to promise something, just as a musical prelude promises a greater movement to come, a greater song. It's almost a religious feeling, perceptible only to oneself, and instead of wondering how to prolong it, she wonders how to make her life better in a more general way.

She considers the idea of leaving. She can let the current lease on her apartment expire, sell some furniture, pack her bags. It's an exciting idea, and an uncomplicated one; simply buy a ticket, get on a bus. She can conclude, like Holly, that this town is not the right place to live, that happiness is easier to find elsewhere. She can move to the mountainous west coast, where the weather is milder. Or she can live near her sister, rebuild that relationship, immerse herself in a language and a place she has always been curious about. She can dine in downtown restaurants with Holly and her writer friends, wander through a maze of streets until she's lost and has to find her way back again. After a year or two, just before the city starts to inhabit her, she can buy another ticket, get on another bus headed farther east. She can experience what it means to breathe salt in the air while exploring lighthouses on the tips of rocky islands or the abandoned shells of ships and fisheries of the eastern coast. It sounds very romantic, and very doable. With the paper bag swinging at her side, she vaguely thinks to herself, it is not horrible to be alone; in fact, it is wonderful to be alone because anything and everything is ahead of you when you are alone.

But as exciting and possible as all of those may be, those thoughts reveal a plain truth—she wants to stay. As much as she enjoys the idea of packing up and fleeing into the sunset like a downtrodden protagonist set free at the end of a novel, it isn't what her heart is telling her to do. She loves this place, loves it hopelessly, and believes she can survive here better than anywhere. She also decides, despite the attached memories, both good and bad, that she will stay in her apartment. She enjoys the relative quietness of the location, the hardwood floors, the wide casement windows that allow the sun to thoroughly light up the main room.

Beth slips off her shoes and enters the park. She notices, affectionately, the streams of sunlight hitting the grass in a sidelong and wistful way, and finds herself almost unconsciously veering west, toward the nursing home. As she steps slowly through the cool blades of grass, she thinks of what Sally said in the café about happiness. Rather it was what Mary had told Sally about happiness, that it is less a fate, and more a choice. To a degree that's true, but happiness can't simply be something that one passively chooses while standing still. It must be actively strived for, worked for, protected, and once found, have high yet porous walls built around it, a fortress built to stave off certain invaders while allowing inside anything amenable to one's continued well-being. Because as she knows, it is very easy to let things fall the other way, to allow invaders to strip her spirit of hope the way a thief raids a home in search of gold and silver. Hope, like the spirit, can be a very tenuous, delicate thing. Melancholy and happiness exist very close together. They live side by side, on either side of a vacillating thin line, as are life and death. The line is fickle and faithless, shifts place without notice, blurs without reason, is impossible to define in a clear way from one day to the next. She could still easily sway toward the dark, and sometimes it's the smallest of things that can sway her mood one way or the other—

the break of a shoelace, a shared look, the significant or insignificant touch of a hand, a cool draft wafting through a window. When someone finds it difficult to be happy, entrenched in a daily battle to simply be okay, these things are as powerful as they are precarious.

Her feeling of hopefulness this morning, then, is frighteningly delicate.

This is without a doubt a very universal thing, the ebbs and flows of the spirit, feeling dispassioned then impassioned, warmed then unmoved, to be overthrown by the absolute splendidness and beauty of a bird swooping elegantly above the tree line, only to feel something in your soul drop, shift its weight, as the bird gets smaller and smaller in the distance before vanishing from sight. The soul rather easily lifts, then contracts; coils in uncertainty, then uncoils and reaches out again. Just like her mood in the café, which started with lightness, shifted to sadness, then back to lightness, the spirit fluctuates, grows brighter in phases, then slowly dimmer, then bright again. There is room and time for growth, and she takes great comfort in these thoughts of metamorphose, that when one page ends, there is battlement of the new—while one thing withers, another blooms; while one thing is lost, another is reclaimed; while one thing falters, another recovers. We are continually made then remade again, we weaken then wake in altered forms, and for someone living without hope, can there be a more hopeful statement than that?

Beth thinks again of the backward spring, of the autumn rain that makes the prairie seem new and clean. She envisages the tranquility of the river near the old oak tree, its running drops of water that are never in the same place twice, for it moves at a constant until it freezes in motion, crystallized by the winter in little frozen waves, then thaws again before continuing its sweep across the bedrock, changing its tints and colours and shapes a million times. And all the while, many of the bigger aspects of life perpetually stay the same—night, day, death, life. But inside of those big things are a myriad of little things moving and changing in perpetuity; a single night, day, life or death can never be classified as being precisely the same as another. Everything is in a perpetual state of metabolism, all is transient, all is temporary. And so if change is incessant, then it's incessantly possible that things will change for the better.

She'll start by going to Sally's opening. It's a first step, but a big one. She will write in her journal, she will take walks and read stories with happy endings, she will visit Millie and her fable-like apple tree. Two unaccompanied women keeping each other in good company. And then maybe, one day, she will meet someone. Maybe she'll be with James, or maybe someone new. Maybe they'll have a baby. Maybe, and just as possible, she will never again be with anyone romantically. Maybe she'll never have the chance to be a mother. All she can do is be open to either path, be as grateful as she can, and accept whatever happens along the way. She might even have, still ahead of her, a moment or two of feeling happy, or almost happy. That is a distinct possibility, and there is always possibility. She'll try as hard as she can to appreciate her life from this day forward. Step by step, day by day, and on it goes.

The rare and singular moment passes, and again she is just a woman, holding a paper bag in the park, on her way to visit her mother. The moment is simply whisked away as she knew it would be, like something caught in one's field of vision that fades inexplicably when one turns to see it more clearly. Beth slips on her shoes and exits onto the sidewalk. She sighs peacefully as she looks around at the town in which she will spend the rest of her life, and waits to cross Main Street. When she is able to cross, she steps into dappled sunlight, and as she steps onto the curb, hears the soft melody of a piano issuing quietly from somewhere inside the florist shop, and feels her mind rush in that direction. She stops on the pavement. There is, quite simply, no sound more captivating or beautiful.

She envisages, as she takes in the music and the bloomy scents of the florist shop, not the piano covered in emerald lichen being lowered down by glittery golden vines, but her own piano, the piano of her childhood, dusty and propped in her apartment, waiting for her return. The old instrument presents itself ethereally in her mind now, yet in a wonderfully perceptible way, for she had truly touched and played its keys, smelled its musty splendid wood, and these more tangible memories weaved more positively through her mind now than anything she could conjure up in emerald or golden-tinged daydreams, no matter how pretty, no matter how whimsical. The musty instrument of her childhood was solid and true and abundant. She feels almost giddy at the thought of her feet resting once again upon the pedal while a sheet of music sits upon the bracket, and the feel of the keys as she hears those resonant sounds that stir her soul; major and minor, staccato and rest, sharp then flat, because in between the jumps and lilts of the notes, somehow, was the thing that brought life to its knees.

Beth continues unhurriedly along the pavement, recalls the evening she had cried over the row of keys, long ago, her small fingers sore from hours of practice. Indeed, she sat frustrated in front of the instrument many times as a child, yet she remembers clearly this evening in particular, for it was slightly different from the others. Her mother must have heard her crying, for she came into the room and sat beside her on the bench. She took her daughter in her arms, gently wiped away a tear, and said to Beth the words that are perhaps the most comforting for anyone to hear.

"Don't worry. Everything will be alright."

About the Author

Nettie Marie Magnan is a writer turned nurse, turned writer again. Raised on the vast and rural prairie landscape that inspires her stories, it wasn't until years of nursing that she felt compelled to write about loss, hope, the complexities of human relationships, and the beauty and torment and strangeness of being alive. Stories with a healthy mix of melancholy  and optimism are the ones she's always been drawn to, after all.

When she's not busy working as a nurse or writing sad but optimistic tales, she can be found sketching the pretty elements of the prairie landscape, spending time with her family and cats, failing at both gardening and cooking, and as a lover of antiques, she enjoys volunteering at a local heritage museum.

9 781990 336744